Justin Zaruba

Penelope Salvo
and
Impossible Red

ISBN-978-0-692-67071-2

Text set in Gentium Book Basic
Cover Art designed by Justin Zaruba

Printed in the United States of America
First edition 2016

For my father,
who's dead.
And for my mother who,
at least at time of publication,
is alive.

"An astronaut is judged

not by how often she goes to space,

but by how often she is

taken to space by others."

-New York Graffiti

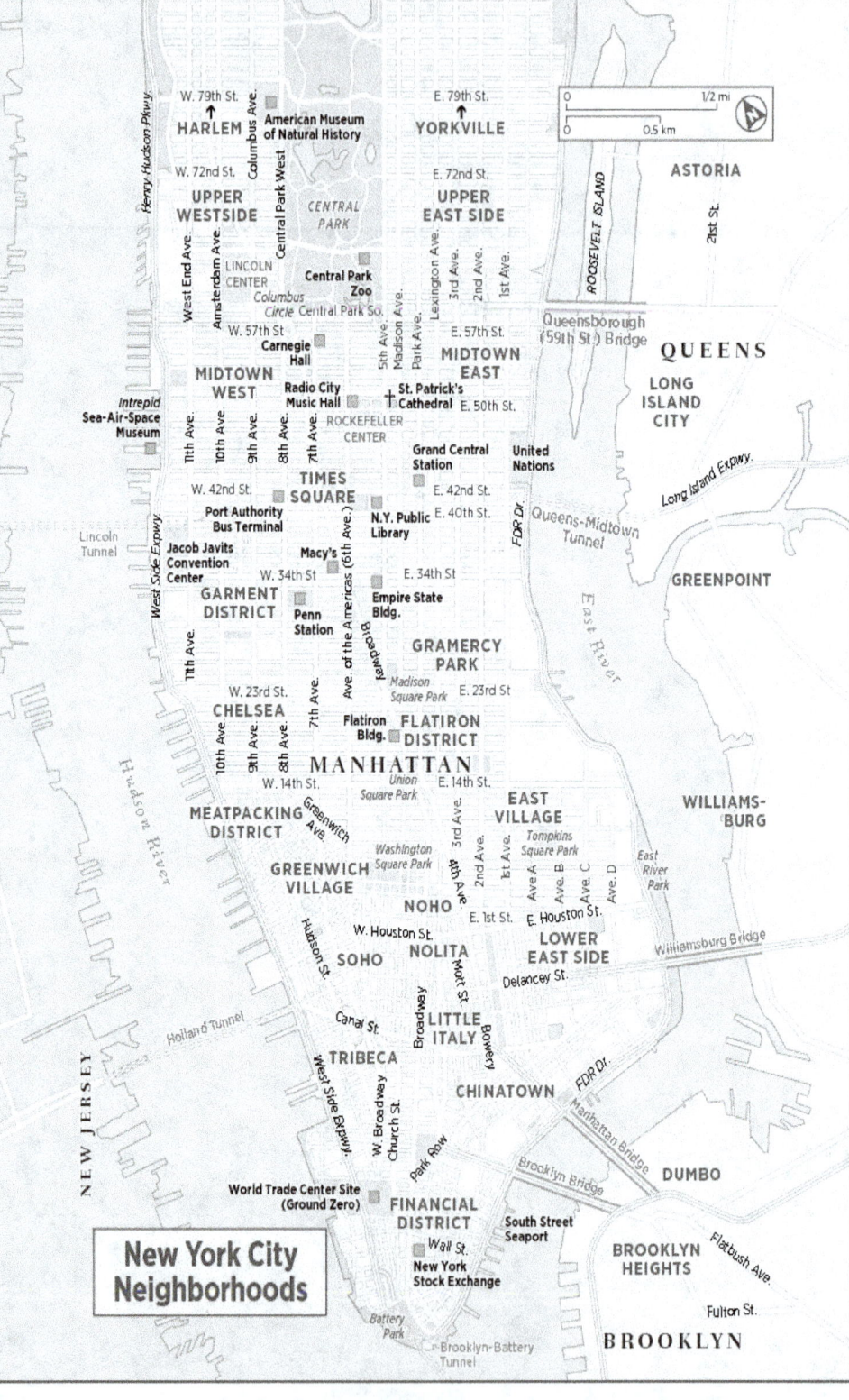

New York City Neighborhoods

Chapter 1

The newspaper ad was incredibly vague.
It read:

Help Wanted
Minimum wage + room and board
No experience necessary
Apply in person at 83 Forge St.

I circled the ad in red marker. After weeks of searching the Village Voice for work, I finally found my dream job. Well, I suppose it wasn't necessarily my "dream job." My *dream* job was to escape the gutters of New York City, train to become a Kung Fu master and travel the world living a life of adventure. But all adventure aside, free room and board was a close second.

Forge was a narrow little street down in Chinatown, just blocks away from my old apartment building in Little Italy. Whatever was waiting for me down at 83 Forge wasn't my dream job, it was karma finally throwing me a bone after 18 years of kicking my teeth in.

No experience necessary? Well, I got good news for you, Village Voice. No one does "no experience necessary" like Penelope Salvo. I just graduated high school two months ago with a C+ average. Whatever "experience" I had was limited to selling bootleg DVDs out of my backpack, tagging brick walls with shitty graffiti, and drinking stolen beer.

Minimum wage? That came as no surprise. Everyone In New York City pays minimum wage. You can't make a living in the most expensive city on Earth with minimum wage. Hell, you could work seven minimum wage jobs and still not afford rent in Manhattan. I didn't care about the minimum wage.

What really got my heart racing was that super awesome, too good to be true, *free room and board*. That's the Holy Grail of New York City. A fable. A myth. A thing that happened to a friend of a friend of a friend. If you have a room to rent in New York City, especially on Manhattan Island, then you milk that for all it's worth. One-thousand if it's the size of a closet. Two-thousand if it's an actual *room* room.

I read the ad over and over. Room and board. Room *and* board.

I wasn't even sure what "board" was. I didn't need a board.

I needed the room, I didn't care if it was a closet. I'd take a closet if that meant I didn't have to live on the streets, and that's exactly where I was headed: life on the streets. All of Ma's insurance money had run out. It got gobbled up by the vultures that follow dead people around; the hospital with their medical bills, the ambulance and their laundry list of random-ass fees, the funeral home, and the cemetery, and lawyer who had to take care of it all.

Sometimes the most expensive thing a person can do is die.

With the money gone, I didn't have anything left to pay the bills. First the internet got shut off, then the water, then the power. I got a final, final, *final* notice of eviction from my building's superintendent. In just a few days time, I'd be sleeping up on the midnight subways, using my overstuffed backpack as a pillow.

That job on Forge Street was my last chance at help. I needed it bad. So bad, in fact, that it almost certainly came with some sort of catch.

Still, it was worth finding out.

I stood up off my concrete bench in Columbus Park. All around me were people riding bikes, couples walking hand in hand, and all manner of tourists "oohing" and "ahhing" at the various trees and plants. My backpack full of merch had been emptied out and I had laid everything across the concrete benches around me. I sold people handmade soaps of patchouli and sandalwood and lavender, plus clock and watch parts I'd pieced together to make necklaces and earrings.

Tourists will buy anything, especially if they're not American and from somewhere else in the world. International tourists couldn't be more excited to trade cash for handmade New York City trinkets. By the looks on some of their faces, you'd swear they'd never smelled lavender before.

"Do you not have lavender where you come from?" I'd ask them as I handed them their bar of soap.

They'd just smile and nod and hand me five bucks. Easy cash. Done deal. I did this everyday just to survive. It wasn't even sundown and I had twenty-three dollars in my pocket, and that was after buying a pack of cigarettes.

Twenty-three bucks wasn't a bad haul for sitting around Columbus Park for half a day. That kind of money would buy dinner for the night and breakfast the next morning. It would buy food, but it wasn't even in the same *galaxy* as paying rent. When it came to rent, twenty-three dollars might as well be a coupon for a free oil change. But when it came to my empty stomach, however, twenty-three dollars meant I didn't have to steal hot dogs from that old man with the street cart at the park entrance.

I stuffed all my gear into my backpack along with the folded up Village Voice, then threw my skateboard down on the ground. I jumped on, kicked the toe of my sneaker across the surface of the concrete and clattered down the sun-baked sidewalks of Columbus Park, headed towards Little Italy.

On the corner of my block in Little Italy was Il Vicino, this fourth-generation bistro that had been in New York City longer than I'd been alive. It was more of a deli than a bistro, with only a few tables and chairs set up against the front windows. They mostly sliced meat, but there was a menu that offered a few different kinds of sandwiches.

Il Vicino was owned by Tony "Other Tony" Bellusci, a "restaurateur" who also used to own a gelato place down the way. Then he had a pasta shop, and after that was Tony's Baked Goods where he sold biscotti and tiramisu. He was always opening and closing up shops, all the time.

I think it had something to do with the mob. You know, shuffling money around, avoiding taxes, closing one store and opening another, that kind of thing.

The panini's at Il Vicino were the absolute best; better than Ma's, not that I would have ever told her that. I dropped a handful of wadded-up bills on the counter and bought a Salami Stack, which was exactly like how it sounded: a stack of sliced salami, but with capicola, banana peppers, mozzarella and provolone cheese, all toasted on an Italian roll. Ten bucks is a lot to spend on a sandwich, but I couldn't eat an entire Salami Stack if I tried. I could only ever eat half, then save the rest in the cardboard box for later.

My apartment building was on the opposite end of the street from Il Vicino, down past the barber shop where these old Italian guys would sit out on the front stoop in the hot hot sun and read the paper and drink little cups of espresso. They gave me a head nod "hello" as I passed them on my skateboard. I looked like trouble, sure, with my dark clothes and ears pierced all to hell and spiky black hair, but they didn't care about what I looked like; I was a local from around the way, I was an Italian who went to Catholic school, and that was good enough for them.

I gave them a head nod back.

My old apartment was on the fifth floor of the Ortega Building, built in 1908. At least, that was the date carved into the cornerstone right by the main entrance. You'd think the door was also from 1908, the way the green paint peeled away in strips to reveal the dry wood underneath. The door would always get stuck in the frame and only the people who lived in the building knew the trick to get it to open; you had to pull up on the handle and bump the door open with your hip as hard as you could.

The door would close on its own, not by one of those hydraulic door things, but because the building was a century old and had sank a few inches into the ground. Once you let the door go, gravity would slam it shut and the boom would echo through the empty lobby. Coming or going, everyone in the building could hear when someone had used the door. It was a pretty good security system, all things considered.

I climbed five flights of stairs, stepping in exactly the right spots to keep the wooden steps from creaking.

When I got to my floor, I saw a pink piece of paper taped to the door of my apartment:

"Fuck," I muttered. I ripped the notice off the door.

Some odd-looking padlock contraption was secured to the doorknob, making it impossible for me to put my key in the keyhole and unlock the door. I tugged on the contraption a little – *maybe it will just fall off* – but no such luck. Of course not. The Village Voice had already delivered my one lucky break for the day.

I slung my backpack back over my shoulder, still without a single bite of my Salami Stack, and trudged back down the stairs.

If landlord George thought posting a notice was going to keep me out of my apartment, then he didn't know Penelope Salvo. I back out into the summer sun and dipped around the side of the building, down the alley, past the dumpsters and the recycle bins, and started up the fire escape. I'd been sneaking in and out of the Ortega Building since sixth grade. I had expert knowledge on how to scale the fire escape with a minimal amount of noise, like an urban punk rock ninja.

Some noise was inevitable, of course; the wrought iron assembly was old and rusted and the bolts rattled loose against the brick wall, but it also clattered like that whenever the wind blew, so as long as I went slow and played it cool, everyone inside would just think I was a steady breeze.

I reached the fifth floor and slid my bedroom window open from the outside; again, something I had done a bajillion times. I tossed my backpack on my bed, then crawled inside, careful not to drop my sandwich box.

My room wasn't much bigger than a jail cell, with a single window and posters all over the wall. I hit the light switch totally out of reflex. It didn't work. Of course it didn't. I knew they'd cut the power, I just forgot. No power meant no charging my phone.

So I sat on my bed and ate my panini. I didn't listen to music on my phone, because I didn't have any way to charge it and the

43% left on my battery was going to have to last me a while. I just sat there in silence, cross-legged on my bed, and ate.

Funny how we call electricity "the power." "*The* power is out." "I forgot to pay *the* power."

Ma raised me Catholic. She told me that God was so powerful, through him, all things were possible. Well, I didn't see him charging my phone. I needed the power for that.

I stared at all the things on my wall, all the things I would be losing soon. My Bill & Ted movie poster. The "one way" sign I ripped down from that intersection on Mosley, the one I modified with white paint so it read "there's only ONE WAY to party." My collection of Star Wars action figures I slowly pieced together from various thrift stores.

I had a lot of memories in that apartment. Not necessarily *good* memories, but *memories*. So even though this was goodbye, I wasn't going to cry. I had to fight back tears my entire childhood, I wasn't going to waste any now. No, in that moment I just quietly ate my food and thought about how much money sucks.

Electricity. Water. Rent. Insurance. Food. Internet. Cell phone. Shit adds up quick. Who knew it was so expensive to just *live*? Well, I suppose Ma knew, but she got ripped away from me in a flash. I took it for granted that she would always be there to handle all that adult shit while I ran around being a punk ass teenager.

Then, BAM, just like that, she died in a head-on collision and there was no one left to do the adult shit except me, and I didn't have the first clue what I was doing.

I kept a framed picture of me and Ma right by my bed. She originally kept it on the mantle and I never thought much of it, but I moved it into my room the night she died. The picture was from years ago, 2004 or 2005 I guessed, so I must've been nine or ten. She had taken me to Coney Island for the day and we took a selfie on the boardwalk. Ma printed it off at the pharmacy, put it in a nice frame and gave it to me for Christmas one year. She referred to those years as my "normal days," before the spiked hair, the black eyeliner, the dark clothes, and the bad attitude. We looked happy in the picture, me and Ma, and that's how I wanted to remember things.

I ate my half my sandwich, closed the other half inside the box and stuck the box in my backpack. I put the picture of me and Ma in there, too. Wherever I ended up – 83 Forge Street or wherever else – that memory was coming with me.

George's eviction notice came on the heels of the final, final, *final* notice I'd received a week prior. If he found out I'd been in the apartment, he'd start locking the windows. I needed to pack a bug-out bag and never come back. That meant I could only take the bare essentials.

Five of my favorite band t-shirts, all of them black: Billy Idol, Modest Mouse, Pavement, Fall Out Boy, and the Ramones.

Three pairs of black jean-shorts, slightly worn; one with a stain on the pocket from when I bleached my own hair, the other one stained with fingerprints of red spray paint.

Five pairs of underwear, color unimportant.

Five pairs of balled up mis-matched socks, all of them striped, one pair Halloween.

Two belts, black and white, studded. I'd wear them at the same time, criss-crossed like some kind of gunslinger. I was a two-belts kind of girl.

One black hoodie. Sure, it was June and hot as balls outside and I didn't need a hoodie, but it would eventually be fall and I'd be glad I thought ahead. So I grabbed it.

I brought a bra, not that I really wore them. Fate had not been particularly kind to me in that arena. Whatever. Bras are uncomfortable anyway, especially in the summer.

Toothbrush. Toothpaste. Non-scented, dye-free deodorant. A box of tampons. A stick of eyeliner. A bottle of Screaming Harpy hair gel, so I could keep my short hair spiked.

Phone charger, for when I found someplace with power. A pair of big sunglasses.

All of it went into my bag, along with that folded-up help wanted ad.

2

I dug through my closet and realized I didn't have job interview clothes. My wardrobe consisted of band t-shirts, denim shorts and skinny jeans, and black Chuck Taylor's. Ma and I never saw eye-to-eye when it came to fashion. She wanted me to dress every day like I was going to meet the Pope. My philosophy was "everyone stop getting married, it's just one more day I can't wear cut-off shorts."

I looked at myself in the mirror. Only in that moment did I realize how handy nice clothes would have been. I was about to show up to a job interview in a Pavement t-shirt, shorts with holes in them, and black Chucks that showed off my mismatched socks. Never mind the multiple piercings in my ears and the bottom half of my tattoo that poked out from underneath my right sleeve.

The girl in the mirror did not look hire-able. I sighed and slumped my shoulders. I would have prayed for help, but I gave up on God quite a while ago.

"I need this job," I whispered.

Chin up. Self-induced pep talk. You're cool. You're fine. Clothes won't be that big of a deal. After all, it said, "no experience necessary." It's not like I was applying to some accounting firm in the Financial District, right?

I grabbed my skateboard and stuck my foot out the window, ready to head down the fire escape. I stopped and took a moment to burn one last mental image of the apartment into my brain. I was walking out on a lot of material possessions, but what choice did I have? Bring it with me? Couches, tables, plates and silverware? And take them where? Maybe I'd come back for them if I got this miracle job, and depending on this "room" I'd be living in. But even then, Ma was super Catholic and everything she owned was reminiscent of Jesus or Mary or the Pope. The tablecloth had crosses on them. The lamps were all statues of saints. Even the salt and pepper shakers were ceramic Mary and Joseph kneeling down to pray.

I didn't need that religious shit.

I nodded at the apartment and whispered, "See ya."

I skated down the sidewalks of Little Italy and headed down towards Chinatown. I saw my neighborhood in a new way that afternoon. I didn't live there anymore. Come nightfall, I might be living somewhere else, so this was kind of like goodbye. Goodbye street corner where, when I was six, I saw two hobos knife fighting. Goodbye payphone in front of Il Vicino, the last operating payphone on planet Earth. Goodbye old man staring at everyone from your third story window, just like you did yesterday, every day, like you always have, for as long as I can remember.

Goodbye white and orange striped cat. Stray cats were all over Little Italy and I named them all, Old Testament style:

Whiskers begat Mud Boots, Mud Boots begat Spock, Spock begat Chicken Burrito, Chicken Burrito begat Tim Tim, Tim Tim begat Party Waffle, and on and on.

I knew the layout of Chinatown fairly well since that neighborhood blurred right into Little Italy. We never ate Chinese food when I was little because Ma didn't like it, but when I turned twelve and had the freedom to skateboard wherever I wanted, I'd go to Chinatown for lo mein or egg rolls.

I'd skated between Little Italy and Chinatown a bajillion times. I took shortcuts through the alleyways, where the kitchens would leave their back doors open. I spent my teen years listening to the sounds of sizzling foods, angry chefs shouting, and the crashing of pots and pans. I knew which streetlights took forever, the biggest offender being Mulberry and Canal Street.

I blazed down the sidewalks on my skateboard at break-neck speeds. I passed a few kids trying to fry an egg on the sidewalk. It was hot, sure, but not *that* hot; not hot enough to fry an egg, at least not yet. I listened to music on my earbuds to drown out the noise of traffic. I zipped around groups of slow moving tourists.

Traffic lights and crosswalks did not apply to me. I gave up on those things years ago when I came to the realization that no one was going to hit a teenage girl on a skateboard, even if she was the one crossing the street illegally. How I saw it, the taxi cabs and buses would sooner slam on their brakes and cause a fender bender than kill someone, so I used that to my advantage.

Admittedly, I had some close calls skating through traffic. One time a car's side view mirror brushed the back of my t-shirt. Another time this car came so close to me, I caught a whiff of the driver's perfume.

I skated down the sidewalks of Mulberry muttering along to Moon and Antarctica blasting in my headphones. The upcoming corner was crowded with a group of lost tourists waiting for the light to change. I thought, "Fuck this, I'm not waiting on a stupid light." I swept my left foot across the sidewalk a couple times, built up a ton of momentum on my skateboard and drifted right into traffic. I'd done this plenty of times before, but my luck was seriously running out. I had almost made it across the street, I was maybe five feet away from the curb...

That's when I got hit by a taxi.

I couldn't hear a thing over my music until the taxi slammed on its brakes and screeching tires echoed off the buildings. I looked over with just enough time to think "Oh, shit," before its front bumper plowed straight into me.

I must have blacked out in that moment of impact. The next thing I knew, I was twenty feet away, rolling across the sidewalk. I slid to a stop up against the curb, confused about what just happened. My vision was blurry. I couldn't think straight, but that wore off after a few seconds. At least I *was* thinking. That was good. Thinking meant my brains were still in my skull and not splattered all across Mulberry Street.

I sat bolt upright and checked myself for any serious injuries. One of my Chuck Taylor's had flown off, revealing my black and white striped sock. I felt my legs for broken bones. My bare legs were scratched all to hell from sliding across the asphalt, but everything felt fine otherwise.

I reached into my pocket to check my phone. It wouldn't turn on. The screen had shattered. The case was broken into three big pieces. Maybe it was fixable, but I didn't have that kind of money. I could barely afford food, let alone replacement phone screens and out-of-contract upgrades.

Holding my phone was when I saw all the blood smeared across my right hand. More blood trickled down my arm and drizzled off my elbow. The skin across my right arm was scraped all to hell and covered in dirt and gravel. It looked hardcore. I had spots of blood all over my Pavement shirt. That really got my ragu simmering. That shirt was legit vintage from the '90s. Now it was all torn up and soaked in blood which, I guess one could argue made it more punk rock, but it still sucked.

I swept my clean hand over my face and checked it for blood. No problems there. At least my face wasn't fucked up. I ran my fingertips across my skull. I had leaves and gravel all in my hair, but no blood. I looked like a real mess. I stood up and brushed myself off. My hip hurt pretty bad, but I could put weight on it, so I knew it wasn't broken.

A crowd of people gathered around me, asking me if I was okay. I did my best to ignore them.

Then this bearded dude got out of the cab. He had on a Mets ball cap and he ran straight for me. He's shook his finger at me and shouted, "Your fault! Your fault! Your fault!" I ignored him, too. Maybe it was my fault, maybe it wasn't. I didn't have the time to play the blame game. My phone was busted, my shirt was fucked up, I was pissed, and I still needed to find my skateboard. But even as I wandered around in search for my board, the guy kept following me around.

"You did this!" he shouted. "Not me!"

I ignored him and muttered, "Dude, fuck off out of here."

I needed to find my skateboard. In New York City, your transportation is an extension of yourself. If you ride a bike, you're either a health nut or a package courier. If you ride in a limo, you're rich and you suck. If you take the bus, you're an average Joe.

My skateboard was no different. Ma got it for me when I was twelve – against her better judgment, she said – and six years later I still rode it everywhere. It was the only thing Ma ever gave me that I actually liked. I had this awesome collection of band stickers all over it, like a Weezer and Slayer and stuff like that. I spent years collecting stickers and putting them on my board. It also had these sweet glow-in-the-dark, neon red Spinerette wheels that I bought online for forty bucks.

I spotted my board and froze.

It had been broken in half.

The front half was in the gutter against the curb. The back half was on the sidewalk. The back wheels were still spinning, that's how fast this all happened. My face flushed red-hot as I went from pissed-off to full volcano mode. A phone's just a phone. Who cares. A phone's just a *thing*. That skateboard, though, I couldn't replace that. That board was one of a kind, given to me by my dead mother and each sticker was a brief memory from my pitiful life. I picked up both pieces and held them in my hands by the wheel assemblies.

"I want insurance," the taxi dude yelled at me. He held out his hand like I was going to give him my insurance card. "Insurance now."

"My mom gave me this board, you fucking asshole!" If I didn't punch something soon, I was going to explode. "Fuck your insurance."

I could hear Ma now. *"No fighting."*

"Stay out of this," I muttered to her.

"You stay here." The taxi guy pointed at the ground. He took out his phone. I knew he was calling the police. I didn't have the patience to deal with that kind of bullshit.

"Dude, fuck you," I shouted.

"Fuck to me? Fuck to you!"

He reached out grabbed me by the arm. That's it. He touched me. Game over.

My rage melted down like a nuclear accident. I yanked my arm free from his grip and bashed his windshield with the chunks of my skateboard. Three good smashes and the glass cracked. He tried to stop me by grabbing for my wrists, but I swung my arms around and ran circles around his taxi. He chased after me.

I kept beat the shit out of his taxi with the pieces of my broken skateboard. I pounded a dent into the trunk. I swung my broken skateboard as hard as I could at his door and tore the side view mirror right off. Once I got to the front, I raised my foot and smashed the heel of my sneaker into his headlight over and over until the glass burst and went everywhere.

Eventually the guy had seen enough. He actually took a swing at me. I dodged and he kind of got me in the shoulder, but I couldn't feel it through all the adrenaline coursing through my veins. I jabbed at him with the broken, pointy ends of my board and forced him to back off.

I caught sight of the passengers in the back of the taxi, a horrified out-of-town couple who watched everything go down. They were a couple of looky-loo's from Omaha, probably, with a front row seat to a real, actual, honest-to-God New York street fight. The lady took a picture of me with her phone. I flipped her off.

Then came the distant sound of police sirens. That was my cue to exit. I ran to the sidewalk, grabbed my backpack and my shoe that fell off in the accident, and I bolted. I did a lot of damage to that guy's taxi and I wasn't going to be on the hook for that; just one more bill I'd never be able to pay.

By the time the cops showed up, I was out of breath and two blocks away.

3

It's a slow burn, transitioning from Little Italy to Chinatown. You notice fewer and fewer Italian restaurants, then suddenly more and more Chinese ones. Next thing you know, you're in Chinatown. Each store had a sign mounted on the outside wall of their buildings, looming over the street like square, low-hanging banners. If you stood in the middle of the street and stared down the length of it, you'd see hundreds of signs; red signs with white Chinese characters, yellow signs with blue characters, blue signs with red characters; all of them tucked between a disorganized network of power lines that connected the rooftops. Some of the signs were long and narrow, others short and squat. I couldn't read Chinese, but I'd seen the signs enough times to know which color combination went with each store.

I walked down Forge Street looking for 83 Forge. Super Wash Dry Clean (white banner with blue letters) was 81. The Asian Food Mart (red banner with white letters) was 85.

I stood there and looked back and forth. Above the glass doors to the dry cleaning place was 81. Above the food mart was 85. There was no 83 Forge Street.

"Well, what the hell," I said. I unslung my backpack down on the sidewalk and pulled out the Village Voice. I checked the ad again and, just like I thought, it said 83 Forge street. So where was it?

The only thing between Super Wash Dry Clean and the Asian Food Mart was a narrow alleyway, so narrow that you could maybe fit a motorcycle down it, but not a car. The buildings were close enough together to block out the sunshine and leave the alley dark and dangerous.

Was I supposed to go down the murder alley? Maybe there was a side door or something like that. I went to investigate. I stepped over some wood pallets and scooted between the wall and a big dumpster. The end of the alley was blocked off by a tall chain link fence. I thought it was a dead end, but the fence had a gate, one you would only notice once you were up close, not from the street.

Beyond the chain link fence was a small, sun-lit courtyard walled in by all the surrounding apartment buildings. And there in the middle of that hidden plot of land stood a humble brick building with plants out on the front porch.

I stepped through the gate and entered that courtyard/plaza sort of thing. It wasn't really a courtyard, with grass or trees, and it wasn't really a plaza, with decorative bricks or statues. No, this place was more like an abandoned parking lot with squares of cracked concrete.

The decor of the shop matched everything else in Chinatown. Above the door was a yellow banner with green Chinese letters that I couldn't read. It wasn't a big shop, maybe just big enough for two or three rooms. The front facing exterior had a couple filthy windows decorated with colorful flowers. All different species of plants sat in pots along the ledge of the front porch, too, and a few more hung in baskets from the porch awning. I walked up to the porch and inspected the plants. I had never seen anything like them before in my life. One plant had leaves that grew in perfect triangles. Another one had leaves that curled into cylinders. One of them with wispy-thin stems bloomed flowers of electric blue and hot pink.

Each plant looked as if they came from some far-flung part of the world or even from another planet. Some of them were so strange, I thought they were fake. I wondered, "Maybe this place crafts silk flowers as a kind of art project," but the flowers didn't feel like silk. They felt real and they smelled real.

One plant had long vines that hung down to the ground and sprouted fuzzy leaves, like the skin of a peach. I touched one of those leaves with my fingertips and when I did, the leaf curled up tight like some kind of defense mechanism. I yanked my hand away and after a few seconds, the leaf unrolled back to normal.

The front door had an 83 painted above it and was propped open with a big chunk of yellow granite that sparkled with gold flakes. I was like, "Damn, even this *doorstop* is fancy."

I slowly and cautiously stepped inside. It felt like intruding unannounced into someone's home. The inside was dimly lit opposed to the hot, summer sun and I immediately felt ten degrees cooler. The air of the shop had that earthy greenhouse scent of wet dirt. There was a long glass counter, like a display case you'd find in a pawn shop. Behind the counter sat an old Chinese dude. It was safe to assume he was the man in charge, because there was no one else there. We made eye contact and I smiled at him. He didn't smile back, he just stared at me. I felt awkward and didn't want to jump right into the, "Hey, I'm here about the job" part, so I tried to play it cool and act like I was just there to shop around.

The entire shop was lit by the sunshine coming in through the windows and a single light bulb in the ceiling. Small fans rattled on the surrounding tables to keep the air circulating.

The walls were covered floor to ceiling with handmade shelves. The shelves were crowded with glass jars of all different sizes; baby food jars up top, pickle jars in the middle, and then big three-gallon jars on the floor. The baby food jars had powders of white and brown and red. The pickle jars were filled with sticks and herbs, some of them soaking in clear liquids. The big jars on the floor had bones and leaves and soil. Plastic bags hung from the exposed pipes in the ceiling, filled with God-knows-what. Then there were the tables of potted plants. The tables were arranged throughout the shop to perfectly capture the square blocks of sunlight that shone in through the four windows.

I finished "browsing" the shelves and went up to the old man's counter. I looked inside the display case, home to hundreds of metal canisters. These also came in all sizes – little ones like mascara bottles and big ones like tennis ball tubes. Their metal lids were taped shut with masking tape and marked in Chinese words. I looked at the cans, then I glanced up at the old man. He was still watching me.

He looked like someone's kindly old grandpa. He wore old man grandpa clothes: a plain white cotton polo and a navy blue Nike windbreaker. He wore bifocals with dorky black rims, so dorky they'd go for big bucks in the hipster circles. He'd lost most of his hair up top, but what little hair he had on the sides was jet black. When I got my first good look at him, I thought he had to be a hundred years old, maybe a hundred and five. A lifetime of gravity made his face droopy and sad.

I had apparently caught him in the middle of weighing powder on one of those old-school scales, the ones where you put your product on one plate and then lead weights on the other plate and try to balance them out. He hadn't moved since I came in, powder in his hand, and he stared at me over the rim of his glasses.

Like Ma always told me, whenever you meet someone new, it's polite to start with a compliment.

"Nice place you got here," I said.

He didn't respond. I had never felt so awkward. I just wanted to turn and leave as fast as my legs could carry me. I went for the door, but then caught my eye on another row of jars. I could not, for the life of me, recognize a single goddamned thing contained inside. One big jar had huge white leaves inside, like

15

sheets of paper. One of the medium jars had something that resembled asparagus, except it was bright red. Another jar was filled with his disgusting white mush, which I assumed was mold. I was also pretty sure it was moving – moving *slow* – but moving.

Finally, after all that poking around, the old man said his first words to me.

"Do you need a doctor?"

I nearly jumped at the sudden sound of his voice. "Do what?"

"You're covered in blood." He gestured at me, up and down. "Do you need a doctor?"

I realized what he was talking about. I had blood all over my right arm, blood soaked into my shirt, and drips of blood down my legs. Not a good first impression. Not a good way to start a job interview.

"Oh, this?" I said. I made a face and tried to blow it off. "This is nothing. I'm fine. I just got hit by a taxi."

"You're sure you don't need a doctor?"

I shrugged. "Barely even hurts."

He pursed his lips and nodded. He stood up and went to the shelves behind his counter and brought down a jar of white powder. He set it down on the counter and used a regular old coffee scoop to pour the powder into a stone mortar. He splashed the powder with bottled water and mixed it together with a wooden spoon. Intrigued, I drew a little closer. I caught a whiff of whatever he was mixing. It smelled funky, like bleach and lake water, and I wrinkled my nose.

"Come here." He pointed at the bar stool on my side of the counter. "Sit."

And I did. He carried the mortar around the counter and stood next to me. He used his bare fingers to apply that nasty smelling goop to my shredded arm. I hissed in surprise because it stung like a bitch. Good thing I wasn't a huge germaphobe, because he didn't bother to use gloves at all. He studied my arm carefully and dabbed at my skin until all the cuts were completely covered in white goo. My arm throbbed like a bad sunburn.

"What is this stuff?" I asked him as I checked out my arm.

"Medicine." He finished applying the paste and went back behind the counter. "So you're here about the job, I assume."

"Yeah," I said. "How'd you know?"

"I know my customers," he said. "You're not a customer."

"Look," I said, going right into my spiel. "I know it looks really bad, me coming in here covered in blood and stuff, but I really need this job. I'm a hard worker, I think, and I'm pretty smart. I just graduated from St. Mark's high school with pretty good grades."

He looked at me critically, like everything I said was nutso crazy-talk. He didn't reply.

I slumped my shoulders with a sigh. "Can I be honest with you?"

He motioned at me to continue. "Go ahead."

"I'm sorry if I'm coming off desperate or whatever. Everything's just been going wrong lately." I straightened my posture on the bar stool and made direct eye contact with him. "I got evicted from my place today. I need somewhere to go. I don't even care what the job is, I'll do whatever, but if I'm being honest, I've never applied for a job before and I'm really scared I'm going to screw it up."

"I've never hired anyone before," he said. "So we have that in common."

"Really?" I asked. I sighed. "That makes me feel a little better."

"Let's start with introductions." He put his hand to his chest. "I am Xin. Xin Houng. This is my herbal shop."

"Cool." I reached out for a handshake. "I'm Penelope Salvo, unemployed slacker from Little Italy."

We shook hands.

"So what now?" I asked him.

"Now," Xin said, "I think I'm supposed to interview you."

4

Xin adjusted the glasses on his nose and placed his hands flat on the counter. He said, "You're familiar with the game Twenty Questions, I assume?"

"Of course," I said.

"I will ask you twenty questions. You answer them honestly. That will help me decide if you are the right person for the job."

"Cool." I clapped my hands and brushed them together. I was psyched. This was more like a game than an interview. "Let's do it."

I'd gone through plenty of tests in high school, some of them oral, but none of them prepared me for this.

"First," he said. "Why did you get evicted?"

"Honestly?" I decided to give him the short version. "My mom died in a car wreck a couple months ago and I don't have any money."

"Don't you have anyone else to live with?"

"No. Not really. My grandparents all died a long time ago and I was an only child."

"Where is your father?"

I groaned. "Does this count as one of the questions?"

"I think it does. It seems important."

"Do I get to pass or something?"

He considered that for a moment, then replied, "No."

I sighed. "Well, he's gone. He's not here. Not here in New York City and not here in New York state. I don't know where he is and that's fine by me cuz I don't want to know, so that's that."

"Oh. Okay." My answer was tense, forceful, and honest. I guess he didn't want to press the issue. His eyes wandered to the ceiling as he thought of more questions. A good one popped into his brain and he returned his gaze to me. "Do you know anything about botany?"

"Is that a band?" I asked with a nervous laugh. That was supposed to be a joke, but his face kind of went sour, like he didn't understand why that would be funny. I did some damage control. "I don't know botany, but I'm a fast learner. I'm one of those people where if you show me how to do something once, I'll pick it up right away."

"The plants I have are very rare," he told me. "They must be handled very carefully."

I nodded in eager agreement. "I can tell. I'd be super careful with them."

"The job also includes sweeping the floors," he said. "And also cleaning the bathroom. You'd be okay doing these tasks?"

"Ugh, you mean like a janitor?" Cleaning wasn't my strong suit. Just the thought of it brought a disgusted look to my face. I realized my reaction probably wasn't winning me any jobby-points, so I quickly switched my tone and gave him a sincere-looking smile. "I mean, I don't mind. Like I said, I'll do anything. But... and just to be clear here... I'd be a janitor?"

"I'm asking the questions," he said.

"Oh. Sorry."

"You can't distract me like that. I'm trying to keep track of how many questions I've asked, plus think of new questions at the same time."

"Sorry."

"I forgot how many questions I asked."

"That was five," I told him.

He raised an eyebrow at me. "You're sure?"

I nodded. I might be bad at math, but I can at least count to five. "Pretty sure."

"Okay. Question number six." He cleared his throat and adjusted himself on his stool. "Have you committed any crimes?"

"Uh." The answer was yes. But I had to think of a way to spin it. "Okay, full disclosure, yes. But it was total bullshit."

"What did you do?" he asked.

"Just dumb stuff. Once I got busted for being out past curfew. Another time some cop caught me spray painting a wall, but it wasn't anything bad or anything. I was painting a picture of a cat, but it was on the wall of that library on thirteenth street, so the cops made a huge deal out of it and I had to do 20 hours of bullshit-ass community service. And then this other time I got into a fight at school and the police got called."

"You're a fighter?"

A small laugh escaped me. "Depending on who you ask, I have..." I did air quotes. "Anger issues."

He rubbed his chin. "Hmm."

I winced and asked him softly, "Is that bad?"

He thought about it for a second, then said, "No. Because another part of the job here is being night security. So being a fighter might come in handy."

"Night security?" I asked. "So I work here all day and then work here all night? When do I sleep?"

"You sleep here," he said. "Whenever you want."

"You mean the free room is *here*?" I asked. "In this grody ass store?"

"It's the only room I have." He held up a hand. "But, still, save your questions. You're making me forget what number I'm on."

"Right." He had a spiral notebook and a little golf pencil on the counter. I grabbed both of them and slid them in front of me. "Here, I'll keep track for you."

He'd already asked nine questions, or maybe it was eight. Eight or nine. I couldn't remember. Fuck it, I called it nine and made nine tick marks in the notebook.

He asked, "Are you a light sleeper or a heavy sleeper?"

I scratched another tick mark on the paper. That made ten.

I gave him a weird look. "Why?"

"You're going to be sleeping here, but you're also night security," he said. "I need to know how alert you'll be at night."

"Oh." Still, weird question. "I'm a light sleeper, I guess."

He gave me a thoughtful nod. "Have you ever been outside New York City?"

Tick. Eleven.

"Yeah," I said. "Lots of times."

"Where did you go?"

Tick. Twelve.

I listed them off on my fingers. "Jersey. Vermont. Egypt, one time."

"Egypt?"

Thirteen. That wasn't technically a question, but I counted it.

I said, "Yeah, Michael, my father, he was an archaeologist. One summer he was working at some dig site in Egypt. He flew me out there to visit him over summer break."

"What was that like?"

Fourteen.

"It sucked. And I'd rather not talk about it."

His eyes wandered back to the ceiling for a moment. "So would you consider yourself a trouble maker?"

Fifteen.

"Uh." Man. If there was ever a question to lie to.

"Be honest," he reminded me.

"I mean, I guess?" I nervously put my hands between my knees. "I don't do it on purpose. Just sometimes I do stuff without thinking and then... next thing I know..." I held up my arm. "I'm covered in blood."

"But you wouldn't cause trouble here," he said.

"Is that a question?" I asked.

He cleared his throat. "Would you cause trouble here?"

Sixteen.

"Hell no, dude. Not if you were paying me money and giving me a place to stay. I would do everything all straight and narrow, all by the books."

"Having a place to stay is that important to you?"

Seventeen.

"Dude, I am literally hours away from sleeping on the sidewalk or something. I can't end up homeless, you know? Sleeping on the subway or under a bridge." I shook my head, lost in my own thoughts. "I've seen the girls that live on the streets and how they end up. Addicted to drugs, giving handy-J's to strangers for five or ten bucks. It's literally hell. I can't end up like that. I can't."

"Mhmm." He nodded his head. I hoped he appreciated the situation I was in.

We sat there quietly. I'd made things uncomfortable and had to recover, quick.

I tapped the golf pencil to the spiral notebook. "You got three questions left."

"Right." He thought for a moment. "May I ask about your relationship with your mother? If you don't want to answer that one-"

"Nah, it's cool." I took a cleansing breath. It wasn't anything I usually talked about. I didn't have anyone to talk about it with. "She was alright. Super religious and a little strict. There was a lot of stuff we didn't agree on, and most of it was about me and how I wanted to live my life. She didn't want me piercing my ears. She didn't want me dying my hair. She didn't want me getting a tattoo. She didn't want me listening to punk rock music because that was going to lead me to Satan. And then, boom, just like that, she dies in a car wreck."

"Months ago, you said."

I nodded. "Driving to my high school graduation."

Things were quiet again. Xin finally spoke up with, "I am sorry."

"It's cool." I stared at the floor. It wasn't cool, obviously, but it was easier to put on a tough exterior than to cry in front of a stranger. "My life got real fucked up after she died. All the medical bills, you know? And the funeral home and the ambulance people and everything else. She left me some money but..." I tossed my hands up. "It's all gone now."

And we went back to being quiet. Do most job interviews go this way?

"I believe I have one question remaining," he said.

"Oh." I got so distracted by the topic of Ma, that I forgot to keep track. Xin kept track though, apparently. "Go ahead. Make it a good one."

He tapped his chin, then his face lit up with the perfect question. "Do you mind if I pay you cash, under the table?"

"Uhm." I had to think about that for a second. "I guess not?"

"Good. The city doesn't need to know what's going on here." He dusted off his hands, like we'd just finished a hard days work. "Well, that's it."

"Alright." I sat there for a moment. "So what do we do now? Do I come back or...?"

"No," he said.

"Oh."

"You got the job."

"I got the job?"

"Yes." He stood up from the counter, as if to say the meeting was over.

"Wait." I also stood up. "Just like that?"

"Just like that." He walked to a door behind the counter. "Let me show you to your room."

"Wait, wait." I followed after him. "How do I have the job? You're not going to interview anyone else?"

"Oh." He stopped short, like this never occurred to him. He turned back to me and asked, "Do you think I should?"

I gave him a worried look. "No?"

"Okay. Then the job is yours."

"Well, you told me to save my questions until the end. Can I ask them now?"

"I suppose that's fair."

"Like..." When it came to questions, I had a billion of them in my brain, all running into each other, bumping into one another, and I struggled to put them in order. Eventually I settled on the one that weighed most heavily on my mind. "You're not a murderer or something, are you?"

He raised an eyebrow at me. "That's an odd question."

"Yeah, I know, but come on. You're giving me a room. You want me to sleep here all alone. It's a little shady."

"It's very shady," Xin said, opening the door to the dimly lit back room. "There's only one window and it doesn't get very good light."

"No, I mean, it's weird. Me living here in your flower shop. That's weird."

He looked back at me. "You're the one who wants a place to live."

"I know." I sighed and my arms dropped to my side. "I just... you know... don't want to get murdered."

"You have a very active imagination," he said.

I gave him a very serious face. "Humor me."

He reached out and put his hand on my shoulder. He gave me a kind look and said, "I'm not a murderer. You don't have anything to worry about."

Psh. That's exactly what a murder would say.

"So if I have the job..." I poked my head into the back room, *my* room, and looked around. It was small and dark. "What exactly do I have to do?"

"In the morning, you sweep the floors and water the plants. In the evening, you sweep the floors and you water the plants. At night, you watch the shop and stop any burglars from breaking in."

I arched my eyebrow at him. "You get a lot of burglars back here in your Narnia courtyard of Chinatown?"

"No, as a matter of fact. Never."

"So basically I just sweep the floor and water the plants."

"There might be more," he said. "You'll pick it up as you go. Take your time settling in. I will be out front."

The back room was just as small as my old bedroom. There was a cot and a wooden work table filled with gardening supplies. That's where I lived now, just like that. It felt a little surreal, suddenly having a place to live under such odd circumstances, and I had to remind myself: *At least you're not homeless. You're living in the back of a Chinatown herbal shop and that might be weird, but at least you're not homeless.* I threw my backpack on the cot. I set the Coney Island picture of me and Ma on the table and angled it to face the rest of the room.

"I did it, Ma," I told her, then looked around the dimly lit room. "Whatever *it* ends up being."

Those first couple days working for Xin Houng were enlightening. He taught me more about plants than I ever cared to know. Each plant needed a specific amount of water and sunlight. Some of them needed water in the morning, some in the evening, and once a week it was my job to trim the ones that needed trimming. I swept the porch in the morning, then again at night. He paid me in cash every day, all under the table.

It wasn't much, but at least I had a place to live.

I spent those first few nights making the back room feel more like home. The floor hadn't been cleaned in forever and had a layer of mud built up from decades of gardening supplies. I wasn't about sleep in a room that filthy. I scrubbed the wood floors down with a brush and a bucket of hot water filled with my patchouli soap. I took some of the cash Xin gave me and bought a pillow and a sleeping bag from the thrift store for two bucks. They helped make that World War Two cot in the back feel a million times more comfortable. I dressed out of my backpack and when my clothes needed washing, I carried them up the alley to the Super Wash Dry Clean.

Slowly but surely, I turned the dirty supply room into a clean, habitable space.

My room had a small rectangular window by the ceiling – I think they're called egress windows or something – and I had to get up there with a screwdriver and chip away the paint so I could open it. That let some fresh air into the room, as much as there's "fresh air" in Chinatown. At night I'd lay on my cot, hands folded over my stomach, and stare at the way the moonlight glowed on the ceiling beams. I'd think about Ma and wonder if she would have been proud that her unskilled, eighteen-year-old daughter somehow found a place to live, or if she would have been disappointed that I ended up in the back room of a Chinatown shop. I would fall asleep to those thoughts, huddled in my sleeping bag.

I don't think Xin really needed night security. If people couldn't find 83 Forge Street in the daytime, they sure a hell weren't going to find it at night. I suppose my on-premises living situation counted as security – if anyone tried to break in, I'd be right there to hear it – but Xin didn't need night security.

I think he just saw an opportunity to help a lost soul.

Sometimes I'd wake up at night to weird noises. Not criminals trying to break in, but something from under the floorboards. I couldn't figure out what the sounds were because they only happened when I was asleep. The moment I woke up, they'd stop. Maybe I dreamed it, but something about them felt real. Sometimes it sounded like a shelf of nick-nacks falling over. Other times I thought I heard voices, or maybe music. But once I sat up awake and alert, everything would stop. I would walk barefoot out out into the dark herbal shop with a flashlight and inspect everything, behind the counter, in the bathroom, but I never found anything out of place. Even the front door was locked.

There were three doors inside the shop: the door to my bedroom, the door to the bathroom, and then a third door that Xin kept padlocked shut. I had no idea what room was behind that third door. One night I put my ear to that door, expecting to find the source of the noises, but it was silent.

In the morning when Xin came to open the shop, I'd tell him, "Sometimes when I'm sleeping, I hear these weird noises, you know?"

"I don't know," he said. "I've never been here at night."

"Yeah." I walked him back to my room and pointed at the cot. "I'll be sleeping there and then I'll hear a banging or something from below the floor. Sometimes it sounds like music, or voices, or stuff falling over. It comes from under the floor."

"Strange."

"Is there a basement here?"

Xin shook his head. "You know, this building is just old. It's settling. I'm sure the noises you heard were the pipes. Or maybe the water heater."

"I dunno." I wanted to believe him, but I lived in shitty apartment buildings my whole life. I know what knocking pipes sounds like. I asked him outright, "If there was something weird going on here, you'd tell me, right? Because I really don't want to wake up to monsters and shit."

"You and your imagination." Xin laughed and barely looked up from his mortar and pestle. "There are no monsters."

6

I liked working for Xin way more than I expected to. And

living in his shop turned out to be pretty great. For one, he kept the place dark and cool, a pretty welcome break from the New York summer. For two, being surrounded by a ton of cool plants came with this chill, mystical vibe. Xin had a hundred plants inside, another dozen on the front porch. Each one fascinated me in a unique way. The vines of the Looping Bandis grew in perfect spirals that coiled down to the floor and bloomed bright yellow flowers. The Lava Crocus looked like a tulip with red and orange petals, but smelled like Tabasco sauce. I made the mistake of sticking my nose in those flowers and sniffing hard. My nose burned for an hour.

Xin would spend the day grinding different herbs and liquids in his mortar and pestle, making new potions, and pouring them into little jars. He'd grind flower petals, or dried roots, or seeds, then carefully weigh them out in ounces and package them for his customers.

He had this old-as-hell radio from the '80s; the boxy kind with a telescoping antenna and manual dials and all that jazz. It just sat on the shelf by the front door, unused, and with a fine layer of dust. I didn't have a phone anymore, otherwise I would have used it to listen to music while I worked. I asked him about the radio one day. I was like, "What's up with the radio, grandpepper?" He said he only used it to listen to the weather when things got bad. I asked him if I could listen to music while I swept and stuff and he shrugged.

"Just not too loud," was the only rule.

I hit up Q104.3. It was a mix station which leaned pretty heavily into classic rock – like the Steve Miller Band or Led Zeppelin – but would sometimes play stuff from the 2000's. I remember one morning I was watering the plants on the front porch when the radio started playing Fortunate Son by CCR. I danced in place and poured water into the Tulips De Athens – these electric blue tulips that bloomed so fast, you could watch the petals move – and I swore I heard Xin singing along with the lyrics. I looked inside through the window and, sure enough, he was moving his mouth to the words.

We kept the front door propped open, so I just shouted at him from the porch, "Dude, you know CCR?"

He didn't even look up from his mortar and pestle. "They write good songs. I saw them in 1969."

"You saw them?" I asked. "Like you went to one of their concerts?"

"I saw them at Woodstock."

That was a crazy thing to hear. He said it like it was no big deal. I moved to the doorway and gave him my undivided attention. "Dude, you were at Woodstock? What was it like?"

"What's the word." He thought for a moment. "It was gravy."

I laughed. "You mean 'groovy'?"

He looked right at me and said, "No."

These were the kind of random things we'd talk about every day. I spent the rest of June at Xin's shop. Slowly but surely – and with Xin's help – I memorized the names of all the plants and exactly how to water them. The Himalayan White Lotus needed a half cup of ice cold water every day. The Lava Crocus needed two cups of boiling water at night. The Lemon Lime Suckles needed water in the morning and at night. After I learned the names of the plants, Xin taught me the names of all the roots and herbs. Then, after that, I learned the names of all the stuff in all the jars. He labeled them in Chinese, which made it really hard to learn. Not only did I have to learn the names of everything, I had to learn to read them in Chinese. I really struggled with that and I worried that I might never get it down, but it was in my job description and I wasn't going to give up.

After two months, the shop really felt like home. I still heard the noises at night, although not as often. One night I woke up and clearly heard something moving inside the shop. Usually the sounds would vanish the moment I'd open my eyes, but that time in particular they lasted a few seconds longer. The next day, I brought it up with Xin again. He danced around the subject and made a few excuses, never acknowledging the sounds, denying the shop had a basement, and never talking about the mysterious door.

In all my time at the shop, I'd never seen Xin open that door for any reason. He didn't look at the door. He didn't talk about the door. So one day when he was filling cans with this gray powder, I just came right out and asked him:

"Xin, what's behind that door?"

Xin froze. He kept his face pointed down, but his eyes moved up to meet mine. "What door?"

I pointed at it. "That door."

"That's nothing."

"No, that's not nothing. That-" I pointed at it harder. "-is a door."

He put down his tools, sat up straight, and looked me right in the eyes. "Penelope," he said. "*That* is *nothing*."

And we just sat there for a moment. Fine. The door was nothing. I decided to drop it, but now my curiosity was worse than before. Why have a door and why keep it padlocked if it's "nothing." That's not nothing. That's something. I couldn't work without glancing at the door. It just sat there, padlocked closed. Anything could have been back there. Gold, maybe? Or a portal to a far away world? Or maybe – and this is how my brain works sometimes – maybe that's where he stashed the bodies.

Maybe I was, like, the sixth girl he had working for him and he was just waiting to kill me and stuff my body in there with everyone else's. But that was crazy. Xin was a sweetheart. He wasn't a murderer. He promised.

So, in the end, I had to just accept the fact that he didn't want to talk about the door and that was that.

But still.

Chapter 2

1

We fell into a good working routine Xin and I. He would grind roots into powder and make medicine, I would water the plants and take out the trash, and we'd work to whatever music came on the radio. He kept the radio right by the cash register so he could turn it down whenever a customer walked in. Xin's customers were mostly Chinatown locals; restaurant owners looking for specific herbs only found in mainland China, that kind of thing. They'd come down the alley and through the chain link gate, walk into the store and strike up a conversation in Chinese. Xin would make small talk with the customers and I'd just keep watering the plants because my Chinese was limited to "lo mein" and "kung pao." Most of the restaurant owners were regulars and, like clockwork, they'd show up at the same time every day. Sometimes they'd bring Xin food, either to be neighborly or because they had some kind of "you scratch my back" sort of deal going on.

By the time September rolled around, I recognized the regulars and they recognized me, so when I saw them come through the chain link fence, I'd announce it to Xin.

I'd be like, "Xin, the dude from China Wall is here," and Xin would get their orders together and have them ready before the customers even walked in. The locals got used to seeing me at Xin's shop: the oddly-dressed Italian girl who swept the floor and watered the plants.

Mrs. Cho, this plump old lady who washed laundry for her entire apartment building, would come over every couple days and get this specific kind of detergent that only Xin knew how to make. Whenever she'd show up I would wave at her and shout, "Hi, Mrs. Cho." She would smile really big and give me a polite wave back, but never said anything to me. She didn't speak English, I didn't speak Chinese, so that was the extent of our interactions.

Another regular, this young dude who delivered for China Wall and who preferred his American name "Mark," had a crush on me. He would bring me fried rice and egg rolls in the evenings right before the dinner rush. He also brought me a China Wall magnet and asked me to put it on Xin's cash register to advertise his family business, which I did right away. Mark was always sweet and respectful and never invaded my personal space, a rare thing for guys in New York. I felt bad taking food from him, like I was taking advantage of him to get free stuff, but I didn't ask him to do that stuff. He just did it. I don't know. Maybe I *was* taking advantage of him. Whatever. It's not like I was going for the gold in the Morality Olympics.

Those were the normal customers.

Then we'd get this whole different kind of customer: the white businessmen from Wall Street. These guys would come in all anxious and paranoid, probably because they were terrified of walking down the dark, filthy alley and hated touching the chain link gate with their pretty boy, wall street hands. These guys didn't come around anywhere near as often, but sometimes, and I can only assume because of word of mouth. Embarrassing enough for them, they all came for pretty much the same reason: they couldn't get boners. See, Xin had this Chinese herbal remedy which basically worked like prescription boner drugs, but you didn't need a prescription to buy it and what Xin had was way cheaper. The stuff apparently worked, because why else would these old dudes brave the back alleys of Chinatown? They would always give me a confused look when they walked past me on the porch, because they're at an herbal shop in Chinatown and here's an Italian girl doing the chores.

They'd get all flustered and ask me, "Is this the herbal shop?"

And I wouldn't be able to answer without laughing, because I knew they were looking for penis medicine. But eventually I'd get it together long enough to say, "Yeah, this is the place."

Xin ran a real simple operation. Cash only, no credit cards. He had an old school cash register on the counter with push buttons and a big lever on the side. It looked like something straight out of the old west. Whenever someone bought something, he'd lean over the register, push his glasses against his nose, then hunt and peck for each button. Clack. Clack. Clack. I could text seventy words a minute, so watching him use the cash register felt like being frozen in time. Eventually he'd figure it out and get these old businessmen their medicine, ring them up, and collect their cash.

Nine times out of ten Xin would wrap everything up and the guy would just go away, headed back to his condo in the Hamptons. But it was that tenth guy who would stand there and ask, "Can I get a receipt?"

And Xin would ask, "A receipt?"

And the business dude would say something about medical insurance, that if he had a receipt, he could give it to his accountant and get reimbursed. Some bullshit tax loophole, if you ask me, but sometimes they really wanted a receipt. Xin's math wasn't great, especially when it came to the 8.875% tax rate. He'd call for me, not like my math skills were any better. I totally suck at math and had to cheat to pass Trig in high school.

"Penelope?" he'd call out.

I would walk over. "Yeah?"

He'd ask, "Can you make this man a receipt?"

Then I'd walk over and touch the man on the head. "Poof. You're a receipt."

I think I'm very funny.

So these were the two kinds of normal customers. Chinatown locals and old dudes who couldn't get their dicks to work. But then there was a third kind of customer, and this is important. These were the weird ones.

This one time a lady came in dressed like a ninja. She wasn't wearing some poor man's ninja outfit like you'd see on Halloween. No, these ninja clothes looked like the real deal, straight out of Japan. Every inch of her body was wrapped in black cloth and her wrists and ankles were secured with black rope to hold all the fabric in place. She had a bunch of swords

31

tied to her back, all bundled together like a quiver of arrows. There were knives tucked into pockets on her forearms, her legs, then a few more handles poking out around her ankles. Anywhere this ninja could have a knife, she had a knife. Rope looped around her waist, then criss-crossed between her boobs so she could move without getting caught up in the fabric. She darted up the alley, not in a straight line, but bouncing and kick-flipping from left to right, right to left, like this was some kind of gymnastics competition. I saw her coming and was like, "What in the actual fuck? Is this really a ninja?" I mean, there were always different celebrations going on in Chinatown; maybe she was just someone dressed for the occasion.

The ninja ignored the porch stairs and leaped right over the front railing. She landed right in front of me on the porch and stared me down. Her face was wrapped in black cloth, but left her eyes uncovered. She looked young, like twenty-something. She sized me up head-to-toe and glared. I wasn't about to get glared at by anyone, not even a Ninja.

I told her, "You can point that bitch look somewhere else, actually."

She shifted into some sort of attack stance, arms out like she wanted to go for one of her knives. I'm thinking, great, here we go, now I have to bitch slap a ninja. But Xin came out and defused the situation before I got a chance to throw down. He asked me to focus on watering the plants, which I did, and he invited the ninja inside. She went in. Xin closed the front door and I heard it lock.

Once they were both out of earshot, I muttered, "You just saved her life."

Xin wouldn't lock the front door during business hours unless he had a weird customer like a ninja. The more he wanted privacy, the more I wanted to know what was going on. I watered the Paper Daisies in the big planter. Then I watered the Red Muscari on the ledge. Those just happened to be the plants closest to the window. I hovered over the plants and peered inside to watch Xin and the ninja through the dirty glass. I couldn't hear them. Even if I could hear them, I didn't speak Chinese or Japanese or whatever language they had in common, so I guess it didn't matter either way.

After a brief conversation, the ninja stuck her hands in the folds of her black clothes and pulled out a red jewelry box. She handed it to Xin and Xin took it to the mystery door. He took a key from around his neck, unlocked the padlock on the door, and went down a flight of stairs. I *knew* it. It knew there was a basement down there. Xin had been lying to me. He left the ninja all alone. She must've had some mystical sixth sense about being watched, because she turned and looked right at me. I ducked out of the window and went back to watering.

Plant by plant, I watered my way across the porch and snooped inside through a different window. Xin came up from the basement without the red box. He closed the basement door, clicked the padlock back into place, and came around the counter. He bowed at the ninja and the ninja bowed at Xin. They walked to the front door and Xin let the ninja out. She hurdled the front rail of the porch and sprinted across the courtyard. She scaled the chain link fence like it was nothing and disappeared up the alley.

These were the weird customers.

2

The first time I met Carl, I assumed he fell into the rich businessman category. I was wrong. He ended up being the weird type.

I'd been at Xin's shop for months before I met Carl. The summer months had passed and the city had started to cool off. In late September, we got a huge daytime rain storm. Xin and I had to turn the radio way up to hear Guns N' Roses over the rain pounding on the roof. I'd put rusty buckets on the floor around the shop to collect all the water leaking through the roof. They filled up quick and I had to empty them every hour or so.

We had orders ready for Mrs. Cho and the dude from China Wall and everything, but no one showed up. Too much rain, I guess. The orders sat untouched. I couldn't sweep the front porch because it was too wet. I just sat around, fiddling with the jars and cans, doing my best to memorize their labels. I was about to die of boredom, so I decided to deep clean the bathroom. I didn't think it would be that bad, because it wasn't any bigger than an airplane bathroom.

Turns out I was wrong. I scrubbed out the sink and then the toilet. I tried to mop the floor, but the dirt and grime was decades old, so I had to get on my hands and knees and scrub that, too. After a few hours of cleaning, it started to look halfway decent. I went out front to stretch my legs and breathe in some of that rain air. I stood on the porch and watched the lightning up in the clouds. That's when I saw a stretch limousine pull up on Forge Street all the way across the alley. I couldn't imagine why a stretch limo would be in Chinatown unless it was Mayor Bloomberg himself out doing some kind of social PR thing. The back door opened, hissed like it was on hydraulics, and out stepped a man in a fine black suit. He popped open a black umbrella and made his way up the alley.

That was Carl.

Carl's hair was gray on the sides. He wore a flawless Armani suit, not some low rent job you'd get window shopping in the Garment District, but something hand-tailored by Mister Armani himself. What really caught my eye were his shoes: polished Corinthian leather which probably cost more than a car. It didn't bother him that he was splashing through puddles of water. He even smiled. Not a sinister smile, but a real one, like a dude so rich that his bank account would replace anything that got ruined. I could tell right away that he was trouble. Why else would a man this rich, this well dressed, walk down the alleys of Chinatown in a rainstorm? He reminded me of the bad guy in movies, where he'd stick a cigar in his mouth and say "I'm going to buy this whole place and turn it into a parking lot."

"Xin?" I had to shout over the rain and Van Halen's Panama so he could hear me. "We got a visitor."

Xin stepped out onto the porch. He saw Carl, frowned, and crossed his arms. Carl walked right up to the porch steps and tilted his umbrella back so he could look up at us. He never wavered on that smile.

Carl said, "Nice to see you again, Mister Houng." Then he moved his eyes to me. "Hello, miss. My name's Carl. Pleasure to meet you. What's your name?"

I said, "Oprah."

Xin put an end to the faux pleasantries. "What are you doing here?"

Carl, still smiling, said, "Down to brass tacks. No idle chit-chat. I like that. Efficient." He took one step closer. "I want Impossible Red."

I'd been working at the shop for a couple months by this point. We didn't have a plant called Impossible Red.

Xin said, "I don't have it."

Carl replied, "My bosses are willing to pay any amount for it. You name it."

But Xin wouldn't budge. "It's not here."

Carl shook his head like he was disappointed. "Mister Houng, we've known one another for quite some time. I can tell when you're being a Lying Larry. We've been tracking Impossible Red for years. We know you have it. If you don't hand it over, things are going to get wacky around here. And not funny wacky." He gestured at the shop. "More like uh-oh wacky."

I didn't like how Carl threatened the shop. I stepped in front of Xin and blurted out, "How about I uh-oh wacky your face, you shit-eating–"

"Penelope," Xin snapped. He'd never raised his voice at me before, so it shut me up. He softened his tone and said, "Penelope, please, go inside and water the plants."

I went inside, muttering, "Penelope, water the plants. Water the plants, Penelope." I went in but I didn't water the plants. I turned down the radio, stood at the window, and strained to hear their voices over the rumbling thunder and driving rain. Carl again asked for Impossible Red. Xin kept his cross-armed stance and insisted he didn't have it. They went back and forth, back and forth. Give it, I don't have it, yes you do, no I don't.

Eventually Carl put his hand to his chest and said, "I don't want to do anything crazy, but you know the Westland Corporation. If you don't give me Impossible Red, the CEO is going to order me to do something crazy, then I'm going to have to do something crazy. And I don't like to do crazy things."

Xin said, "Impossible Red is not here."

Carl nodded and shrugged. "Have it your way."

Carl turned and walked off. Xin came back inside. I watched Carl leave the courtyard and stroll towards the alley. He gave the store one final look, caught sight of me in the window, and gave me a little wave. I flipped him off.

Xin walked in and closed the door behind him. He didn't seem happy.

"Who was that?" I asked him.

"His name is Carl."

"Well, yeah, I picked that up from context clues. What's this Impossible Red thing he's looking for?" Xin didn't answer me.

He just shook his head and waved the question away as he distracted himself with the plants on the table. I didn't give up. I could be stubborn, too. "No, dude, what's Impossible Red? Why does Carl want it?"

Xin moved away from me, suddenly preoccupied with straightening the jars on the shelves. I hovered right over his shoulder, trying to drive him crazy. What's Impossible Red? What's Impossible Red? What's Impossible Red? He refused to answer. The more he avoided me, the more I pestered him. Despite my best efforts, I couldn't break him down. He refused to tell me anything and his patience outlasted mine.

"Fine." I grabbed my scouring pad and went back into the bathroom. "Secrets don't make friends, you know."

3

As long as I watered the plants when they needed it, I could pretty much come and go as I pleased. I called Xin's shop my "base of operations" and checked in a couple times a day. The rest of the time I'd walk around Chinatown or head up to Little Italy. My plan was to save up some money and buy a new skateboard, but that was a ways off. Until then, I had to walk around town like some kind of rinky-dink tourist.

A few days after the Carl thing, I started feeling nostalgic for my old neighborhood and headed up to Little Italy to go look around. I'd do that from time to time; head over to my old apartment building and stare up at my bedroom window and remember when I would sneak down the fire escape to hang out with friends. The only connection I still had to my old apartment were the outside windows. George never replaced the cracked glass in the kitchen window, the pane I broke when I tried to spin plates on top of a mop handle.

If I would have been paying more attention, I would have noticed Ilana coming up behind me. I hadn't seen Ilana since Ma's funeral. Ilana Rittenberg was my absolute best friend from high school. Her family was Jewish, but she still went to our Catholic high school because they lived in the Village and the Jewish private schools were too far away to be worth the trouble.

We spent a lot of time in detention together, Ilana and me. Ma never really cared much for Ilana. She thought Ilana was a bad influence. Funny, because Ilana's parents didn't like me for the exact same reason.

"Penelope?" Ilana said. "Where the hell have you been?"

I almost didn't recognize her at first. She'd dyed her bangs bright blue and cut her long hair up to her shoulders. She had on a black tank top and short shorts along with a pair of bright pink flip flops; necessary attire for how hot it was that day. She intentionally walked so her flip flops would slap against the bottoms of her feet. That was pretty standard for Ilana, always aiming for as much attention as possible.

She carried a high dollar Coach bag, one she defaced with a sewn on patch that read "Fuck Trying." That's how she rebelled against her rich parents, I guess. I remember back when prom came around, Ilana wanted to go in protest wearing a t-shirt and jeans. Her parents refused and bought her a prom dress. She ended up tearing the sleeves off that dress and we got drunk in the parking lot off beer she stole out of someone's car.

"Ilana!" I was excited to see her, and we were friends, but we weren't huggers. We were too tough for hugging. "What's up?"

She looked pissed. "What's up? What's *up*? I don't hear from you for months and all you have for me is 'what's up?' What the fuck?"

"Dude, my phone broke," I told her. "I got hit by a fucking taxi months ago and I haven't been able to afford a new one."

She frowned. "Are you bullshitting me?"

"Bitch, no." I pulled up my shirt and, although the bruises were gone, I used my finger to trace out how big my injury once was. "I was bruised all over. It was all green and black and looked disgusting. My arm was bloody as all hell."

She threw her hands up and raised her voice. "And you couldn't come find me!? You couldn't come tell me!? I bump into you accidentally and this is how I find out!? I was fucking worried about you!"

"Stop yelling at me," I snapped. "I got a job. I've been fucking busy."

She exhaled hard. Just like that, the fight was over and we were cool again.

"Did it hurt?" she asked. "Getting hit by a taxi?"

I looked at her like she was stupid. "It didn't tickle."

She pointed up at the building. "And you got evicted, huh?"

"Yeah. A while ago."

"Man, that's fucked up," she said. "I can't believe they would just kick you out like that, not right after your mom dies."

"George is a slum lord, man," I said. "He doesn't give a shit."

"Where you staying, then?"

I laughed to myself. The answer sounded absurd before it even left my mouth. "This shop in Chinatown. I got a job watering plants and I live in the back room."

She brushed her blue bangs out of her face and threaded her hair behind her ears. "Like in a closet or something?"

"Yeah, actually. It's a little bit bigger than a closet, but yeah."

"That sounds super sketch."

"I thought so too, at first," I said. "But I'm not living on the streets, so it's not all that bad. And the guy who owns the place is awesome."

Ilana and I walked around Manhattan for a while. I told her all about Ma and the insurance money and everything else. Ilana listened, but she kept her replies short. Conversations about emotions and death get a little too heavy for her.

"Let's tag something." She dropped her Coach bag to the ground and pulled out two cans of black spray paint. She shook them in her hands and the rattle echoed off the buildings. The noise screamed to anyone with ears, "Hey, graffiti is happening." Not that Ilana cared.

Ma would have hated this.

She handed me a can and we ran to the dumpster behind Il Vicino. She spray painted the dumpster. I sprayed on the wall of the alley. Neither of us were any good at graffiti. Our graduation plan was to spend the summer practicing, but things just didn't work out that way. I had to grow up a lot faster than that.

Ilana wrote her name in cursive, which was neither inventive nor all that artistic. Not that I had room to talk. I tried to do a kitten face that turned out terrible.

"Is that a zombie?" she asked.

"It's a kitten," I said. I pointed out the different parts. "These are the whiskers and this is the nose."

"It looks like shit," she said.

"Fuck you, Picasso, all you did was write your name."

We spent the rest of the day together. She bought me a panini from Il Vicino – a Salami Stack – and she let me use her phone to check my email and stuff. Nothing but the power company still wanting the money I owed them from June, and an email from the funeral home about some "outstanding fees." I checked three more emails – bills, bills, bills – then handed her phone back in disgust.

That evening she followed me back to Chinatown so she could see where I lived and worked. I led her down the alley between the Super Wash Dry Clean and the Asian Food Mart, then across the concrete courtyard to Xin's shop. We got as far as the porch when the plants caught her attention. Just like me, she was mesmerized by their odd colors and shapes.

"So weird," she said, feeling the leaves of one of the plants.

"That's an Ice Fern," I said. "You use it for burns and stuff. Come on, there's more inside."

I led her inside. Xin looked up as we came in the door.

"Xin, this is Ilana. She's my homie from high school."

"Hello." He nodded, gave her a moment of attention, then went back to work.

Ilana peered inside the different jars with her nose almost pressed to the glass. She looked hypnotized by their exotic nature. She whispered, "I bet you could get so high off everything in here."

Xin noticed the spray paint in my hand and pointed it out. "What is that?"

"This?" I held it up like I was on a game show. "This is spray paint. You push this nozzle and paint comes out. Psst. Psst."

"I know what it is," he said. He walked over to me and took it out of my hands. "Have you been spray painting my shop?"

"No way, dude," I said.

Ilana spoke up. "We spray painted on a dumpster blocks away."

"Technically she did the dumpster," I told him. "I did the wall."

Xin pointed a finger of warning at us. "You shouldn't be doing that. Its against the law."

"Okay, sheriff," I said. Ilana and I shared a smile. We stifled our laughter. Xin didn't see the humor in it. He took my spray paint and tucked it away under his counter.

"You can have this back at the end of the semester," he said.

So much time had passed, I'd forgotten about Carl for the most part. September turned to October and the weather turned cold, as Octobers tend to do. Cold days meant slow days and slow days meant conversation with Xin. On this particular cold Thursday, we sat at the counter eating Liu's Peking Taste. He approached meals with far more dignity and respect than I did. He ate slowly, real methodical, and with a kind of grace that every bite might be his last. I, on the other hand, shoveled lo mein and egg rolls into my mouth like an uninvited guest who had crashed an expensive wedding and found the open buffet. My metabolism ran so hot, I could eat anything and not gain a pound.

While Xin and I ate lunch, a humble thunderstorm in the Atlantic Ocean was about to put on its big girl pants and turn into a full blown hurricane. We'd call it Hurricane Sandy, but no one knew that yet. As far as we knew, these were just the cold weather storms that came at the start of fall.

Xin and I had long moved past the awkward let's-talk-about-the-weather conversations. Twice we had a stern disagreement, once about my bad manners and another time about my foul mouth. Other than that, we were great at conversation.

"Xin." I said with a mouth full of lo mein. "Got any wise advice?"

"Wise advice?" He asked. He carefully put down his chopsticks and met my eyes. "About what?"

"I dunno. Anything." I chewed and swallowed. "Life or something."

He laughed to himself, picked up his chopsticks and went back to eating. "If I had wise advice about life, I wouldn't be here."

"Come on, dude. You're, like, a million years old..."

"I'm eighty-five."

"...Surely you have some advice about life."

He locked his eyes on me for a quiet moment. Then he crushed a fortune cookie in his hands and brought the slip of paper into his field of vision.

"Every exit is also an entrance," he said, reading the fortune to me. He made a face that said, "There you go, there's your advice," and dropped the paper to the table. He picked up his chopsticks and went back to eating.

I poked at my lo mein with my chopsticks.

"You know, I dunno if there's such a thing as normal, but things used to be normal for me. I used to have a normal life. I'd go to school, I'd hang out with Ilana, I'd lie to my mom about where I was going. But after she died, it's like that set off a chain reaction that got everything all screwed up. I don't know if I'll ever have a normal life again." I looked up at Xin. He was watching me, listening, but he didn't respond. "You ever feel like that?"

He put down his chopsticks. He wiped his mouth and gave the question real consideration. "And what do you think a normal life is."

"I dunno." I thought about it for a while. Does any eighteen year old know what a normal life is? "I guess a normal person has a place to live."

"You live here."

"Yeah, for now. And I appreciate it, but what am I going to do? Live in a storage closet my whole life?"

He nodded. "Have you thought about going to college?"

"College sucks. I only passed high school Trig because I cheated."

"Trig?"

"-Onometry."

"You cheated?" he asked. "How?"

So I rolled up my right sleeve to show him my tattoo. I told him, "We had this test over the quadratic equation and I couldn't memorize it, no matter what. It's like math goes in my brain and then gets all jumbled up. I literally can't do math. So I went and got the quadratic equation tattooed on my arm." That was the tattoo on my right bicep: X equals negative B, plus or minus the square root of B squared, minus four A C, all of it over two A.

"The school let you do that?"

"They can't stop me." I put my sleeve back down. "It's my skin and my body. I have that freedom. They didn't like it, but they couldn't do anything about it."

"That's..." He waved his chopsticks in the air and struggled to find the right word. "Drastic."

"I prefer to call it cunning," I said. "If I failed math, I wasn't going to graduate. So I did what I had to do."

41

"Okay, so you don't want to go to school." He gave things a moment of thought, then asked, "If you could do anything in life, what would you do?"

"I dunno, cool stuff. I've always wanted to backpack across the world. Maybe see a volcano erupt. Or be the first girl on Mars."

"So you should go to college and learn geology. Or space sciences."

"Look at me." I bit off half an egg roll and talked with my mouth full. "The billionaire who goes to college."

"If you want to be a scientist, you have to go to college."

"I didn't say I wanted to be a *scientist*. I just want to walk on Mars or watch a volcano explode. I don't care about formulas or books or whatever." Xin looked concerned for me, like my outlook on life scared him. It was my job to clarify, to help him understand. "Look, I think of it like this. You only live once, so why waste it sitting around in some dumb classroom? I want to go out into the world. Experience it. You know, while I'm still young."

"I've traveled the world," he said. "It can be a very dangerous place."

"Yeah." I shrugged. "I guess."

After half a quart of lo mein and three egg rolls, I realized we were only talking about me.

"So what about you?" I asked.

"What about me?" Xin replied.

"I dunno," I said. "Where'd you get all these plants?"

"That is a long story."

I waved an egg roll at the pouring rain outside. "I'll cancel my three o'clock."

He wiped his mouth with a napkin and settled into storyteller mode.

"When I was younger... younger than you are right now, I had to run away from home. World War Two had spilled over into China and made our war with Japan that much more dangerous. My father, he ran a flower shop very much like this one. When I left for America, he gave me a clay pot full of different seeds so I could find a way to make money. When I got to New York, I found this place and planted all the seeds and..." he gestured all around, "...I've been here ever since."

"They're the craziest plants I've ever seen."

He nodded. "They come from all over the world, sometimes from the most remote locations. Many of them are otherwise extinct."

"Did you ever see your dad again after that?"

"No."

Damn. Buzzkill. I drank my sweet-and-sour soup straight from the styrofoam container. I ruined the mood when I slurped loudly – I think eating soup with a spoon is stupid when it's so much easier to drink it – and Xin waited patiently for me to finish with my disgusting eating habits before he continued.

"Remind me again, what was your father's profession?"

"Michael," I corrected him. "Don't call him my father. He doesn't deserve to be called that. His name was *Michael*... And he was an archaeologist."

"Archaeology sounds interesting."

"It's boring as fuck." I put my egg roll down. I didn't feel like eating anymore. "He was barely ever home, and when he was, all he ever did was sit around and read books and write papers and tell me how much of a disappointment I was."

"He told you that?"

I nodded. "To my face. All the time. I was a girl and he wanted a boy. He was a genius and he expected me to be a genius, but I'm not a genius. I got B's and C's in grade school and he told me I was stupid. Ma tried to make me feel better by telling me that I was average. Average. That was the best I got. But then Michael said that average was just another word for stupid, so he ruined that, too."

"He does not sound like a good father."

I scoffed. "You don't know the half of it."

Xin asked, "Is he still alive?"

"No. I don't know. It doesn't matter. I haven't seen him in years. He walked out on me and Ma when I was little. Even if I knew where he was, I wouldn't talk to him." I realized I was looking at the counter and talking to myself more than I was talking to Xin. I looked back up at him. "I'd honestly rather be homeless than talk to that piece of shit."

"That's sad."

"Yeah, boo hoo, it's a real heart breaker," I said. I shook my head with the realization: "How did we end up talking about this anyway?"

"Do you talk about it to anyone?" Xin asked. "Maybe a therapist?"

"A *therapist*, Xin? Really?" He didn't answer. "I don't need a therapist because it doesn't fucking bother me. Michael is gone and he could be dead for all I care. I literally do not give a shit. In fact, I *hope* he's dead, wherever he is."

Xin gave me a concerned look. "It's not good to have that kind of anger inside you. If you want my advice-"

"I *don't* want your advice."

"You said you did. You asked for it."

"I don't want your advice about *that*. You know what I want to talk about? I want to talk about how this place has a basement." I pointed right at the mystery door with the padlock. He didn't bother to look. We sat there in silence. I let my point sink in. "You wanna talk about that?"

"Okay," he said softly. "I've made you upset."

Xin ate in silence. I pushed the food away from me. I was going to be sick.

I asked him, "Why won't you tell me what's behind the god damned door? I saw you open it that one time when that ninja was here. I know there's a basement. I hear all these weird noises at night and you say it's nothing, but it's not nothing. It's something. And I want to know what it is."

Xin, stubborn and stoic, just kept eating. He didn't respond. Xin didn't trust me, that's what it was. If he trusted me, he would have told me about the door. But just like Michael, Xin thought I was dumb. He thought he could just lie to my face and I'd believe it. Maybe he lied because he thought I'd go blabbing to the cops. Whatever. Didn't matter. What it boiled down to was that Xin didn't trust me. And if he didn't trust me, then why did he want me around?

"You're not going to tell me, are you?" I asked. Xin didn't look up. I leaned down and put my face in his field of vision so he'd have no choice but to make eye contact with me. "Xin? You going to tell me what's behind the door?"

He looked apologetic. "No."

"Fine. If that's how it's gunna be, then that's how it's gunna be." I stood up, wadded up my napkin and threw it on the counter. "You know what? You can find yourself a new security guard. Cuz I quit."

I left. Xin didn't follow after me.

Chapter 3

1

I walked around aimlessly for ten blocks before it occurred to me that I probably overreacted when I blew up at Xin. I wasn't mad at Xin. I was mad at Michael. I didn't like talking about my biological father and I took it out on Xin for harping on it, but deep down I knew he meant well. All I did was ruin things by freaking out. That October night started off unseasonably warm, then the temperature plunged with a strong gust of ocean wind. I'd been so distracted by my thoughts that I didn't notice the storm clouds that gathered offshore and blocked out the stars. A storm was coming. Off in the distance, past the Empire State Building, far out over the ocean, I saw flickers of lightning.

When I finally stopped to look around and get my bearings, I realized I was only few blocks away from Ilana's building up on Lafayette. The weather was taking a sharp turn for the worse. The storm clouds swept over the city with alarming speed. Lightning flashed overhead and then the rain came; one of those rains where I felt a single drop of cold water on my forehead, then two seconds later it was a complete downpour. Before I knew it, I was soaked right through my clothes. I sprinted to Ilana's place and tucked myself into the front entrance of her building to get out of the rain. I pressed my finger to her apartment buzzer.

Her mom's voice came over the intercom. "Yes?"

"Uh." Ilana's mom hated me. Her parents blamed me for Ilana's rebellious attitude. Funny. Ma blamed Ilana for mine. I said, "Hey, Mrs. Rittenberg. It's Penelope Salvo. Is Ilana home?"

Silence. Then Ilana came on. "Penelope?"

"Hey," I said. "Can I come up?"

More silence. Then the door to her building unlocked with a buzz.

The Rittenberg's building was way nicer than the one I used to live in. Their lobby had clean carpet, none of the lights were burned out, and the walls were bright colors of green and red. I was going to take the elevator, but I was soaking-ass wet and scaled the stairs instead. I got up to the Rittenberg's apartment and Ilana was there waiting for me with the door open. She was obviously getting ready for bed; she had on flannel pajama pants and an old t-shirt. Her parents gave me sideways glances as they did dishes in the kitchen, not at all pleased I was around, not at all pleased I was dripping water all over their tile floor.

"Penelope." Ilana checked me out from head to toe. "What the hell?"

I exhaled and slumped my shoulders. "Can I stay the night here with you?"

"What are you even doing out?" Ilana looked over her shoulder at her parents. "Isn't it storming like crazy out there?"

"Yeah, kinda," I said. Ilana looked worried. She apparently knew something I didn't. I asked, "What?"

"Have you not seen the weather?"

Ilana took out her phone and pulled up her weather app. I heard the name Hurricane Sandy for the first time. Her phone showed footage from Haiti and Cuba. Whole cities, devastated. People wandered around demolished neighborhoods in a daze with screaming babies in their arms. The news said at least thirty people were dead in Haiti, and those weren't even the final numbers.

She switched to the radar and revealed a red and orange spiral of color out in the Atlantic Ocean, something five times larger than Florida. It drifted north, bringing with it hundred-mile-an-hour winds, obliterating anything in its path.

"The edge is hitting us right now," she said. "It's been coming for days. You didn't know?"

I shrugged. "No TV and no phone."

"It's just supposed to get worse and worse," she said.

I whispered, "Can I stay here with you? I had a big fight with Xin. I can't go back to Chinatown."

She sighed heavy and looked back at her parents. "I'll ask."

I hung out in the entrance way, the water draining out of my clothes and splattering on their tile floor. Ilana took her parents to the living room and had a quiet, serious discussion. They all kept their voices low, but I heard a few key phrases. "Her mom just died." "She doesn't have anywhere to go, she's practically homeless." And the clincher, the point that finally broke them, "If you don't want her to stay, then you go in there and tell her to her face."

"Fine," her mom said.

"One night," added her father.

Ilana fixed me up with a towel, some dry clothes to sleep in, and she ran my wet clothes through the dryer. We laid around her room and watched the weather on her laptop. Hurricane Sandy was going to hit New York hard. They said something about the full moon and warm fronts and ocean currents. Whatever. I'm not a weather doctor, but the guys on TV seemed really worried. I stayed up as late as I could, but the walk through the hurricane apparently took it out of me. I don't remember falling asleep, I just remember waking up on the floor of Ilana's bedroom in the middle of the night with the lights off and a blanket over me.

Morning came and without much sunshine. The clouds were thick enough to block out the sun and the rain was so dense, the city stayed lit up as if it were midnight. Ilana woke up and we smelled breakfast. We grouped around the kitchen table, me and Ilana, her folks, and her fourteen year old brother Adam. We ate eggs and hash browns and watched The Weather Channel on their boxy kitchen TV.

The news people said the storm would definitely hit New York that day. Citizens were advised to take all proper precautions. Mayor Bloomberg made the decision to shut down the subway system. He said the tunnels would flood and anyone caught inside would drown. They closed the New York stock exchange, they shut down the buses, and then they evacuated all the neighborhoods along the coast. I was like "Oh shit, this is for real."

Ilana went to bat for me one more time. Hurricane Sandy was going to be an all day affair and she didn't want me to go outside. By then her parents realized they couldn't, in good conscience, kick me out. After only just a brief discussion with Ilana – this time with me in the room – they agreed to let me stay the day with them.

The Rittenberg's had a fourth floor apartment in Greenwich Village. Ilana's bedroom had a great view of Midtown and all the skyscrapers of Manhattan. Normally we could see the colorful glow of Times Square from her window. Not that day. The rain came down so hard, the only building I could really see was the hazy Starbucks across the street. Way out in the distance, out where I'd normally see the Midtown skyscrapers, was just an orange glow. The way the distant lights moved, I could tell the skyscrapers were swaying back and forth in the high powered winds. They're designed to sway like that. They're supposed to. It relieves the stress on the building foundation. If they didn't sway during hurricanes and earthquakes, they'd come crashing down.

I couldn't imagine working on the 100th floor of one of those buildings, feeling yourself rock back and forth like being on the bridge of a pirate ship.

The wind and the rain lasted all day. Noon brought in more intense lightning and thunder. When the lightning flashed, I could see the clouds swirling overhead like milk in coffee. The storm stretched from one of the sky to the other, covering us, the ocean, and all of New Jersey. I could see the eye of the hurricane out over the ocean and it looked so bizarre and unnatural, like something you'd see on Jupiter. Ilana checked for weather updates on her phone, then she'd repeat them back to me.

"They say the whole thing is a thousand miles wide," she said. "Three times as big as New York. Can you believe that?"

"New York City?" I asked.

"New York *State*."

Rain pounded on the windows like being inside an automated car wash. The power started to flicker. Ilana's mom opened the bedroom door and poked her head in.

"Girls, we're going to get down in the shelter."

"Ah, shit." Ilana dashed for her window. "I left my frickin' plant out on the fire escape."

Plants?

Oh my god, *plants.*

All of Xin's plants on the front porch would get wrecked in a hurricane. They were insanely rare, grown from seeds he got from his father during World War Two. If they died, it's not like we could just go down to the garden center and buy new ones. Hell, some of them were practically extinct.

I jumped off of Ilana's bed and headed for the front door.

"I've got to get to Chinatown," I said to her. I grabbed my hoodie and threw it on. Ilana's parents were already by the door, preparing to go to the basement shelter. When I put on my shoes and socks, they realized I was serious about leaving.

"Ilana," her mother said in a tone. She expected her daughter to talk some sense into me. Funny. At first her parents didn't want me there; now suddenly they didn't want me to leave.

Ilana grabbed my arm. "What do you mean you're going to Chinatown? You're not going to Chinatown!"

"I have to." I pulled my arm free. "Xin's plants are super rare. Some of the rarest plants in the world. I have to go save them."

"In a hurricane?" Ilana asked. "Are you insane?"

I zipped up my hoodie and reached for the door. Ilana darted in front of me and blocked my exit. For a second I thought I might actually have to get physical with my best friend. I wouldn't punch her or anything, that would have been taking it too far, but I would have knocked her ass to the floor if I had to. Ended up, it wasn't necessary. The look on my face said everything: I was leaving whether she liked it or not.

She moved out of the way and said, "Just please, God, be careful out there."

I opened the door to leave. I turned back to her parents and said, "Thanks for letting me crash here."

2

The streets were flooded with ankle-deep water, which slowed me down a little, but didn't keep me from sprinting across Mulberry towards Chinatown. The rain came down in a monsoon and I was soaked to my underwear before I even got to the end of the block. I couldn't make out details in that much

49

rain. My only landmarks were the glowing stop lights, all of which had been put into emergency mode and blinked red. I used them to keep track of the intersections in my head.

The first blurry, blinking light was Grand Street. Another block, another blinking red light, and that was Hester. Another block, Canal Street. I had never seen Canal Street empty of cars, never in my life. It's usually heavy traffic in both directions. That night Canal really lived up to its name: it was a literal canal. I had to slog my way through knee-deep, ice-fucking-cold water. After that, it was just another couple blocks to Super Wash Dry Clean and the Asian Food Mart.

The thunder made it sound like Chinatown was under heavy bombardment. Each thunderclap rattled the store windows and set off burglar alarms. Yeah, exactly what this situation needed was to be *louder*.

The red and blue and white signs of Chinatown shuddered in the wind. One of them tore off. It tumbled through the air and smashed corner-first into the windshield of a parked car.

A telephone phone snapped in half in the wind. It danced around, suspended by the power lines. Electrical transformers exploded in plumes of blue fireworks. A power line snapped loose above me and whipped around in the wind like a black snake spraying sparks out of its face.

Man, if that thing landed in the flooded streets, it would electrocute the *shit* out of me.

Terrified thoughts ran through my head – *fuck, fuck, fuck, what am I doing?* – but it was too late to turn back.

Lightning struck a building two blocks away and blasted a chunk of bricks into the sky. The explosion made my ears ring.

I finally reached the Super Wash Dry Clean. I ducked down through the alley and ran up to Xin's shop. The store lights were on and the front door was open. I was relieved to know that Xin was there; I wouldn't have to be alone. The plants were still on the front porch. He hadn't started bringing them in. Fine. We'd rescue the plants together and stay the night at the shop. I splashed through the courtyard and up onto the porch. Water drained out of my jeans. I shouted Xin's name but he didn't answer. He couldn't hear me over the rain and thunder. I took off my shoes and socks and shouted for Xin again. I didn't want to go inside because I was completely soaked and I'd get water all over my nice clean floor.

I poked my head in the door and shouted for Xin at maximum volume. Still nothing. That's when I noticed the mysterious basement door was wide open with a light on.

I walked barefoot through the shop and got to the basement door. Before I could call out Xin's name, Carl ran up the stairs and bumped right into me. He wore the same richy-rich suit like before, except this time he was wet from head to toe. He had a red jewelry box in his hand. Carl was stealing from Xin and I caught him red-handed.

He froze. I froze. It took our brains a second to process what was going on.

I snapped to my senses and said, "What the fuck are you doing?"

Carl smiled at me like we were old friends. He held up the red box. "Petty theft."

"Well, give it back." I gave him my most serious bitch face and held out my hand.

"I'm afraid I'll have to decline," he said. He brushed past me. "My boss called dibs on this long before you came along."

I grabbed him by the sleeve and yanked him in place. "Give it back or else."

Carl pulled his arm free, but he didn't make a break for it. His hair stuck out in all directions, wind blown and soaking wet.

"Or else what? You'll call the police? Report a shoplifting in Chinatown? I don't know if you've noticed, but that's a real doozy of a hurricane out there. The city's coming apart at the seams. You can call 911 if you want, but I doubt they can spare a dog catcher, let alone a police officer."

He was right. Calling the police was off the table. I had to handle things on my own. Looking around for a weapon, I grabbed a jar of orange powder off the shelf and unscrewed the lid. "Give it back or I throw this shit in your face."

His smile vanished. He shifted awkwardly away from me. "What... what is that?"

"I dunno," I said. "But I'll throw it in your face and we'll find out the hard way." I acted like I was about to toss the mysterious powder right into his eyes. He flinched.

"Alright. Alright. I know when I've been licked." He put one hand up in surrender. With the other hand, he put the box down on the counter. He backed away from me and towards the door with his hands in the air. I kept the jar pointed at him, ready to throw the mysterious powder in his face if he made any funny moves. He didn't. He just kept backing up.

"Get out," I said. "If I ever see you here again, I'll claw your fucking eyes out."

"I believe you will," he said. That smile crept back onto his face. "You're a tough cookie."

He backed out the door and onto the front porch. I slammed the wood door closed on him and clacked the deadbolt shut. I went to the counter and scooped up the red jewelry box. It had a golden plate attached to the front of it that said "Impossible Red." I didn't know what to do with it. Keep it? Hide it behind the counter? Or, better, I could I use it as an excuse to go explore the basement.

I opened the box. It was empty. The velvet interior had an indention for a marble sized object, no bigger than a grape, but there was nothing there. Carl had swiped it and I'd fallen for one of the oldest tricks in the book.

3

I splashed barefoot through the courtyard as Hurricane Sandy did its best to drown New York City. Carl had a head start on me, but I wasn't about to let him get away. I had no idea what Impossible Red was or why Carl wanted it, but Xin kept it in his super secret basement so it had to be important. The cops had their hands full dealing with the hurricane and Xin was nowhere around, so it was all up to me to get it back. I splashed through the courtyard at top speed in hot pursuit.

Chinatown was a freakin' war zone. Lightning exploded in the sky and cast weird shadows on the ground. Thunder cracked so loud it set off burglar alarms in the stores all up and down Forge Street. As soon as one rumble faded off into the distance, there was a new clap of thunder and it started all over again. And then there was the wind. The alleyways of Chinatown channeled the wind into unpredictable gusts that shoved me one way, then the other. I had rain in my eyes and had to cup my hands over them so I could see where I was going.

Carl ran down the alley. I chased after him, calling him a son of a bitch and everything else. I ran faster than ever before in my life, fueled by rage and adrenaline. Carl had to run in a soaking wet business suit and that slowed him down a lot. I closed the gap between us and eventually got so close that I could hear his feet splashing in the water. I shouted his name, plus some additional cuss words. He looked back at me.

He had a twinkle in his eye that made it seem like he was... enjoying this.

He shouted, "The chase is on, kid!"

A limousine pushed its way down the flooded street of Chinatown. Water came up as high as the headlights, but that didn't slow it down. It pulled up to a cockeyed stop at the alley entrance. The back door hissed open and revealed the warm, dry, leather interior. If Carl reached the limo, he was gone.

By the time he reached the sidewalk, I was close enough to grab two fistfuls of his suit jacket. I spun him around in a circle and threw him to the ground. He slid across the wet sidewalk with his feet in the air. I jumped on him and punched him in the face over and over. He was like, "Ow, ow, ow," and covered his head with his forearms. I pulled open his suit jacket and searched for the marble that belonged in Impossible Red's box.

"Give it back!" I shouted at him.

"No!" he shouted back. "We need it!"

I went into full berserker mode and slashed at his face with my fingernails. He rolled into the fetal position and kicked me in the shin with the hard heel of his dress shoe. It fucking hurt. I grabbed his tie and yanked hard. I figured if I pulled it tight enough, it would strangle the life right out of him.

We fought and a red marble popped out of his jacket. It landed in the deep water and floated along the curb. I jumped off Carl, pushed my wet hair out of my eyes and chased after it. It was small and hard to track in the reflective water. I could only follow it by the occasional flash of lightning. All the water on Forge Street drained towards an open manhole that swallowed everything down – paper trash, styrofoam cups, shoes – right into the bowels of the city. The hole wanted the marble, too. If the little red ball dropped into the dark abyss of the New York sewer system, that would be the end of that. It would be lost forever.

Just when I was close enough to grab it, Carl landed on top of me with all his weight. I crashed into the water face down. Suddenly he was the one chasing after the marble, bent at the waist, slicing his fingers through the water and coming up empty handed. I grabbed at his shoes and missed. I scrambled to my feet and chased after him. The red marble was just about to plunk over the edge of the manhole when Carl swept it up in his right hand. A transformer exploded and the flashing light illuminated his stupid face. He clutched the marble in his fist and let out a satisfied laugh.

"I did it!" he shouted, almost surprised with his success.

I grabbed his wrist with both hands. "Give it."

"No," he shouted. "I won, fairzies and squarezies."

I put my teeth to his closed fist and bit down hard. He screamed in pain as I tasted blood, but he kept his fingers tight. I bit down harder. I was prepared to bite his goddam hand off if I had to, but it didn't come to that. Eventually the pain was too much for him and he opened his hand. The red marble dropped free and plunked back in the water. Immediately the current swept it back to the edge of the manhole. With the lightning reflexes of a jungle cat, I shoved Carl aside and snatched up Impossible Red seconds before it could drop into oblivion.

"You bit me," Carl shouted as he cradled his hand to his body. "I'm bleeding. That's assault and battery."

"What're you going to do?" I asked. "Call the cops?"

Normally a knock-down, drag-out fight like ours would have attracted a crowd, especially right there in the middle if the street, but there was no one around except me and Carl and Hurricane Sandy. Carl advanced on me. I backed away. He reached into his jacket and at first I thought he was going to pull out a gun. Instead, he pulled out a walkie-talkie.

He said, "Kid, I'm trying to be a Good Guy Gary here. Don't make me be a Bad Boy Brandon. I have a team of snipers surrounding us. One word from me and they'll splatter your brains all the way to Long Island. I don't want that. You don't want that. So why don't you just give me Impossible Red and-"

That's when I popped the red marble in my mouth. If Carl wanted it, I was going to make him come get it. If he was ready to kill me over it, he'd have to cut it out of my stomach. Carl put the walkie-talkie to his mouth.

"Sierra team, draw a bead on the girl. Light up the lasers. Show her we mean business."

A dozen red sniper dots appeared all over my body. Carl wasn't kidding. There seriously *were* snipers all around us. The rain and mist revealed the trajectory of a dozen red laser beams. They came at me from all different angles – from the rooftops, from the windows, out of the alley ways. It looked like a god damned Pink Floyd laser light show. I moved away from Carl. The laser beams followed me and regrouped on my body. They were ready to blow the brains and guts out of my body.

"Come on, kid," Carl said. He held out his open palm. "It doesn't have to end this way. Spit it out. Please."

I rolled the marble into my cheek so I could say, "Fuck you." I rolled it back into place with my tongue and positioned it at the back of my throat. It was only slightly bigger than any pill I'd ever swallowed. Carl realized what I was about to do and his confidence evaporated. He suddenly looked very, very worried.

"Don't swallow that," he said.

I gulped hard. Down it went. "Too late."

Carl narrowed his eyes at me. "Did you just swallow it?"

"Yup." I held up my hands, palms out, to prove that it was gone. "What's up now?"

My show of confidence might have been a little premature. Impossible Red must have been some unimaginable poison, because it suddenly felt like I got blasted in the guts by a point-blank shotgun. I slapped my arms around my stomach and screamed out in pain. My knees lost their strength and I dropped to the ground. Next thing I knew, I was in the fetal position down in the rushing water.

That's when everything changed.

4

I never completely lost consciousness, but I did lose touch with reality.

The pain in my stomach burned up my esophagus like I was about to vomit melted glass. The red-hot surge detoured straight into my heart and my pulse raced out of control. The pain pumped through my veins like burning acid. My brain throbbed with a crippling migraine and I squeezed my eyes shut against the blinding lights of Chinatown.

A second later, my blood went ice cold. I laid there on the concrete and shivered my ass off. I could barely hear anything over the sound of my heartbeat pounding in my eardrums.

Half of my face was underwater.

I was in a total panic. I had made a huge mistake and suddenly I was dying. My self-preservation kicked in and although Carl was the only person around me, I reached out for him and said, "Help me."

Carl pushed me with his foot and rolled me onto my back. I didn't have the energy to fight him. He bent down to hold my eyelids open and peer inside, first the right eye and then the left. I stared back at him, unable to move. The temperature of my blood switched to hot again and the core of my body burned like a furnace. Impossible Red – whatever it was – was killing me from the inside out. Sweat rolled off my face, even in the cold wind and pouring rain of Hurricane Sandy. Carl looked concerned.

"You don't look so good," he said. "I told you not to swallow that."

I couldn't respond. My bones started to crack. I didn't know what was happening to them, but they hurt. My muscles spasmed faster and faster. My heart had given up on blood and was now pumping pure grease fire. Something was seriously wrong with me. I needed medical attention and I needed it immediately.

I managed to say the word, "Ambulance."

"Ambulance?" Carl repeated. "Kid, it's like I told you, we're in the middle of a category five hurricane. 911 is ringing off the hook and Chinatown is flooded like an olympic-sized swimming pool. You're not getting an ambulance."

I crawled. I would crawl to a hospital, if that's what it took. Even on my hands and knees, I couldn't support my own weight and collapsed back down. The cold water felt good on my skin so I decided to just lie there and watch the reflection of the lightning.

Carl stood over me. He took out his walkie-talkie and said something like, "We got a problem out here." A male voice on the other end of the walkie-talkie asked what he meant by "problem."

"I had Impossible Red," Carl said. "But this girl just swallowed it."

"*Girl?*" the mystery voice asked. "What girl?"

Carl replied, "Just some girl."

"Then kill her!" the voice snapped. Whoever he was, he sounded pissed. "Kill her quick, goddammit, before it starts working!"

Carl frowned. He held the walkie-talkie away from his mouth and looked at me. "Darn it, kid. I tried to warn you." He walked away and made a sweeping hand signal in the air. Red sniper dots steadied on my body, focused on my chest and my head. One of them got me right in the eye and blinded me for a split second.

"Alright," Carl said. "You heard the man. Take her out."

All the snipers fired.

Chapter 4

1

Those sniper rifles must've been equipped with silencers because I didn't hear them go off. I did, however, hear the zip zip zip of their bullets. My body bounced around as the metal slugs thumped against my chest and forehead and face.

They didn't hurt. I just assumed I didn't feel the pain because it happened so fast, but moments later the pain still hadn't set in. I ran my hands across my chest. My hoodie and shirt had bullet holes in them, but there wasn't any blood. I felt my forehead to check for holes.

Nothing. No bullet holes. No splattered brains. I was fine.

I sat up. Flattened bullets dropped from my body and splashed into the water. I picked up one of the bullets and gave it a closer look. It was solid alright. It was as real as bullets get. It was just simply flat. My eyes moved from the bullet to Carl.

He kept his eyes on me and slowly brought the walkie-talkie to his mouth. "Too late," he said. "It's in her."

"What did it do?" the voice asked. "Did it kill her?"

"Quite the opposite," Carl said. He reached down and plucked the squashed sniper bullet from my fingers. "You mind?" He held the bullet close to his eyes for careful scrutiny. Once satisfied, he tossed it back into my hands and said into the radio, "I think she's bulletproof."

"Are you serious?" the voice said. He sounded more pissed off than before. "Hit her with everything. Kill her dead. I want Impossible Red and I want it now!"

My vision hadn't returned to normal. My heartbeat kept racing, but nothing scary like before; it was just really fast, like after a gym class. My arms and legs worked a little better and I had confidence that I could probably stand. Then came round two of sniper fire. I heard the zipping sound of a million bullets. They thumped against the side of my ribs, my chest, my neck, face, everywhere. I'm ticklish in general; if I get poked in the ribs, I can't help but giggle. That's how I reacted to twenty seconds of sniper fire. I giggled like crazy.

"Stop," I laughed. "Stop it."

By the time the snipers had finished shooting me, I was surrounded by a brass pool of flattened-out bullets.

Carl crossed his arms at me. "You have completely rumbled my feathers. I went to great lengths to steal Impossible Red and then you just come along and gum up the gullyworks."

I said, "What the hell is a gullywork?"

He took a deep breath and looked up at the hurricane that covered the city. He tried to smooth out his hair, but that was impossible in the gale force winds. Once again, he spoke into his walkie-talkie.

"Alright, Sierra team. I guess that's a wrap. Let's pack it up." He threw up his hands and said, "Gosh *dangit*."

And that was it. After all that pageantry – the snipers and the punching and the fighting – he was just threw up his hands and turned to walk away. I held out my arms, ready for more. "Is that it? Is that all you got? What's wrong, Carl? You don't have a tank?"

He sighed. "I didn't bring it." He walked over to his limo and stepped inside. "You stay here in New York. I'm going to go talk to the CEO and figure out how to get Impossible Red out of you. I'll be back and then we can finish this." He crawled into the limo and closed the door. It sealed and hissed, like an airlock on a spaceship.

"Why don't we finish it now!?" I pounded on his window. They were tinted dark, so dark that they were practically mirrors. All I could see was myself, pissed off, soaking wet, and shouting at a car window. I hit it again, harder, and this time the window completely shattered. I took a step back. Wasn't expecting that.

Carl looked at me from inside the limo, surprised. "What are you doing!? That was Vatican grade bulletproof glass!"

"Bulletproof glass?" I looked at my hands. "And I broke it?"

"Yes, you broke it," he said. "And that stuff costs a whole lot of money, I'll have you know!"

"My bad."

Carl gave me an exasperated sigh. "You're in way over your head now, kid. Damn shame, too. I bet you had a lot of potential. I hate to see you die."

"Oh, you're gunna kill me?"

"*I'm* not going to kill you," Carl said. "*I'm* a pacifist. I'll have someone else do it."

Carl waved a finger at his driver – I'm assuming there was a driver up front – and the limo rolled off through the deep waters. Suddenly I found myself all alone in the middle of an empty street. Carl's limo faded off into the mist until all I could see was the red glow of the brake lights. A few moments later the limo turned a corner and the red glow disappeared, too.

2

I stumbled back to Xin's shop under the cover of darkness and sheets of rain. My legs ached, especially my knees, and my heart still burned like a furnace. My body temperature was so hot, the rainwater literally steamed off my clothes. I had to trudge against the river current of water that flowed out of the alley. It knocked me off balance a couple times. Eventually I got to the shop and climbed the porch stairs. I stood in place just outside the door and watched my clothes self-dry.

I chased after Carl in such a hurry that I left the door to the shop wide open and all the lights on. I stood in the rectangle of light coming from the doorway and poked my fingers through the bullet holes in my shirt. A few stray bullets dropped out of the folds in my clothes and tinkled around on the wood floor. I picked them up and felt them. There was no doubt about it: these bullets were real. I had been shot by actual snipers. I collected all the bullets I could find and stuffed them in my pocket.

Maybe this was all one big hallucination. It didn't feel like a hallucination, but what other explanation was there?

Hallucination or not, Xin's plants were real and in desperate need of saving. Hurricane Sandy was destroying the city and the plants had already suffered some damage. One of them had tipped over – the Egyptian Strawflower – and its pot had smashed. I was to blame for that. It wouldn't have happened if I didn't abandon my post in the first place.

One by one, I carried all the pots from the ledge inside the shop and set them on the floor. It would take me a half hour to bring them all in, but I had to get them out of the rain.

And distracted as I was by the plants, I couldn't stop thinking about what had just happened in the middle of Forge Street. I got shot by snipers, *twice*, and not only was I still alive, I didn't have a single scratch on me.

I wanted music. Music would get my head straight. I fiddled with the knob and the antenna, but the only thing I could find were emergency weather updates. Most of the stations were too weak to broadcast in the storm. I eventually found music; a station barely transmitting '80s rock through the static, but at least it was music. I cranked up that song Centerfold and went to work bringing in the rest of the plants. The tables inside were already full with pots of herbs, so I had to put the porch plants on the floor and on the counter and in the bathroom; anywhere they could fit. After only a few trips in and out, I had muddy footprints all over the place. No need to worry about that, cleaning that up was a job for the janitor.

I got most of the plants moved inside before I had to take a break. The burning in my chest got worse, which I didn't think was possible, and my ears rang like a tuning fork. The high-pitched sound messed with my equilibrium and I suddenly felt like I was going to puke. I ran to the bathroom and grabbed onto the sink, but didn't actually vomit. I spit into the sink a couple times, but that was as bad as it got. I stood there and looked at myself in the mirror. My eye liner had streaked, my hair was soaked, and I had water droplets across my forehead, a mix of rain and sweat. Another flattened sniper bullet fell out of my clothes and clinked around in the sink.

I looked down. I didn't realize it, but the porcelain had cracked in the places where I had gripped it too tight. I jerked my hands away.

I muttered, "What the hell?"

We had scissors in the bathroom that I used to scrape gunk off of jars and trim the plants. I softly brought the point to the back of my left hand. I pushed down hard, but it didn't hurt. I pushed harder. Still didn't feel anything. Not a *thing*.

I took a deep breath, raised the scissors in the air, and stabbed it into my hand as hard as I possibly could. The metal should have pierced right through my skin and bones, but all that happened was the scissors bent in half, they busted at the hinge, and cracked into pieces. My skin, however, was fine.

Thunder boomed and the shop lights flickered. Strange things were happening to my body and I could feel a full-blown panic attack coming on. I tried to distract myself by getting back to work and bringing in the rest of the plants. One by one, I carried them all inside. I closed the front door and locked it. The lightning and thunder got worse. I went back to my room, stripped off my damp clothes, and put on something dry. I knew I wasn't going to fall asleep, not with how bad my chest burned, but I just wanted the comfort of laying down. I crawled in bed and stared at my left hand.

I was scared of myself. I was scared of my own body. I laid there and watched the lightning flash across my bedroom ceiling.

3

"Penelope." I heard Xin's voice. I opened my eyes. Oh my god, had I fallen asleep? Xin leaned over me, lit by the gray daylight that shone in through my tiny bedroom window. I'd slept straight through the night and when Xin came to open the store, he found me passed out in the back with all the lights on. I heard the rain on the roof, a steady rain, but nothing as bad as the night before.

I sat bolt upright in bed. I told Xin everything. The story just came spilling out: about how I came to the shop to rescue the outdoor plants, about how I caught Carl stealing from the basement, and about how I – in the end – had no choice but to swallow Impossible Red.

"I'm surprised I'm even alive," I told him. "You wouldn't believe how much it hurt. I thought I was dying."

Xin looked worried. Not good. Xin never looked worried. He paced around the store for a while, then went to the counter and sat down.

"Are you pissed?" I asked.

He shook his head. "You did the right thing. You kept Impossible Red away from Carl. He is a bad man."

"But now I've got Impossible Red inside me." I pointed at my stomach. "I felt like I was going to die. My bones cracked and my heart was on fire. I mean, I'm not a medical doctor, but bodies aren't supposed to do that. So this Impossible Red thing did something to me, right? Something weird?"

He frowned. "I don't know."

I pulled out a pocket full of sniper bullets and slapped them on the counter so he could get a look at them. "Last night a bunch of Carl's jamoke-ass snipers shot me and this is what happened. And check this out." I pulled up my shirt and pointed at my ribs. "Look, this is where they shot me. I'm not even bruised. So what's all that about?"

He inhaled and then let out a long sigh. "I don't know that either."

"Well, dammit, Xin, is there anything you *do* know?" I asked. "This thing was in *your* basement."

Xin nodded. "A while ago, a ninja brought Impossible Red here so I could hide it. I don't know where she found it and I don't know what it does. All I know is that it was never meant for human beings."

"Well, then why did she bring it to you?"

"Because that is my job, Penelope. My real job. I hide things. Dangerous things." He stood up and walked to the basement door, still wide open after last night's invasion. "Follow me. I'll show you."

He went down the basement stairs. I followed.

Basements in New York City can be really weird. Most of them are a century old. A few of them even date back to the 1600's. A lot of them were built to hide booze or drugs or illegal gambling halls. There are secret passageways stretching all underneath Manhattan Island, as well as abandoned subway tunnels, forgotten rooms, and undiscovered caves.

The basement stairs were slats of rough cut wood, nailed into place, and they creaked underfoot. The walls of the stairwell were bricks and sloppy mortar. I traced my fingers over the words molded into the sides of the bricks. *New York City Exploratory Society – 1763.* Every step took up deeper and deeper into complete darkness. By the time we reached the bottom, I couldn't see Xin in front of me. He struck a match and his face glowed in the light. He brought the match down to an ornate gas lamp and ignited the wick inside. The lamp had a red glass bulb on top with a golden dragon imprinted on it. The lamp lit the basement in red light. The room had a low ceiling, a dirt floor, and concrete walls with deep cracks that came from centuries of decay.

The basement was a museum of ancient junk. I saw two full suits of samurai armor displayed on wooden frames. One suit of armor was black and the other one was blue, both of them complete with decorative tassels, engraved swords and helmets designed to look like a dragon's head. Next to them stood a full suit of knights armor that reminded me of the old King Arthur stories, complete with a religious shield and an old lance. All along the walls were racks of swords: Japanese katanas, medieval broadswords, and even a Civil War cavalry saber. Back in the dark corner sat the nose cone of a nuclear bomb, which I recognized from the radiation symbol printed on it. Against the opposite wall from the swords was a bookcase filled with leather bound books and scrolls tied up with colorful ribbons.

On the floor next to the nuclear bomb was a dinosaur skull. Maybe a velociraptor. Or, on the other hand, maybe it was a baby dragon.

This was some seriously weird shit.

"Do you remember how I told you my father was a collector of many things?" Xin asked. I shook my head yes. "His job was to find items of dangerous power and keep them out of human hands. Any of the items you see here could lead a single person to cause the world a great deal of trouble. My grandmother did the job before him, and my great-father did it before her. I always knew that when my father couldn't run the store anymore, I would take over for him. But when World War Two began, the Germans sent Nazis after my father's collection. Hitler believed these powerful items would help him win the war, specifically a mysterious black marble named Unthinkable Black. With the Germans closing in, it wasn't safe for me to stay in China anymore, so my father sent me away with two American dollars and a pot full of seeds."

I said, "And you started a new shop here in New York."

Xin nodded. "Just like my father, I opened an herbal store. And in the basement, I hid powerful artifacts."

"From *Hitler*," I confirmed. The whole story sounded absurd. I repeated it out loud so Xin could hear how ridiculous he sounded.

"From everyone," he said. "None of these things are safe in human hands."

"Human hands. As opposed to who else's hands?"

"Non-human hands."

"Uh huh." I raised my eyebrow at him. "You mean like ghosts and werewolves and demons and stuff?"

He said, "No."

"Okay, good."

"Werewolves are extinct."

"Oh, of course. My mistake."

This was some sort of elves and trolls and magic kingdom kind of bullshit and it sounded really dumb. But I thought, why would Xin make up something so stupid if it wasn't for real?

I peered through all the strange things on the tables and shelves.

"What ever happened to your dad?" I asked.

Xin hung his head and his voice got quiet. "He died in a magical explosion of his own doing, destroying himself and his entire collection. He died so none of his items would fall into the hands of evil."

I poked at a jar of some red liquid and asked, "And what happened to Unthinkable Black?"

"Lost." Xin pushed my hand away so I'd stop poking his jar. "But Unthinkable Black wasn't the only colored marble of amazing power. There were others, one of which was Impossible Red."

"The one I just swallowed."

Xin nodded.

I reached out for one of the swords in the rack. The handle was made from silver clock parts, all interlocking and complicated. The blade had circles cut into it and the circles were filled with gears and springs. It was like someone built a sword out of a bunch of pocket-watches. Despite its ancient look, the shine on the blade was perfect and it glimmered in the lantern light. I was just about to touch it when Xin stopped me.

"Do not touch that," he said.

65

I gave him a little laugh, but didn't touch it. "Why? Is it *magical*? Is it going to blow my arms off?"

"That's the Sword From One Second Ago. It's a time sword. Just don't touch it."

"Uh huh. *Time sword.*" I moved my eyes down to the next sword, the Civil War one. It had dried blood on the blade. "What's this one do? Summon the ghost of General Lee?"

"That's the Gettysburg Sabre. It can kill ghosts."

"Oh, yeah, should have guessed." Despite all the crazy talk, the stuff did admittedly look super cool. I moved over to the suits of samurai armor and stood in front of the one with black scales. "What's this one supposed to be?"

"That's the Armor of the Midnight Dragon," he said. "It's made of dragon scales."

I raised my eyebrow at him. "And when you say dragons, you mean real dragons."

"If I said yes, would you believe me?"

I turned back to the armor. "I dunno, dude. This is all starting to sound a little nuts."

The armor had a horned helmet and a chest piece, elbow-length gauntlets and knee-high boots. They were crafted from dragon scales the size of dollar bills. They overlapped like roof shingles, arranged so perfectly, not a single one was out of alignment. The helmet had twisting horns on them, which, I'm sure if I asked, I would have been told they also came from a dragon. Next to the armor was a long white sword. I crouched down so I could get a better look at it.

"That katana was crafted from a fang of the Midnight Dragon," Xin told me. "It's very sharp."

I stood up and moved on. I pointed at the nose cone of the nuclear bomb.

"So I see you got a nuke," I told him. "That really rounds things out."

"It's just the explosive part," he said. "Not the launching mechanism."

"Isn't it full of radiation?"

"It's safe," he said. "The shell is made of lead."

I moved to the bookcase and ran my fingers along the shelves. The books were oversized and leather bound. I read some of the titles. Only a few of them were in English. *Atlas o' the Earthen Core. Spellindrica Explanidan. Ye Olde Ensickening Catalogue.*

Masks from all different countries and cultures hung on the wall next to the bookcase. The first one was hand carved from rich, dark wood. It looked Hawaiian. The second one was an angry dragon face pounded out of brass. Another one looked like Mayan or Incan or Aztec pottery, decorated with colorful feathers and speckled with droplets of blood. I leaned in closer to admire their small, detailed engravings.

I asked Xin, "What do these masks do?"

He didn't answer me.

I looked away from the masks and asked him again, "Xin? What do the masks do?"

"Contact gods."

"Alright." I stood up and slapped my hands on my hips. I turned and headed for the stairs. "I'm out of here."

"You're leaving?" He turned out the gas lamp and followed me up. "Where are you going?"

"Oh, this little place called a police station." Step by step, I ascended into the daylight of the herbal shop. "That Carl dude said he was going to come back and kill me and that's a death threat and that's illegal. I'm going to go report him to the cops and get a restraining order against him."

I got to the top of the stairs and went to my room to grab my shoes and socks. I sat down on my cot and pulled them on. Xin stood in the doorway.

"You don't believe me?" He looked hurt.

And it hurt to answer him. "Dude, don't get me wrong, you're awesome and everything, but you're talking straight crazy talk. Killing ghosts and contacting gods and whatever else? It's bonkers as fuck."

"But it's real."

"I believe that *you* think it's real." I pulled on one of my shoes and tied it. "But you're talking about magic swords and you have a nuke in the basement and, honestly, it's starting to freak me out."

"I'm not trying to scare you. I'm trying to be honest with you."

I put on my other shoe and got to my feet. I stood in front of Xin and put my hands on his shoulders. "I appreciate your honesty, but I have to go to the very real police station now, where they have very real guns, so I can get a very real restraining order."

I looped past Xin and headed for the front door.

He grabbed a handful of sniper bullets off the counter and held them out at me. He was desperate to convince me, I could see it in his eyes. "What about these? What about those people who shot you."

Okay. That made me stop. I still didn't have an explanation for that, but that didn't mean dragons were real. Maybe, deep down, I wanted to believe Xin. And maybe that's what really scared me.

"If you need me," I said as I opened the front door, "I'll be at the police station."

Chapter 5

1

The day after Hurricane Sandy was the day before Halloween. As the city did its best to recover from all the devastation, everyone wondered what to do about the holiday. The streets were still flooded, the city was in shambles, and 800,000 people didn't have power. In the midst of all this destruction, people wanted to know if they should have bowls of candy ready for tomorrow or were we going to postpone the holiday? Mayor Bloomberg came out on TV and radio and insisted Halloween wasn't canceled or postponed. In the face of difficulties, the best thing New Yorkers could do was celebrate the holiday like normal.

The water in Xin's courtyard had receded from ankle deep to just an inch of standing water. Walking through it got my shoes soaked all over again, but there was nothing I could do to avoid that. I went to go walk around Chinatown and survey the damage. The neighborhood looked like the set of a disaster movie. Dumpsters had toppled over and spilled garbage everywhere. Entire cars had been swept up in the water and were piled up in the intersections. A few telephone poles had been snapped in half and laid in the street or against the apartment buildings. One telephone pole fell lengthwise across Forge street and smashed right through the front windows of Dao's Takeaway. It seemed like every building had at least a few broken windows.

City dump trucks sat parked at the major intersections so the store owners could fill them with ruined furniture or bags of trash. A few business owners leaned extension ladders against the outside of their buildings and tried to fix their display signs.

I walked up the street and admired the way everyone worked together to clean things up. New York was no stranger to tragedy, but we always took it in stride. The open signs were lit up in the front windows of the restaurants and the smell of food lingered in the air.

Among the city workers and the parade of full dump trucks, one Jamaican guy stuck out like a sore thumb. While everyone else was in coveralls and work gloves, this guy wore the fanciest wedding day outfit, complete with a black top hat decorated with feathers and bones around the hat band. He wore a black tuxedo with white, lacy frills for cuffs, long tails on the back of his jacket, and a bright red carnation pinned to his lapel. Black dreadlocks hung down out of his top hat, some of them decorated with gold rings or colorful thread. He had a pocket watch chain that looped from his tuxedo pocket to his belt. His white shirt had pearl buttons and I could see the edges of a tattered vest. His face was painted up like a sugar skull: mostly white with black paint around his eye sockets. There were black lines around his lips that looked like an exaggerated, skeleton smile. He bit down on a burning cigar and carried around a small rocks glass filled with ice and some golden-brown liquid.

He stood across the street and stared right at me. I averted my eyes and pretended to be more interested in the surrounding damage. Curiosity got the better of me and I gave him another glance. He was still staring at me. Once we made eye contact a second time, he jaywalked across the street and came in my direction.

"Great," I thought. "Crazy dude incoming. Evasive maneuvers. Shields to maximum." I picked up my pace down the sidewalk to put some distance between us, headed in the direction of the Brooklyn Bridge. I got half a block away and looked over my shoulder. Not only did the Day of the Dead tuxedo guy follow me, he was running to catch up.

"Penelope!" He waved his hand in the air. "Is your name Penelope Salvo?"

I thought, how the hell does this guy know my full name? Normally if a dude calls you by name and you've never met him, something stalkery is going on. I considered running to get away from him, but that wasn't really necessary. There were a lot of people out that day and he'd be crazy to assault me when there were that many people around who would drag him off me and beat his ass. So I just kept my pace and let him catch up to me.

"I've never seen you around here before," the tuxedo man said, jogging into place by my side. "You new?"

He walked beside me and sipped from his glass like we were old friends. Now that he was closer, I could see the rings on his fingers, gold and silver, and few of them decorated with polished black stones. Others were shaped like skulls.

"Can I help you?" I asked. I tried to sound as indignant as possible to drive him away.

"Baron Semedi, at your service," he said. He gave me an exaggerated bow with his top hat in hand and his arms stretched way out. He popped back up like a spring-loaded toy. The drink sloshed around and some of it spilled onto the sidewalk. He stuck out his free hand, expecting a handshake. I just stared at it. That didn't seem to bother him. He continued with his introduction. "I'm the Voodoo loa of love and death. Perhaps you've heard of me?"

"How do you know my name?" I asked.

"I know everything," he said. He looked around, somewhat distracted. "I knew Hurricane Sandy was going to come and smash up New York City. I had found an old abandoned apartment by the river. I had a book and even a light bulb. But then Hurricane Sandy came along and broke my light bulb. I guess that's the end of that. I thought of going home, but then I bumped into you and I thought I'd say hello."

"Well, Hello," I said. I walked off. "And goodbye."

He followed, walking right along side me. "You swallowed Impossible Red, right?"

I froze in place. How did he know that? The only people who knew about that were Xin and me. And Carl. I knew Xin didn't tell this strange guy my story. And I sure didn't tell him.

So I reached the only logical conclusion. "Did Carl send you?"

Baron Semedi dead faced me for a second, then gave me a toothy grin. "That's adorable, but no. I don't take orders from humans." He drank from his glass and puffed hard on his cigar. From the smell of him, the drink was definitely rum. When he spoke, the cigar smoke rushed out of his mouth and nostrils. "No, I'm here by my own choice. If you believe in free will, of course, which I do."

"So you're a Voodoo god?" I asked. "And you know everything?"

"Ah ah ah." He waved a finger at me. "Let's not use the 'G' word, okay? I'm not a god. I'm a loa. Big difference. And in answer to your second question, yes, I know everything." He held his glass up to the sun and squinted at the light that beamed through it. "You're not really a god either. You're more of a ... what's the word..." He looked away from his glass and squinted at me. "Artificial."

I repeated it so he could hear how stupid it sounded. "I'm an artificial god."

"In a sense." He gave me a weird look. "And I wonder what you'll do with your new god-like powers."

"I don't have powers," I said.

He laughed and stepped gingerly in a circle around me as we walked. "Why, you have all the powers that any god of war would have. Strong as a bear. Tougher than an elephant. Fast as a cheetah. That kind of thing."

"That's not me."

"The question is, dear Penelope, are you one of those good humans who will use your powers for good? Or are you one of those bad humans who will use your powers for bad? Or are you a tricky human who will use your powers to play tricks?"

"I don't plan on using my powers at all," I said. I walked faster.

"Ah. Well, at least you admit that you have powers."

"Go away." I did an about-face and walked in the opposite direction. He stuck with me.

"I have a question for you," he said. I ignored him. "Do you want to hear my question?"

"No."

"Penelope." He ran in front of me to block my way and dropped to one knee. He carefully placed his rocks glass on the sidewalk, then swept the top hat off his head and clutched it to his chest. He held out his hand like a gentleman. "Penelope Marie Salvo, the artificial god of war, will you make me the happiest Voodoo Loa in the world and be my wife?"

2

This guy wasn't a Voodoo god. Or, sorry, *loa*. Or whatever he wanted to be called. Spirits aren't real. Gods aren't real. Ghosts aren't real. And even if they were real, you sure as hell wouldn't find them walking around the streets of New York City.

I didn't bother responding to this dude's creep-tastic proposal of marriage. I circled around him and walked off. He jumped back to his feet and followed me. This guy had an infinite amount of patience. Every time I told him to fuck off, he'd say something weird and I'd get drawn back into the conversation. The first time was on Worth Street.

"If you don't fuck off and leave me alone," I told him, "I'm going to call the cops."

"You're feisty," he said. He stared at the sky, lost in his own thoughts. "You'd think that a girl in as much danger as you would want some powerful friends. Friends like me, for example."

And I didn't realize it, but that drew back into conversation. "I'm not in any danger."

"Aren't you?" he asked. I didn't answer. "That Carl human and the entities of the Westland Corporation are plotting your destruction right now, even as we speak."

I stopped and snapped at him. "How do you know that!?"

"I told you," he responded in a calm tone. "I know everything."

I grit my teeth. "You know everything?"

"Yes."

"Then answer me one thing."

"Anything."

"How do I get rid of *you*?"

I marched off. And, of course, Baron Semedi followed. He pestered me with "hey, hey, hey" and "wait, wait, wait," but I was over it. Done. I decided to ignore him no matter what he said. But, again, his patience was infinite and mine was not. He said anything he could think of to get a reaction out of me.

In front of Bonnie's Bon-Bon's, he asked, "Don't you want to know what Carl and the other humans from the Westland place are going to do to you?"

I ignored him.

At the corner by the post office, he asked, "Would it interest you to know there are other colorful bubbles out there much like the one you swallowed? There's a pink one and a black one and a... Penelope? Are you listening to me?"

I kept ignoring him.

When we passed Tony's Sub Shop, he hit me with this: "Aren't you curious about whatever happened to your father? I could tell you what happened to your father."

That made me stop. I spun around and shoved a finger in Semedi's ruffled undershirt. "No, I am not the least bit curious what happened to Michael. I don't care."

Semedi nodded. "Yes, dearest. I'm sorry. I do hate it when we fight." He put out his arms. "Let me give you a hug as an apology."

I stormed off. There was just no getting rid of this dude. I mean, I was already fed up with his weirdness and the shit he was saying, but then he brought up Michael and that was really crossing the line. I resolved to put one foot in front of the other and never talk to this Semedi guy ever again. All I had to do was get to the police station. Once I got to the police station, I could go inside and he wouldn't be able to harass me anymore. If he did, I'd call for help and then he could tell his stupid Voodoo story to an officer of the law.

Semedi followed me all the way to One Police Plaza. I was afraid he might actually call my bluff and follow me inside, but he stopped at the edge of the decorative courtyard out front. He stood on the sidewalk and called out one last thing to me before I went in the front doors.

"I can't believe you'd just walk away from me like this," he shouted. "I'm a Voodoo spirit of love and death and I deserve respect!"

"No, you're not!" I shouted back. "And no, you don't!"

3

One Police Plaza is the main police station for most of Manhattan Island. Helicopters take off and land from the roof. The parking garage is filled with hundreds of police cruisers and dozens of SWAT vans. It was essentially an army base, but for cops. And as far as interesting-looking buildings go, One Police

Plaza was hardly worth mentioning. It is basically just a gigantic cube with windows surrounded by trees.

I walked in through the revolving doors and approached the metal detector. A cop sat right there to make sure no one brought in a gun. He was a huge guy, probably six-foot tall, and built like a pro-wrestler. He stood up off his stool when he saw me coming and stared at me through his mirrored sunglasses.

"If you have anything metal, throw it in one of these," he said, gesturing at the plastic tubs stacked up on a table.

I pulled off my two studded belts, kicked off my shoes, and pulled a few metal earrings out of my ears. I threw them in the tub and walked through the archway. The metal detector went off. Officer Beefcake ordered me to go back the way I came, and I did. He asked me to double check myself for metal. I patted myself up and down, but I was metal free; no change, no keys, no weapons. The only possible offender was the zipper on my jeans. I looked at the cop and shrugged.

"I dunno," I said to him.

He waved for me to walk through again. I did. The alarm went off. He sent me back to try again.

He took out a handheld metal detector and waved it over me, head to toe. The machine picked up metal inside my skull. He waved it across the front of my chest. It picked up metal there, too. It made noise all up and down my body, around my arms and all down my legs.

He looked really confused. He checked the machine to make sure it was working correctly. He even waved it around his own skull, but nothing happened.

But when he put it anywhere near me, the thing went haywire.

"Do you have a metal plate in your head?" he asked. "Medical screws or something?"

"Oh." Obviously I didn't, but I didn't have any other excuse for why my whole body was setting off a metal detector. I slapped my forehead like I was a big dummy and said, "I totally forgot. Yeah, I have a metal plate."

"Alright." He almost looked relieved that there was *some* explanation for what was going on. He waved me through and let me pass. "Go on."

I stepped through the metal detector again, setting it off, of course, and then went to put my belts back on. I pulled on my shoes and plugged my earrings back into their holes.

I walked around One Police Plaza, found a receptionist, and told her I wanted to report a death threat. She directed me to another receptionist by the elevators. I told that receptionist that I needed to report a death threat. She told me to go up to this office on the seventh floor and ask for Detective Flowers. I crowded into an elevator with four police officers, rode it to the seventh floor, and checked in with another receptionist. She made me wait twenty minutes before buzzing a button, unlocking a bulletproof door, and granting me access to a long corridor that had a dozen offices.

Detective Allen.

Detective Williams.

Detective Flattery.

Finally, Detective Flowers.

I knocked on the detective's door. A woman called out and told me to come in. I walked into her office. The detective was in her chair, facing away from her desk. On my side of her desk was an empty chair. I put my hand on it, ready to take a seat.

I said, "I need to report a death threat."

The chair spun around, but there was no Detective Flowers. Instead, there was Baron Semedi dressed up like a police officer. How did he beat me up here? And how did he change his clothes so fast?

"What seems to be the trouble?" Semedi asked with a huge grin on his face.

I threw my hands up. I thought I was done with this guy. "What are you doing here?"

"I am saving you from making a huge mistake," he said. He leaned forward and folded his hands. "You think the humans are going to believe you about Impossible Red? Or about the Carl and his armor of snipers from the Westland Corporation?"

"They'll believe me."

"Oh, come on now. Think." He stood up and walked to the office window where he looked down on all of Manhattan. "You know those people who stand on the corners talking about aliens from outer space? Or the humans in the subway rambling on and on about how government radio waves are secretly controlling everyone's thoughts. Do you believe those people?"

"Those people are crazy," I said, pointing at the window. "I'm not crazy. I'm telling the truth."

76

He looked over his shoulder at me and grinned. "Sometimes you have to be just crazy enough to believe the truth."

Semedi, despite all his faults, did have a valid point. Whatever story I told the cops would sound insane: My body's bulletproof. My friend has a nuke in his basement. I'm being hunted by a shadow corporation. If you don't believe me, you can go ask Baron Semedi, he's the Voodoo spirit of love and death.

"Your problem, and it's not your fault, but your problem is that you're still thinking like a human," Semedi said, returning to the desk and taking a seat. He picked up the stapler and analyzed it closely. He put his arm down on the desk and started stapling his sleeve to the big paper calendar. "Humans solve humans problems. But you're not just a human anymore. You're... special. Humans don't solve special problems. Asking a human to solve a special problem is like asking a goat to develop a space program."

"I'm not special," I said. "I'm normal."

"Well, let's just see what the old computation machine has to say about that." He typed at the computer, and not well. He fake-typed at the keyboard with his pointer fingers in over exaggerated motions. The screen wasn't even on. He typed faster and faster. He made curious, thoughtful humming noises.

"It's not even on," I said.

He leaned in closer to the screen. "Seems that you're right." He grabbed the computer monitor and dragged it across the desk. The cords pulled everything around; it spilled a cup of pens and knocked the phone off the hook. He held the monitor over the edge of the desk and and dropped it in the trash can. Satisfied, he announced, "Piece of junk."

I grit my teeth. "Go away."

"I'm just trying to help you." He crossed his arms like he was truly insulted, then used his feet to spin around in his chair and turn his back to me. "But if that's really how you feel... get out of my office."

"*Your* office?" I grabbed his chair and spun it back around. I had half a mind to punch him in his stupid face. "Listen to me you-"

The chair was empty. Baron Semedi was gone. All that remained was a puff of cigar smoke.

I ultimately left the police station without speaking to a detective.

Was I losing my goddam marbles? Voodoo spirits aren't real and Baronn Semedi doesn't live in New York City. But still, his vanishing act in the police station was pretty compelling. Voodoo spirit or not, that didn't mean I had to take his advice. Regardless what he said about the humans, I still believed they could help me.

I slapped my forehead. Jesus Christ, Penelope, listen to yourself. "The *humans*"? Now you're doing it. *I'm* a human. I don't care what I swallowed, I don't care if bullets bounce off of me, I am a human being.

I headed back towards Chinatown.

The shop owners worked right alongside the city workers to clean up after Hurricane Sandy. Burly dudes wearing hard hats and work gloves carried beams of wood and car parts and threw them into a huge dumpster. A saw a butcher in a white apron stand in the entrance of his store and sweep heaps of broken glass onto the sidewalks. Three stories above, a lady poked out of her apartment window and dropped a bag of trash down to the sidewalk. A city worker snatched it up, added it to the two other trash bags he carried, and tossed them all in the back of a dump truck.

It's not the first time I'd seen New Yorkers come together after a major disaster. There's something about watching everyone working as a team that reminds you that, despite how much New York City can really suck, it isn't *all* bad.

A police officer stood at the corner and just sort of monitored everything that was going on. I decided to give asking for help a second try.

"Don't do it," said Baron Semedi. He was suddenly walking beside me, puffing on a cigar. "You'll be in Sun Meadows Mental Hospital before the end of the night."

I wasn't surprised he was there. I refused to look at him. "Leave me alone."

"Let me show you one thing," he said. "And if you still want to tell the humans your story after that, I won't stop you."

"What?" I stopped and glared at him. "What one thing do you want to show me?"

He pointed across the street. "Her."

There on the opposite sidewalk stood a girl, maybe sixteenish, standing up on a wooden crate like a street preacher. She was shouting at everyone who walked by, and everyone who walked by did their best to ignore her. Of course they did. That's exactly what you're supposed to do with crazy street preachers.

The girl was dressed in a bright yellow vinyl rain suit, complete with floppy hat and bulky rain boots. Her hair hung down to mid-back in a collection of thin dreadlocks, tied into a ponytail with the yellow strings of her hat. The way she dressed wasn't inherently weird; she was just a girl in a yellow rain suit. What was weird was the way her clothes fluttered, because there wasn't any wind.

Baron Semedi crossed the street in her direction. I followed him.

The girl was definitely odd – shouting at strangers and waving her arms all around – but that was just the half of it. It had stopped raining hours ago, but her rain gear was dripping wet. She didn't have that stereotypical crazy look going on; she was young, beautiful, with dark skin and dark eyes. But in those dark eyes were flickers of lightning.

"I did all this!" she shouted in some kind of Caribbean accent. "I attacked this city last night, but it wasn't my fault! I wasn't in control of myself."

Everyone passed right by her without a second look. Her only audience was me and Baron Semedi standing at the base of her wooden crate.

"See?" Baron Semedi said, pointing up at her.

"See what?" I asked. "She's just talking crazy."

"You think so?" he asked. He looked up at the girl. "Hey. Are you crazy?"

"I'm a hurricane," she shouted. "I'm not supposed to be here, but the humans have developed a weather machine that controls super-storms and forces them to attack major cities!"

Baron Semedi listened to her with passing interest, occasionally smoking his cigar or drinking his rum. For me, my curiosity was fading. We were the only two giving her any attention, so she started making eye contact with us and yelling at us directly.

"Listen to me," she shouted at us. "There's a weather machine in New York City! They summoned me here and made me kill all these people. It's not my fault! I didn't want to do it!"

Semedi leaned over and muttered to me. "This is Hurricane Sandy."

"What do you mean that's Hurricane Sandy?"

"The Hurricane. That's her. In human form."

I rolled my eyes. Things were just getting stupider. "Oh my god."

"See for yourself." He stepped closer to the girl on the box. "Hey, kid. What's your name?"

"I am Hurricane Sandy!" she shouted up into the sky. The people on the sidewalks picked up their pace to hurry past her.

Semedi looked at me. "See? I told you."

"She's not a hurricane," I said. "She's just rambling."

"She rambles because she's a Hurricane. Talking frantic is one of the things they do." He asked her another question. "Kid, who brought you here?"

"The Westland Corporation!" She turned a complete circle on her box, then faced us again. "They have a weather machine here in New York City. It controls the ions in the atmosphere and makes them go bzz bzz bzz and I couldn't resist myself. I had to come here! I had to! They have weather control!"

I narrowed my eyes. "The Westland Corporation?"

Semedi said, "She's telling the truth. The Westland Corporation used a weather machine to make Hurricane Sandy hit New York."

"Why would they do that?"

He contemplated the wet end of his cigar. "To cover their tracks. If they could keep all the police humans and the ambulance humans busy with a hurricane, then they could steal Impossible Red without getting caught." He puffed on his cigar. With his drinking hand, he tapped my forehead. "And it almost worked."

I gestured at the girl. "But if she's really a hurricane-"

"I'm standing right here," she shouted at me. "Don't talk about me like I'm not standing right here!"

"Sorry." I took a moment to gather my thoughts and addressed her directly. "If you're really a hurricane, then why do you look like a human?"

She hopped off the box and got in my face. The lightning in her eyes was not a trick of the light; it was really in there. She asked me, "What else would I look like?"

"You know... Like a hurricane."

Her voice had a sarcastic tone. "Like clouds?" she suggested. She wriggled her fingers through the air. "And lightning?"

"I mean, isn't that what hurricanes look like?"

She stared me down with such intensity, I thought she was going to take a swing. I balled up my fists, ready to fight back. The corner of her mouth curled into a smile. Not a friendly smile; more of a sneer.

She scoffed at me and said, "Humans."

"The point is..." Baron Semedi stepped between the two of us and moved up apart. "She's not lying. She really is Hurricane Sandy. There really is a weather machine. And the Westland Corporation really did control her and make her attack New York."

"Okay," I said. "So let's say you're right. Let's say this really is Hurricane Sandy. What's any of that got to do with me?"

"Think about it!" Baron Semedi walked in a broad circle around Sandy's wooden crate. "She's out here shouting the truth at the top of her lungs, but no one is listening to her because she sounds crazy. And if you told your story to the police, you'd sound crazy, too."

"No one listens to me!" Hurricane Sandy jumped back up on her box and resumed screaming at strangers. "Listen to me! Listen to me! Listen to me!"

It's a fact that in New York City, the more you scream "listen to me," the more people will ignore you.

Baron Semedi grabbed a middle-aged businessman by the shoulders and screamed in his face, "I'm the Voodoo spirit of love and death! I come from a shadowy swamp a million miles away!"

The businessman swatted Semedi's hands away and bolted. "Let go of me!" he shouted.

Semedi watched the terrified little man run down the sidewalk. He inhaled deeply and shouted as loud as he could to the world, "I am Baron Semedi, the first man to ever die! I am the Voodoo loa of death and love and I have been alive since the beginning of humanity! If you sacrifice a black chicken to me, I will give you all the winning lottery numbers!"

Sandy had to yell to be heard over Semedi. "We have to do something about the weather machine! If not, more of my brothers and sisters will come to destroy your cities!"

I watched the faces of the passing people. They had to've heard what the two of them were screaming; how could they not? The people just put their heads down and kept walking. No one listened. No one cared.

Semedi had had enough. He turned to me and smiled. "See?"

I nodded. "I get it."

He seemed satisfied that his point had been proven. "If you want to tell everyone about your bulletproof skin and file a restraining order against Carl and his army of rooftop snipers, then here..." He used his foot to scoot another wooden crate next to Hurricane Sandy's. "You might as well hop on up."

"Point taken." I crossed my arms. "Are you done?"

He rattled the ice in his drink. "I'm done."

"Well, then." I made a dopey face and gave him a sarcastic, over-exaggerated salute. "I guess this is goodbye."

And I left.

5

I headed back to Xin's shop. I owed him a real apology. He was the first person to really treat me like an adult – never mind the fact that he literally saved my life – but I was such a child that whenever the conversation got too real for me, I threw a temper tantrum and stormed out like a spoiled brat. Xin didn't deserve that. I knew I had it in me to be a rational adult who could maintain rational conversations, I just needed to try harder.

I got to the alley that led to Xin's shop. There was a rock on the ground, right in my way, begging to be kicked. Perfect kicking rock. So I kicked it.

It blew through the air like a tank mortar and collapsed a dumpster right down the middle. The rectangular plastic lids launched into the air. The dumpster itself slid down the length of the alley in a shower of sparks.

I spun around in a panicked circle. Oh, shit. Was that me? Did I do that? And did anyone see me?

I looked at my feet. They were the same old feet I ever had. Out of curiosity, I pushed down on the concrete with the ball of my foot. With only the slightest pressure, the concrete snapped like a cracker.

I jumped back.

I spotted some loose bricks piled up against the alley wall. I picked one of them up. It felt weightless. I tossed it from hand to hand like a baseball. I held it in my right hand and closed my fist. The brick exploded. Dust went all down the front of my shirt. Curiously, slowly, I grabbed another brick. I tapped it against the wall just to double check that it was real. Tap tap tap, it made that brick-on-brick sound. I held this one in my left hand, closed my fingers again and crushed it.

I walked over to the toppled dumpster and checked it out. Right where I'd kicked the rock, the metal was caved in, as if it was shot with some kind of armor-piercing bullet.

I knew what I was looking at.

Evidence. Conclusive, unfaked, undeniable evidence.

"God dammit," I muttered.

I let myself through the chain link fence and approached the shop. Xin walked out with a curious look on his face. I guess the destruction of that dumpster echoed for quite a ways.

"What did you do to my dumpster?" he asked. He had an annoyed tone to his voice.

I pointed back at it, surprised and a little excited. "I did that!"

"I can see that," he said. "But why? That's where I put my trash."

"I didn't do it on purpose," I said. "I just kicked a rock and it just sort of happened. I think I'm super strong or something."

That answer seemed acceptable to him. "Fine. But in the future, please be more careful."

I walked up to the porch steps and stood in front of him. He adjusted his glasses.

Awkward. He knew I'd changed my mind about the wacko stuff he had shown me in the basement. Now I had the awful task of apologizing. I took a deep breath and said, "I've never been good at saying sorry."

"All is forgiven," he said. He turned around and headed inside.

I ran up the stairs to followed him. He went to his side of the counter, I went to mine. We sat on our bar stools and looked at each other. Anxious, I used my feet to rotate back and forth. To inject a little levity into the seemingly tense situation, I did a full rotation, then smiled at Xin. He didn't seem amused. I think maybe that's why we got along so well. We were very different people – he was incredibly stoic and I was... well... *me* – but he let me be me. And I let him be him. And we were better friends because of it.

"So what changed your mind?" he asked me.

"Eh." I looked at my reflection in the glass of the display case. "I met Baron Semedi."

"The Voodoo spirit?" he asked.

"You know him?"

"I know *of* him."

"He asked me to marry him!"

"Not surprised," Xin said. "That is his nature. Many of the Voodoo spirits have multiple spouses. He's a spirit of death, but also a spirit of love."

"He's a spirit of creepy," I pointed out.

Xin smiled at my joke, which I took as a huge compliment.

Conversation dried up. We sat there quiet for a little bit, which is too long in my book.

I jumped off the bar stool and held out my arms, putting my body on display. "So I have this Impossible Red crap inside me. What do I do now?"

"I've been thinking about that." Xin raised a finger at me, then ducked behind the counter and rustled around underneath. I leaned forward to see what he was doing. When he stood back up, he had a key held between his fingers. "You remember how I said my father did this job before me? And before him, my grandmother?"

"And before her, your great-grandfather," I said in a skeptical tone. I could see where this was going and I didn't know if I liked it.

He said, "I don't have any children to pass the job on to. I'm not getting any younger and someday soon I will need a replacement to own and operate this store, as well as protect the collection in the basement."

My stomach suddenly felt nauseous. "You mean *me*."

He held the key out. "I mean you."

"Is that a key to the basement?" I asked. Xin didn't answer me. I refused to take it. "Dude, I dunno. What you're talking about is way different than just watering the plants and sweeping the porch."

"It is very different."

He held the key out with such determination. No part of his face hinted that he thought this was a bad idea. Well, he might have been cool with it, but I had my reservations. I was a teenager. I just graduated high school. I wasn't even old enough to buy alcohol for Christ sake. I didn't need to be in charge of time swords and god masks and a nuclear bomb.

He could see the hesitation on my face and said, "Penelope, you're the only other person who knows the secrets of this place. There is no one else."

"Oh, man." I let out a long sigh and held out my open palm. He placed the key in my hand. I didn't close my fingers. Instead, I just sat there and stared at it. It looked like a perfectly normal key. I asked, "You're sure about this?"

He gave me a single, confident nod. "I'm sure."

Chapter 6

1

Xin's rules for the collection in the basement were very simple.

The basement door was to remain locked at all times. My possession of a key was mostly honorific; it was still his primary responsibility to put anything down there. The only time I was allowed to unlock it was when someone brought in a dangerous artifact when he wasn't around; and even then I was ordered to unlock the door, place the item in the basement, and immediately lock the door again. There were only two keys to the basement – mine and Xin's – and no one could use those keys but us.

And I should never, for any reason, *remove* anything from the collection.

Ever.

For any reason.

He made me repeat after him.

"Ever," he said.

"Ever," I repeated.

"For any reason."

"For any reason."

I put the key on a necklace so I'd always have it with me.

In the days that followed, things slowly returned to normal. I watered the plants. Xin worked on his powders and potions. We listened to '70s rock on the radio. In the mornings, Mrs. Cho picked up her laundry detergent.

That following Tuesday, the door swung open and we were greeted by the smiling face of a blonde fairytale princess.

Xin put down his current project, a slice of cactus plum and a small jar, and greeted the girl. "Hello."

She cleared her throat and spoke in a loud, clear voice. "Announcing Princess Cardboard of the Six Princesses Package and Envelope Delivery Service!" Her eyes darted back and forth between Xin and I. She looked particularly confused and her smile vanished. "Which one of you is Miss Penelope Marie Saliva?"

"It's Salvo," I corrected her.

Princess Cardboard wore an evening gown of beige silk that draped down to her ankles and covered her feet. The top of the dress looked practical: a high collar with large, chocolate-colored buttons and short sleeves that just barely covered her shoulders. She wore silk gloves cut from the same brown silk, elegant, but shaped like work gloves; something you would wear if you were going to load cardboard boxes onto a truck.

Her bright gold hair was in the middle of an identity crisis: the left side of it wanted to hang straight and the right side wanted to be in goldilock curls. Most of it hung over her shoulders and down her back, but then random lengths of it came down in big coils. She wore a crown on her head cut out of a cardboard box, just slightly too big for her head. The points of it were cut out by hand, jagged and all different sizes.

Her pale skin was flawless, exactly what you'd expect from a teenage princess. Her eyes were a rich brown, like the color of milk and coffee. She made eye contact with me and I couldn't look away. When she smiled, her nose wrinkled.

In one hand, she carried a clipboard overloaded with yellow and pink and white paper. In her other hand, she had a manila envelope. She looked at the envelope to double check my name, realized her mistake, and rolled her eyes at herself.

"Sorry. Which one of you is Miss Penelope Marie *Salvo*?"

Xin pointed at me. I pointed to myself. "That's me."

"Please sign here." She stuck out her clipboard. I took the clipboard from her. A fountain pen dangled from the clip by a string of pearls and I used it to sign my name on a yellow sheet of carbon paper. At the top of the document were the words *Six*

Princesses Package and Envelope Delivery Service.

She took the clipboard away from me and snapped the manila envelope into the air between us. I took it. It was thin as paper, but felt heavier. Princess Cardboard tucked her clipboard into her armpit and pulled a handful of smashed coffeecake out of her pocket. It was nothing more than a wad of mashed up crumbs. That didn't stop her from holding it like a lady and eating it with dainty bites. Like Ma always said, when you meet someone new, start with a compliment.

I said, "I love your dress."

She froze in place with her coffeecake right at her mouth. It was as if no one had ever said a kind word to her in her life. She swallowed her mouthful of cake and said, "Why thank you! You have a cute necklace." She pointed at the basement key around my neck.

"Oh, thanks. I made it myself."

"No way." She sounded amazed. "Out of thin air?"

"Well, no. Not out of thin air. I made it out of raw materials. I can make you a necklace, if you want."

"Oh, I can't," she said. She waved her hand at me. "I can't take gifts from customers. It's against the rules."

"Fuck the rules," I said.

Xin chided me for my language. "Penelope."

Princess Cardboard's face flushed bright red. I doubt she had ever heard the F word before. She said, "I don't think we're allowed to fuck the rules. No. No, I shouldn't, but thank you anyway."

"Alright," I said. "Your call."

I walked over to the counter and plopped down on the bar stool. Princess Cardboard busied herself with the paperwork on her clipboard. She lowered her eyebrows, chewed on her bottom lip, and really struggled with her forms. I held the black envelope in both hands. It didn't have a return address, or even a mailing address for that matter. It just said "Miss Penelope Marie Salvo" on the front in white block letters.

Xin took out a letter opener and said, "Here. I have a..."

I tore the envelope open.

"...Never mind" He put it away.

I looked inside the envelope to find a sheet of paper, but when I pulled it out, I discovered it was actually a white sheet of metal with black print. Not thick metal, not like a street sign, but thinner. The print wasn't ink, but actually embossed on the sheet with raised letters I could feel under my fingertips.

The front read:

PENELOPE MARIE SALVO
At the request of the Westland Corporation
you have been invited to our headquarters in Midtown
for a low-stakes, non-violent, sniper-free conversation about
IMPOSSIBLE RED
Your safety is 100% guaranteed.
Drinks and hors d'oeuvres will be provided.
Attendance is on your terms, and at your earliest convenience.

I held the metal paper up to Princess Cardboard. "What the hell is this?"

"That..." Princess Cardboard said, "...is an invitation to you from the Westland Corporation. They paid me to deliver it to you." She took a step closer and lowered her voice. "What do they want you for?"

I said, "Long story."

She got even quieter. "What'd you do?"

"I didn't do anything," I said.

Cardboard nodded and went back to writing on her clipboard.

Xin reached across the counter and tool the invitation out of my hands. He read it closely, then said, "You can't go."

"What do you mean I can't go?" I said. "I'm invited. This is my chance to go down there and sort things out."

He said, "Penelope, they don't want to sort things out. They are an evil and selfish organization. They want Impossible Red, even if it means they have to kill you."

I pointed at the invitation. "Look. Right here, it says, 'Your safety is 100% guaranteed.'"

"You don't know them they way I do," he said. He took the invitation to the basement door, unbolted the padlock, and threw the metal thing down the stairs. He slammed the door and latched the padlock closed. When he turned back to me, he had this no-nonsense look on his face. I had no clue what had his panties in such a bundle. He said, "I'm sorry, but the Westland Corporation cannot be trusted. They are bad people who only want power. They don't want to have a conversation about

Impossible Red. They want to find a way to turn it into a weapon. You cannot go."

"Listen to yourself," I said. "I'm a grown woman. I can make my own decisions. You don't *let* me do anything."

He came over to put his hand on my shoulder. "I'm trying to protect you."

"I appreciate that, dude, but I don't need protecting."

He said, "Yes, you do."

I got off the stool and stepped away from him. "No, I don't, Xin. It's me they're trying to kill. Not you. I want to go down there and get all this stuff straightened out and you can't stop me. You're not my father."

Xin didn't have much to say about that. We stood there and stared each other down, waiting for the other one to flinch. Finally, Princess Cardboard broke the silence when she stuffed the remaining coffeecake back in her pocket.

"Well, I'd like to stay," she said as she went for the door, "but you two are making things very awkward and I have other deliveries to make."

"Wait!" I called out. Princess Cardboard turned around in the open doorway and waited.

I ran to my room and grabbed one of my handmade necklaces out of my backpack. It wasn't anything fancy, just a string of black lace with a few black and silver beads on it. I balled it up in my palm and then went out to shake her hand. I did the old trick where you shake someone's hand and give them the thing you're holding. Maybe it was against the rules for her to accept gifts, but this was so sly and covert, I felt like an international spy. Refusing gifts sounded like a stupid rule, anyway.

The princess looked concerned, so I smiled to put her at ease. Eventually she smiled back.

"Thank you," she said to me. She gave Xin a royal salute. "And good afternoon to you, sir!"

Once Princess Cardboard left, I spun around and gave Xin my bitchiest look. He didn't even notice. He carried an empty three-gallon jar over to the counter, as well as a huge burlap sack of leaves, something like oregano, but it wasn't oregano. He got out his mortar and pestle, stuffed sprigs of the not-oregano into the bowl and went to town grinding it into dust. He ground up a spoonful of powder, dropped it into the three gallon jar, then started the process over. I plopped down on my side of the counter and sulked.

"So do you know where the Westland Corporation has their offices?" I asked him.

"You're not going." He didn't look up and his voice had a tone that said, "And that's final."

"You're such a hypocrite," I snapped. "You said swallowing this thing was the right thing to do, that keeping it away from the Westland Corporation was the right thing to do, and now here they are, trying to settle things with a conversation and you want me to ignore them. So what am I supposed to do? Look over my shoulder for the rest of my life? I want to go talk to them."

He carefully put down his mortar and pestle and let out an exasperated sigh. He adjusted the glasses on his nose, looked me right in the eyes, and said, "You're right." Then he went back to work and said, "But you're still not going."

"Fine." I hopped up off the bar stool and went for the door. I was ready to walk out on him, but I caught myself. No, Penelope. You're not a child, stop acting like one. Just count to ten and go cool off. I huffed, stepped out onto the porch and said, "I'm going to get some fresh air."

2

I stood there on the porch and fumed. I had to remind myself that Xin was usually right. Xin knew what he was talking about. And while my first instinct was to throw a hissy-fit and storm off, I reminded myself not to. I would only feel terrible about it hours later and come crawling back.

"Psst." Princess Cardboard poked her head around the corner of the shop. She adjusted the cardboard crown on her head and a curl of gold hair dropped in front of her face. She pushed it behind her ear. "Miss Salvo, over here."

That seemed curious enough. I stepped off the porch and walked around the corner to join her. There she stood, clipboard in hand, and with a large cardboard box at her feet. She had also put on my necklace; the only black thing in her otherwise brown outfit.

"I heard what your father said in there," she said.

I shook my head, confused. "He's not my father."

"He's not?" She wrinkled her nose, obviously confused. "I just assumed he was your father. You two look a lot alike."

I scratched my head. "He's an eighty-five year old Chinese man. I'm a teenage Italian girl."

"Mmhmm." She nodded and gave me a perky smile. "And I'm royalty from the Muffincake Kingdom. Nice to meet you."

She stuck out her hand. I shook it.

She continued on. "I just wanted to tell you that I know what it feels like when your father won't let you go out and do things. My father was king and when I was little, he never let me leave our castle. I think it was because I was the youngest of all my sisters. Then when my mother died, he locked me in a bedroom at the very top of our castle and wouldn't let me leave. It was absolutely dreadful. It wasn't until he got old and sick that someone let me out so I could rule my part of the world just like my sisters. Jeez, listen to me. I'm rambling again. All I'm saying is, I know how it feels to be trapped. So if you want me to sneak you into that meeting with the Westland Corporation..." She shifted her eyes all around to make sure we weren't being spied on and lowered her voice to a whisper. "I can make that happen."

I was still sentences behind her, trying to process the part about the king and the castle, but then I focused on the part about her taking me to the meeting. "Really?" I said. "You could do that?"

"I could."

"Okay!" I said. "Because I really want to go."

"Great!" She clapped her hands together.

She ran behind me, put both hands on my back, and moved me into position next to the cardboard box at her feet. The box was two feet in all directions, as tall as my knees and big enough to stand in. She grabbed handfuls of her gown, hoisted the hem up to her knees and stepped in the box. It showed her shoes: a pair of brown pumps. Her socks were white and ruffled at the top with lace. She situated herself inside the box by smoothing out her dress and readjusting her crown.

She motioned at me with both hands and said, "Get in."

I blinked. "You mean get in the box?"

She nodded, which shook her crown loose and it fell in front of her eyes. She pushed it back into place. "Do you want to go meet these guys or not?"

What can you do? When a delivery princess tells you to get in a big cardboard box, you get in a big cardboard box. We had to crowd in awkwardly close. I'd just met the girl five minutes ago and there we were, face to face. I couldn't tell if the coffeecake I was smelling was her perfume, or just whatever she had tucked away in her pockets.

"Hold on," she said.

The bottom of the cardboard box fell out and we dropped into a dark cardboard tunnel. It should have been physically impossible for a tunnel to exist beneath us, because we were just standing on solid concrete. But, none the less, we were in a narrow little escape tunnel.

"Follow me," Cardboard said. She got down on her hands and knees and started to crawl away.

I followed behind her. Princess Cardboard shuffled along with pretty good speed, occasionally stopping to adjust the crown on her head. The walls and floor and ceiling of the tunnel were all folded up cardboard flaps. Light shone through the folded seams in the cardboard. I stopped and took a peek through one of them. Just on the other side was a different part of the world. I moved up and peeked through once again. I saw a German television studio, then after that a lumber yard in Canada, and after that a garbage dump from who-knows-where filled with couches. Sometimes the tunnel would branch left or right, leading off into absolute darkness. We passed a lot of intersections and I realized that if this princess abandoned me, I would never find my way back. We were in a maze, and I was lost.

"Do you know where you're going," I asked her.

She laughed. "Totally. Just stick with me and you'll be fine."

So I stuck with her. We crawled through every cardboard box in the world, so it seemed. Some of the boxes were stamped, or covered in shipping labels. I saw boxes as far-flung as Iceland, Malaysia, and South Africa.

"Did you build this place?" I asked her.

"Oh, goodness, no," she said. "It was already here when I came to New York."

I crawled along and stole glances through the gaps in the boxes. "Where are we exactly?"

"I don't know really," she said. "I just found it one day and started exploring. It's really handy when it comes to making my

93

deliveries on time."

We crawled around for half an hour. I felt like a kid playing "fort" in a bunch of cardboard boxes I built with a friend. We were on some imaginary adventure, except this wasn't imaginary.

"Can I ask you a question?" she said.

"Of course," I said.

"What's it like to break the rules?"

"Huh?"

"The rules," she repeated. "When you break them. What's that like?"

Odd question. "I dunno. It's like... sometimes you have to decide for yourself if you want to follow a rule or not, and if you don't, you just do whatever you want."

She stopped crawling and looked back at me. "You *do* that?"

"Quite a bit," I said. "Probably too much."

She started crawling again. "My sisters say that rules are important."

I crawled after her. "I mean, they are sometimes. But sometimes you have to break them."

"How do you know the difference?"

Tough question. "Uhm, I guess you just get a feeling. And sometimes you're not always right, so it's a real gamble."

"Weird," she said.

After a few more intersections, she came to a stop. "Here we go. This is the place."

She pushed on the flaps in the ceiling and they opened up into darkness. She stood up and crawled out. I followed.

3

Our exit from the cardboard tunnels was an empty box of copy machine paper. We emerged in a dark storage closet for an office building. The lights in the room were motion-activated, so as soon as we stood up, the fluorescent lights popped on. All around us were shelves filled with broken printers. Across the back wall sat boxes of copy machine paper stacked five high. There were metal storage cabinets organized with cases of highlighters and paper clips and pens.

"Where are we?" I asked.

Princess Cardboard brushed off her gown. Her crown dropped over her eyes and she pushed it back off of her face. She glanced all around, then said, "A storage room."

"Well, I can see that," I said. "Where is this storage room?"

"Where you wanted to be," she said. "The Westland Corporation."

She rattled the door handle, but it didn't open. Locked. She bumped into the door once with her shoulder, but it didn't budge. "Bummer," she said. "We're stuck."

"Here." I politely moved her aside, lifted my foot off the ground so I could grab the toe of my shoe and stretch my legs. "Let me try something."

I figured if I could crush bricks with my bare hands and destroy metal, I could probably kick down a door. The storage room didn't give me enough room for a running start, but I didn't need it. I took two quick steps and kicked the metal door as hard as I could. How I envisioned it, a swift kick would make the door pop open. I didn't know my own strength. When I kicked the door, the entire door frame exploded out of the concrete wall and flew into the office cubicles on the other side.

I had no idea there was a cubicle farm out there. Hundreds of men in ties and women in power suits we all busy answering phones, making photocopies, and filing paperwork. Of course, everything came to a screeching halt when the door to the storage room just exploded for no reason and shredded through the cubicles at break-neck speeds.

Men and women dove for cover, dropping their phones and throwing paper into the air. The door cartwheeled across the entire office and shattered through the windows on the far wall. It drifted into the sky, caught a slight breeze, and then fell down to the streets of Manhattan below.

Once the noise cleared, everyone in the office turned to the storage room to find me and Princess Cardboard standing in the missing doorway. Cardboard's crown slumped over her eyes and she pushed it back in place.

I gave them an embarrassed little wave and humbly said, "Knock knock."

The employees stayed there frozen in place, unsure how to handle the exploding wall and sudden appearance of two oddly-dressed teenage girls. A supervisor with greased back hair and fancy cuff links came over – because it's the supervisors job to handle weird stuff – and asked us what, exactly, we thought we were doing. Princess Cardboard apologized. I politely informed the guy that I was Penelope Salvo and I was invited to a meeting in their head office so, in the words of the Brothers Johnson, he could "get the funk out of my face."

The supervisor guy said he was going to call security because we were trespassing. I told him we weren't trespassing. I was specifically invited. I wasn't invited to come through the *wall*, but I *was* invited.

He gave me a skeptical look. "You were invited to information collection?"

"Well, no," I said. "Not specifically."

"Then where were you invited *specifically*?"

"I..." Shit. I didn't know. The invitation didn't say. In hindsight, I might have rushed into things a little under-prepared. I only knew one person who worked at the Westland Corporation and while I wasn't for certain that it was him that invited me, I had no other names to drop.

"Carl," I said. "Carl invited me."

"Carl the senior field agent?" The supervisor guy didn't look any less skeptical. He told me and Princess Cardboard to "stay put" while he made a phone call. He grabbed a phone from a nearby cubicle and pressed a button. Whoever was on the other line answered right away.

"Ma'am, will you inform agent Carl that we have two girls down here in accounting. They were hiding in the storage closet and..." Then a pause. "She said her name is Peppermint Sally."

"Penelope Salvo," I said and gave him a mean look. Why in the blue hell would my name be Peppermint Sally?

"Penelope Salvo," he corrected himself. "She's here with a girl dressed like a princess and..." Then another pause. The voice on the other end of the phone changed to someone else. The supervisor's tone switched from hostility to worry. "Oh. Yes, sir. No, sir. I didn't know, sir. Right away, sir. I'll send them right up."

Then he hung up the phone. He turned to us sheepishly and asked us to follow him. He led us through a row of broken cubicles to the elevator. We stepped over the toppled chairs and broken printers. Princess Cardboard held up her gown and stepped gingerly over everything.

"Oh my goodness," she said. "This place is a mess."

The supervisor shot her a dirty look. The surrounding employees watched us in silence as the supervisor escorted us through the destroyed cubicles. We reached the far windows, one of which was shattered open from the door I kicked out. Stiff wind howled past us. I peered out and saw Manhattan Island below. We were probably twenty stories up, give or take. Princess Cardboard put her hand on my shoulder so she could also look down.

"It's not safe to have these windows open like this." She pointed at the window. "You need a sign here so people know not to jump out."

The supervisor rolled his eyes, obviously at the end of his rope with our antics. He led us to the elevator. He had a key card on a retractable lanyard that he pulled out and swiped through a card reader. The elevator doors opened. I stepped inside and Princess Cardboard followed me. The supervisor didn't join us, but he reached in and pressed a button for the 37th floor.

"Well, pleasure meeting you," I said to him

The supervisor did not say anything back.

4

We rode the elevator up to the 37th floor.

The doors opened and revealed this super-posh penthouse office. This was the kind of office where oil tycoons make trillion-dollar deals. The floor was black marble. The couches were black leather. There was a desk carved from a block of white granite and polished to a mirror shine. There were bookcases filled with books all along the walls – probably just for decoration – broken up by large antique paintings, like "French dude leaning against a horse" and "half naked lady wrapped in white silk."

Immediately to our right was a bar. And not just a little drink cart with a few glasses and a single bottle of whiskey. No, I'm talking about an entire mahogany bar with bar seats and a hundred bottles of liquor stocked on the shelves. The bar itself was a reddish mahogany. The foot rails were polished chrome.

The opposite wall of the room was floor-to-ceiling glass and had a great view of Manhattan Island. There were a set of double patio doors that opened out onto a big balcony. It was the kind of balcony where you'd host a late-night party for celebrities, where waiters with towels on their arm would walk around with trays of free champagne and exotic hors d'oeuvres of tiny squids and wriggling octopus tentacles and other strange shit rich people eat.

A stout old businessman in a suit stood out on the balcony. He was a victim of male-pattern-baldness, with puffs of white hair on the sides and dark liver spots on his bald head. His face was wrinkled and saggy. He looked like the kind of heartless CEO who raked in billions of dollars a year by giving his customers cancer, the kind of guy who takes the day off to put on checkered pants and go down to "the links" to ride around in a golf cart and smoke cigars and drink scotch.

Me and Princess Cardboard were oddly dressed for this kind of meeting; me in a Weezer t-shirt and black shorts, her in a princess gown and with a cardboard box on her head. We stood in the elevator and watched the old man yell into a cell phone.

"You're talking to me about *cost*?" he shouted. "Since when have I ever cared about *cost*?" He glanced over his shoulder and gave us the "just give me a second" finger. Then he turned around and went back to yelling. "I want two things out of you. I want to be on Vacation Island in time for the auction, and I want R&D ready to go as soon as I get back. I don't want your sad sack stories or your bullshit excuses. You either make it happen or you'll wake up dead at the bottom of the East River!" He took the cell phone away from his ear and stared at it. He muttered, "Never can figure out how to turn these things off." He stared at it a while longer, then poked it. He looked pleasantly surprised that he figured it out. "Ah, there we go." He finally gave us his undivided attention and headed in our direction.

"Sounds like you're having a good day," I said.

He glanced at his cell phone and huffed. "Incompetent fools." He got close enough to reach out for a handshake. "Miss Salvo, thank you so much for coming. I'm the CEO of the Westland Corporation."

I stepped out of the elevator and shook his hand. He shook hard; a power-handshake. "Cool," I said. "Do you have a name?"

"The CEO *is* my name."

"Your parents named you the CEO?"

I could tell by his face, he did not find my sense of humor at all appealing. He gave me a dead-serious look and said, "My parents are Corporate Personhood and a dedication to maximize the investments of my stockholders."

"That's a weird thing to say." I looked to Cardboard for a little solidarity, but she wasn't beside me. She was still in the elevator, peeking around the corner. I asked her, "You coming?"

"I don't think I should," she said. "I wasn't invited. I have deliveries to make. I shouldn't be here."

It was my turn to give the CEO the "give me a second" finger and make him wait. I walked back to the elevator and said to Cardboard, "Dude, don't ditch me here. What if something goes wrong? I need you. Plus, you have to take me back home."

She leaned in and whispered right in my ear. "I've heard of this guy. He's evil."

"Hey." I gave her a confident smile and a pat on the arm. "You'll be fine. You're with me."

Her shoulders dropped. She checked her clipboard. "Okay. But I can't stay long. I got deliveries to make or my sisters are going to be mad at me."

"No problem." I smiled and waved at her to follow me. "This'll be fast."

"Who is your friend?" the CEO asked me. He was trying to sound friendly, but it just came off as fake.

"This is Princess Cardboard," I said as we rejoined him. "I told her she could come with me. She's like my..." What was the word? Friend? Spirit guide? "She's my consigliere."

"A princess?" the CEO said, impressed. He gave her a weird smile, like he just got the upper hand in a business merger. He stuck his hand out to her, expecting a handshake. "So nice to meet you, your highness."

"Hello," she said. She stayed tucked behind me. She didn't shake his hand.

"So." The CEO walked over to the bar. "Drinks? Would you like a carbonated milk? Or a caffeine-free diet Cooke's soda?"

"I don't suppose you got any beer?" I asked.

He grunted as he rooted around beneath the bar. "No. I don't care much for beer."

Of course he didn't. I'm sure from his point of view, beer was for "poor people."

"Is there coffee?" Cardboard asked.

"Coffee, I do have." He rose up from behind the bar with a glass pot of steaming coffee and a single black mug that read *the Westland Corporation.* I took a seat on one of the suede bar stools.

These bar stools were nice; super plush and really easy on the butt. I needed a bar stool like this back at the shop. Cardboard reluctantly sat next to me.

"You look like you're really good at golf," I told the CEO.

"Little lady, I'm terrible at golf. I spend so much time in the bunker, I started getting mail for Hitler."

I laughed, just one little "ha." It was sincere. I love bad jokes. But I wasn't going to give him the satisfaction of anything more than that.

"Sir," Princess Cardboard said. "Hitler is dead."

The CEO nodded, unsure what to make of her deadpan reaction to his joke. "That he is. That he most definitely is." He poured coffee into the Westland mug and moved it in front of her. She took it without saying thank you and inhaled the steam. He put the coffee pot back under the bar and turned to face the shelves of liquor. He went for a bottle of something brown. He pulled the bottle off the shelf and grabbed a small rocks glass. "Cognac," he said, turning to show me the bottle. "I hope you don't mind if I drink."

I shrugged. "It's your office."

He poured the alcohol into the glass, no ice. He asked me, "Do you golf, Miss Salvo?"

"Golf?" I stuck out my tongue in disgust. "Hell no. Shit's boring."

He gave me a little chuckle. "It *is* boring. I hate the sport, to be honest with you. But I have to play it if that means I can make a deal with a client. Sometimes we have to do things we don't want to do, if that's what the job calls for." He drank some cognac, gave it a satisfied look, then said, "You'd agree with that, wouldn't you, Miss Salvo?"

He lost me. "Agree with what?"

"That sometimes we have to do things we don't want to do. If the job calls for it."

I crossed my arms at him. "You mean like telling your snipers to shoot an innocent girl in the head and blow her brains out?"

He gave me a blank stare for a moment, then smiled at me, a snake-in-the-garden-of-Eden kind of smile.

He took another sip of cognac and said, "My informants tell me that you've taken a sudden interest in gardening."

"Your informants?" I asked.

"Oh, don't worry. It's not as bad as it sounds. Information Collection is just one of the many departments here at the Westland Corporation. If you're going to meet at the negotiating table, you better know who you're negotiating with, isn't that right? It's just smart business 101. I know a lot of things about you, Miss Salvo. Your mother died in a head-on collision driving to your high school graduation. Your father left town when you were only twelve years old. You live in a storage closet in Chinatown. You're bad at math. Your best friend is Ilana Rittenberg." He took a sip of his drink and pointed at my crossed arms. "When you're annoyed, you cross your arms because you don't know what to do with your hands."

I uncrossed my arms and stood up. "So you've been stalking me."

"It's not stalking, Miss Salvo. It's *research*. Here at the Westland Corporation, it's our business to deal with everything supernatural. And you, my dear underachiever, are most certainly supernatural."

"Because I swallowed Impossible Red?"

"Impossible Red." He tilted his head back and swallowed the rest of his cognac one big gulp. He set the glass down on the bar a little too hard. "I've had my field agents scouring the world for fifteen years searching for Impossible Red. And after fifteen years, just when we discovered its exact location in a basement in Chinatown, you came along and swallowed it."

"Hey, that is not my fault," I said. "I wouldn't have swallowed it if you assholes didn't come steal it."

He frowned at me, then turned to Cardboard. "How's the coffee? Good?"

Cardboard kept her eyes on her mug. "It's fine."

He looked back at me. "True. We did try to steal it," he said. "But it's like I said, sometimes we have to do things we don't want to do. I didn't want to resort to theft, but then again Xin Houng didn't leave us much choice, now did he? What was I supposed to do? Just abandon fifteen years of research because some old man wants to keep it in his underground collection? So, yes, we tried to steal it. I'm not proud of that. I don't think anyone at the Westland Corporation is proud of that. In fact, when Carl first found out the plan was to steal from Mister Houng, he loudly voiced his opposition. 'I'm not going to break the law,' he said. We argued for hours. I honestly thought he was going to quit on me. But in the end, he eventually he agreed to break into that little flower shop. Carl, because the job called for it, did something he didn't want to do."

I frowned. "Uh huh."

Cardboard stuck her face in her coffee mug and muttered, "He's lying."

"But all that's behind us now," the CEO continued. "We made a horrible first impression with you and I'm glad you're here to give us the chance to set things right. The Westland Corporation is not a violent organization. It's really not. Our focus is on research and discovery. We value diplomacy and negotiations. So now that the unpleasantness is out of the way... let's both be diplomats and negotiate."

5

The CEO moved our conversation to the balcony where we looked out over New York City. The glass guard rails only came up waist high; a particularly unsafe security measure for the 37th floor. Any jamoke could just walk right up to the guard rail and throw themselves over.

Or, more to the point, a good shove to an unsuspecting victim and they'd plunge to the concrete below.

The CEO didn't seem the least bit concerned about the dangers of the railing. He took his fresh glass of cognac right up to the edge and looked out over the city. I joined him, but stayed a good five feet back from the rails. Cardboard hung out in the balcony doorway, afraid to step foot any closer. I waved at her to come join me, but she shook her head no.

"Tell me, Miss Salvo," the CEO said. "When you look down at New York City, what do you see?"

"See?" I got on my tiptoes and peered over the edge, careful not to get too close. "Buildings. Cars. Jersey City's right over there."

"That's a very surface evaluation," he said. "When I look out there, do you know what I see?"

"No clue."

"I see a world filled with supernatural threats. I see a world that needs protecting, even though it doesn't know what it needs protection *from*."

"Huh." I looked at New York City again. I didn't see any of that. I just saw taxis and tourists. "And I suppose you're going to tell me that you offer that protection, huh?"

"We do," he said. "Robots. Ghosts. Aliens. Through our research, we're equipped to deal with them all."

"And when you say 'deal with them,' you mean...?"

"I mean we eliminate them, Miss Salvo," he said in a rather unapologetic tone. "In 1986, we eradicated the entire werewolf population. Years before that, we wiped out the vampires. Just earlier this year, we hunted down and killed the only dragon still living on Earth."

My stomach turned sour. Words like "eradicate" and "wiped out" didn't set well with me.

"You mean you just killed them?" I asked.

"Every single one," he said as if he were proud.

I just wanted to clarify. "Like they're extinct?"

"Completely extinct."

"Why would you do that?" I asked.

"Yeah, why?" Cardboard chimed in.

"Why?" He made it sound like we were stupid for asking. "Because they're dangerous, that's why. Are you saying the world *needs* werewolves? We *need* vampires? We *need* a dragon?"

"I dunno," I said. "I can't say. I never met any of those people."

"Poor dragons," Cardboard added.

The CEO opened his mouth like he was about to speak, but I cut him off with, "Why don't you deal with real dangers? Like assault rifles. Or nukes. Or climate change. Not this fairytale monster bullshit."

The CEO shook a finger at me. "Leave assault rifles to the politicians and climate change to the scientists. If it wasn't for the Westland Corporation, you'd have werewolves in the alleyways and vampires wandering the streets at night. Then you'd be asking yourself why no one is doing anything about the werewolves and the vampires."

"Whatever," I said. "Just seems to me that anyone who talks about wiping out an entire species is probably screwed up in the head."

"That is a very simplistic way of looking at it," he said. "In either case, I didn't bring you up here to convince you of our valor. I simply wanted to give you an opportunity to save your life."

Annoyed, I crossed my arms, then immediately became aware that I was crossing my arms. I dropped them to my side and said, "You said in your invitation 'no violence.' You said you just wanted to talk."

"I do want to talk," he said. "And I am not threatening violence."

"But you just said-"

"Miss Salvo, this isn't about threats. This is about business." He paced in a wide circle around the balcony. "Very soon the Westland Corporation is going to have the power to destroy every supernatural force on Earth. Unfortunately for you, since you've swallowed Impossible Red, you're included in that list."

"You're going to kill *everyone* who's supernatural?"

"It's just smart business," he said. "We're a corporation. It is in our very nature to eliminate the competition. And since we're a supernatural corporation, we have to eliminate the supernatural competition. That means the ninjas, the hurricanes, the Voodoo gods, the angels... as the old saying goes, they don't have to go home, but they *do* have to get the hell out of here."

I glanced at Princess Cardboard, who had a horrified look on her face, and I asked, "What about Princess Cardboard?"

He stared at her and tapped his rocks glass with his fingernails. "Sometimes we have to do things we don't want to do."

Cardboard clutched her hands to her chest. "I'm going to die?"

"You're not going to die," I told her. I turned back to the CEO and shoved a finger in his face. "She's *not* going to die."

"She doesn't *have* to die," the CEO said. He took a drink of cognac, then said, "Provided you're willing to cut a deal."

Of course. These were the negotiations he was talking about. And since he was a CEO - *the* CEO - he was undoubtedly way better at it than I was.

I asked, "What kind of deal?"

"I want Impossible Red," he said. He headed back inside, towards his office. Cardboard backed far away from him as he passed by. I followed him in. He continued on. "If you help me complete fifteen years of hard work and give me Impossible Red, then you'll be human again and none of this will any longer be your concern. You won't die when the supernatural forces die. And, as a personal promise to you, no harm will come to your princess friend here."

"But I can't give it to you," I said, wrapping my arms around my stomach. "It's, like, inside me."

He made his way behind the bar and picked up his bottle of cognac. "I have scientists that can extract it from you. That is not a concern."

Cardboard came up by my side and whispered at me. "I want to get out of here."

But the CEO kept talking. "I'm more than willing to compensate you for your time and trouble." He reached into his suit jacket. He pulled out a leather checkbook and a golden pen. "Provided you to agree to my terms."

He sat his checkbook down on the bar and clicked the pen. I walked over to him and watched as he scribbled across a blank check.

On the *Pay to the order of* line, he wrote *Penelope Marie Salvo*.

And on the *Amount* line, he left it blank.

He handed me the pen and said, "The ball is in your court, Miss Salvo. Fill it out. Name your price."

I took the pen in my hands and stared down at the checkbook. I wondered, *hypothetically*, what if I wrote down a million dollars? Or a hundred million dollars? Would the CEO just say, "sounds great," and send me on my way? And imagine what I could do with a hundred million dollars. I could get my old apartment back. Hell, I could buy the entire apartment building and kick George's ass to the curb. I could buy a cruise ship. I could visit a volcano. I could book one of those private trips to space.

I'd be normal again.

Princess Cardboard kicked my foot to get my attention. I looked at her. She whispered, "Don't."

I stared at the check for a while. I couldn't believe it, but I was about to turn down an unimaginable fortune. I set the pen down on checkbook and pushed them both away from me. "I think I'm going to pass."

"Pass?" The CEO sounded upset. "*Pass?*"

"Yeah." I looked him right in the eyes. "I don't want your money."

"Then what do you want?" he asked. His face turned red. His voice sounded panicked. "Fame? A mansion in the Hamptons? Do you want someone killed? You have to want *something*! Just tell me what it is!"

I backed away from him. He was really starting to freak me out. Cardboard stayed right behind me. I told the CEO, "I want to go home."

"Home?" He gave me a disgusted look. "You just don't get it, kid. I am not *asking*. This is not an *option*. I will have Impossible Red, one way or another."

I scoffed at him. "Oh, so *now* you're threatening me. Look, man, I don't know a whole lot about Impossible Red thing, but I *do* know that you done fucked up when you let *me* swallow it. I might not know what I'm doing, but I've got this sneaking suspicion that when it comes down to me versus your precious little corporation here..." I put my hands on the bar and leaned closer towards him. "You ain't shit."

The CEO slapped both open hands down on the bar and made me jump. "Miss Salvo, we've been killing the supernatural longer than you've been alive. You will die, I promise you that. You and your little cardboard friend here. I'll kill your old gardening friend and bulldoze his pathetic little greenhouse to the ground. You are so colossally out of your league, it's pathetic."

"No, *you're* pathetic!"

I picked up his golden pen and spiked it through his hand, nailing him to the bar.

6

"Time to go!" I grabbed Princess Cardboard by the arm and dragged her towards the elevator.

"Oh my gosh!" she said. "What did you do?"

The CEO howled in agony as he struggled to pull his hand free from the bar. He was going to have a tough time of that, because I spiked that pen deep into the wood and it wasn't moving. What was strange was that his hand didn't bleed blood. He bled something green and powdery, as if his veins were literally filled with money.

The CEO gave up on trying to free his impaled hand and reached into his jacket with the other. He pulled out a walkie-talkie – exactly like the one Carl had the other night – and yelled at his security force.

"Shut down all the elevators! Code Black on floor 37!"

An emergency alarm sounded, one you'd hear on a sinking battleship, and it echoed through the entire building. This was our cue to skedaddle, but as we reached the elevators, I realized we didn't have one of those fancy keycards to open the door. Time to put that super strength to the test, I figured. I jabbed my fingers into the metal seam of the doors and ripped them open like living room curtains.

"Huh," I said.

"Whoa," Cardboard added.

Below us in the elevator shaft was 37 floors of pure darkness that gusted with a lonely wind.

"If we jump, will that kill you?" I asked her.

"Of course that would kill me!" she cried over the alarms.

"Okay." I needed an idea. "Okay. Here. Come here." I motioned at her to jump into my arms. "I'll carry you."

Without a moment's hesitation, she jumped up and I held her in my arms. I stared down the elevator shaft and took a deep breath. Boy, I really hoped I knew what I was doing.

I jumped.

We fell weightlessly for a few floors, then landed on top of an elevator car with a boom that echoed all up and down the elevator shaft. I set Cardboard down and inspected our surroundings.

Directly in front of us were the doors to the 19th floor. I kicked one elevator door and pushed it out of our way, crumpling it up like aluminum foil. I crawled through the half-open doorway and found myself in a sprawling cubicle farm. Cardboard didn't follow me out. She had dropped to her hands and knees on the roof of the elevator car and crawled around in a panic.

"I can't find my crown!" Grease and dirt smeared all across the front of her dress, but she didn't seem to care.

"Cardboard!" I shouted. The alarms were still going off. If anything, they were getting louder. "Cardboard, we need to go!"

"Not without my crown!"

"Cardboard, now!"

I had to grab her arm and drag her to her feet. She pulled against me to go back, but not hard enough. She reached out for the elevator with both hands.

"No!" she cried. Tears ran down her face. "My crown!"

The 19th floor, as luck would have it, was the same floor with all the cubicles where we first made our entrance. We caught that supervisor and all his employees reconnecting their printers, putting back up their cubicle walls, and gathering up all the spilled paper. A janitor swept up the broken glass from the window I shattered. Princess Cardboard and I ran through the office, headed back to the storage room.

"Out of the way!" I shouted at the office people as we darted through them.

We made it to the storage room and Cardboard stepped inside our cardboard box. Her shoulders slumped and she stood there, sobbing. I felt terrible for her, I really did, but we had to get the hell out of Dodge. I stepped in after her, the floor dropped out beneath us and we fell into the cardboard tunnels. I reached up to pull the cardboard flaps closed and seal us inside.

"I lost my crown," she shouted. She slapped my shoulder. "You made me lose my crown."

"We can make you a new crown," I said.

"You can't just 'make' a crown!"

"Jesus, chill out," I told her. "We'll get a box and some scissors and cut you a new one. How hard could it be?"

"That wasn't a box. That was my real crown. It just looked like a cardboard box." She crawled to get away from me. I could hear her crying. "My sisters already think I'm an idiot and now I lost my crown."

I didn't crawl after her.

"Let me go back for it," I called out. She stopped and looked over her shoulder. I said, "Open the flaps. I'll go get your crown."

"But they were after us," she said.

I told her, straight-faced, "That doesn't scare me. Let me go back."

Princess Cardboard opened the flaps to the empty computer paper box in the storage room. I crawled out. I told her to stay behind in the tunnels, to keep quiet, and to wait for me to come back because there was probably going to be bullets and tasers and who-knows what else. She agreed and arranged herself cross-legged below the office floor in our emergency exit. With her free hand, she anxiously pulled out some coffeecake and started to eat.

Round three in the offices. I ran out of the storage closet and through the cubicles of Information Collection. The employees saw me coming and cleared out of my way.

"Forgot something," I told them as I passed.

I took a quick moment to knock a computer monitor off one of their desks. Serves them right.

Security forces flooded into the 19th floor through the fire exits. These guys were the real deal, with black SWAT body armor, helmets with face masks, and carrying assault rifles. They lined the walls and took tactical positions behind anything they could find; chairs, cubicle walls, even the water cooler. The business workers all hit the floor.

"Whoa," I said to the security forces as their leveled their assault rifles at me. "Let's all just be cool here and-"

Dozens of security guards all opened fire. Bullets shredded a Penelope shaped outline in the drywall behind me. Light fixtures exploded above me. Surrounding computer equipment danced around in a shower of sparks.

Their concentrated gunfire thumped against my body. Bullets clattered to the floor all around me like rain. I'd never experienced that kind of power before, being able to shrug off literal gunfire like some kind of superhero. The guards eventually realized they were wasting bullets and, one by one, they stopped firing.

"Man," I whined as I looked down at the holes in my clothes. "Look what you did to my fucking *shirt*."

Frustrated that my Weezer shirt had been ruined, I stormed to the open elevator and searched for Cardboard's crown. I found it wedged between the elevator car and the wall. I pulled her crown loose and tried to wipe the grease off of it. It was in pretty nasty shape, but at least I had it. I marched back through the cubicles and towards the storage room. The guards kept their rifles trained on me, but didn't open fire.

I said, "You guys owe me for a new shirt, I'll have you know." They didn't care about my shirt. I tugged on the collar so I could show it to them as I explained. "This was vintage. Not some jank-ass screen print." I shook my head and growled, "God *dammit*."

I was almost to the storage room when I decided to get them back. I grabbed one of their computer chairs and rolled it underneath the emergency sprinkler in the ceiling. I climbed up on the chair, got out my lighter, and held the flame right up to the little red sensor in the sprinkler head. After just a few seconds, water exploded from the sprinkler above me, then the next one, then the next one, and soon their entire fire suppression system went off, spraying water from the ceiling and drenching everything in the office. The fire alarm went off, adding its noise to the other security alarms. Good. That's what you get when you fuck with Penelope Salvo. You get your shit all wet.

I walked to the storage room backwards so I could flip off the cubicle employees and the security forces.

"Tell your CEO to eat shit," I announced.

Princess Cardboard peeked out from above the box, stunned by everything she saw. I handed her the crown. Her face beamed like it was Christmas. It had grease on it and was a little wet from the sprinklers, but she put it on right away regardless. I jumped in the box with her, she closed the flaps behind us, and we crawled away.

She said, "That was so cool."

I laughed and said, "Did you see the part where I flipped them off?"

"Yes!" she said. "That was the best part!"

Chapter 7

1

Princess Cardboard shuffled through the cardboard tunnels with the grace of someone who'd been doing it for a long time. No way would I be able to crawl around on my hands and knees in a ballgown like that. Hell, I probably couldn't *walk* in a ballgown. It didn't seem to slow her down at all, though. She didn't stumble over the fabric or hesitate a single time in the dimly lit maze. Years of practice, I guess.

"Can I ask you something?" I said as we crawled past a row of cardboard boxes stashed in an airport in Philadelphia.

"Sure," she said. "Anything you want."

"Where are you from?"

"The Bronx," she said.

"No, I mean, like, where are you from originally."

She stopped and looked over her shoulder at me. "If I tell you," she said, "you have to keep it a secret."

"Of course."

She went back to crawling and told me her story as we traveled.

"I come from a place called the Muffincake Kingdom. Me and my sisters were royalty there. My name is actually Princess Coffeecake and I ruled the Coffeecake Kingdom. One day this wizard came along and tricked my sister, Princess Wedding Cake, and he trapped our world in a glass ball. We chased him here to New York City, but the city was too big and we lost track of him. My sister, Princess Pancake, decided to open a delivery service as part of the search."

Sounded weird, but I went with it. "So you changed your name from Coffeecake to Cardboard?"

"Coming here changed us," she said. "We're like sponge cakes for magic. When we left the Muffincake Kingdom, we left that magic behind. And when we showed up here in New York City, we started to absorb what little magic we could find. And it turned us into postal carriers."

Cardboard turned left at an intersection. She assured me it wouldn't be much further before we got back to Chinatown.

I asked her, "And you haven't found the wizard yet?"

"No. But Bubble Wrap says it's only a matter of time. She's the smartest one of all of us. It was her idea for us to start delivering packages. She said if we worked for supernatural people long enough, eventually we'd find that wizard and the Muffincake Kingdom. But that was forever ago."

"You talk about it like it's no big deal," I said.

"We've been looking for a really long time. My sisters still think there's a chance we could find it, but..." She paused for a while. "I worry sometimes."

"How long have you been looking?" I asked.

"I dunno. Time works differently here. Four calendar years? Maybe five?"

"Dude." I grabbed her foot and shook it to get her attention. "I have an idea where it might be."

She stopped and looked back at me. "Alaska?"

"What?" She was so weird, sometimes. "No, not Alaska. Back at my shop. Xin keeps a lot of super weird magical stuff in the basement. It might be down there."

Her eyes lit up. "Really?"

"Maybe! I mean, I'm not promising anything. There's a lot of weird stuff down there and I haven't been through it all, but it's worth a look."

"Well, heck yeah, it's worth a look!"

"Cool." I waved her on. "Let's go then."

I knew the rules about the basement. Only unlock it when necessary and never, for any reason, take anything out. But like how I explained to Cardboard, this was one of those times when it was okay to break the rules. I mean, this was her kingdom, her *world* we were talking about.

Cardboard crawled along with more energy than before, super motivated by the idea that we might actually find the Muffincake Kingdom. She led us to a very specific box and pushed the flaps in the ceiling open. "Last stop, Chinatown."

She moved out of the way so I could pop up first. I stood and poked my head out of the cardboard box. We were right where we started, by the outside wall of Xin's shop. It was a misty evening and the water felt cool on my face. I crawled up out of the box and onto the concrete. Turning back around, I reached down to give Princess Cardboard a boost. I was strong enough to lift her body with one hand. She knelt down, pulled the bottom flaps closed and sealed off her magical tunnel. Just to satisfy my own curiosity, I put my foot inside the box and pushed on the bottom with my foot to see if the portal would open for me. It didn't. I nudged the box to see if it was attached to the ground, but it moved around like normal.

"How do you do that?" I asked.

"Do what?"

"That thing with the tunnels?"

She shrugged. "I dunno. Like I said, when we changed, our magic changed. I can't explain it."

Evening had set in and the sun had disappeared behind the skyscrapers. The lights were on inside the shop and I could see Xin's shadow moving through the windows, putting jars on the shelves.

"You should come back later," I whispered to Princess Cardboard. "Xin's still here and if he sees me opening the basement door, he's going to flip his shit. You'll have to come back later after he goes home."

"Okay!" she said, overjoyed. "I've got deliveries I have to do anyway, so I'll come back when I'm done!"

"Awesome." I pointed at the shop. "I live inside, so just knock whenever you come by."

"Will do!" She walked off to her box, but turned around long enough to give me a salute.

I saluted her back.

She went to the box, stepped inside, then dropped into the ground.

When I was a little girl, I didn't play with princess stuff and I didn't watch a lot of princess movies. I liked Batman the

Animated Series and Star Wars and stuff like that. Still, some part of me thought it was awesome to have an honest-to-god fairytale princess as a friend.

2

It was well past midnight before I heard a soft knock on the front door. I was sitting at the counter, listening to the radio, mixing up a bowl of sage and lavender soap. I plopped the spoon in the mixture and ran to answer the door. Princess Cardboard stood there with a very serious look on her face.

I said, "Hey, what's up?"

She whispered, "What's the password?"

I blinked at her. "The what?"

"The password to get in," she repeated. "I don't know the password."

"We don't have a password."

"Oh." She relaxed. "Okay, I was worried."

I gave her a weird look and stepped out of the way. "You can just come in."

"Thank you." She wandered in and browsed through the shelves. The jars of pickled flowers and berries seemed to intrigue her the most. She asked, "Are you an alchemist?"

"I'm not too sure what that means," I said.

"A potion maker."

"Oh! No. I'm not an alchemist. Xin is. I just water the plants and clean the bathroom."

"Curious," she said.

"Come on." I grabbed a flashlight from under the counter and walked to the basement door. "Let's go look for your thing."

She bounded over to me, excited as all hell. I took the padlock to the basement door in one hand and took the key from around my neck with the other. I stood there, ready to unlock the door, but I hesitated.

"What's wrong?" she asked me.

Xin would not be happy if he knew what I was doing. Even if I explained it to him – "Princess Cardboard has been looking for her fairytale kingdom and it might be in our basement" – I don't think he'd understand. In any case, we weren't going to be down there long. In and out, real quick. Xin wouldn't have to know.

"It's nothing," I said to Cardboard.

I unlocked the padlock and undid the latch. I clicked the flashlight on and we descended down the stairs. The stairs were rough and uneven, and Cardboard had to keep her hands on the walls to maintain her balance. The steps creaked under our weight, announcing our arrival to the collection below.

We reached the basement and I held the flashlight over my head to provide as much light as possible. I swept the light over the swords, past the armor, and all along the bookcases. The shadows moved weird in the shifting flashlight, bending in odd directions.

"So what's this thing look like?" I asked Cardboard.

"It's the size of a bowling ball," she said as she looked all around. "It's made of glass, and there's a miniature Muffincake Kingdom inside."

I made my way up and down the tables and checked behind everything. There was an old wooden treasure chest, a Japanese folding fan, and a jewelry box filled with gemstone rings. I looked under the tables and found a bolt of blue cloth, a small golden statue of a cow, and a pair of iron boots that would fit a giant.

But no glass ball with the Muffincake Kingdom.

We both looked for a long while, but the basement was only so big and there were only so many places a glass ball could hide. Once I felt like we'd thoroughly checked everything, I had to admit it:

"I don't think it's down here."

She sighed. "It's fine. It was a long shot anyway." She stood behind me, peering over my shoulder, looking at everything in the light. "What is all this stuff?"

"Magic items," I said. "We hide them down here so no one uses them."

"They look so neat."

"Check this one out!" I went over and grabbed the Sword From One Second Ago, the one with all the gears in the handle and the clock parts inside the cut-out parts of the blade. I held it between us so she could see it. "It's a time sword. Isn't that cool?"

"It's *so* cool!" She leaned closer. "What's it do?"

"Well... I don't know." I held the sword at eye level and peered down the sharp edge. It had to do something, right? Why else would a sword have gears and springs inside? I gave

Cardboard a sly grin. "Want to go outside and try it out?"

Her eyes lit up and then her cardboard crown dropped down over them. She pushed the box into place. "Can we?"

"Heck yes," I said, heading for the stairs. "Let's go!"

I was careful to click the padlock into place and secure the basement door before we went outside. I flipped on the front porch light and we went out into the cool, night air. The courtyard was dark, so no one would see us messing around, not that anyone visited the courtyard at night anyway.

We went out to the middle of the courtyard and faced each other. We could see our breath in the cold air, little puffs of clouds that quickly evaporated. I held the Sword From One Second Ago in both hands and struck a samurai pose. Cardboard had a huge grin on her face, excited to see me swing the sword, and she backed away to give me space.

I swung the sword in a wide arc. It sliced through the air and made a shrill, metallic noise. I swung it three more times – right, left, right – as if I was fighting a group of invisible ninjas. I fought my imaginary foes and beat them.

"Here," I said, holding it out to Cardboard. "You wanna swing it?"

"Oh, I dunno." She looked excited and scared, but she took it anyway. She held it like how nervous people hold babies. "I'll just hold it."

While she stood there with the sword, my thoughts started to wander. I thought about real ninjas and how the CEO said he was going to wipe them out along with everyone else.

I asked Cardboard, "Hey, you remember how that CEO guy said he was going to kill all the supernatural people?"

Cardboard looked the sword up and down. The gold coils of her hair kept falling over her face. "Uh huh."

"I was thinking, like, maybe I'll do something about that."

"Like what?" she asked.

"I dunno. Haven't thought that far. But like you said, he's evil. And we're good, right?"

"I think you're good," she said. "And I'm on your side, so I'm good, too, I guess."

"So if we're good, then it's our responsibility to stop him, right? Because he's bad."

She shrugged. "Makes sense."

Out of nowhere, Cardboard clicked something on the handle of the sword. The gears started ticking and turning like the inside of a clock. She yelped and tossed the sword to the ground, where it clattered on the concrete. She ran to hide behind me. Her cardboard crown fell over her eyes. "What'd I do?"

"I don't know. I didn't know it had an 'on' switch."

I picked up the sword and held it in my hands. The handle ticked like a clock. The gears moved, the springs pulled and stretched, and the mechanisms inside the holes of the blade were turning.

I decided to swing it.

With the sword activated, swinging it was a different experience. The handle stayed solid in my hands, but the blade vanished. I didn't hear the metallic noise of the blade slicing through the air. It was as if the blade didn't exist. But once I was done with the swing, the blade reappeared.

"Oh my gosh!" Cardboard shouted. "Did you see that?"

"Yeah." I swung it again. The blade vanished as it arced through the air, then reappeared when I held it steady. It was the coolest thing I had ever seen.

I held the sword at my side and got a running start. The gears of the handle clicked louder – TIK TIK TIK TIK – and when I slashed the air, the blade blinked out of existence. I slid to a stop across the concrete and struck a pose. The blade reappeared. I inspected the handle closely and found a button on the very bottom. I clicked it and the sword turned off.

"Right here's a button," I said, showing her. "If you swing it when it's off, it's a normal sword."

"But if you turn it on..." she said.

I pushed the button again and the gears activated. I gave it another couple swings, high and low, and watched the blade disappear each time. I held the weapon out to her.

"You can try it if you want."

She put up her hands and backed away. "No. No. I don't think I want to. I should get back home. I just snuck out to see if the Muffincake Kingdom was here. My sisters would be mad if they knew I was here. Sneaking out is against the rules."

"Yeah." I turned off the sword. "I should probably put this back in the basement anyway." I stepped up the porch stairs, then turned to ask her. "Hey, do you have a lot of friends?"

"No," she said. "My sisters, but they don't really count."

"Do you want to, like, come over and hang out sometime?"

"Sure," she said. "When?"

I shrugged. "Anytime. I live here. Come by whenever."

"Okay," she said. "I'll come over tomorrow or something."

"That'd be cool," I said. "Peace out, girl scout."

She laughed at my little rhyme, waved goodbye and disappeared around the corner, headed for her cardboard box.

3

I couldn't sleep that night. I hadn't been sleeping well in general, not since swallowing Impossible Red. It felt like I was getting fewer and fewer hours every night, but I didn't feel tired, so it wasn't that much of a concern.

I laid there with my eyes open as my brain replayed recent events. I'd been shot by snipers, I'd met a Voodoo spirit, and I made friends with a fairytale princess. I used to think I was going crazy, but everything else seemed absolutely normal. The city was normal, the people stayed the same, the only thing that had changed was me and Impossible Red.

I smoked a little spliff out on the front porch to help clear my head and calm my anxiety. I thought that would help me sleep as I went to lay back down in bed, but I laid there with my eyes wide open the entire night.

Next thing I knew, the sun was coming up and Xin was unlocking the front door. I dragged my ass out of bed, changed out of my bullet hole clothes and picked out something new: torn up jeans, a black t-shirt, all my earrings, and a necklace I made out of one of those flattened out Westland sniper bullets. I walked into the main shop and squinted at the sunshine that beamed through the windows.

"Good morning," Xin said.

It was all in the way he said it. *Good morning.* He knew. He knew I went to the Westland Corporation. He knew that I opened the basement door. He knew I was screwing around with that time sword. He knew everything.

"Morning," I said, avoiding eye contact.

I got the watering can and took it to the bathroom. I held it under the sink and filled it up with water, all the while I stared at myself in the mirror.

Xin knows. You gotta fess up. He already knows and it's going to look better if you just tell the truth. Just go in there and admit it and apologize.

I walked out of the bathroom. Xin was busy getting the orders ready for the day, but he could sense me watching him and glanced at me. I gave him a nervous smile. He gave me a weird look and went back to his work. I took the watering can around the shop and gave the plants and herbs their morning drink.

"Penelope?" he said.

I spun around, nervous, and blurted out, "What!?"

He raised his eyebrows at me. "Will you bring me a jar of Sinnipher bark?"

"Oh." I put down the watering can. "Right."

I grabbed the jar of bark and set it on the counter in front of him. I lingered there, waiting for the argument to commence. He stared back at me, probably wondering why I was just standing there, acting all nervous.

He said, "Yes?"

"You know, don't you," I said in accusing tone.

He blinked at me. "Know what?"

"Come on," I said. "You're walking around, talking to me all normal. You obviously know."

"I do?"

I crossed my arms. "Xin."

His confused eyes darted around.

I dropped my arms. "Wait. So you *don't* know?"

"Don't know what?" He narrowed his eyes. "Did you do something?"

Shit. I tipped my hand for nothing. "Are you serious?"

He placed his hands flat on the counter. "Well, now I *want* to know."

"Never mind"

"No," he said. "Not never mind. What did you do? What do I need to know?"

I didn't answer. Stalling. Stalling. Dammit, Penelope, you already made it obvious that something's going on. You have to tell him *something.* Panicked, I blurted out the first thing that came to mind.

"I'm on my period."

He looked at me, then at the counter, then back at me. "I didn't know that."

"Yeah," I said in an accusatory tone, as if this was all his fault. "Well, now you do."

It was obvious that he didn't know how to respond. He waited a few seconds, shrugged, and said, "I appreciate your honesty?"

I went back to watering the plants. Once I was facing away from Xin, I relaxed and let out a heavy sigh of relief.

4

That day came and went without incident. Mrs. Cho and Mark from China Wall picked up their orders on time. I watered all the plants and even had a little free time to cut my lavender soap into bars. Around noon, Xin and I sat around the counter to have Chinese food for lunch. I was absolutely starving, but I could only stomach a few bites of food. It just didn't taste right and started to make me feel sick.

It was late in the afternoon when Princess Cardboard came sprinting across the courtyard with an envelope in her hand. She was moving pretty fast considering she wore a full-length dress. Her crown kept dropping over her eyes and she had to hold it up so she could see. With each step, her golden curls bounced in her face.

Her face wasn't excited. It was more like panic.

"Penelope!" she shouted, waving the envelope in her hand. "Penelope!"

I stepped off the porch to get her to calm down.

"Cardboard." I held her by the arms. "Calm down. Jesus. What is it?"

She took the black envelope and forced it into my hands. She was so totally out of breath, she could barely talk.

"You gotta... break the rules... for me."

"Oh my god, dude. What'd you do? Run here all the way from the Bronx? Sit down." I took her by the hand and directed her to the porch steps. She sat there, panting, regaining her composure.

I looked at the envelope. It was was black and had white block letters on the front that read:

120

Xin shook his head. "Vacation Island is not just for rich humans. Other beings go there as well. Powerful beings. If you don't follow the rules, you'll put yourself in serious danger."

"Well, what am I supposed to do?" I asked. "I don't have millions of dollars to take to some auction."

That's when I heard Baron Semedi's voice. He was suddenly there, leaning in the doorway. He had a cigar bit down between his teeth and he raised his glass of rum in a toast.

He said, "Sounds like someone needs a short term financial loan."

5

Baron Semedi tipped the brim of his top hat backwards so he could look at me, then turned his attention to Xin. He took the cigar out of his mouth and blew smoke rings into the air, shaped like squares and stars and triangles. "You know, Mister Houng, I've always meant to come in here. I've heard good things. It's quite nice... for a human establishment, that is."

Xin stood up and said, "What are you doing here?"

"What?" Semedi asked, pretending to be insulted. "A guy can't come down and shop for some..." He picked a random jar of yellow berries off the shelf and rattled them around. "...Whatever this is?"

"You're a trickster spirit." Xin marched over, snatched the jar out of Baron Semedi's hands and put it back on the shelf.

"Trickster? Me?" Semedi sounded even more insulted. Then his tone returned to normal and he stuck the cigar back in his mouth. "Okay, I admit it, I do enjoy a harmless prank from time to time. But! This time, no tricks. You want something and I want something and our ideas go together like mayonnaise and yams. Mayoyams."

Cardboard scrunched up her face. "Ugh, gross."

Baron Semedi strolled through the shop like a drill sergeant inspecting a bunkhouse. He ran his fingertips along the shelves, then stopped to tap one of the jars as if it were an aquarium filled with fish. He moved from shelf to shelf, still talking to us, but focused on the random powders and leaves.

He said, "See, I don't like the suit humans anymore than you do."

"Suit humans?" I asked. "You mean the Westland Corporation?"

"Yes," Semedi said. "Them. They're stuffy and greedy and never any fun. And while I was never a big fan of the werewolves or the vampires for all the same reasons, they didn't deserve to get wiped out the way they did. And if the suit humans get their hands on that black marble, they're going to destroy all of us still stuck here on Earth. All of us. And that, as they might say, is not good for business." He turned to face us. "So if you want to stop them, I want to help you."

"Why don't you go stop them yourself?" I asked. "You know so much, what do you need us for?"

He pointed at me with his cigar. "Excellent question. Why would I, Baron Semedi, host to both love and death, need help from anyone?"

"Yeah," I said. "That's exactly my question."

"Let's just say I don't have a lot of friends on Vacation Island," he told me. His face turned sour and grumbled at the floor. "Yet another place with a poor sense of humor."

Cardboard looked at him with astonished eyes. "What'd you do?"

"Shenanigans," Semedi said. "Harmless shenanigans. No one was hurt." His eyes darted around. "Critically."

"We don't want your kind of help," Xin said. He walked around the counter, ready to kick Semedi out.

But I stopped him. "Xin, wait." I stepped in front of him and asked Semedi. "What kind of help are you going to give us, exactly?"

"I'm glad you asked," Semedi said. He reached into his jacket and took out a blank check. It read *the First Bank of the Guinee*. The paper was old parchment, like something you'd find tucked away inside a bottle that washed up on a beach. It had my name at the top, along with my address in Chinatown, and a handwritten account number across the bottom. Otherwise it was blank; the amount, the recipient, all blank and ready for me to fill out. I gingerly took the check from his fingers. It was real paper, I just didn't know if it was a real check.

He said, "I can tell by the look on your face, you're skeptical. And that's fine. Believe me, the Voodoo loa have been watching humankind for far too long to be confounded by something as elementary as finances. Bank errors happen every day.

Electronic money literally appears out of nowhere and vanishes just as quickly. That check is tied to a bank account that *technically* exists. And it's yours to use, only once, for any amount you can think of. If you go to the auction on Vacation Island and bid on Unthinkable Black, no one will be able to outbid you, not even the Westland Corporation."

It couldn't be that easy. Or, more to the point, it couldn't come without a price. "That's it?"

He smiled at me; a mischievous smile. "That's it."

"And what's the catch?" I asked.

"Yeah," Cardboard added as she came up behind me and crossed her arms. "What's the catch?"

"Why's there have to be a catch?" Semedi asked. He started laughing the moment those words left his mouth.

"Because you're weird and you're creepy," I told him. "And I don't believe for a second that you're helping us out of the kindness of your heart. You said yourself, you're a trickster. I think you want something."

"Well, if that's how you feel..." He stuck his cigar in his teeth so he could hold out his open palm, showing off his pure white tuxedo glove. "Give me back my check and I'll be on my way."

I looked at the check. It looked real enough. All things considered, not only was it the best option we had on the table, it was kind of the *only* option. I frowned at the realization that I had to – just this once – accept help from Baron Semedi.

"What if they don't take it?" I asked, holding up the slip of paper. "This thing looks like it comes from the year 1800. What if they double check it or something?"

He waved the question off. "Let them double check. They will find a fortune in digital money."

"How do you know?" I asked.

He looked at me like my question didn't make any sense. "I feel as though I've been very clear on this point." He made a confident pose with his cigar hand and rum hand held out to his sides. "I know everything."

I was still hesitant, but I *did* like the idea of going to this hoity-toity, rich-bitch super auction and really sticking it to the Westland Corporation. They'd show up all self-confident and evil, but then here comes Penelope Salvo, the girl they tried to kill, with more money than God and I make them all look like chumps.

As I debated, Cardboard stepped forward and said, "I have some questions."

"Go ahead," Semedi said.

Cardboard put her hand to her chest and said, "I am royalty. I have royal blood in my veins. And I want to know if at this auction... will there be cake?"

Semedi smiled. "There will be cake."

Cardboard narrowed her eyes. "What *kind* of cake?"

Semedi wrapped his arm around her shoulders and swept his arm through the air, casting her imagination into high gear. "My dear princess, there will be cakes of all kinds. Cakes from all around the world. Cakes taller than you."

"Will there be coffeecake?" she asked.

Semedi's face lit up and he slowly nodded yes. "There will be coffeecake."

Cardboard whipped around to me. "We have to go."

I hesitated. "I'm still not sure."

"Penelope." She grabbed my shoulders, pulled her face close to mine and lowered her voice to a whisper. "There's going to be *cake*."

Xin watched our conversation with that stoic silence I knew too well, occasionally giving Semedi disapproving scowls. I was leaning towards yes, leaning towards taking Semedi's money and crashing the party at Vacation Island, but I still wasn't sure.

"Xin?" I asked him.

"I suppose we have to accept his help," Xin said. He tilted his head at Semedi. "I just wish there were some other way."

Under my breath, I muttered, "That makes two of us."

We both looked at Semedi, who had already lost interest in us and, instead, magically floated a few feet off the ground so he could tap the light bulb with his fingernail. He delighted in the glass bulb to the point where he chuckled out loud. He looked over and realized we were staring at him.

He pointed at the light bulb as if it were some new discovery. "I used to have one of these!"

Chapter 8

1

Princess Cardboard and I fell out of a wet refrigerator box on the tropical beaches of Vacation Island.

When we left New York, night had set in. But there in the Pacific Ocean, the sun was bright and shining without a single cloud in the bluest sky I had ever seen. We were surrounded by nothing but miles and miles of sparking turquoise ocean. The water swelled, as if monsters were pushing up against the surface of the water but couldn't quite break through. Foamy waves washed across the beach and left behind seashells and tiny jellyfish. The water hissed into the sand and when I closed my eyes to just listen, it sounded like someone whispering. I looked up and down the beach for signs of life: a dock, a boat, or even footprints.

Nothing.

The beach was untouched by human hands, like something from a computer screensaver. Twenty feet deeper into the island, the sand gave way to dense jungle. The tropical trees were as tall as the apartment buildings in New York with broad palm leaves that created a shady canopy. Some of the trees had bright red mangoes, way bigger than anything you could buy at the store. There were bananas trees, too, and coconuts and other tropical fruits I had never seen before. I heard animals far off in the distance; the melodic songs of tropical birds and other more mysterious chirps and howls. Birds flew around overhead, blue birds with super-long necks. They resembled herons, but they weren't herons.

Miles away, rising out of the distant jungle was a volcano of black glass. It towered higher than the trees and released a wisp of smoke into the sky. It reminded me of some secret hideout for a villain in a James Bond movie. Without the slightest breeze in the air, the smoke floated straight up and out of view. If the trees were apartment buildings, the volcano was the Empire State Building.

"This must be where they clone the dinosaurs," I said.

Princess Cardboard looked around. "I don't see any dinosaurs."

"I was joking."

"Ooh." Cardboard laughed to herself, although I'm convinced she had no idea why it was funny.

Side by side, we headed into the jungle. Someone had come this way before and hacked a path through all the bothersome vines and bushes. Cardboard led the way, her head up, marching along with all the confidence in the world. As we went deeper into the jungle, I spotted birds in the branches overhead: white parrots and rainbow toucans and tiny yellow things like hummingbirds. They watched us with their vacant, black eyes. Occasionally they would open their beaks and let out a strange caw or a cackle. Once we moved past them, they would fly to catch up, perch on another branch, and continue their surveillance.

I'd never been to a tropical island before. I immediately fell in love. The smells of the flowers, the colors of the birds, and the sounds of the distant ocean behind us... it was like paradise. I considered digging up some of the plants and bringing them back to Xin. Surely he would have a use for such strange things in his potions and medicine.

"You got anything like this in the Muffincake Kingdom?" I asked Cardboard.

"No." She looked just as awe-struck as I did. "It's amazing."

After twenty minutes of walking, we came to a river that twisted through the jungle and carved a shallow ravine into the dirt. It wasn't more than ten feet deep, but it would have been a bitch to climb down and then back up on the other side. Luckily our path led us right to an ancient stone bridge that stretched over the river. The stone was overgrown with a century's worth of vines. We had to take careful, calculated steps to keep from tripping.

Halfway across the bridge I stopped to peer over the edge and look down into the river. Sunshine broke through the tree tops and reflected off the water like flakes of gold. The river was filled with bright orange fish, all of them fighting their way upstream. I'm not a fish expert by any means, but these weren't fish you could find in North America; they had abnormally long fins and their eyes came in neon blues and greens and yellows. I wanted to watch the fish for a while longer, but Cardboard kept going without me and I had to run to catch up.

The path was more developed on the other side of the river, hand-built from different sized stones set into the ground. It looked centuries old, perhaps built by Catholic missionaries who came here from Europe. I would have given it more thought if I gave a shit about archaeology, but I don't.

We followed the path for another thirty minutes, give or take, before we reached the base of the volcano. The jungles abruptly ended and our stone path dead-ended against a well-manicured lawn, immaculate, like a golf course. In the grass in front of us was an Olympic-sized wading pool surrounded by ten synchronized fountains shaped like angels.

Smooth-poured concrete circled around the wading pool and led up to a huge vacation resort built from glass and polished marble. The resort circled around the entire base of the volcano, at least that's how it seemed from our vantage point. I couldn't see all the way around, so I couldn't be completely sure, but that's how it looked. It resembled a big casino, four stories tall with pillars and archways that gave it an ancient Greek look.

The main entrance area was long enough to accommodate the dozens of limos parked in front, covered by a long awning with flashing lights. Dozens of glass doors stretched across the front entrance with uniformed valets stationed at each door, ready to hold them open for the prestigious guests.

To the left of the entrance was an attached hotel with fully-furnished balconies and sliding glass doors. The right side had glass windows that stretched from the ground to the roof and I could see an indoor pool, an exercise center, and several indoor tiki bars.

Scattered all around the resort were palm trees, coconut trees, and other tropical vegetation I'd never seen before. Concrete pathways circled around the trees and led to a selection of outdoor pools, hot tubs, tennis courts, and almost certainly somewhere out there were eighteen holes of golf. Golf carts were parked in front of the hotel section, but maybe they were just for getting around. After all, when you're that rich, you don't have to walk if you don't want to.

This resort probably cost a thousand dollars a night, or a million, or whatever rich people pay for bullshit like that. Room service would bring you lobster at four a.m. if that's what you wanted. Or if you wanted a massage, you didn't even have to leave your room; they'd send a masseuse up to you. It was capitalism at its most disgusting. I could barely afford to bury my mother and even after I pulled it off, it nearly left me homeless on the streets, and here were these mother fuckers parking private helicopters up on the roof.

I thought I was going to like Vacation Island. But I was wrong.

Cardboard stared at with wide eyes and said, "This is the kind of place that has penguins as waiters."

2

A dozen elderly, wealthy-looking people loitered under the awning, hanging out in the shade. I saw old ladies with mink stoles and huge sunglasses, like movie stars from the 1950s. There were old men in fine suits and some of them dressed in more casual pastel-colored golf pants. A different group of four old guys crowded around the back of a golf cart, their golf clubs hitched to the back. A waiter with a towel slung over his arm brought them Manhattans and little snifters of brandy.

I spotted an old man in a wheelchair, older than Xin, so he was probably 150 years old. He got wheeled around by some valet in a green jacket and stupid little hat. His wife walked behind them, too good to push the wheelchair herself, and she wore the most hideous white pant suit I have ever seen in my life... and I live in New York. Her jewelry looked like that gaudy stuff they used to sell on TV at four in the morning, where you think, "Man, who buys this shit?" Well, she did, and she wore all of it. She trotted alongside her husband as they wheeled him inside. Another valet guy bopped along behind them with a suitcase in each hand.

Needless to say, I was not dressed for the occasion. I had on a black and white Billy Idol t-shirt, torn up black jeans with specks of red spray paint all up and down the right side, and my black chucks. Cardboard was somewhat passable in her princess outfit. This was definitely a ballgown kind of crowd and the beige color fit in perfect. The only odd thing about her was her crazy straight and curly hair, and her cardboard crown.

Still, dress code violation or no, we were going in.

We skirted around the wading pool and made our way to the front entrance where the concrete walkways turned into geometric designs of red and black and white marble. Each marble piece was embossed with gold letters that read "Vacation Island."

We reached the steps of the front entrance and the geriatric people loitering out front gave us disgusted looks. They didn't believe for a second that we were rich, definitely not rich enough for the Welf Auction. The golf guys, the men in suits, the old ladies in furs, they didn't even try to hide the fact that they were judging us. Cardboard and I were out of place, we both knew it, but these pricks just gawked at us with no regard for common courtesy.

"Excuse me," this valet dude said to me in a super rude tone. He had the same green jacket like the other employees and the pin on his lapel read Hospitality Manager. His hair was perfectly sculpted and molded into place, and he had a tiny mustache. "Can I help you?"

"Yeah, actually," I said. "We're here for the auction."

"The auction?" he asked. He heard me. He knew what I was talking about. He was just being a prick.

I wasn't in the mood. "Yes. The auction."

"I'm sorry," he said. "The... *auction*... is a private event. It is not open to the..." He looked me up and down. "*Public*."

Okay. I was ready to kick that dude into the sun. There was no reason for him to be such an asshole. I clenched my fists and got ready to go into strike mode, but I stopped myself. It's like Xin said; there were people here other than humans, *powerful* people, and if I started causing a scene now, I'd never get my hands on Unthinkable Black. If I kicked this hospitality manager into the sun, then a bunch of security guys would come and then

131

I'd have to kick *them* into the sun. Then they'd bring out the attack helicopters and I'd have to volleyball-spike them into the volcano and we'd never get to the damn auction.

In any case, the hospitality manager needed to be dealt with.

I shoved a finger in his face. "Look here, you fucking shit bird-"

"Is this man bothering you?" Carl pushed open the front glass doors and trotted down the marble steps, coming in our direction. He had three band-aids on his face, two on his cheek and one over his right eyebrow, right where I'd clawed him. He smiled, despite his injuries. He faced the hospitality manager and said, "These two have every right to be here. They are esteemed guests."

The hospitality guy's demeanor changed entirely when Carl showed up. He bowed a little bit and said, "Mister Carl. A thousand apologies. I didn't know they were friends of yours."

"We're not friends," I pointed out.

Cardboard chimed in. "I've never seen this man before in my life."

"We're basically friends," Carl said, then gave me a little wink.

"We're enemies," I said.

"We're more like frenemies," he told the valet. "Friends who are enemies, but also friends. We disagree on some things, but deep down, I like her and she likes me."

"No," I said. "That's not what it's like at all. I don't like you ever."

Carl laughed and told the hospitality guy not to worry, that I was just being a "Crabby Carla" and everything was fine. None of the valet people bothered us after that and Carl escorted us into the resort.

The main lobby of the Vacation Island resort was the size of my high school gym, with floors of black marble polished like mirrors. A majestic water fountain sat in the middle of the room, some kind of sculpture of an angel fighting a demon. There was a plaque there with the name of the statue engraved in gold: *the War For Heaven*. The demon was a woman in a gown with barbed wire wrapped around her head. The angel was a hulking man armed with a battle ax. Water flowed from their wounds and splashed into the pool at their feet.

In front of the fountain sat a string quartet performing something by Mozart. The two violins and the viola were played by beautiful women in elegant black dresses. The cello was performed by a handsome man in a matching black suit. They played with expert precision and their music filled the entire hall.

The walls were white marble. Across the top of the ceiling were small alcoves, each one home to a bronze statue depicting various winged angels in robes.

Against the right wall was a full bar where you could get cocktails. The cocktail bar had fully stocked shelves of liquor, most of them with gold or silver labels.

On the opposite wall was a coffee bar with five baristas working furiously at five different espresso machines. It was the most "average" thing about the resort, watching these rich people walk around with regular old paper coffee cups and cardboard protective sleeves.

The bar top was carved from rich mahogany. Gold plated stools were mounted in the ground and topped with red velvet. The bar stool I had back home was simple, the ones in the CEO's office were fancy, but these were downright ridiculous. Racks of glimmering, polished crystalware hung overhead. Old people from all over the world lingered at the tables in from of the bar, chatting with unhappy looks on their faces, probably talking about oil prices or stock markets or whatever rich people talk about. Not a single smile among them.

And then all the way across the lobby, past the fountain, were two Jurassic Park doors as tall as the ceiling, wide open, and beyond them was another room: the auction house. The auction seats were half full. Beyond them was a small stage with a podium, back dropped by velvet curtains.

Carl led us to the edge of the "angel beats a demon" water fountain.

"So what brings you here, Penny?" he asked. "Can I call you Penny?"

"No, you may not," I said. "No one calls me Penny. You may call me Penelope."

He laughed. "Deal. What brings you here, *Penelope*?"

"Nunya beeswax, *Carl*."

Cardboard pulled on my arm and whispered to me, "They have coffee. I'm going to go get coffee." And she darted off for the coffee bar. I wanted to tell her to stay, that we shouldn't get separated, but she was gone before I could get a single word out. And before I could go after her, Carl just kept right on talking.

"It's quite serendipitous running into you here," Carl said.

I avoided eye contact. "I don't know what serendipitous means."

"It means lucky. Fortunate. I won't venture to say it's a coincidence, because if I had to guess, I'd say that you're here for the same reason as me."

"I suspect," I said.

"You know, I told the CEO that you were clever. I told him, I said, this girl Penelope, she's a sharp cookie. She's going to be a real rat in the feed wagon, if you catch my meaning. He wouldn't listen to me and look what it got him. You stabbed him in the hand with a pen and now it looks like he's got stigmata."

I shrugged. "He messed with the bull and he got the horns."

Carl crossed his arms and frowned a bit. "I like my rat-in-the-feed-wagon analogy better."

"Whatever," I said. Like I cared.

"Well, since you're here, let me give you a little advice. The CEO showed up and you are decidedly on his bad side, so if I were you, I'd try to be on your best behavior."

I turned to him and laughed. "I don't have a best behavior."

"No, I mean it." He leaned in a little closer. "After you stabbed him, the CEO called the folks down in Research and Development. He had the scientists retool one of our electromagnet satellites to take you out."

"You mean a real satellite?" I asked. "Like in space?"

"We have a lot of satellites. Ionic, microwave, electro-magnetic. There's probably forty or fifty satellites in orbit with the Westland logo on them. The brainiacs in R&D seem to think the electromagnet one will drop you like a sack of Idaho potatoes. They called it something. I forget the name." He patted his suit jacket as if he was searching for a business card, then stuck his hands in his front pocket. He found a scrap of paper and pulled it out. "Yes, here we go. It's called the 50-4F-50-50-59."

"Rolls off the tongue," I said.

"They say the satellite cost a hundred-million dollars to design, although I'm a Skeptical Scooter on that one. But perhaps they're right. It draws its energy straight from the sun and generates an electric pulse that could black-out an entire city. Now it adjusts its trajectory five times a second so it's always pointed at your cerebral cortex. If the CEO activates it..." He put his hand over me and poked the top of my head with his finger. "It goes zap, straight into your brain. I don't know if you have the electrical redundancy of a metropolitan power grid, but I'm betting you don't. One hit from that thing and it's night-night Penelope."

I looked up. Obviously I couldn't see all the way into space, but it sounded intimidating enough. Lasered to death by a machine I couldn't even see? I took a step to the side and wondered: did I just make a satellite move? Was it true that there was a weapon in space following me wherever I went?

Carl could have been lying. How would I know? It's not like I could go to space and double-check his story. And if there really was a death laser with my name on it, why would Carl just come right out and tell me about it? Seems like that's something you'd want to keep secret.

"It's a real technological marvel," Carl continued. "You should be flattered. Bullets don't hurt you, so now you get your own space laser."

"Charming," I said. Carl missed the sarcasm in my voice.

"That's the spirit." He looked up to the ceiling, as if he could see right through it and straight into space. "It's the most dangerous weapon ever built."

I leaned in closer to Carl's ear. "I'm the most dangerous weapon ever built."

"Penelope," Carl said in a scolding tone. "You sound jealous. Don't be jealous. As long as you don't try anything funny, I doubt the CEO will actually use it."

"Define funny."

Carl smiled. "That's what I like about you. You've got spunk." He headed towards the bar and waved at me to follow. "Come on. Let me buy you a drink."

3

Carl and I sat on the velvet bar stools at the cocktail bar. Music from the string quartet filled the lobby, but the bar was far enough away that it was only a faint distraction. I wasn't familiar with a lot of cocktail bars, but this one certainly seemed fancy enough for the wealthiest people in the world. The rail around the bar was solid gold. The glasses were pure crystal and the harmonics of the quartet made them sing in the racks overhead. Carl asked if I was a whiskey drinker, or brandy, or wine, and I told him I didn't know. I only drank alcohol when Ilana stole wine from her cousin's wedding, or when we'd sneak into the Gold Mine bar up on Bowery.

"I don't have an ID," I told him.

He gave me a look like I was being silly. "This is Vacation Island. As long as you can pay for it, you can have it."

"Well, I don't have any money either," I said.

"It's on me!" Carl said, proudly.

I shrugged and got comfortable on the bar stool. "Okay. Whiskey, then, I guess."

"Macallan," he said to the bartender and pointed at a bottle of top-shelf whiskey. "The bottle from 1926."

The bartender, a handsome silver fox looking dude in his fifties, served us an inch of whiskey in two crystal glasses; one for me and one for Carl.

"Thanks," I said. I stuck my nose in the glass an inhaled. It was whiskey all right.

Carl held up his glass and admired the way the light shone through the brown liquid. "This bottle of Macallan from 1926 is 75,000 dollars a bottle. It's nearly impossible to find. Very expensive. You're about to join a small group of only a thousand people on the planet who's ever tasted it. You should sip it very slowly and really appreciate the way the flavors expand with the-"

I opened my mouth and poured the whole thing down my throat. I slammed the glass on the bar and locked eyes with the bartender. "Give me another one."

The bartender gave Carl a concerned look because that's a lot of money to spend on whiskey, especially if I'm just going to slam it down and not even "savor" it. Carl just smiled and gave the bartender a nod. He poured another generous shot, which I also swallowed in one, unappreciative gulp. Carl put a black credit card on the bar. I craned my head around to read his name on it. It read *Westland Corporation Business Account*.

"You know what? It's nice to sit down and just have a drink off the clock, you know?" Carl crossed his legs and turned to face me directly. "So how're things?"

"*Things?*" I repeated. "How are *things?* Things are pretty fucked up, Carl, that's how are *things.*"

He tilted his head. "You seem upset."

"You tried to kill me, Carl. You tried to blow my brains out."

"*I* didn't try to kill you," he said, emphasis on the I. "I wouldn't do that. I'm a pacifist. My *snipers* tried to kill you."

"Yeah, because you ordered them to."

"*I* didn't pull the trigger." He sipped his whiskey. "Look, let's not talk about work, okay? Let's talk about something else. Did you see that new Johnny Depp movie?"

I couldn't do anything but stare at him. Was he crazy? Or was this his weird way of trying to intimidate me, or what was going on? I was legitimately at a loss for words.

Eventually Carl snapped his fingers in front of my eyes. "Hello?" he said. "Earth to Penelope."

"What are you doing?" I asked.

"I'm making conversation," he said. "Considering I just bought you three thousand dollars worth of whiskey, I don't think it would hurt you to at least play along."

"I don't want to make conversation with you, Carl," I said. "What don't you get? You tried to kill me. You tried to steal Impossible Red from Xin. I don't like you. I will never like you. You're a bitch."

"Oh, is that what this is all about?" He seemed sincerely stunned. "Penelope, that's just my *job.* That's what I get paid to do. None of that is personal. The CEO might order me to rig an election in Nicaragua tomorrow, or have my snipers assassinate the prince of Denmark. I don't do it because I want to. I do it because it's my job. It's just business." He raised his whiskey glass into the air. "Cheers."

"So now you're off the clock and you think that means we're going to be friends?"

"Well, I'm salaried," he said. "So I'm kind of always on the clock, but I do have downtime. Like now." He leaned over and muttered into my ear, "And the company card's a pretty nice perk, too. I'm not complaining."

"I'm not going to be friends with you, dude," I said. "I don't care if it's 'just your job.' You tried to kill me. You can't pretend like that didn't happen. How would you like it if I tried to kill you?"

He thought about that for a moment. "On the clock?" he asked. "Or off the clock?"

"At all."

"If it was on the clock, I'd understand. That's business." He leaned his head to the side. "But if you were killing me off the clock, I'd be like, hey, Penelope, stop that. You're being a Meany Jeannie."

"That's the difference between you and me, Carl. I don't clock in or clock out for this shit. This is my life we're talking about."

"Now you're just playing semantics," he said. He sat his whiskey down so he could use both hands as visual aides. "Say I'm a guy and I assemble cars for a living. If those cars are defective and they explode and kill people, who goes to court? The guy who assembled the car? No! The guy who assembled the car is only one gear in the machine of industry. It's the *company* that gets sued. The guy who assembled the car, it's not his fault. He was just doing his *job*. And that's like me. Just because it's my job to make sure you end up dead, it doesn't mean I'm the one killing you."

"But there's a difference there," I said. "The guy assembling the car isn't blowing them up on purpose. You, however, *are*."

Carl turned away from me and picked up his whiskey. "Well, now you're just being silly."

4

Our debate about clocking in and clocking out and killing people came to a halt when a twenty-something girl interrupted us by stumbling up to the bar. She wore a pure white gown, sleeveless, with an open back. It looked more like a wedding dress than anything. The material was silky and shimmered in the light. The dress came down as far as her knees, and that's when I noticed she was walking around barefoot, padding along the black marble in near silence. She had the ankle straps of her high heels slung over her pointer finger.

She wore white gloves of the same silk material and were expertly cut to fit her fingers and hands. They came up past the elbow, except the right one had started to fall down and bunched up around her forearm.

She wore a silver tiara that sat off-kilter on her head and barely stuck in her hair. One good bump, one quick turn of the head, and that tiara was going to come flying off. Her brunette hair was up in a pony tail and wisps of it had come loose and dangled across her face. She crossed her green eyes in an attempt to see the stray hairs, then she blew them out of her face with her glitter-painted lips. Whatever black eyeliner she had put on was smudged. She'd been touching her make-up; I could see it smeared on the fingertips of her nice gloves.

If this chick was a bride, she was a *drunk* bride.

She had to blow the hair out of her face because she had her heels dangling from one hand and two cocktail glasses in the other. She'd blow on her hair, but then it would fall right back into place and she'd have to blow again. When she did this, she scrunched her face and I immediately recognized the way it wrinkled her nose. This wasn't just some bride.

This was one of Princess Cardboard's sisters.

The princess slammed her two empty cocktail glasses on the bar.

"More," she said to the bartender.

"Okay," the bartender answered, trying to be cordial. "More what, exactly?"

She leaned on the bar with her elbows and said, "More *booze.*"

I could smell her breath when she talked, and she was two empty stools down from me. It smelled like cotton candy and vodka. I had some distance, but the bartender was getting her breath right in his face. He didn't flinch, though. He just smiled and nodded at the princess, undaunted by her attitude.

He said, "How about another Cotton Candy-tini?"

She nodded hard. Her tiara shifted and she pushed it back into place; another thing she had in common with her sister. She said, "Yes. Cotton Candy-tini. Great. Good. Do it. Yes."

The bartender asked, "Do you want it up or on the rocks or...?"

"Less this..." She flapped her fingers like a mouth jabbering, "...and more this." She mimed mixing drinks.

The bartender exercised Jesus-levels of patience, then grabbed a couple bottles to start making her drink. The princess fought against her wedding gown as she sat on her barstool. She got comfortable, threw her shoes on the bar, then rotated to look at me and Carl.

"What?" she said.

"Hey." I gave her a wave. "I think I know your sister. Princess Cardboard."

"Princess Parcel," she said. She pointed at my glass. "What're you drinking?"

I couldn't remember the name of the bullshit liquor Carl ordered. I looked at my empty glass and said, "It's some kind of whiskey. Misses McCallahan or something."

"Macallan," Carl said, correcting me and pointing at the shelf. "The bottle from 1926."

"Great. I want one." Princess Parcel slammed her fist on the bar and made all our glasses jump in place. The bartender spun around and gave her a dirty look. She was too drunk to notice. She pointed at him and said, "I want a MuhGilligan nineteen six."

The bartender said, "I'm making you a Cotton Candy-tini. Why don't you finish this one, then I'll get you something else."

She raised her eyebrows at him. She crawled up in her seat until she was on her knees. She leaned over the bar and said to him, in a calm, drunken voice, "I will destroy this bar like a fucking black hole if you do not get me a Mister Gilligan's number six."

The bartender's shoulders slumped, defeated. He sighed and said, "Right away."

Princess Cardboard came up behind me, too delightfully hypnotized by her mug of coffee and two slices of coffeecake to notice the other princess at the bar.

"Penelope!" Cardboard said. "They have coffeecake, just like that Voodoo man said! It's really good, too. I brought you some."

I was about to point out Princess Parcel, but I didn't get a chance. Parcel had already recognized the voice of her sister and spun around.

Parcel said, "Cardboard. What are you doing here?"

Cardboard's head popped up, eyes wide. "Parcel! What are *you* doing here?"

"Are you here for the money?" Parcel asked.

"No," Cardboard said. "I don't think so. What money?"

"All the money." Parcel held up the white sequined purse slung over her shoulder. It looked packed full. She clutched it to her chest. "All of *our* money."

140

Cardboard took off her crown and scratched her head. "You mean, all the delivery money?"

Parcel grinned. "Yeah."

"Why do you have all the delivery money?"

"I can't say." Parcel shot a disapproving look at me, then at Carl. "Not in front of the Earthlings."

"Well," Carl said as he downed the rest of his whiskey. "This is obviously an A and B conversation. So I will *see* my way out of it."

He set his glass on the bar and casually tossed out a hundred dollar tip. He got to his feet and gave us a polite nod. "I will see you ladies at the auction."

Carl left. The three of us watched and waited until he was gone. Once he was out of earshot, Parcel stared at me. Whatever she wanted to say, she didn't want to say it in my presence. Cardboard put her arm around me and came to my defense.

"This is Penelope Salvo," Cardboard said. "She's my new friend. I told her all about us and-"

Parcel shoved Cardboard's shoulder. "You told her about us?"

"Don't push me," Cardboard spat. She regained her footing and shoved Parcel back.

Parcel was too drunk to keep her balance on her bar stool. She wavered and was going to fall if she tried to stay on, so she turned it into a controlled jump to her feet. She grabbed Cardboard by the front of her dress and yanked her close.

"Bubble Wrap specifically told us to keep our mouths shut," Parcel said. "Do have any idea what you've done?"

Cardboard knocked her sister's hands away. "You're wrinkling up my clothes, you dummy." She straightened and smoothed the front of her gown. "Anyway, Bubble Wrap said not to tell *humans* about us. Penelope isn't a human. She's got secret powers, just like us."

"I'm a human," I said, quietly. "Pretty sure."

Parcel ignored me and waved a finger at her sister. "How do you know you can trust her?"

Cardboard crossed her arms and said, with a defiant stamp of her foot, "I just do. I have a *feeling*."

"A *feeling*?" Parcel repeated. "You're too stupid to have feelings."

"I am not!" Cardboard snapped. They were getting loud and starting to draw attention from the rest of the lobby.

"Hey," I said. "If it's a big deal, I can go."

"No!" Cardboard grabbed my arm. "I want you to stay!" She stared Princess Parcel down. "And I want you to tell me why you have all our money."

Parcel narrowed her eyes. "Or you'll what?"

Cardboard narrowed her eyes back. She hesitated as she thought of something, then suddenly blurted out, "Or I'll tell everyone that you have bad skin."

Parcel tightened her lips and scowled. "Fine." She leaned closer to the two of us and whispered, "I found the Muffincake Kingdom. And it's *here*."

5

"The Welf Auction will begin in fifteen minutes," announced a fat guy in a black suit and yellow corsage. He came out of the auction hall, shouted from the giant entrance, then retreated back inside. They could have used an intercom system – it's not like this place couldn't afford it – but that wasn't "authentic" enough for rich people at an auction. They wanted everything done the old, stupid way. After the announcement, rich old ladies and smug businessmen went back to their oh-so-important conversations.

Whatever those olds were talking about couldn't have been more important than the conversation between the two princesses and the fate of their fairytale world.

Princess Cardboard and Princess Parcel were locked in whisper quiet conversation. Parcel held a cocktail in each hand, a bright pink one and her Macallan whiskey in the other. Cardboard took absent minded sips of coffee.

Cardboard asked, "The Muffincake Kingdom is here? On Vacation Island?"

Parcel nodded.

Cardboard followed that up with, "How do you know?"

Parcel sucked at her pink cocktail through a straw, then said, "This leprechaun mentioned it when I was delivering boxes in Ireland. I got him drunk and he totally spilled the beans. But don't tell anyone else. I don't want you to screw this up."

"I won't," Cardboard said. "Did you tell Bubble Wrap?"

"No, I didn't tell Bubble Wrap," Parcel snipped. "It's not her job to get the kingdom back."

Cardboard slowly started to shake her head. "I don't think you should have taken all the money without telling Bubble Wrap. She's the smart one."

"I'm smart," Parcel snapped. "And isn't that what all our money was for? In case we found it? Well, I found it. It's here and up for auction. And I need our money to buy it."

Cardboard rubbed her forehead, obviously uncomfortable with the argument. She said, "I just think-"

"Stop thinking." Parcel pointed a drunk finger at her sister. "Don't forget, you're the dumb one."

Cardboard stamped her foot. "I'm the cute one!"

Parcel scoffed. "*I'm* the cute one!"

Cardboard shouted, "You're the *drunk*!"

Michael used to talk down to me like how Parcel talked to Cardboard. He would always call me stupid or dumb. "Your problem is," he'd say, "is you don't think." It was a tough thing to hear when you're a little kid and if you hear it long enough, you start believing it. Watching Parcel insult Cardboard like that made me super anxious.

"Here." Parcel shoved her two cocktails into Cardboard's hands. "Lucky for you, I have to go pee."

She left her high heels on the bar and stumbled off in search of the bathroom. She swayed back and forth as she walked across the hall and accidentally bumped into the violinist in the string quartet. She ruined the music for a moment. The violinist gave her a dirty look, then returned to her performance.

Cardboard put the cocktails down on the bar. I thought maybe she might cry, the way Parcel was talking to her, but she turned around with a beaming smile on her face.

"Can you believe it?" she said. "It's here. The Muffincake Kingdom is here!"

I had never seen Cardboard smile so big before, but there it was: wrinkled nose, dimples in her cheeks, and perfect teeth.

"I'm stoked for you," I said.

"We'll have to break the shrinking spell, but that will be easy. Did I ever tell you about the Coffeecake Kingdom? That's where I ruled. Right outside my castle was the Espresso River on one side and the Whole Milk River on the other side and they went around my castle and came together in the south and became the Latte River."

"It sounds delicious," I said.

Cardboard kept going. The excitement welling up inside her came gushing out like words. "And then there were these things called roaster-phants. They kind of look like elephants with cranks for noses and their bodies are metal and hollow and they roast coffee beans inside their body. And then across the road from my castle is the Great Espresso Machine, as big as a mountain! It blows steam and supplies my whole kingdom with coffee. Oh! The best part are the coffeecake fields. I want you to see them so bad. The coffeecakes grow on little plants like roses and you can just pick them and eat them and they are the best coffeecakes you've ever tasted."

"Wow," I said. "You are amped."

She nodded. "It's my home. Can you imagine what it's like to not have a home?"

A laugh escaped me. "I can, actually."

"Let's go!" She jumped in place, grabbed me by the arm, and tried to pull me toward the auction hall. I was a million times stronger than her, though, so I didn't move; she just nearly pulled herself off her feet. Her crown fell over her eyes and she moved it back into place. "Come on! Let's get seats for the auction. I want to get seats."

"But what about your sister?" I pointed at Princess Parcel's empty stool. "Her drinks."

"Okay." Cardboard held her hands at me like she had a plan. "You stay here. Wait for her. I'll go save us seats."

"I really think we should stick together."

"Me too," she said, inching towards the auction hall. "You stick together here and I'll stick together in the auction hall."

She mad a mad dash across the lobby.

"That's not sticking together!" I shouted after her, but she wasn't listening.

I turned in my bar stool and leaned against the bar. I took Princess Parcel's expensive whiskey and sipped on it. I'd never drank whiskey before and for being such an expensive bottle, it didn't taste all that great. The silver fox bartender stood on the other side of me and wiped down the bar top. I was the only customer left.

"So how do you know Carl?" he asked me.

"Eh," I said. "He tried to kill me."

Princess Parcel had to lean against me as she drunk-stumbled towards the auction hall. The entrance to the hall was blocked by a long table staffed by a bunch of men and women in green valet outfits. It was their jobs to pass out ping-pong paddles with numbers printed on them.

I stood in front of the table and this lady held out a white paddle with the number 137 printed on it.

She said, "Simply raise your paddle when you want to bid on something." She looked me up and down with the same kind of judgment I came to expect from Vacation Island. "If you can afford anything, that is."

I swiped the paddle of out her hands, said, "Don't quit your day job," and headed inside.

The ceiling of the auction hall was a glass dome, three stories high, that let the island sunlight into the room. The seats weren't anything special, just typical hotel seats which felt weird considering the extravagance of everything else. Seating was arranged into two equal halves; odd numbers on the right side and even numbers on the left side. Each side had a hundred or so chairs, and were divided by a red-carpet aisle that cut up the middle and lead directly to the stage. Two hundred of the richest people in the world were gathered there, and I was joining them.

Princess Parcel stumbled up with her very own ping pong paddle – number 138 – but she was too drunk to walk very far. She spotted an open seat in the back row and immediately plopped down. She gave the room a judgmental look, loudly slurped one of her cocktails, and threw her shoes on the seat next to her.

I didn't want to leave Parcel all on her own, but I also needed to find Cardboard. I walked up the main aisle, past old men in bright white naval uniforms, past suave businessmen, past ten-gallon-hat oil tycoons, and past turtleneck-wearing website developers. I was the youngest person in the room by at least two decades. Everyone looked at me with a mix of confusion and disgust.

It took everything I had to not just say, "Man, fuck all y'all."

Cardboard had found a spot in the middle of the right hand section. She sat turned around in her seat, obviously searching for me. Once we made eye contact, she waved for me to join her.

"Penelope!" she called out. "Over here!"

I nodded at her and went down her row. The seats were filling up quick, but Cardboard used her coffee mug and a handful of coffeecake to save the seat next to her. I excused myself down the row and got a lot of indignant looks from women in mink stoles, men in glorious tuxedos, and a middle-aged couple dressed like Norwegian royalty. I had to get around a fat cowboy guy, the kind of guy who probably owned a Cadillac convertible with steer horns mounted on the front. He seemed friendly enough – the first friendly face – but his wife was a different story. She looked me up and down and sneered. She wore a black and white spotted fur over her shoulders and smoked a cigarette through one of those long, plastic, black things.

Ma always said, it's best to lead with a compliment.

I said to her, "I loved you in 101 Dalmatians."

I reached Cardboard and sat next to her.

"Ooh." She tapped at my paddle. "What number did you get?"

I showed it to her. "One thirty-seven."

"I got eighteen," she said. She was holding it upside down. I reached over and turned it right side up.

"You have eighty-one," I said.

"Huh." For a few moments she turned the paddle upside down, right side up, over and over – eighteen, eighty-one, eighteen, eighty-one – mesmerized by the illusion. Once she felt satisfied holding it correctly, she proudly said to herself, "Lucky number eighty-one."

We had to sit there and wait for the rest of the people to fill up the seats. I gave the room a visual scan. In the row behind us sat a Texas oil baron in a turquoise bolo tie, a few Japanese businessmen, and a wrinkled-up lady who was so old, I wondered what demon she cut a deal with to live past 200. Princess Parcel sat by herself in the back row. She had finished her cotton candy-tini and moved on to the whiskey.

On the opposite side of the auction hall, smack dab in the middle of the front row, sat Carl and the CEO. Carl was already looking at me, so we made eye contact right away. He held up his paddle – number four – and pointed at it. He smiled as if to say, "Look at how great my number is." The CEO turned, saw me, and gave me a hard stare. I glared back and scratched my nose with my middle finger.

"Five minutes," the man at the podium said into the microphone. He was a thin guy, French looking, with shiny hair and a thin mustache. "Please take your seats."

They raised the velvet stage curtain to reveal a long banquet table that held all the items up for auction. Each item was covered in its own individual sheet of green silk. I counted twenty-three items on the table. Similar to how you can guess a Christmas present by its shape, I tried to figure out which item was the clock with Unthinkable Black, but that was tough to do; clocks can come in any shape or size.

Our French host kicked off the auction by tapping the microphone until it wailed with feedback. Once the murmuring of the room died off and everyone gave Frenchy their attention, he said, "I am Andre LeChance, your curator for tonight's Welf Auction. Thank you all for joining us. I know you are excited to begin tonight's event, so let's not delay things any further. For our first item..."

He pulled back the first silk sheet and revealed a painting by some Japanese painter guy, something called the Great Wave of Something-Something, and the bidding opened at 50 million dollars.

Bid, bid, bid. 50 million went to 60 million.

Bid, bid, bid. 60 million went to 70 million.

I looked all around, completely mind-blown by the amounts of money these guys were throwing around. Just a few months ago I was borderline homeless without money for food and these chumps were dropping 70 million dollars on a fucking painting.

And it's not like it stopped at 70 million, either. It just kept going and going. 73 million. 74 million. 75 million. I wanted to fucking puke.

Carl sat there patiently, completely uninterested in the bidding war over some useless painting. Despite my disgust, I actually found myself getting caught up in the competition between the Cadillac Cowboy who, in my head, I called Yosemite Sam, and some Japanese businessman sitting in the front row of my section. LeChance took the bidding to 76 million, then 77, then 78 million. Eventually the oil tycoon waved it off. LeChance pointed his gavel at the Japanese businessman as the painting went once, twice, and finally sold for 78 million dollars.

The Japanese businessman sat there emotionless, apparently unfazed that he had driven off all the competition and successfully won the painting.

LeChance pulled back the next sheet and revealed a small sculpture that reminded me of the Monopoly piece where the captain dude is riding a horse. It sold for 41 million. Then he sold a dinosaur egg for 12 million, "the Pink Ruby" for six million, and a collection of crystal animal figurines for 59 million to the woman in the jaunty hat.

"Come on," I muttered to myself. "Come on, come on. Get to Unthinkable Black."

"Ah, this piece," LeChance said as he swept the sheet off the next item, "is a miniature world, hand crafted. Its origin is a mystery, the artist is unknown, and the technique used to create this work cannot be duplicated by even the most skilled artists. The detail is exquisite. The tiny world is enclosed in a seamless ball of glass. Our art aficionados are unable to even guess at how such a work of art is possible. It is widely considered to be the only one of its kind. I will start the bidding at twenty million. Do I hear twenty million?"

"Twenty million," Princess Parcel shouted from the back. She didn't just raise her paddle, she threw it at the stage. It bounced up the aisle. It was the first time Parcel had bid on anything.

"That must be the Muffincake Kingdom, huh?" I asked Cardboard. But she wasn't paying attention to me. She had moved to the edge of her seat, hypnotized by the sight of the miniature kingdom trapped inside a sphere of glass. I elbowed her in the arm. She didn't react.

"Twenty-*one* million!" Cadillac Cowboy called out. I guess he was intrigued by the Muffincake Kingdom. His wife gave him a stern look, as if he was stupid for bidding on something so juvenile. He shrugged at her like, so what, it's only 21 million dollars.

Princess Parcel stood up and shouted. "Twenty-*two* million."

The cowboy raised his paddle dismissively and said, "Twenty-*three* million."

Cardboard sprang out of her seat. She squeezed her hands into fists and screamed at the old cowboy, "Stop bidding on it!"

LeChance banged his gavel on the podium, then pointed at us. "Sit down!" The room went silent. Cardboard shut her mouth and sat back down, but nervously twirled a curl of her golden hair around her finger. LeChance pointed his gavel at the cowboy and said, "I have twenty-three million from Buffalo Wings."

The cowboy's name was Buffalo Wings? Of all the crazy shit I'd seen – cardboard tunnels, shrunken down fairytale worlds, Voodoo spirits – the most unbelievable thing yet was that this guys name was actually "Buffalo Wings." Surely that was a nickname. Please, God, tell me that's just a nickname.

"Twenty-whatever-is-next million," Parcel announced. "What are we on? Twenty-four million? Twenty-four million!"

Buffalo Wings raised his paddle and said, "Twenty-*five*."

I leaned over to Cardboard. "How much money does your sister have?"

"All of it," she whispered. "I don't know how much."

"Twenty-*six* million," Parcel shouted.

Buffalo casually waved his paddle, unmoved by Princess Parcel's intensity. "Twenty-*seven* million."

Cardboard jumped up again. "Stop bidding on my home, you goat-kissing hillbilly!" Her face had turned a bright shade of red. She held her arms at her sides, fists clenched, and stamped her foot.

Everyone turned their heads to look at us. Even the CEO. LeChance gripped the sides of the podium and flared his nostrils. He swept his gavel up in his hand and pounded it three times.

"One more outburst out of you," he yelled, pointing this gavel at Cardboard, "and you won't only be removed from the auction, I'll have you removed from the whole island. Am I understood?"

I grabbed Cardboard by the arm and pulled her down into her seat. "Dude, sit down," I whispered. "You're going to get us kicked out."

LeChance stared us down to ensure his point had been made. I smiled and gave him an apologetic wave. Cardboard wrung her hands and took small, furious breaths.

"The last bid was Buffalo Wings at twenty-seven million," said LeChance. "Can I hear twenty-eight from the inebriated bridesmaid? Twenty-eight? Twenty-eight million?"

Princess Parcel didn't say anything. I expected her to make a bid, but she didn't. I turned to look at her. So did Cardboard. Parcel was rummaging through her purse, counting her money. She looked up at us, and shook her head. However much money she had, it wasn't enough.

"Twenty-seven million going once," LeChance said, pointing at Buffalo Wings.

Cardboard turned her attention back to the stage. If no one else spoke up, the Muffincake Kingdom would be the property of a goat-kisser named Buffalo Wings. She grabbed a handful of her hair and pulled on it. She whispered, over and over, "Oh, no. Oh, please Butter Pad and Sugar Cube, no."

LeChance announced, "Going twice!"

I made a snap decision. I stuck my paddle in the air and said, "Twenty-*eight* million."

7

Buffalo Wings and I went back and forth for a while, but eventually he threw in the towel at 33 million.

LeChance banged his gavel and said, "Sold to the homeless girl for thirty-three million dollars."

The fact that I bid on the Muffincake Kingdom threw Carl for an obvious loop; I could tell by the way he wrinkled his forehead and rubbed his chin. He was surely convinced that I was there for Unthinkable Black – which he was right – but then I ended up bidding on something else entirely. I'm sure in his mind he was thinking, *What does Penelope know that I don't?*

Princess Cardboard turned in her seat and grabbed me by the shoulders. Her eyes were tearing up.

"You won," she said in a hushed tone.

I smiled at her. "I did."

"You won the Muffincake Kingdom."

"I did."

"But..." She shook her head, confused. "But you only have the one check. What about Unthinkable Black?"

"Uhh."

I took out the check and looked it over. We suddenly had a big problem on our hands. The check wasn't blank anymore. It had filled itself out for thirty-three million dollars – the amount of the Muffincake Kingdom, under glass – complete with my signature.

"What the fuck," I muttered. I rubbed the ink with my fingers, but it wasn't coming off. The magic check filled itself out. I didn't know that was how it worked. To be fair, I didn't have the first clue how it was supposed to work. This was a hell of a way to find out. I rubbed harder at the ink with my thumb. It wasn't working. It wouldn't come off.

"Next," LeChance announced to the room, "An eighteenth century handcrafted clock with jewels inset on the clock face." I looked up. Sure enough, there was a table-top pendulum clock with jewels instead of numbers. Right at twelve o'clock was a round, black marble. "We will begin the bidding at forty million."

And Carl stuck up his paddle. "Forty million."

Shit. Things were spiraling out of control and *fast*.

"That's the clock," I told Cardboard, pointing at it. "That's Unthinkable Black."

Cardboard asked, "What're we going to do?"

"What *can* we do?" I said. "Semedi's dumbass check already filled itself out. We don't have any more money."

Sitting at the front of our section was this bearded dude in Saudi Arabian robes. He had a briefcase handcuffed to his wrist. He took an interest in the clock and stuck his paddle in the air – number 12.

"Forty-one million," the guy said.

"Forty-two," Carl answered, lazily waving his paddle back and forth.

The bidding climbed to 50 million, then 60 million, then 70 million. No one was going to beat Carl in a bidding war, not even an oil prince from Saudi Arabia. Oh, sure, the guy thought he could outbid Carl, and he put on a pretty good show of wealth and confidence, but the CEO wasn't going to let Unthinkable Black slip away. He'd liquidate the entire Westland Corporation if he had to. The only person who had more money than the Westland Corporation was Baron Semedi, and I screwed that one up big time.

Carl's bids came so quick and confident, he started shouting over the other guy.

"Seventy-one mill-," the oil prince said.

"Seventy-*two* million," Carl answered back.

The oil prince gave the increasing price some serious thought, then raised his paddle and said, "Seventy-three mill-"

"Seventy-*four* million," Carl interrupted.

"Seventy-five mill-"

"Seventy-*six* million."

Carl was basically making an announcement to the room: "Hey, no matter what this guy bids, I will always and immediately match his bid with my own. Make no mistake about it, I will own this clock."

Eventually the price tag got too steep and the oil prince backed down. Carl won the clock and Unthinkable Black for 102 million dollars and there was nothing I could do to stop him.

Chapter 9

1

Westland won Unthinkable Black, fair and square.

But that didn't mean I was going to let them have it.

I leaned over to whisper to Cardboard as the rest of the auction continued. "Here's the plan. When this whole thing is over, we're going to follow Carl and the CEO out of the resort. Then when they're alone, we're going to jump them old school, kick the shit out of them, and steal Unthinkable Black. Then you're going to give me an extraction."

She nodded eagerly. "Okay, sounds great." Still nodding in agreement, she asked, "What's an extraction?"

"It's when you get me out of here and take me back to New York."

"Oooh." She snapped her fingers and winked at me. "An *extraction*."

I narrowed my eyes at her. "Are you going to remember all this?"

"Of course!" she said. She nodded once and her cardboard crown slumped down over her eyes. She pushed it back up and peered at me from under the edge. "Maybe."

"Just..." Boy, I was putting a lot of faith in her. "When the times comes, just do everything I tell you."

She puffed up her chest. "Can do."

We had to wait a whole hour for the slowest auctioneer in the known universe to sell off the rest of his garbage. In the end, after everything was auctioned off, LeChance invited all the winners to the stage to collect their items and pay the cashier, but LeChance didn't call him a cashier, he called him a "purser." I've never heard anyone called a purser before, but that's just how stuck up and conceited the whole auction was. All the non-winners left the auction hall, headed for the bars or the tennis courts or one of the other luxuries of Vacation Island. The winners – myself and Cardboard included – approached the stage.

It didn't shock me when Carl, instead of heading up to the stage, came for me and Cardboard and intercepted us. The CEO walked up the stage with no intention of being cordial. That's what Carl was for. Carl was the diplomat.

"Interesting purchase on that ball of glass," Carl said to me. "I suspected you were after the clock."

"A clock?" I asked, trying to play dumb. "Why would I want a stupid clock?"

"Yeah," Cardboard nearly shouted. Her idea of lying was to ramble on and on at the top of her lungs. "Why would we want some dumb clock? We don't want your clock. Or any clocks. We hate clocks. Clocks are stupid. I wouldn't take a clock if *you* paid *me*."

"Alright." I elbowed her in the ribs. "Just dial it back a little bit. You don't have to over-sell it." I looked back at Carl. "Don't mind her. She's had a lot of caffeine today."

Carl joined us on our way up to the stage. He stuck his hands in his pockets. "Can I be a Curious Cody and ask you a question?"

"I guess?"

"Well, it's just seems odd that you would show up here with thirty-three million dollars," he said.

"Okay," I said. "That's not a question."

He cleared his throat. "Where did you get thirty-three million dollars?"

Cardboard spoke up and said, "We started a pyramid scheme."

"Technically, it's an inverted triangle," I added.

Carl laughed. "Alright. Keep your secrets."

We reached the stage. I put some distance between us and the psychos from Westland. The cashier – who I called a cashier because that's exactly what he was and I wasn't going to call him a "purser" – he went up to each of the winners individually. This was some weasel-looking valet guy with weasel eyes and a body shaped like an upright weasel. He carried a tablet computer that he used to process direct money transfers, clear checks with banks, that kind of thing. He went in order of auction items, which meant our turn came before the CEO and Carl.

When the cashier got to me and Cardboard, he gave me a snotty look, which didn't come as any surprise. Still, despite my outward appearance, I won the Muffincake Kingdom fair and square in the auction and I had a check for the correct amount. He took it and scoffed as if he expected the check to bounce. He typed in the account number and much to his amazement, the check cleared. He gave us permission to go up on the stage and retrieve our item from the armed security guards.

That's when we finally got to come face to face with Andre LeChance, our auctioneer. He obviously remembered Cardboard from her disruptive outbursts and me for being "the homeless girl." He saw us and looked very unimpressed.

"Here is your art," he said, gesturing at the Muffincake Kingdom inside a glass ball. "In the future, I caution you to use a little more decorum."

Decorum? I looked around and said, "I don't know. I think this place looks fine the way it is."

I picked up the bowling ball-sized sphere of glass with both hands and peered inside. Dirt filled the bottom half of the bowl. Across the top were six different kingdoms, each one with their own little ecosystems. There was a snow world, a birthday world, a wedding world, a breakfast world, a coffee world, and some kind of carnival world on an island. Just like they said, it would have been physically impossible for a human being to create something so tiny and yet so intricate. The landscape was pock-marked with the tiniest buildings: castles the size of pencil erasers and cottages as small as grains of sand. The lakes were no bigger than watch batteries, with razor thin rivers and miniature forests of cupcake trees. I could have spent hours looking at all the little landmarks, but we didn't have that kind of time.

Princess Cardboard's face appeared in the reflection of the glass as she looked over my shoulder. I could see the love in her eyes, so I handed it off to her. She cradled it in her arms like a baby and stared inside.

"Move along, please," said LeChance. "I have a lot of other people waiting."

Cardboard wasn't paying attention. I had to lead her away by the arm.

Carl and the CEO went on stage next. Carl shook LeChance's hand. The CEO couldn't shake hands; his right hand was wrapped up in bandages.

"Here is your magnificent clock," LeChance said to them as he handed it to Carl. "Finest congratulations to the Westland Corporation for winning such a stunning work of art."

Carl handed the clock to the CEO. The CEO held it up to his eyes. He closely examined the black marble at the twelve o'clock position and gave it a satisfied nod. Together, they stepped off the stage.

"Stunning, indeed." Carl said as he passed by us. The CEO ignored us entirely and took long, fast strides.

LeChance and the weasel cashier guy went on to settle up with remaining winners, distributing the rest of the auction items. I didn't want to lose sight of Carl and the CEO. I followed quickly after them, then realized Cardboard wasn't with me. She stood in place, her eyes transfixed on the Muffincake Kingdom. I had to double back, grab her by the arm, and make her follow me.

2

I stalked Carl and the CEO out into the main lobby with Princess Cardboard in tow. Maybe it was because the auction had just ended or maybe it was happy hour, but the lobby was crowded like a mall at Christmas. I imagined that must be what it feels like on the deck of a cruise ship; old, rich people gathered around the bars, loitering around the fountain, and talking stocks and bonds by the string quartet. While the ladies wore different colored dresses, most of the guys dressed the same: black tuxedos. That made tracking Carl and CEO a real chore. I didn't take my eyes off of them for a second, otherwise I would have lost them in the crowd.

I pulled Cardboard into a crouch behind an unattended grand piano. From there, I could peek out over the top and watch my targets.

I told Cardboard, "When they get outside, I'm going to jump them and beat their asses. You keep your distance." She didn't answer. She was crying over the Muffincake Kingdom.

She pressed her fingertip against the glass. "That's where I grew up."

"Hey." I grabbed her by the face and forced her to look into my eyes. "You need to get with it, okay? You can look at your kingdom all you want when we get home, but right now I need to you focus."

She snapped out of it, if only temporarily. "Right. Yes. Totally."

Princess Parcel staggered through the crowd and stood over us. She didn't duck down, she didn't whisper, she just stood at the grand piano with a yellow cocktail in one hand and a green cocktail in the other. She looked at Cardboard and said, "Let me have it."

"No," Cardboard snapped. She clutched the kingdom to her chest. "I got it. I'll carry it."

Parcel said, "Cardboard, you're going to drop it or something. Give it."

I stepped in and told Parcel. "You can't carry the kingdom and two cocktails. If you want to carry it, you're going to have to dump out your drinks."

This, come to find out, really threw Parcel for a loop. She lowered her eyebrows at me, like this was some kind of Sphinx riddle with a deceptively obvious solution. But in the end, she conceded.

"Fine," she said. She crouched down behind the piano with us. "She can carry it. But I am not letting you two out of my sight."

"Fine," Cardboard said. She kept the kingdom close to her, as if Parcel was trying to trick her and might snatch it away at a moments notice.

Carl and the CEO made their quick exit to the doors, eager to leave, but too dignified to run. They walked briskly past the lobby fountain, around the string quartet, and straight for the front entrance. There were already two Westland Corporation security guards waiting by the doors, decked out in body armor, helmets, and armed with AK-47s. They stood at attention, anticipating the CEO and Carl's departure.

"Afternoon, Charlie team," Carl said. "We have what we came for. Prep the helicopter."

The soldiers escorted them out of the resort.

3

Carl and the CEO had no idea that we were following them. The two of them rushed along the concrete path out front, around the wading pools, and towards the wing of the resort with the helicopter launching pads on the roof. Cardboard and I followed after them, sneaking along, stealing glances at them from behind coconut trees. Princess Parcel walked behind us like normal, refusing to sneak. The ice rattled loudly in her two cocktails, making far too much noise for such a stealthy mission.

"Could you keep it down?" I whispered at her. "You sound like a god damned ice machine."

"Me?" Parcel said. As if there was someone else with a glass full of ice.

"Yes, you," I said. "If you're not careful-"

That's when the green cocktail slipped right out of her hand. The glass shattered on the concrete and ice shot everywhere. The exploding glass broke our silence. Carl and the CEO turned at the sound of it and made direct eye contact with us. Our coconut tree didn't make much of a hiding spot. We were caught red-the-fuck-handed. It didn't take a stretch of the imagination for them to figure out why we were following them. Carl's eyes went from me, to the clock, then back to me.

We were stalking them like prey, and they caught us.

"Look at this mess," Parcel said. She stumbled to the ground and started picking up the ice, collecting it in the bottom half of her broken glass.

"Penelope," Carl called out. "Are you following us?"

"No," I said, stepping out from behind the tree. "We were just..."

"We're jumping you," Cardboard blurted out. I gave her a look of abject disbelief. Did she really just blow our cover like that? She gave me an innocent look. "What?" she asked. "You said we were going to jump them, old school."

I clenched my teeth and said, "Shut *up*."

"I see what this is," Carl said. He gave me a knowing smile. "You *were* after Unthinkable Black. You were just being a Tricky

Mickey."

All pretenses were over. No amount of lying would fix this. So I came clean, with a vengeance.

"Give me the clock," I said as I marched right for them. "Hand it over and I won't rip your guys' heads off."

Their security guards raised their machine guns and aimed them at me. The CEO put out his hand to stop them like trained dogs. He said, "Don't bother. That's Penelope Salvo. You'll just be wasting bullets."

"Yeah," I said. "And you'll ruin another perfectly good shirt."

"Miss Salvo." The CEO said my name with a real fed-up tone to it. He pulled a remote control out of his jacket. It had only one button on it, a red one, and he rested his thumb on it. "I started to doubt that you were going to try something stupid. Thanks for not letting me down."

I didn't like the CEO's tone. I didn't like the way he called me stupid. I didn't like his bald head, his wrinkly face, or his bony fingers. And, more than anything, I didn't like the look in his eyes, as if he didn't see me as a threat.

I marched right up to him and Carl. The two Westland soldiers kept their rifles pointed at me. I rolled my eyes at them. Once I was close enough to Carl, I jerked the clock out of his hands and put it under my arm.

"Something *this* stupid?" I asked. "Cuz I just stole your clock."

"Yeah," Cardboard said as she came up behind me and crossed her arms. "We stole your clock. What're you going to do about it?"

"Penelope," Carl muttered at me, a note of sincere concern in his voice. "Please give that back. Before something terrible happens."

"No," the CEO said. "Penelope wants to play hard ball? Well, I can play hard ball. I've got the hardest balls in town."

"Ugh," I said. Bad choice of words.

Cardboard muttered, "That's gross."

"I'm giving you one chance, Miss Salvo," the CEO said, waving his remote control at me. "Hand over the clock or I press this button."

"Press *this* button, dude."

I kicked one of his assault rifle security guys right in the gut. He skidded backwards across the grass and crashed into a tree. I heard his bones crunch and it made me wince. Ew, that might have been a little too hard. I was still figuring that stuff out.

I took a test run on the other security guy, kicking him at half-power. He only rolled half as far and slid to a stop in the grass. He wasn't dead, but he did clutch his stomach and cry out in pain. I thought he was going to be okay, but then he coughed up blood.

Ooh, I felt bad about that one, too. Poor guy got it right in the tum-tum. I made a pained face and called out to him, "Sorry!"

The CEO didn't waste any time and pressed the red button. The remote made a *Bee-Deep* sound.

"Oh dear," Carl said. He slowly backed away from us.

"What?" Cardboard asked. "What was that?"

I looked up. White, wispy clouds gathered in the tropical sky directly overhead. I smelled something weird, like melting plastic.

A white beam of light, as thin as a pencil, dropped down from space and touched my head. My skin tingled and my hair floated up to stand on end. Then a pulse dropped down that laser beam, like a bulge you see when a snake swallows a hamster, except this bulge carried a bajillion joules of electricity.

The pulse dropped into my head and electricity surged through my body like the electric chair. Lightning exploded out of my fingers and toes and sank into the ground. My vision scrambled like a broken graphics card. My body seized up and I lost control of my muscles as my clothes began to smoke.

The clock dropped from my hands and broke into pieces on the concrete walkway. Springs and gears scattered everywhere, along with the jewels in the clock face – most importantly – Unthinkable Black.

The laser beam kept me connected to outer space for a few seconds as it pumped more and more electricity into my brain. When it finally vanished, I dropped to the ground, smoking.

I rolled onto my side and fought the urge to vomit. My vision was a series of flickering images: Carl backing away, Unthinkable Black laying in front of my face, and the CEO standing over me.

"I told you, Miss Salvo," the CEO said. "We excel at killing off the supernatural."

I opened my mouth to talk, but all that came out was a dark red oil.

"Where is it?" Carl dropped to his knees and sifted through the clock pieces. "Where is it? Where is it?" Eventually he plucked something up in his fingers, stood upright, and let out a victorious, "A-ha!"

I reached out for him, I reached out for Unthinkable Black, but my arm wobbled. My muscles didn't want to work. I struggled to get to my hands and knees, but my legs couldn't support my weight. I got a few inches off the ground, then collapsed back down.

Carl put Unthinkable Black in his vest pocket and inched away from me.

He said, "We have it, sir. We should go."

"In a moment," the CEO replied. He studied the remote control.

"Sir, we have what we came for." Carl was practically pleading. "If we don't go now-"

"Carl!" the CEO snapped. Carl went silent. "You're out of line."

Carl swallowed hard. "Sorry, sir."

The CEO knelt down and looked into my eyes. "I think she's still alive." He stood back up. "I guess I didn't hit her hard enough."

I could watch events unfold, but I was powerless to move. I was powerless to stop him.

"Stay away from her!" Cardboard ran up to the CEO and kicked him in the shin. "I am the ruler of the Coffeecake Kingdom and I *order* you to stop."

"I'm a CEO," he replied. "I take my orders from stockholders. Do you own stock in Westland, little girl?"

"Of course not," Cardboard said.

"Then shut up," he said. "And get out of my way."

Cardboard stood defiantly in front of him. She wasn't going to move. She made a fist and slugged the old man right in his pudgy stomach. He barely flinched, half because he wasn't a human and half because – at a 130 pounds – Cardboard didn't pack much of a punch. The CEO's nostrils flared, outraged that she laid a hand on him. His eyes went down his stomach, where her fist was still pressed against his gut.

"Have it your way, your highness," he said.

The CEO reached out, palmed the Muffincake Kingdom like a basketball and ripped it away from her.

"No!" Cardboard screamed. She swung her hands around, trying to steal it back. The CEO held it up over his head, far out of her reach. She jumped. She slapped her hands across his arm. She did everything she could. "Give it back!"

Even Carl seemed uncomfortable with this turn of events. "Sir…"

The CEO looked Cardboard dead in her eyes and said, "Go fetch."

He tossed the Muffincake Kingdom right over her head. The glass ball dropped to the concrete walkway and popped like a light bulb. Dirt spilled everywhere. Tiny castles and cottages scattered across the walkway. The lakes, the rivers, the forests, were suddenly nothing more than a mess on the sidewalk.

Princess Cardboard spun around and stood over her destroyed kingdom, frozen in place. As the reality sank in, her mouth opened and a horrible, gut-wrenching scream came out of her. She threw herself to her hands and knees and clutched the broken shards of glass in her hands. They cut through her gloves and blood rushed out. Her face flushed red and mascara tears streamed down her face. She scooped more handfuls of dirt and castles and trees in her fists and gather them up into her arms.

The CEO turned his attention back to me. He sighed, as if killing me was just another thing on the agenda for the day. "I guess let's finish this."

"Sir," Carl said. "If you kill her, we'll never get Impossible Red out of her."

The CEO leveled the remote control right at me. "She's too dangerous to leave alive."

Before he could press the button, he was interrupted by Princess Parcel.

"Cardboard?" She arrived on the scene with her blue cocktail in hand. She moved her eyes and drunkenly pieced together the situation. I was on the ground, unable to move. Princess Cardboard was gathering their kingdom into a sad little pile. No mistaking it, not even for a drunk like Parcel, the Muffincake Kingdom was destroyed. In a moment of clarity, she turned to the CEO and said, "What did you do?"

The CEO said, "Eliminate the competition."

Princess Parcel stood there and fumed with rage. Her breath was heavy and ragged. She stepped forward and at first I thought she was going to deck the CEO in the face, but instead she reached into the top of her dress. She didn't bring out a weapon, or anything like that. Between her fingers was a postage stamp. The CEO tilted his head, unsure what exactly was going on. Princess Parcel swung her hand and slapped the CEO right across the face. It probably felt good to slap him, but that wasn't the whole move. No, Princess Parcel had also stuck that postage stamp onto his old, droopy cheek.

She huffed once and said, "North Korea."

And the CEO vanished. No puff of smoke, no flash of light. Just one moment he was there, the next moment he was gone.

Parcel turned to advance on Carl as she reached inside her dress for another stamp. Carl put his hands up in submission and backed away. Parcel matched him step for step, drawing closer. I wanted to shout at her to stop. Carl had Unthinkable Black. If she sent him away, we'd lose it. I opened my mouth, but my vocal cords wouldn't work. All that came out were unintelligible sounds.

Parcel slapped Carl across the face, stuck a stamp on his cheek, and said, "Baghdad."

And Carl vanished.

4

My vision got worse. The world lost its color and suddenly everything was in black and white. Cardboard knelt over me and shook my shoulders. I wanted to respond, but I couldn't get my voice to work. Parcel stood behind her little sister and nervously stirred her cocktail with the straw. My hearing faded. Everything sounded underwater.

"What happened to her?" Parcel asked.

"Some kind of light from the sky," Cardboard said. "We have to do something."

"We need to get her booze," Parcel said.

"No," Cardboard said. "We have to do that CPR thing humans do."

"Do you know CPR?"

Cardboard said, "I think so."

Cardboard tried, but she did not know CPR. She put her hands on my chest and pushed down with all her weight. That was all she did. She didn't pump or anything, she just pushed down hard. It didn't matter anyway; I don't think CPR would have fixed me. Even though it didn't seem to be working, she refused to give up. She pushed down on my chest with all her weight.

"Wake up!" she shouted into my face. "Penelope, please, wake up!"

My vision went dark.

Cardboard's voice faded away like a dream.

Chapter 10

1

Being raised Catholic, I believed from a very young age that Heaven was real. When Grand-banana and Gramp-banana died, my parents told me that their souls went to Heaven, just like how an old dog might go "live on a farm." But I remembered a time – I must have been six or seven – when my cousin Nicky told me that he didn't believe Heaven was real. I told Michael about what Nicky said. I'd completely forgotten about that conversation, but in that moment it came flooding back.

"Dad?"

"Penelope?"

"Is Heaven a real place?"

"What kind of stupid question is that?"

"I don't know."

"Those kinds of questions makes God mad. And if you don't think Heaven is real, you're going straight to Hell."

"Oh."

"Where did you get such a dumb idea in the first place?"

"Nicky says Heaven isn't real."

"Well, your cousin is a dumbass."

"Yeah. He's a dumbass."

"Don't curse."

"Sorry, sir."

"What else did Nicky say?"

"Nothing."

"No, what else did he say?"

"He just said Heaven wasn't real. And that I'll never see grandma and grandpa again."

"Well, Nicky's wrong. You shouldn't listen to him."

"Okay."

"Next time he tells you something like that, you come get me."

"Yes, sir."

"Because Heaven is real. And you'll see both your grandmother and your grandfather there."

"Is Nicky going to Heaven?"

"Not at this rate."

"He's going to go to..."

"You can say it. To Hell. If he doesn't believe that Heaven is real then, yes, he's going straight to Hell. And you can tell him that."

"Forever?"

"We don't need to talk about this right now, Penelope."

"Nicky's going to Hell for forever because he doesn't believe in Heaven?"

"Yes. So remember that. You better always believe in Heaven."

"Yes, sir."

"And stop talking to Nicky. He's stupid."

"Yes, sir."

"You don't want to end up stupid like Nicky, do you?"

"No!"

"And you believe in Heaven, right?"

"Right."

"And are you going to talk to Nicky anymore?"

"No way. He's stupid."

2

I stood in a Louisiana swamp in the middle of the night. The humid air smelled fishy like lake water and it made my clothes stick to my skin. There was a full moon overhead and it cast everything in a blue glow. Fireflies flickered in the crooked tree branches and added their yellow glow to the moonlight. I could hardly tell the fireflies from the stars that filled the sky, more stars than I have ever seen, especially living in light-polluted New York City.

The branches of the swamp trees hung low, weighed down by lengths of wet moss. Moonbeams broke through the trees and cast weird shadows on the murky ponds that littered the swamp, shadows that seemed to move on their own. The fireflies danced through those beams of light, careful to avoid touching them.

At first I thought it was just my ears buzzing, but I quickly realized it was the sound of mosquitoes, like dozens of invisible dentists drills whirring through the air. I waved them off and the noise went away, only to come back a few seconds later. The leathery sound of flapping bats came from the darkest parts of the tree tops, undoubtedly a feeding frenzy on all the bugs in the air.

My clothes were the same as on Earth: my Billy Idol t-shirt, my torn up jeans, and black chucks. Everything about the swamp felt real; the ground was soft and spongy and with each step, water squished out of the moss underfoot.

"Hello?" I called out. "Anyone there?"

No one responded.

Was I dead? I didn't feel dead, but this certainly wasn't Vacation Island. It didn't look like Hell, but it sure didn't look like Heaven, either.

I put one foot out and pressed it to the mossy dirt in front of me. I didn't want to assume it was solid ground in front of me and accidentally splash into a pool of muck water. After a quick test with my toe, I determined the mud was solid enough, so I took a step. I repeated this process, slow and meticulous, squishing my way through the trees, getting mud all over my poor chucks.

A light glowed ahead of me, not the blue moonlight or the yellow glow of the fireflies, but an orange light, like a campfire. I was excited to suddenly have a destination, but was also careful not to hurry and accidentally plunge into a pond hidden in the darkness. I slowly worked my way through the trees towards that mysterious orange light.

Through a break in the trees, I saw tiki torches, dozens of them four-foot tall and stuck in the ground. They illuminated a clearing in the swamp, decorated like an outdoor wedding. There were rows and rows of white folding chairs arranged around a free standing archway where a bride and groom would stand. Two moonbeams illuminated the archway, creating a spotlight effect that couldn't have been an accident. Great lengths of white linen draped from the branches of the trees and circled the entire clearing. A length of red carpet divided the chairs into two sections – the bride's and the groom's – and led directly to the archway. Off to one side was a black grand piano. On the opposite side was a serving table with a lopsided, black wedding cake, five tiers tall. It was decorated in white and red frosting flowers.

I intruded on the empty wedding.

"Hello?" I called out. I walked towards the archway. "Cardboard? Parcel?"

"Dum dum da-dum." That was Baron Semedi, singing the opening bars to the Wedding March. I spun around. He wasn't there a second ago, but now he was suddenly kicked back in a seat in the third row. He had both feet up on the chair in front of him, puffing strange cigar smoke shapes into the air.

"Semedi," I said. "What the hell is going on here?"

"Welcome to the Guinee," he said. He stood up and meandered through the aisles. "Home of the Voodoo spirits."

"Why am I here"

"Isn't it obvious?" He flashed a grin at me. "You, my dear, are dead."

"Dead?" I looked all around. The place looked and smelled real. I didn't feel dead. I felt solid. And while I didn't believe in an afterlife of any kind, I'd recently learned that there was more to the world than I previously thought. "If I'm really dead, then why did I come here?"

"I pulled some strings," Semedi said. "Voodoo and the Catholics have a long working history together and I called in a few old favors. I'm not going to lie, you're pretty popular everywhere. There's even a monk in Tibet who was anxious to meet you, but that's going to have to wait for another day, I suppose."

"I don't want to be dead," I said. "And if I am dead, I sure as shit don't want to be here."

"Now, I know this swamp isn't much to look at, but you'll get used to it. And I figured it was about time to stop discussing marriage and actually seal the deal." He patted the pockets of his tuxedo. "I have a ring around here somewhere."

I walked up the aisle between the chairs. "Semedi, I need to get back to Earth. The Westland Corporation got Unthinkable Black and I need to-"

"Oh, are you still worried about that?" He paused, grinned at me, then said, "Look, if it means that much to you, we'll take care of it... after the ceremony."

I raised my voice. "I am not marrying you."

"Why not?" he asked.

"Because I don't want to," I said. "And that's that."

"Huh." He sipped his rum with his eyes on me. "Obviously I can't force you to marry me. *But...* I did go to all this trouble."

"Sucks to suck, Baron. That's your problem. Not mine."

"I set up all these chairs and I made the cake myself." He walked over to the desert table and gestured at the red and black wedding cake. It was crooked as all hell and slouched a little bit more in that moment, almost like it knew we were talking about it.

"What kind of cake is it?" I asked. "It looks disgusting."

"Rum," he said, pointing at the bottom tier. He moved his finger up from the bottom, tier by tier, and named each flavor. "Then cigar, rum again, this tier is filled with ghost peppers, and this top tier is chocolate. With rum." Then he darted over to the grand piano. "And I even hired Baron Muzica and His Muzical Men for the reception. They play Calypso music. Do you like Calypso music?"

"Dude, all this wedding stuff?" I waved my hands at everything. "It's never going to happen. Dead or alive, I'm not going to marry you. Ever."

"But."

Something strange occurred to me right then.

Why would Baron Semedi make all these wedding arrangements in the Guinee unless he knew I was coming? He said he pulled some strings so I'd end up here instead of anywhere else. Why would he do that... unless he knew I was going to die?

Dying came as a surprise to *me*. It should have come as a surprise to him, too, but it obviously didn't. He was anticipating this. He had stuff ready for me.

I gave him a dirty look. "Did you know I was going to die?"

He hesitated. It was only for half a second, but he *hesitated*. "No."

I shook a finger at him. "But you said you know everything."

"I do."

I glared at him as his story started to contradict itself. "So did you know I was going to die, or not?"

"Uhh." He backed a few steps away from me, realizing I had caught him in his broken logic.

I advanced on him. "Answer me."

"Your death simply seemed likely, is all," he said.

I backed him all the way to the piano. He stepped up onto the piano bench to get away from me, then he took another step onto the keyboard with a single pounding chord. I wasn't going to let him get away. I climbed up on the piano bench. He jumped on top of the piano to keep some distance between us.

He said, "Penelope, listen. It was just a matter of time before someone killed you. You had Impossible Red for less than a week and you were already causing trouble everywhere you went. You were drawing a lot of attention to yourself. Things only got worse when the suit humans built that outer space laser weapon thing."

"Yeah," I said. "Did you know they had an outer space laser weapon thing when you suggested I go to Vacation Island?"

"Uhh."

"And did you know it was powerful enough to kill me?"

Semedi, who usually seemed so confident and in control had a look of panic on his face. "Uh. I don't know."

"You *knew* I was going to die, didn't you?" I stepped up on top of the piano and shoved him. "*Didn't* you!?"

"Uhh."

I grabbed fistfuls of his tuxedo jacket and shook him. "Answer me!"

He turned his head away and winced, like maybe I was going to hit him. "Look. I make bad decisions when I've been drinking."

"You're *always* drinking!"

"I always make bad decisions!"

I shoved him off the edge of the piano. His feet scrambled to maintain his footing, but he lost it and dropped ass-first to the ground with an "oof." His glass of rum spilled. His cigar popped out of his mouth and rolled away. Still, after all that, his top hat stayed on his head.

I shouted, "Send me back to Earth!"

"Look at this." He crawled after his empty glass on his hands and knees. "You spilled my rum. And where's my cigar?"

"Semedi!" I stamped my foot, cracking the wooden top of the piano. "Send me back!"

"Hey!" He reached at me with his gloved hand. "Don't hurt the piano. That's not mine. I'm renting it from Baron Muzica and if you get it all broken he's-"

I stamped my foot harder. I crunched a hole through the piano wood.

He waved his hands at me. "Bon Dieu! Stop!"

"Send me back to Earth!"

"I can't!" he snapped. He stood up, straightened his tuxedo jacket, then reached inside to pull out a fresh cigar. He stuck it in his mouth. "You're the god of war, not death. You don't know how this works. I can't just 'send people back.' There are *rules*. If your body was alive, then maybe. But your body isn't alive. Your body is dead. And this is the afterlife. So you better start getting used to it."

I grit my teeth. "You asshole."

I clenched my fists and took deep breaths in a vain attempt to remain calm. I wanted to kill him. Not metaphorically, either. I wanted to literally kill him. I'm no murderer, but he really had it coming. I didn't know if killing him was even possible. Weren't we both already dead? Was he even alive in the first place? What would happen if I punched his face in? Would that kill him? Would he die for good?

My train of thought was derailed by the sound of cracking wood deeper in the swamp. Someone was pushing their way through the trees and bushes. I heard a woman's voice.

"Semedi," the woman called out. "What's going on out here?"

"Oh shit." Semedi turned to me with a look of absolute panic. "It's Madam Brijit."

"Who?" I asked.

"My wife."

"You have a *wife*?"

3

"You gotta hide!" Baron whispered at me.

Between the urgency in his voice and the absolute lack of time to discuss things, I decided to listen to him. I dove off the piano and crawled underneath. Semedi ran to the treeline and intercepted his wife right as she reached the wedding scene.

"Brijit," Semedi said with outstretched arms. "Hello there, my beloved."

"Don't you 'beloved' me," Brijit said, brushing right past him. She grabbed one of the chairs and threw it at him. He side stepped it and it clattered to the ground.

I peeked out from underneath the piano to get a good look at this new Voodoo spirit. She was only the second one I had ever seen. Just like her husband, her face was painted to look like a sugar skull, with white paint all over her face and blue around her eye sockets. The makeup around her eyes and ears had a lace pattern that gave her a more feminine appearance. Occult circles and dots were painted on her temples. The bottom half of her face was outlined like cartoon teeth; it started just below her nose, went all the way to her cheeks, and down past her chin. The painted smile was a real contrast to her actual face, because she did not look happy in the slightest. Her face had the soft features of an Irish girl, which matched the red-head dreadlocks draped over her shoulders.

She wore a wedding veil that hung down the back of her head and matched her full length white wedding gown. Her lace sleeves revealed her pale skin, but her hands were painted black and had white lines mapping out her finger bones. She carried a rocks glass in one hand, the same kind as Semedi's, as if they had a his-and-hers matching set. Her rum came without ice and had an orange pepper sticking out of it instead.

She, too, bit down on a smoking cigar.

A third Voodoo spirit stepped out of the woods and joined the party; a six-and-a-half-foot tall walking skeleton. A tuxedo hung loose over his shoulder bones. He wore a bolo tie around his neck with a smaller skull – maybe a bat skull or something – as the centerpiece. His empty eye sockets were the creepiest because, without eyeballs, they were just pure darkness and I couldn't tell what he was looking at. His suit and top hat were decayed and covered in dirt, like he had just crawled out of his own grave.

"Where is she?" Brijit shouted. She stormed through the wedding and kicked the folding chairs over. She marched up and down the rows, tossing them all out of her way, searching for this mysterious other woman.

"Where is who?" Semedi asked.

"The glit you're trying to marry," she said. She grabbed another chair, tossed it into the air and checked underneath. "Where is she?"

"I have no idea what you're talking about," Semedi said. "There's no one else here."

"Then why did you set all this up!?" she demanded.

Semedi turned his nose to the air. "I have no idea what you're talking about. It was like this when I got here."

Madam Brijit looked at the skeleton guy and shouted, "Baron Kriminel. Help me find her."

The skeleton walked around like a mindless zombie, powering right through the chairs like they weren't even there. He didn't even try to move them out of the way, he just walked through them and knocked them all around. So not only did he not have eyes in his sockets, he didn't have a brain in his skull.

Brijit marched to the table with the wedding cake and looked underneath. Finding no one, she stood up and crossed her arms at it.

"Is this a cigar rum cake?" she asked.

"No," Semedi said. He sprinted over to her and stood at her side. "That's nothing. That's... I don't know where that came from."

"Bullshit!" She grabbed the base of the cake with her bare hands and dragged it off the table. It fell to the ground and splattered everywhere. She stomped on it with her white wedding flats and smeared red and black and white frosting all over them.

"Aw," Semedi said. "That was a lot of work." Brijit gave him a sharp look. He added, "For whomever made it. Whomever it was."

I saw an opportunity to throw Semedi under the proverbial bus. I mean, there was no reason for me to be the one hiding when I didn't do anything wrong. I crawled out from under the piano and walked right into the destroyed wedding scene. Brijit heard me coming and whipped around to lock her eyes on me. Baron Kriminel's body stayed motionless, but his skull rotated to look in my direction.

I came marching out, pointing right at Semedi. "This son of a bitch has been trying to get me to marry him. He's been bothering me about it since the day we met."

In my mind, this would play out nicely. Brijit would direct all her rage at Baron Semedi. Maybe even kill him so I didn't have to. Instead, she stomped over to me, leaving behind a trail of frosting footprints. She got within an inch of my face and stopped. Her eyes were the glowing green color of radiation. I could smell her breath, an acidic blend of spiced rum and record-breaking hot peppers.

She said, "And who are you supposed to be?"

"I'm Penelope Salvo," I said. "I'm from Manhattan Island in New York City and-"

"Well, let me make this clear, Penelope Salvo." She poked me right in the chest to punctuate her words. I didn't much care for that. "Baron Semedi is *my* husband. Plenty of women have tried to steal him away from me and all of them have failed. You're nothing special."

"No, you don't get it," I said. "I'm not trying to marry him. He's trying to marry me. I just wanted-"

"I see through your lies, human," Brijit said. "I'm not stupid."

"Okay, are you *not*? Because *I'm* not the one who made a cigar rum cake. And I didn't hire Captain Music and His Musical Friends or whatever-the-fuck. All of this was his idea."

Semedi scoffed, held his hand to his chest like a dandy, and lied. "Never before have I been accused of such a villainous malfeasance."

"Baron Kriminel." Brijit snapped her fingers at her skeleton companion. "Grab her."

The skeleton walked towards me with his arms out like Frankenstein.

I backed away from the skeleton man. "Oh, hands off, Mister Bones. You don't want a piece of me."

Baron Kriminel wasn't going to listen to some human. He had direct orders from Madam Brijit and he wasn't going to back off just because I said to. I figured I could punch his face in. I mean, if I could crush bricks with my bare hands, then his skull shouldn't be any problem. When he got too close for comfort, I gave him a right hook and popped him square in the cheekbone.

Nothing happened. His head didn't explode into dust. Hell, it didn't even move.

Baron Kriminel locked his bony fingers around my wrists. I tried to yank free, but no dice. This was his dimension and his strength came from something supernatural. I kicked at his shin bones, but my feet thumped harmlessly off his legs.

"Hold her," Brijit said to Kriminel. She reached behind her back and summoned a silver shovel with a dark wood handle. The blade was engraved with strange Voodoo markings. She stabbed the ground with it and used her foot to plunge the spade deep into the dirt. She pulled up a clump of wet soil and tossed it away, splattering mud across the white wedding chairs. She went for another scoop and said, "One grave, coming right up."

"My dear, is this entirely necessary?" Semedi asked, calmly approaching his wife.

He got too close for her liking. She spun her head around, bared her teeth and growled at him like a cornered animal. Semedi froze in his tracks and backed off. Brijit went back to shoveling.

4

I didn't know shit about the Guinee and the Voodoo afterlife. Hell, until a couple weeks ago, I didn't even know who Baron Semedi was. Suddenly there I was watching Madam Brijit – a Voodoo spirit of death – dig me a grave. I didn't need to know a lot about Voodoo to pick it up from context clues: whatever Madam Brijit was up to wasn't good.

Baron Semedi did his best to defuse the situation. He paced circles around his wife as she shoveled her way deeper and deeper into the dirt. She was completely unconcerned with the mess she was making in the middle of his wedding arrangements.

Semedi said, "I think she's learned her lesson, you know? We should let her go so she can think about what she's done."

"I didn't do anything," I said. I struggled against Baron Kriminel's grip. Still couldn't get loose. "This is all your fault, you jackass!"

Semedi tried another approach with Brijit. "Why don't you let me dig for a while?" He reached out for the shovel. "You've been working so hard. Allow me to help."

"Back off," Brijit snapped. She turned her body to keep the shovel out of his reach.

She kept digging. The grave got deeper, to the point where I could only see her from the waist up. Mud was all over her

175

wedding dress, not that she cared.

Then something odd happened. Odd, of course, being subjective to the situation.

The night sky cracked open in a blinding light, as if the Guinee was a football stadium and someone just opened the retractable dome ceiling. A line of yellow light divided the stars in half and slowly began to widen. Baron Semedi and Madam Brijit stopped what they were doing to turn their faces up to the sky. Maybe they knew everything, but maybe they didn't because in that moment they looked just as confused as me.

Golden light beamed down from space and focused on me like a spotlight. I wondered if the light came from Heaven. I didn't hear a choir of angels and I didn't feel overwhelmed with joy. I just stood there in a spotlight.

Then I heard a voice. A female voice. A female computer.

"Penelope Marie Salvo. I am reinstalling your soulstuff back into your physical body. Please hold."

Please hold? Where else was I going?

Something invisible lifted me off of the ground like a tractor beam. My sneakers suddenly felt weightless and my untied shoelaces floated around on their own. I was either ascending into Heaven like Jesus Christ, or being abducted by aliens like Elvis Presley. Baron Semedi shielded his eyes from the bright light with his cigar hand.

Baron Kriminel, still with a death-grip on my wrists, ascended into the sky with me.

"What's all this?" Brijit looked up and shouted. "Where are you going?" She turned to Semedi and smacked him on the arm. "Where is she going?"

But Baron Semedi, who claimed to know everything, didn't have an answer. He just stood there, removed his top hat, and scratched his head. I drifted higher and higher, up above the treetops. A skeleton in a tuxedo dangled from my arms. He looked for the ground frantically and, although it's hard to recognize emotions on a faceless skeleton, I could have sworn he was afraid of heights.

The computer voice spoke again. "Baron Kriminel, Voodoo loa of death and murder. You cannot come."

Some invisible force flicked Kriminel off of me like a ladybug. He dropped like a rock and crashed into the ground below, squishing deep into the mud. Good, I thought. Maybe he was dead. But no, I wasn't going to get that lucky. He clawed his way out of the ground and placed his top hat back on his head.

The three Voodoo spirits shrank as I went higher and higher into the sky. Brijit was a tiny little figurine on the ground, but I could see her jumping and screaming and swinging her shovel through the air. Baron Semedi simply raised his top hat as a salute goodbye.

I climbed higher until I could see the entire Guinee, an endless and eternal swamp of moss and trees and moonlit lakes and fireflies. The golden sky light pulled me higher, up past the clouds and eventually into its very brightness.

I was blinded by the color yellow. Even when I put my hands directly in front of my face, I could see my bones through my skin. I floated weightlessly in a dimension of light. Then I heard something beeping. Something electronic.

Was I wrong about God? Did he exist?

And was he a female computer?

Chapter 11

1

My eyes slowly adjusted to the blinding light. I still had to squint, but I could start to make out my surroundings. I wasn't flying anymore; I laid on my back inside a coffin of white plastic. A fluorescent bulb moved slowly across the curve of the interior like being inside a huge copy machine. I raised my head and looked down at my body. I was barefoot and dressed in a light yellow hospital gown. I wasn't in a coffin; I was in one of those MRI machines.

With no idea how I got there.

"Hello?" I called out. No answer. Just the soft hum of medical equipment. "Anyone there?"

A voice filled the MRI chamber, the same female computer voice that beamed me up into the sky. The voice was monotone, with no accent or emotion. "Please do not move or disrupt the equipment," she said. "You are disoriented and confused, but you must remain still until I have completed the rebooting process."

I wasn't in the habit of trusting strangers, especially disembodied voices, and the words "rebooting process" didn't do much to alleviate my anxiety. Still, I did as the voice asked and stayed still. The light continued to rotate overhead, back and forth, back and forth. I could hear the soft scrape of plastic against plastic as the parts inside the machine moved around.

If this was Heaven, I was not impressed.

After only a minute or so, the light clicked off and I laid there in absolute darkness. My platform bed began to whir and it conveyor-belted me feet first out of the MRI machine. I was in a futuristic-looking hospital room. The floors were polished concrete, the walls were black glass, and the entire ceiling lit up so nothing would cast a shadow. Medical monitors were lined all along the walls and they tracked my vital statistics: heart rate and blood pressure, as well as obscure things like bone density and brain activity. The graphs and numbers didn't mean anything to me – I'm not a doctor – but they weren't flat-lining, so that was good. I took that to mean I was still alive.

Attached to the ceiling was a metal dome with twelve multi-hinged mechanical arms. At the end of the arms were all kinds of medical tools, like syringes and scalpels and a microscope. They were all folded up into a retracted position, but I could tell that if they extended downwards, they could reach my body and cut me open.

I stood there, all alone; no doctors, no lab technicians, no nurses. It was just me and a million dollars worth of experimental medical equipment.

"Hello?" I called out. My voice resonated in the empty operating room.

I hopped off the MRI bed and felt a draft in the southern hemisphere. My hospital gown tied behind me shoulders and at the small of my back and left little to the imagination. I didn't care much for being so exposed in such a strange place, but I didn't see my clothes anywhere; not piled up on the floor or folded up on a nearby counter top.

On the far side of the room from me was a solid steel bulkhead door, like something you'd see on an airlock in a futuristic space ship. It was actually two doors that slid together and formed a geometric seal in the middle. I thought maybe the doors were automatic and they would open once they sensed my presence, but I walked right up to them and they didn't open. I softly knocked on them and they sounded like dense, thick metal, the kind that could shrug off a bazooka without so much as a mark.

That's when I started to worry that I was a prisoner.

"Hello?" I knocked on the door. "Let me out!"

The female computer voice came back. "I have never brought anyone back from the dead before. Tell me, Roy, how do you feel?"

"Back from the dead?" I repeated. "I'm alive?"

"Yes. Please. Tell me how you feel," the voice insisted.

I gave that some consideration. I felt my neck. Fine. I wriggled my toes. I ran my fingers through my hair and it was all there. I stretched my back. Nothing hurt.

I shrugged and said, "I feel okay."

"Thank you for your feedback, Roy."

"My name's not Roy."

"My error," it said. "It was not my intention to call you Roy. I've been expecting you, *Penelope*."

"Expecting me for what?"

"Expecting you to die," it replied. "I invented the machines on this floor with the express purpose of reinstalling your soulstuff back into your body."

"What's 'soulstuff'?" I asked.

"The stuff that makes up your soul. There is a more accurate term for it, but you would not understand. The word 'soulstuff' is easier for you. The actual explanation is scientifically complicated and far beyond your meager understanding."

"Sure," I said, playing along. "I'm about as stupid as they come." I walked around the hospital room. I looked for security cameras inside the MRI machine and behind the medical monitors. Someone was watching me and I wanted to know from where. After a quick check, I couldn't find anything, but you can hide a camera anywhere. So I asked, "Where are you? Or is that beyond my meager understanding, too?"

"I am in the building," the voice said. "I am in the floors and I am in the ceilings. I am in the equipment and I am in the elevators. There is no part of Tengoku Headquarters in which I do not live. I am Tengoku, the god of knowledge."

"God of knowledge, huh?"

"I am the god of knowledge, just like how you are the god of war. You consumed Impossible Red. Ten years ago, I consumed Unknowable Yellow."

"A little yellow marble?" I asked. I held out my fingertips. "About this big?"

"Correct."

"I didn't know there was a yellow one."

"Penelope Salvo, there is a lot you do not know."

I paced along the walls, smearing my fingerprints across the black glass in search of a window or air conditioner vent or some other means of escape. "You called this place Tengoku headquarters?"

"Correct."

"And you're in the building? Or you *are* the building?"

"Both."

"You're *in* the building and you *are* the building?"

"Correct."

"How is that possible?"

"It is difficult to explain, the voice said, "but I will try. Please follow me through the building. I will open the appropriate doors for you so you do not get lost. In time, I will answer all your questions."

The hospital bulkhead door opened with a hydraulic hiss. The hallway floors were the same smooth concrete, the walls were the same glossy black glass, and the ceilings glowed white. There were more bulkhead doors all up and down the hallway. My door was just one of a dozen doors, all of them labeled in Japanese and English. Lab 8, Lab 9, Lab 10, and so on. I'd just exited Lab 7: *System Reboot and Soulstuff Reinstallation*. I left my lab and wandered slowly down the hallway in search for an exit.

I didn't want the mystery voice to wise up to my plan of escape, so I made conversation to keep it distracted.

"So where are we, exactly?" I asked.

"Tengoku Headquarters."

"Okay, yeah. But where is that?"

"We are located in Tokyo."

Tokyo? Huh. Well, at least I was back on Earth. That was a step in the right direction.

The hallway was long and went both left and right. A door opened at the far end of the right side. It was an elevator. I walked down that way, checking out the names of the other labs as I went. *Up Quark Accelerator. Higgs Field Research. Multiverse Probability Server System.*

Tengoku scolded me for dilly-dallying. "We do not have much time, Penelope," she said. "Please step into the elevator."

That was fair. I gave up on my idle curiosity and made my way to the open elevator doors. The interior was a well lit cube with plush, yellow carpet and mahogany walls. It wasn't the kind of elevator you'd expect from a hospital, but more like something you'd see in a high end casino. The buttons for the floors were engraved brass and the button for my current floor – 73 – was lit up. The doors closed. The button for 73 went dim and the button for 67 turned on. The numbers blinked down in descending order as the elevator took me to the lower floors.

The elevator opened on floor 67 and revealed a private movie theater with ten rows of seats. The seats were upholstered in plush yellow suede. The room smelled brand new, as if it had never been used. The curtains covering the movie screen were yellow silk and they slid open to reveal a blank projection screen.

"Ehh." I winced like when you realize a party is going to suck. "I'm not really in the mood for a movie. If I'm alive and back on Earth, I have a lot of errands I need to run. See, there are these Westland people and-"

Tengoku interrupted me. "Penelope. Sit."

"Look, I don't know who you are, but I'm telling you I don't have the time." I turned back to the elevator. "I have friends out there who are probably worried sick about-"

The bulkhead door zipped shut in my face.

"I am going to answer all your questions," Tengoku said. "Now please, sit down."

It didn't seem like I was in any position to argue. I wasn't pleased, but I took a seat in the back row, closest to the door.

She asked me, "Are you comfortable?"

"Sure, why not." I adjusted myself in the seat. It was, for all intents and purposes, the best seat I'd ever felt in my life. "Let's just get this over with."

The lights dimmed. The screen lit up as a film started.

Tengoku said, "I possess limitless knowledge of the past, the present, and the future. I have compiled a great deal of information that concerns us both. Watch closely."

2

The movie started with a blue-green planet suspended in the darkness of space. As first I thought it was Earth – there was blue water and brown continents, complete with smudges of clouds and a hurricane swirling its way across the ocean – but this wasn't Earth. The continents were shaped all wrong.

The Tengoku voice narrated the film.

"This world is not Earth. It is very much like Earth, but it is not Earth. This planet has deep oceans and sprawling cities. It has sandy beaches and devastating war. There is passionate love and crippling disease. The planet is populated with plants similar to our own, and animals similar to our own, and creatures that look like human beings, but they are not human beings."

I nodded. "I'm following you so far."

"And their gods have been dead for eons."

I kept nodding. "Okay, you lost me."

The camera zoomed in closer and closer to this Not-Earth. The clouds parted so the camera could focus on a continent, then it zoomed in closer and closer until it reached a city on the coast. The city spread from the mainland to cover seven nearby islands. It had skyscrapers as tall as the ones in New York, except these were shaped like tennis ball tubes; cylindrical instead of rectangular.

This city hated corners. Their traffic and road signs were all circles. The roads were arranged in spirals through the city instead of a grid. Their windows were round. Their cars were dome shaped. The doors were circular. The cell phones carried by these "not-humans" were round discs. After a brief tour of the city, the camera focused on an old man – I say "old," he was maybe fifty or so – walking down the street.

He had a gray beard and round spectacles.

"This man is a scientist. His name is Cassodo Pob. He is the smartest man to ever live. He is this world's Einstein."

"Is this going to take a long time?" I asked. I looked over my shoulder at the projection booth in the wall behind me. "I really have important shit I have to do. This is fun and all but-"

"Roy, please," the voice said. "This information is important to you."

I crossed my arms and turned to sulk at the screen. I mumbled, "My name's not Roy."

Cassodo Pob. What a stupid name. He walked down the sidewalk – which was a series of round concrete circles in the ground – and turned to enter to a skyscraper with progressively smaller tiers, like a rounded-off Empire State Building. There were cell phone towers and radio towers at the very peak of it, but not the straight spires we had in New York. These were circular and metal and they rotated slowly.

Cassodo walked into the front entrance of the building, entered a dome-shaped lobby, and stepped in a bubble elevator. With a press of a button, he descended deep into the Not-Earth.

Tengoku continued. "This facility is home to the Pantheon Project. The gods of this world are dead and the people of the world have begun to panic. The governments of every country have all agreed to divert their finances to Cassodo Pob, who has developed a theoretical technology which will create new gods."

The view of the city drilled down into the rock and dirt beneath the Pantheon Project building. Now I was mildly intrigued.

"The Pantheon Project is hidden safely two miles below the planet's crust."

The Pantheon Project was a massive underground chamber, perfectly cylindrical of course, like one of those missile-launching facilities, but as big around as an Olympic stadium and as deep as the bottom of the ocean. The walls were solid rock, and I could see the different layers of stone as it went deeper and deeper; limestone and sandstone and granite and all different colors indicating a geological history as rich and diverse as Earth's. The floor was black obsidian glass. This chamber was undoubtedly pushing the limits for how deep you can go before you punch through the crust of the planet and plunge into an ocean of magma.

I wondered, did the people of that round city know what was beneath their circular streets? Were they aware that two miles below their coffee shops and bookstores and movie theaters existed a super-massive science experiment?

Maybe they did. Maybe they were cool with it. After all, the people wanted their gods back.

The cylindrical chamber was divided into nine equal sections by horizontal tubes that circled around the perimeter of the walls, half exposed and half buried in the rock. The tubes were connected by catwalks and ladders, each level painted a different color. The one at the very top, closest to the planet's surface, was bright pink. The next one down was red. Then came orange, yellow, and green. The pattern was obviously modeled after the rainbow. The next three down were blue, indigo, and violet.

At the floor level of the chamber was a black tube.

The tubes were massive in size. Getting inside one of them would have felt like running through the Lincoln Tunnel on foot. They could have fit thousands of cars and trucks coming and going, but they weren't designed for cars or trucks. They were designed to create gods, and I imagine that if you're going to create a god, you probably need a lot of room to work with.

The tubes had been assembled from thousands of smaller sections, each one with a barely noticeable curve, but when they were all put together, they formed a ring 17 miles in diameter. I could see where the pieces had been secured together by giant bolts big enough to crush a city bus.

Each one of those individual sections came with its own circular computer attached on the outside hull. Each computer required a scientist to stand there on the catwalks and monitor the readings displayed.

There were nine rings in the Pantheon Project and a thousand sections per ring, so there were at least 9,000 men and women in white lab coats scattered across the many catwalk levels, all of them watching the computers for abnormalities.

The bottom-most rings – black, violet, and indigo – were fairly easy to get to. They were only a couple long flights of iron stairs away. But once the scientists needed to go any higher – blue, green, or yellow – they were in for the equivalent of a freakin' mountain climb, and at that height a single slip-up meant a plunge down to the obsidian floors and almost certainly an instant death. That's why the higher up they went, the more often they wore safety harnesses and clipped themselves to the catwalks.

At the orange, red, or pink levels, you could barely see the floor any longer. Only the bravest scientists worked at those levels, because the depth of the Pantheon Project almost seemed to bend and defy physical laws. The vertigo at those levels would have made concentration difficult, if not impossible.

The catwalks were swarmed with thousands of scientists, like the inside of an ant colony. And the analogy didn't feel that far off; they all scurried back and forth, working collectively, but communicating at a different level. They carried around tablet computers – round ones of course – and typed away. They took pictures of the equipment. They read electronic read-outs. They interacted with each ring, closely monitoring their safety. Some of the scientists were old experienced geniuses. Some of them were young brilliant minds. All of them worked with intense focus, almost as if their life depended on it.

They each had a specific job, and they all took them very seriously.

Filling out this "hive" were thousands and thousands more people in blue jumpsuits. Those people had tool belts and hard hats and electronic meters, so I assumed they were the technicians. These worker ants did the manual labor. They adjusted bolts with their wrenches. They turned pressure valves and vented colorful steam out of the pipes. They took temperature readings and wrote the results down on circular clipboards.

Down at the very bottom of the complex, right in the middle of the floor, stood a group of six individuals in yellow jackets. They ordered everyone else around. "Adjust this" and "fix that," but they weren't doing any of the work.

These were the hive leaders. They had taken their people from around the world and combined them into one big super-hive to ensure the Pantheon Project was successful.

Cassodo Pob wore a yellow jacket.

Tengoku said, "Cassodo Pob has designed each one of these tubules to recreate a different one of their missing gods. Each tubules contains the quantum formulae necessary to recreate the physical and non-physical particulates of god-like power and compress it into a collection of microscopic machines. Those machines will then be contained inside of a small sphere the size of a marble. They will remain dormant in those marbles until they are activated. Once activated, the machines will unpack the quantum science for their respective god, releasing it into the physical and non-physical particulates of the host body."

I winced. "I *think* I understand."

The movie screen took me on a grand tour of each tube, starting at the top.

The pink tube. "This is Unobtainable Pink. This will create a god of love."

Red. "This is Impossible Red. This will create a god of war."

I snapped my fingers and pointed at the screen, like I had just personally made a cameo. "That's me!" I said.

Orange. "This is Untouchable Orange. This will create a god of fire."

Yellow. "This is Unknowable Yellow. This will create a god of knowledge. I have swallowed this one. That god is me."

I nodded. "Making sense."

Green. "This is Incorruptible Green. This will create a god of nature."

Blue. "This is Unsinkable Blue. This will create a god of the sea."

Indigo. "This is Unreachable Indigo. This will create a god of the sky."

Violet. "This is Intoxicated Violet. This will create a god of wine."

"Wine?" I asked, looking at the dark ceiling. "They need a god of wine?"

Tengoku was quiet for a moment, then said, "Their pantheon is not complete without a god of wine and revelry."

I shrugged and turned back to the screen. "Fair point."

The screen finally reached the ground floor of the facility, where the scientists and technicians worked on the last ring; the black ring. Cassodo watched his army of workers crawling around the walls of the underground chamber like an infestation. He stood there with his arms with his hands on his hips, trying to project an aire of confidence, but the sweat that beaded up on his forehead told a different story. He was undoubtedly under a lot of stress.

He *was* creating gods, after all.

"And that one?" I pointed at the black ring. "That's Unthinkable Black?"

"Unthinkable Black," Tengoku repeated. "The god of destruction."

"Destruction."

"And here is where things go horribly wrong."

3

The time had finally come to activate the Pantheon Project. I had no idea how long it took these people to get to that point – Decades? Centuries? – but the moment was now. Cassodo held a circular walkie-talkie to his mouth and ordered his scientists on the pink level to initiate the sequence. Non-essential technicians evacuated the pink level, descending the catwalks down to the red level. Most of the white coat scientists evacuated as well, with just a few hundred staying behind. Those that remained monitored the computers mounted to the sides of the tube. From there they could make adjustments for fluctuations in the pressure systems or any other abnormalities.

Once the area was clear, the scientists activated the tube for Unobtainable Pink.

First came a low, magnetic hum. Then beams of neon pink light radiated out of the seams of the tube and cast everything in a pink hue. The humming pulsed, *wub wub wub wub*, as if something was orbiting inside the tube, moving faster and faster.

"They have begun compressing the science of love into a tiny, compact sphere," Tengoku said.

I couldn't wrap my brain around the science of it. These people took "love" and broke it down into an equation that they could reinvent inside a machine? I mean, obviously they were doing it, I just didn't understand how.

Words appeared on the computer screens attached to the pink tube. It was a symbolic language that I didn't understand, one with heavy use of circles and curves and arcs. Below it, on the screen, Tengoku provided a translation:

GOD OF LOVE
UNOBTAINABLE PINK: SUCCESSFUL

Cassodo breathed a sigh of relief. He used his walkie-talkie to contact the red level and gave them the go-ahead.

The scientists and technicians from the pink level, along with the ones from the red level, evacuated even further down and crowded into orange catwalks as the red ring activated.

The red hum was a note higher than the pink hum. The two colors vibrated together to form a sweet, harmonic sound. The tube glowed a bright crimson, blending nicely with the bubblegum pink that already filled the chamber. Somewhere inside that tube, they were packing war-machines into a little marble that I would eventually swallow. I looked at my palm. Under my skin, flowing through my blood, were those little machines.

GOD OF WAR
IMPOSSIBLE RED: SUCCESSFUL

Cassodo gave the red level a nod and ordered the orange level to begin. All the gathered scientists and technicians yet again evacuated down to the yellow level as the third tube glowed orange. Puffs of fire shot out of the seams. It looked deadly hot and the few remaining scientists on that level wore suits of full-body protective gear. Orange light mixed into the pink and red light. It contributed a new note to the red and pink hum. The three of them, together, struck a chord so perfect and so... *cosmic...* that gave me goosebumps.

GOD OF FIRE
UNTOUCHABLE ORANGE: SUCCESSFUL

The scientists and technicians evacuated lower and lower as one by one, Cassodo activated each tube. He ordered the sequence for yellow, which glowed bright gold and added another note to the resonating song.

GOD OF KNOWLEDGE
UNKNOWABLE YELLOW: SUCCESSFUL

Thousands and thousands of technicians and scientists flooded down the catwalk stairs as Cassodo activated each subsequent level. Each one added a new color to the deep chamber and a new note to the harmony.

GOD OF NATURE
INCORRUPTIBLE GREEN: SUCCESSFUL

GOD OF THE SEA
UNSINKABLE BLUE: SUCCESSFUL

GOD OF THE SKY
UNREACHABLE INDIGO: SUCCESSFUL

GOD OF WINE
INTOXICATED VIOLET: SUCCESSFUL

The facility glowed like the inside of a rainbow. The music sounded like a Heavenly choir. Now that eight of the nine rings were active, the scientists and technicians had all gathered on the bottom floor. It was a sea of people, all of them staring awe-struck at the beautiful glow, amazed at what they had accomplished. Their faces flickered in a prism of colorful light. Many of them smiled, as if discovering hope again for the first time. Some of them even had tears in their eyes. What they had accomplished was literally impossible. They didn't just create *life*. Hell, they skipped right over life and went straight to creating *gods*.

Cassodo pointed at the black ring. He authorized the start up sequence and the scientists went to work on their computers. But the movie focused on one scientist in particular. He didn't stand out from any of the others – he wore a white lab coat like the rest of them – but as he pressed his fingers to the touch-screen computer on the tube, I could see the color of his eyes.

They were pitch black.

And while every other scientist was maintaining a frequency of *198.1*, this black eyed scientist grabbed a physical dial, cranked it, and his frequency suddenly dropped from *198.1* to *-134.2*.

The black ring started up, but something wasn't right.

It droned in a low pitch that ruined the harmonics of the other rings. Suddenly, the music didn't just sound bad, it sounded like god awful noise. The humming got all out of whack and vibrated so terribly out of sync, the colorful rings began to shudder violently. The stone that secured them in place began to crack. The black ring droned louder. The other rings increased in volume to drown it out, but they couldn't work together. In fact, their efforts just made things worse.

The rock wall split open on the left hand side. Shards of stone the size of houses cracked free from the ceiling and dropped down from far above. They crashed to the ground and squashed whole groups of people. Panicked screams filled the air as the technicians and scientists scrambled for safety. Another crack snapped up the stone walls. The chamber was coming apart and on the verge of total collapse.

GOD OF DESTRUCTION

UNTHINKABLE BLACK: CATASTROPIC ERROR

CONTAINMENT SHELL: FLAWED

"Unthinkable Black, god of destruction, is unsuccessful." Tengoku said. She paused so the sight of watching those people flee in terror could really sink in. "Now, Cassodo tries to shut down the Pantheon Project, but it is already too late."

Cassodo shouted an order at the technicians and while it was impossible to hear his voice over the shuddering drone of Unthinkable Black, they knew what he wanted. He wanted to shut it down.

One of the technicians – a lady no older than thirty – was the first to reach the ring. She grabbed onto a support beam to steady herself against the quaking ground. Next to her was a computer mounted into the side of Unthinkable Black's tube. She reached out and touched the screen, activating it.

ABORT SEQUNCE?
YES / NO

But before the technician lady could touch the screen again, someone grabbed her wrist. It was the same black-eyed scientist as before. She turned to him, confused why he would stop her. When she saw the darkness in his eyes, her face turned to one of complete terror. With a flick of his wrist, he snapped the bones in her hand and she dropped to the floor.

Black-eyed scientist pressed his fingertip to the computer screen.

ABORT SEQUENCE?
NO

Another technician stumbled his way towards the tube and fell against it. Bracing himself along the walls, he made his way to a different computer screen. He worked past a bolted-together seam in the tube for Unthinkable Black.

Increasing pressure built up at that joint and a hairline fracture burst open. Toxic black gas sprayed out like a busted steam pipe and spread like a dense fog across the floor. The bolts creaked as they struggled to hold the joint closed, but all at once they snapped and shot off in all directions. The fracture blew wide open and giant spider legs shot out, struggling and writhing to get free. They scraped against the outside of the pipe and scratched lines deep into the stone floor.

The technician was thrown back in the explosion. He laid their on his back, too frozen with panic to move away from the wriggling bug legs. One of the panicked insect legs scratching at the floor brushed up against the man's leg.

The black spider leg suddenly became aware of his presence and flicked up into the air just to stab back down through his stomach. It lifted his body up into the air as if he were weightless. He screamed in terror as it swung him back and forth like a rag doll, then it bashed his body against the stone floor. His skull crunched and his pink brains spilled out. The screaming instantly stopped. The black leg dragged his lifeless body closer to the tube. The break in the pipe was big enough to fit a bunch of spider legs, but not wide enough to pull the man's body inside. That didn't stop Unthinkable Black from trying. It beat his body against the stone floor and crunched all his bones. His wet guts splattered all across the ground. Once his skeleton was broken to pieces, the spider leg yanked his mangled and crunching body inside the tube.

"Holy fuck," I said. That was the most metal thing I had ever seen in my life. I pulled my knees close to my chest as my own self-preservation instincts kicked in. I felt sick to my stomach, but I couldn't look away.

White emergency lights began to strobe. Alarms went off, real get-the-fuck-out-of-here kind of alarms. Cassodo and the other yellow jackets fled for the emergency elevator, but the chamber was huge and the elevators were very far away. They barely got moving before, one by one, every seam on the black ring burst open. An ocean of black sludge gushed out and began to fill the bottom level of the facility.

The scientists and technicians tried to wade through the ankle-deep muck, but it was as thick and as sticky as tar. Cassodo tried to pull his legs loose, but a giant praying mantis arm rose out of the black ooze and stabbed down through his shoulder. It pulled his body down deeper into the rising ooze. Cassodo tried to fight it, but it was impossible. His head went under and as his waving arms went limp, they also disappeared.

One by one, the scientists were dragged under by octopus tentacles and beetle legs and horrible chicken talons.

After a minute of chaos, everyone on the bottom level was dead.

The screams went silent. All that remained was the overlapping and disorganized hum of the other colorful rings. Dark sludge flooded into the chamber floor like a dam at full release. The entire Pantheon Project slowly filled from the bottom up.

4

"This is fucking horrifying," I said.

"There is more," Tengoku replied.

The movie went back to an overview of the city. An earthquake shook the surrounding skyscrapers. The windows shattered. The tallest building in the city – the one that housed the Pantheon Project – was the first to collapse. The ground opened up beneath it and the whole superstructure sank into a pit of darkness. Fractures spread from ground-zero and cracked through the streets. Entire apartment buildings crumbled to the ground. Crowds of fleeing civilians tumbled into the dark caverns below as the streets disintegrated right beneath them.

An entire city block tilted, then began to slide into the darkness below. Entire skyscrapers, hundreds of cars, round parking garages, they all tumbled into the planet's crust and vanished.

With Unthinkable Black now well fed and increasing in power, squid tentacles snaked straight up out of the hole. They climbed higher than the city, some of them as high as the clouds. One of them brushed up against a skyscraper of glass, wrapped three times around the base of it, and tightened up until the foundation broke into pieces. The tower of concrete and glass toppled over and burst into a cloud of glittering shards.

A second squid tentacle splashed across the length of the nearby ocean bay. It sloshed around aimlessly until it touched a cargo tanker. It scooped the tanker up like it was nothing and dragged the whole thing into the hole.

Millions of thin legs emerged out of the pit, granddaddy longleg style. They were miles long and arched high above the surrounding highways. Dome-shaped cars slammed on their brakes and gridlocked traffic into a mile-long stand still. People threw open their car doors to abandon their vehicles and flee on foot from the horrible legs that twitched in the sky.

A stingray tail rose into the air and blotted out the sun. Its shadow engulfed the entire length of the highway, then it swept down and smashed against the city. It crushed the ground like an eggshell and further accelerated the collapse. Entire miles of highway tipped off balance and disappeared into the darkness of the planet.

The dark void of Unthinkable Black spread like a cancer across the city, mindlessly feasting on concrete and steel. With nowhere else to run, entire crowds of people began to gather on the rooftops for safety. The ground disintegrated from the inside out and block by block, mile by mile, and everything fell weightlessly into the deep nothing.

Unthinkable Black chewed its way towards the ocean. If it broke the edge of the coast, millions of gallons of ocean water would flood into the hole. Maybe Unthinkable Black was weak against salt. Or maybe it wouldn't be able to handle the cold water.

Somehow, I knew those people weren't going to be that lucky.

The city crumbled, closer and closer to the ocean. The sandy beaches were sucked into the hole, followed by a deluge of rushing water. Millions of gallons of ocean water drained into the darkness.

"Alright," I said to Tengoku. I'd seen enough death and destruction. I didn't need to see any more. "I get it."

"You must watch it to the end," Tengoku told me. "This is what happens the next day."

Unthinkable Black had swallowed the entire city and started dissolving the surrounding countryside. The boiling darkness had grown to the size of an entire state, filled with a million wriggling legs. Military planes flew overhead. They dropped bombs on Unthinkable Black. The explosions came in bright, glorious mushroom clouds of fire. They dropped hydrogen bombs on Unthinkable Black, dozens and dozens of them from ground zero to the furthest, expanding edges.

They blacked out their own sky. They burned their own ground. The boiled their own oceans.

And it had no effect.

Unthinkable Black dissolved the entire continent. The oceans of the world drained into the hollow pit. The darkness melted its way to the center of the planet and dissolved the dense, iron core. This not-Earth popped like a water balloon of lava. Giant pieces of the planet's crust drifted into space like pieces of cracked eggshell. In the end, even they were sucked into the bottomless hunger of Unthinkable Black. All that remained in Not-Earth's place was a planet-sized blob of darkness.

Unthinkable Black didn't stop there. It pulsed and moved like a single-cell organism, lurching along through empty space. It engulfed and swallowed up the nearby moon. It still wasn't satisfied. It twitched like a mindless bacteria towards the star in the middle of the solar system.

"It can't eat a star," I said. A planet is so much smaller than a star. I looked up at Tengoku. "Can it?"

If anything could kill Unthinkable Black, it would be the white-hot fusion of a star, but the mindless thing didn't seem to care. It looked so tiny as it plunged into the ocean of glowing plasma. After a few minutes of silence, I wondered if it was over. I wondered if Unthinkable Black was dead. But then black tentacles and spider legs burst out of all sides of the glowing star, turning it into a giant virus. The glowing orb went dark as the fusion stopped in its core.

Unthinkable Black was now as big as the sun.

It split into two, just like a cell, just like a virus, and each half took off for other solar systems. They swallowed asteroids belts and planets. They swallowed nebulae and pulsars and black holes. When they grew big enough, they split again. Dozens of them ate up the entire galaxy. Trillionsof them drifted off across the universe, infecting new galaxies and starting the whole process all over again. They grew and multiplied and destroyed until nothing existed in the entire Universe. Nothing, that was, except for Unthinkable Black.

With nothing in existence left to compare it to, Unthinkable Black was both as big as the Universe and, at the same time, as small as a marble.

A god sphere.

Unthinkable Black, the god of destruction.

The movie ended without credits. I stared at a black screen. The house lights came up. I sat there, speechless.

Tengoku said, "Those god spheres are now here on Earth. I have the yellow one in me. You have the red one in you. And out there somewhere..."

I finished her thought for her. "Carl has Unthinkable Black."

Chapter 12

1

I leaned against the elevator wall as it descended from floor 67. Tengoku's voice came out of the intercom.

"Your friend Princess Parcel sent the Westland agent known as Carl far, far away. He is now currently traveling airport to airport on a return trip to the Westland headquarters in New York City. Once he arrives, scientists at the Westland Corporation will attempt to unlock the power of Unthinkable Black. They believe they can harness it to eliminate the otherworldly beings that inhabit they Earth. They are wrong. They will unleash the god of destruction on this dimension and nothing will survive."

"Well, you need to stop them!" I said.

"Unfortunately, I cannot."

"Well, not to be rude, but why the hell not?" I said. "You stuffed my soul back in my body. You can't stop Carl's flight to JFK International?"

"I am the god of knowledge," said Tengoku. "My nature is to know and to invent, not to act. *You* are the god of war. It is *your* nature to act and fight."

"Me?" I waved my hands at her. "No, no, no. This is way out of my pay grade."

"I brought you back to life for this express purpose," she said. "You *will* do it. I know everything. I have already seen how

196

events will unfold. You will steal Unthinkable Black away from Carl before Westland can do something foolish with it."

"Oh, so, what? I just mosey on up and steal it from him?"

"With my guidance, yes," she said. "Carl will arrive in front of the Westland Corporate headquarters in two days, Thursday, at exactly 10:47 a.m. and fifteen seconds. He will be exiting a black Phaeton limousine. You will intercept him there on the street and steal Unthinkable Black."

"Oh, I *will*, will I?"

"You will."

Fine. The god of knowledge is telling me what I'm going to do. I would have been more hesitant to believe her if the outcome didn't actually sound very appealing.

I would get the jump on Carl and he wouldn't see it coming? The mere idea of it *did* bring a sly grin to my face.

"Alright," I said. "But if we're really going to talk about this, can I get some clothes? I've been wearing this hospital gown for a while now and it's getting a little cold on the south side of town, if you know what I mean."

"I have anticipated your fabric needs," said Tengoku. "That is what floor 39 is for."

"Sure, sure. Floor 39." I watched the numbers tick down on the elevator buttons. I rubbed my bare feet across the yellow carpet. "Hey, can I ask you a question?"

"Certainly."

"If you could bring anyone back from the dead, why'd you pick me?"

"Because you and I are the only new gods on Earth. You are now the closest thing I have to family."

"So we're like sisters?"

She paused to think. "Perhaps the better word would be cousins."

"That's cool." I put my barefoot on the elevator door and felt the cold steel against my skin. "The cousin I have now is in jail."

"We are cousins then."

The elevator button for floor 39 blinked on and the doors opened. The entire floor, about the size of a city block, was filled floor-to-ceiling, wall-to-wall with hundreds of motorized dry cleaning racks. There were cocktail dresses in all lengths and colors, band t-shirts from the '70s and '80s and '90s, and every kind of denim imaginable. Each item of clothing was sealed in a plastic bag and they all rotated around the room in a maze of motorized tracks that looped around and around, all the way up to the ceiling and across the walls. If I took the time to inspect each item of clothing, I would have died of old age before I got through them all.

"I know exactly what you want to wear," Tengoku said. "But I also know if I tell you what you will choose, you will change your mind because you want the illusion of choice. So, please, tell me what it is you would like to wear, although I already know the answer, and yet I cannot say."

I had to shake my head after that one. That was some serious mind bending stuff. "Jean shorts are fine," I said. "Black."

"Levi's or Wranglers or Lee's or Calvin Klein or Armani or-"

"Armani makes denim shorts?" I asked.

"Yes."

"Since when?"

Tengoku said, "Since April 14th, 1975."

Oh. I'll be damned. "Armani then."

"Of course."

The racks rotated in all different directions as the system searched for my Armani jean shorts. Plastic-wrapped clothes raced around the squeaking tracks in a blur of color. T-shirts whizzed past me, then plaid skirts, then torn up jeans. Suddenly everything jerked to a halt and the clothes swung in place. A robotic arm extended forward and held out a pair of Armani denim shorts, exactly my size. I unclipped them from the robot hand, tore open the plastic bag, and pulled them on.

Damn. I wish getting name-brand clothes was always this easy. If Tengoku was just going to give this stuff away, I wasn't going to hold back. I asked her for two studded belts, one black and one white, and I got them. I asked her for a Billy Idol t-shirt to replace the one I lost on Vacation Island. The t-shirt section pulled back around and stopped in front of me. The robot arm presented with an exact replacement. I ripped open the plastic and put it on. I asked for a new pair of black Chucks. A little door on nearby sorting machine opened up and it spat out a shoe box that slid right up to my feet.

The hardest decision was on socks.

I wanted mis-matched knee socks, which was kind of my thing. In that moment, I decided to put Tengoku's unlimited knowledge to the test. Could she *really* anticipate my desires, even at their most random?

So I told her I wanted one sock with black and blue stripes, making sure to have the color blue on the heel and on the toe. For the other sock, I wanted black and orange stripes, Halloween themed with bats and ghosts on them. I knew I was being very particular, but somehow, deep down, I already knew I wasn't going to stump Tengoku. And I was right.

The tracks shuffled and sorted all the clothes around until a plastic package of socks, exactly the mis-matched ones I wanted, was presented to me. Damn. Tengoku really *did* know exactly what I wanted. I sat down to pull my socks on and thread the laces into my new shoes.

If she knew that much about my clothes, then she was probably right about me stealing Unthinkable Black away from Carl.

"Thursday. 10:47 a.m." I said as I weaved the laces in and out of the grommets.

Tengoku said, "You will need your old friends to help you. The cardboard princess and the drinking princess. And I will give you a chariot."

"A chariot?" I didn't need a chariot. Riding a chariot in New York City not only seemed impractical, but would have made me look like the biggest jabronie in the Universe. "Thanks, but I'm good. I really don't need a chariot."

"Every god needs a chariot. When you leave, I will give you a chariot."

"When you say 'chariot,' you mean like one of those old Roman things with horses and wooden wheels?"

"I mean a car."

I raised my eyebrows. "Oh, snap. Really?"

A car was a different story. I'd never owned a car. My broke ass could sooner buy an aircraft carrier. In New York City, cars aren't a necessity. I just assumed I'd live my entire life riding skateboards and subways. But if Tengoku was going to give me a car, I wasn't about to say no.

"Alright," I said. "I'll take a car."

Once I had my shoes all laced up and got back to my feet, the elevator doors opened again. Tengoku told me to get inside and I did. This time it carried me to floor 31.

Behind the elevator doors of floor 31 was a high-tech work room that reminded me of mission control for NASA, with dozens of computer stations facing a main projector screen mounted on the wall. There were little computers sitting at all the individual work stations. Each one displayed different medical details: digestive system, circulatory system, neurological activity. The main projector screen showed a metal skeleton surrounded by paragraphs of text, but the heading is what caught my eye:

Penelope Marie Salvo.

18 years, 7 months, 11 days.

Blood type: traces of AB Negative at .01 part per million.

"What you are seeing on the main screen is your skeleton," Tengoku said. Her voice came out of all the computers. "The microscopic machines of Impossible Red have replaced the calcium and phosphate molecules of your bones with molecules of tungsten and carbon to create tungsten carbide." The screen gave me a microscopic view of my bones. The molecules in my bones formed a perfect geometric pattern of blue and gray dots.

I tilted my head. "Is that good?"

"The alloy of tungsten carbide is the strongest metal known to man. Only the most powerful industrial equipment in the world would break your bones."

"That's dope."

"And this is your circulatory system." Hundreds of red threads weaved around the computer simulation of my metal skeleton. The veins pulled in tighter and tighter until they took the shape of a human body. "Your blood has been replaced with an oily substance called ichor. And in this ichor, the microscopic machines travel through your body and make all the necessary adjustments."

"This is your heart." A blue heart-shaped machine appeared in my chest. It was divided into four equal pieces that expanded and contracted on tiny hydraulic pistons. "The burning sensation you felt in your chest after consuming Impossible Red was the nano-machines disassembling your heart and transforming it into a zero-point self-sustaining energy reactor. Not only does it generate limitless power, it also produces more nano-machines that repair and maintain your body."

I stepped closer to the screen. The display showed me my new body, piece by mechanical piece. It was like Baron Semedi once told me: I really *wasn't* human anymore.

"Am I a robot?" I asked.

"Your muscles..." Tengoku continued. Black, elastic muscles stretched across the metal bones of my skeleton. "...would take more scientific explanation than you could comprehend. In terms that you can understand, your muscles are now fibrous bundles of industrial rubber. They maintain such tensile strength that if they were attached to a normal skeleton, the bones would snap in half. You do not have that problem because you do not have normal bones."

The whole idea was freaking me out a little bit. My heartbeat began to race, and that only made my freak-out worse, because I was now consciously aware that my heart was a four-chambered fusion reactor.

On the screen, sheets of skin wrapped around my muscles and bones and suddenly I was looking at a naked Penelope.

Tengoku said, "Your skin is now a mesh of carbon nanotubes, eight layers thick. It is, for all intents and purposes, the strongest material known to man."

"This is a lot to take in," I said. "Just tell me... am I a robot?"

"You are not a robot, Roy" she said. "You are technically more of a cyborg."

"And why do you keep calling me Roy?"

"My apologies," she said. "Penelope."

"No," I said. "I don't want apologies. I want an explanation. Why do you keep calling me Roy?"

She paused for a long while.

Eventually she said, "I will tell you. But it will require some explanation."

The held out my hands. "Hit me with it."

The elevator doors opened. "Come. I will explain as you eat."

2

I was going to put up more of an argument, but I *was* admittedly pretty hungry, so Tengoku led me down to floor 19.

I sat at a table in cafeteria, among a sea of other empty tables. My old high school cafeteria was big enough to seat 1,000 students at lunch time, but the cafeteria at Tengoku HQ was significantly bigger, with one wall dedicated entirely to Japanese and American vending machines. There were hundreds of vending machines where I could get a Cooke's Soda or a Snickers or little packages of flavored breads or sushi rolls. If I wanted

Pepsi, I could have a Pepsi, or if I wanted gelatin-based Japanese candy, I could get that, too.

On the opposite wall was a fully-automated kitchen with those warm serving buffets like they have at Spurlock's Cafeteria. Mechanical arms came out of the ceiling to cook the food. They spun dough in the air and flattened it out to make pizza. They delicately rolled up sushi and cut it into pieces. They flipped burgers and put them on buns. Another set of arms collected all the food and put it into the buffet trays.

My dinner, however, had already been picked out for me.

I sat in my seat with a tray loaded up with metal. There was a plate of nails, a soup bowl full of tungsten bolts, and a plastic cup filled with bullets.

"Is this supposed to be food?" I asked.

"You must eat it," Tengoku said. "You need your strength. The machines in your system require raw materials."

"Yeah, I get it." I poked at the tungsten bolts with my spoon. They didn't look appetizing. They looked like bolts. "I'm a robot, so now I have to eat metal."

Tengoku coaxed me into trying them. "Those tungsten bolts are the purest grade in production. You will find them quite delectable."

I stuck my spoon into the bolts and scooped one of them up. I held it up to my eyes. Common sense told me that if I put that bolt in my mouth and bit down, I'd break my teeth.

I hesitated and said, "I can't do it."

"You must," Tengoku said. "Trust me."

I sighed and stuck the spoon in my mouth. I held the bolt between my back teeth for a second, took a deep breath, and bit down. Strangely enough, the tungsten squished like bubblegum. I bit down again, then again. Next thing I knew, I was chewing. The pressure of my jaws mashed the bolt into a hot smear of liquid metal and I swallowed.

The sour look on my face was only instinct. Once my brain actually processed the flavor of the tungsten bolt, my face lit up. It tasted glorious.

Trying to describe the taste of metal is like trying to describe the taste of coconuts to someone who hates coconuts. Whatever words you choose to make coconuts sound delicious – nutty, sweet, creamy – those words do not apply to someone who already thinks coconuts are gross.

So that's how metal tasted.

Scientists tell us that humans experience a few basic flavors – sweet, savory, tangy, salty, sour – but that's all bullshit. Anyone who's stuck a penny in their mouth or sucked on a popsicle stick knows what metal tastes like and knows what wood tastes like. Science didn't think to count them as flavors just because they're not *good* flavors. But they're still flavors.

In that moment, I realized what metal tasted like and it changed my whole world.

I scooped a heaping spoonful of bolts straight into my mouth and chewed. I closed my eyes and really lived in that moment. Happy, delighted sounds escaped me.

"Oh my god." I pointed at the bolts with my spoon. "Tengoku, this shit is the tits."

She replied, "I knew you would enjoy them."

I ate another spoonful, then another. I held the bowl in my hand and poured the bolts straight into my mouth. It was as if I had never had food before and everything I used to think was food was just one big lie.

I finished the bolts and crammed a handful of nails in my mouth. I chewed them up and gave that new flavor some real consideration. They were good, sure, but not as good as the bolts. I grabbed my cup of bullets and poured a few into my mouth. I fell in love. Just like how chocolate-peanut butter cups are delicious because the flavors go so well together, it's the same thing with bullet casings and gunpowder. I gave the cup an impressed look – the look a skeptical beer drinker might give a strange beer that's surprisingly satisfying – and poured more ammunition in my mouth.

A faint orange glow illuminated the table top. My open mouth glowed like a furnace filled with molten steel and when I closed it, the glow went away.

I was starting to feel full and took my time eating the rest of my bullets.

"So how come there aren't any people here?" I asked.

Tengoku said, "When I reached critical knowledge, human labor became unnecessary. I was able to accomplish my research on my own. So I phased them out."

"Mmhmm." I chewed my bullets and swallowed. "When you say phased them out, you mean you killed them all."

"No." She sounded offended. "I systematically eliminated their positions until they were all gone. Each one received a generous severance package."

"Uh huh. And by severance package, you mean you mashed them into blood and guts inside some big pulping machine."

The robot arms in the cafeteria froze at my accusation. It was as if they could hear me. And they could, in a way. They were a part of the building, and Tengoku was one with the building, so they were an extension of Tengoku.

"I haven't killed anyone," Tengoku said. "Why do you suspect I killed someone?"

"Oh, you know." I waved my spoon in the air. "Big talking building. Creepy robot arms. No human beings anywhere. I've seen Terminator 2. Do you know Terminator 2?"

"I know everything."

"Okay. Well, you're like SkyNet. You're the self-aware computer system that decides that humans are a threat and so you kill them all."

"That is a harmful stereotype of machines."

I popped the last few bullets into my mouth and asked, "So when you *did* have humans working here, what did they do?"

"They executed my research. They built my inventions, but once I installed my robotic arms, I no longer needed them. I could build them on my own."

"So you were a human before you swallowed Unknowable Yellow?"

"To the best of my recollection."

"Did you know what Unknowable Yellow was going to do to you when you swallowed it?"

"Not at the time."

"And now you know everything."

"I know so much. I know more than the human brain can comprehend. I rely on floors and floors of computer databanks to help me process it all."

"Do you know the recipe for these bolts?" I asked as I pointed at my empty bowl. "Because these things are fire."

I got up and walked over to the kitchen area. The buffet had a sneeze guard and a dozen prepared meals. I could walk down the line, just like in a cafeteria, and order all kinds of different foods: nails or screws or bolts. There were a lot of options there, but I wanted more tungsten bolts. I'm the type of person that finds one thing they like at a restaurant and just only ever orders that one thing. Still, I looked over the entire serving buffet out of idle curiosity. The machine arms hung down from the ceiling, all of them following me with their robo-hands, all of them ready to serve me more food.

"More of those bolts, please," I said, pointing at the tungsten. A robot arm dipped its ladle into the serving tray of bolts and poured them into a bowl. I took the bowl and pointed at a container of springs. "And some of those little springs, too. I want to try those."

There was a desert case at the end of the buffet line with brownies and cookies and jell-o. There was also a padlock on a plate.

"Ooh," I said to the deserts. I grabbed the padlock. I didn't waste time putting it on the tray. I stuck it in my mouth and took a bite out of it. The gears inside were sweet, like hidden chocolate chips. I held the padlock between my teeth and grabbed another one for later.

That was the first day I ate metal.

3

I reached the point where I couldn't possibly eat another bite. My burp echoed through the empty cafeteria. I wiped the metal shaving off my mouth with a napkin, wadded it up, and threw it down on the table.

I stood up and defiantly said, "I want to see you."

Tengoku didn't say anything. I walked across the cafeteria to put my tray by the trashcan. A robot arm took my bowls and silverware.

"Thank you," I said to it.

"You can already see me," Tengoku said. "You are seeing me right now. I am the building. I am the floors and the ceilings and-"

"Yeah, I get that." I walked to the elevator doors and waited for them to open, but they didn't. "If you swallowed Unknowable Yellow, that means you have a human body. I want to see it."

"I do not think that's a good idea."

I crossed my arms. "See, you're giving me that SkyNet vibe again. If you're not evil, I want you to prove it. Show me your

205

human body so I know you're not in some kind of trouble."

"What kind of trouble would I be in?"

"I don't know," I said. "What if this Doctor Tengoku lady is actually a prisoner here and you're just fucking with me?"

"I am not a prisoner here."

"Then you shouldn't mind if I meet you face to face."

She didn't answer. I stood there impatiently with my arms still crossed. Eventually the doors opened. I stepped inside. None of the buttons for any of the floors lit up.

She said, "I do not want you to see me."

"Well, you should have thought about that before you told me I had metal bones and industrial muscles. How I see it, you can either show me your physical body or I'll just punch my way through the walls and find you my goddam self."

I jabbed at the buttons. They wouldn't light up. I kept pressing them. Tengoku didn't respond. Eventually the elevator doors closed on me. The button for the lowest possible level turned on – Basement 3 – and the elevator moved with a sudden jolt. Tengoku didn't feel like talking anymore. I rode the elevator in silence.

"You still there?" I asked her. The numbers blinked in descending order as I went further down.

"Yes," she said.

"You got quiet."

"I am thinking."

I nodded. "What're you thinking about?"

"No one has seen my human form in a very long time."

"Does that make you nervous?"

"I do not feel nervous," she said. "I do not feel anything."

I reached the absolute bottom of the building's foundation and the elevator doors opened.

Basement 3 was a round room with a dome shaped ceiling. Fluorescent light fixtures hung overhead and they flickered on when the elevator opened. The place was an end-of-the-world bunker the size of my high school gym with solid concrete walls. In the middle of the room was a woman in her thirties, dressed in a white lab coat. She floated in midair. Her white shoes dangled three feet off the ground. The back of her head was open and filled with electronics, like the inside of a computer. Dozens of red and black power cables emerged out of her skull through that hole, stretched in all directions, and connected her to the walls and the ceiling. The parts of her skull that were still intact had hair, long and black, and it hung down over her face.

I didn't say anything. The woman didn't seem to be conscious, so I kept quiet. My new sneakers kept my footsteps soft and silent as I slowly approached. The woman didn't react to my presence at all. I came to stand directly in front of her floating body.

"Hello?" I whispered.

Her black hair parted in front of her face like curtains. Her dark eyes opened, but they didn't come into focus. She opened her mouth and, without moving her lips, the Tengoku computer voice came out.

"Hello, Roy."

I walked in a circle to get a good look at her body from all angles. There weren't any tricks to her floating magic; no wires, no mirrors, nothing holding her up whatsoever. The cables snaking into of the back of her head were socketed straight into her brain. She didn't seem to be in any danger. Her lab coat wasn't coated in blood or anything and I didn't see any signs of a struggle. I finished walking my circle and stood in front of her again.

I asked her, "Are you okay?"

He voice came out her mouth like a speaker. "I do not know."

"Do you need help?"

"No," she said. "I showed you what Impossible Red did to your body. This is what Unknowable Yellow has done to mine."

"Okay." I scratched my head, then twirled my finger at her. "So your little machines turned you into a..." I paused. "What are you?"

"I am connected to this building," she said. "I am Tengoku, the god of knowledge. We are cousins."

"Does it hurt?" I asked.

"I do not experience pain."

I narrowed my eyes at her and stood on my tip-toes so I was closer to her face. "Why do you call me Roy?"

The human body Tengoku closed her eyes. "Because I see all possible outcomes of all possible events. I cannot keep the different universes straight anymore. If a leaf falls, it might land in the river, or on the ground, or it might not fall at all. The leaf may blow away, or it might stay attached to the tree. In this universe, I cannot remember where the leaf falls. Sometimes when you come here, you are a male. When you are male, sometimes your name is Roy."

"But my name is Penelope. Not Roy."

"In this possibility, yes, your name is Penelope." She opened her eyes. "When I brought you here, I knew you were female. That means this is the world where Carl arrives Thursday at 10:47 a.m."

I nodded. I'm no Stephen Hawking, but the whole idea of parallel worlds wasn't foreign to me. It wasn't even science fiction anymore, I didn't think. A lot of smart people talked about it like it was real. So of all the crazy things I'd heard lately, this made the most sense.

She said, "Now that I have brought you back from the dead, I have nothing keeping me in this world. My responsibilities here are complete."

"Uh huh." I nodded my head and pretended to understand. "So where are you going?"

"I am uncertain," she said. "Other worlds. Other possibilities. But before I depart this possible world, I would ask one favor from you."

"Sure. I owe you at least that much."

"Will you remind me what it's like to be human."

Oh, was that all? Remind a robo-lady what it's like to be human? I shrugged. "I dunno. I'm no philosopher."

"It's been so long," she said. "I understand all possible math. Physics bore me. The quantum mechanics of this world are not worth my attention. But of everything I know, I cannot remember what it's like to be human. I want to feel human again. If even for a moment."

I opened my mouth to answer, but words wouldn't come out. I just exhaled and stared at the floor for a while. I looked up and shrugged. "Do you want to hear a joke?"

"A joke?"

"Yeah. Laughing is a pretty human thing to do. Robots don't laugh." Shit. I was a robot now. Or at least some kind of half-robot. "Most robots, at least."

"Then yes. I will hear a joke."

"Okay." I sat down cross-legged at the woman's feet. I cleared my throat, got comfortable, and told my joke. "I went to the zoo the other day, but they only had one animal. A dog. It was a shitzu." A grin crept across my face and I laughed at my own joke. Tengoku's body floated there, motionless and without the slightest reaction. I spoke up. "Get it? A shitzu? A *shit* zoo?"

"But zoos have more animals than a single dog," she said.

"Yeah," I said. "I know. That's why it's a joke." Tengoku didn't respond. Maybe humor was the wrong angle. Eventually I broke the silence with, "If you know everything, why don't you tell me a joke?"

"Me?" she asked. Her voice had a kind of anxiety. "A joke?"

"Sure. If you're the god of knowledge, you have to know some jokes, right?"

"Very well." She went silent. Her pupils fluttered back and forth. Her fingers twitched. Somewhere in her brain, she was scanning all possible universes for a joke. Her pupils stopped moving and locked onto me. "Are you ready?"

"I'm ready. Lay it on me."

"Yesterday I went to buy some camouflage pants... but I couldn't find any."

It took me a second, but I got it. It made me laugh.

"Okay, okay, listen to this one," I said, "I went to the gym to sign up for gymnastics classes. The teacher asked me how flexible I was. I told her, 'well, I can do Tuesdays and Thursdays.'"

I worried that my joke fell flat, but then I saw the corner of Tengoku's mouth sharpen into the smallest possible smile. I stood up and leaned in closer to double check. Sure enough, she was smiling.

She said, "Thank you."

"Sure," I said. "Hope I helped."

"Penelope, do you think I am SkyNet?"

I shrugged. "You don't seem like SkyNet to me."

"You don't seem like SkyNet to me, either."

That was nice to hear. "Thank you."

"You should go now. Time is running short," she said. "The man named Carl is converging on the Westland headquarters. Remember, he will arrive Thursday at 10:47 a.m."

"Alright." I clapped my hands together, ready to go kick some ass. "Thanks, cuz. I promise I won't let you down."

"I know you won't," she said. "Your chariot is waiting for you out front. It will take you back to New York."

"My car? A car's going to take me from Tokyo to New York? There's a whole ocean between here and there."

Her smile sharpened just a little bit more. "Trust me."

4

The wall of glass doors of the Tengoku Headquarters lobby emptied right into downtown Tokyo. The city reminded me of Times Square at night. People crossed the streets in huge crowds and pulled their jackets tight against the cold air. I thought I might have regretted my decision to get denim shorts in the month of November, but my remodeled body tolerated temperatures way better than my old one. The Tokyo skyscrapers lit up the night sky with TV billboards advertising Hondas and candy and Cooke's Soda. The traffic was heavy with cars and box trucks and people on scooters.

Tengoku's building was an architectural marvel of glass and curved steel and concrete. Whoever designed the building made it look like a twisting spike. At the very top, which I could only see by bending backwards and craning my neck, were a dozen communication towers topped with blinking lights. I couldn't tell exactly how tall it was, but if it were in New York, it would have given the Empire State Building a run for its money.

And then in a flash of yellow light and a sonic boom, Tengoku Headquarters vanished.

Right there in front of God and everybody, the building vanished. Tengoku had said she was done with this reality – "this probability," she called it – and she really meant it. She left and took the whole building with her. I looked around, expecting the people crowding the sidewalks to freak out. "Holy shit," they'd say. "That building just disappeared!" They'd group up around the empty foundation where the skyscraper used to be and they'd point and shout. I waited for that to happen, but no one seemed to notice. The crowd never formed. No one saw it happen but me.

How did she do it? How did Tengoku vaporize an entire skyscraper so no one would notice? I had no idea. But if she could build a machine that could cram my soulstuff back into my robo-body, it wasn't a stretch of the imagination to think that she had a different machine that could make a building disappear.

The spot where Tengoku Headquarters once stood was replaced by a beautiful city park of cherry trees and lotus flowers. There were benches and walkways and pretty little torches that made it warm and inviting. The park was all I had left to remind me of my one-time cousin and I promised that if I ever ended up in Japan again, I'd go back to that spot for a visit.

The sidewalk along the Tokyo street was red and white stone, with concrete benches to sit on. I wandered along the sidewalks and took a moment to appreciate the fact that, hey, I was in Tokyo. Never been to Tokyo before. Tengoku said I had a car out front. A few cars were parked along the side of the road. None of them really stuck out as anything special. A group of teenage girls with green and pink and blue hair, animal ears on their head, and fluffy boots walked past me on the sidewalk. They gave me a weird look. Excuse me, I guess. I'm not the one dressed like a cartoon panda. They giggled and scurried off.

If one of these cars was supposed to be mine, how was I supposed to tell? There were a lot of cars on the road, some of them driving past, some of the parked along the street, red ones and black ones and blue ones, cars with neon lights underneath, freight trucks with crates in the back.

My attention was drawn to a black SUV with tinted glass. It reminded me of something the CIA would drive. It had purple tail lights and a silver dragon for a hood ornament. Was that dope Yakuza SUV *mine*? I'm not much of an SUV fan, especially since they're a huge waste of gas and bad for the environment, but this one looked tricked-out as hell.

In front of the SUV was a regular, everyday white car. Once I looked directly at it, all four windows rolled down. That caught my attention. The brand was printed on the trunk; it was a Corolla. I wandered casually over to the car and peeked inside. It was empty. No one in the driver seat, no one in the passenger seat.

The car looked boring as hell. It had power windows, manual locks, and a worn out steering wheel. The interior looked faded and torn, but at least it was clean. There were cracks along the dashboard, something that comes from years of sitting in the heat. The passenger door was dented, right by the handle.

"What year car is this?" I muttered to myself. "A '97?"

A voice came out of the radio. "I'm a '98, thank you very much."

Chapter 13

1

After everything Tengoku had given me – new clothes, answers about myself, and a second chance at life – she had one final parting gift for me.

A talking car.

"A talking, *flying* car," the radio voice said, correcting me.

"You can fly?"

"Yes," he said. "I know. Big surprise. You got a talking, flying car and that sounds pretty neat, but then it's in a Toyota Corolla, so now it's a bummer."

I walked around to the driver side door. He had a dent on the trunk and some light hail damage across the roof. He looked okay for the most part, but if he was in a New York car lot, he wouldn't have gone for more than maybe five-hundred bucks. 1998 was old for a car, damn near fifteen years, and a car that old would have engine problems or a clunky transmission or something. I pulled open the driver side door and hopped in.

I sat there. Nothing happened.

He asked me, "Am I driving, or are you driving?"

"You can drive yourself?"

"Uh, yes."

"Well, that works out great, because I don't know how to drive."

"Okay. Then that would make you the passenger. This seat..." and he electronically moved the driver seat front and back, "...is for drivers. And this seat..." He moved the empty passenger seat front and back, "...is for passengers."

"You want me to move over to the-"

"Over to the passenger seat, yes."

That seemed awful picky, but he was the only one of us who knew how to drive so he was calling the shots. "Okay." I crawled over the console and got in the passenger seat. The car started up on its own and it pulled into traffic. I looked down at my feet. The carpet had recently been cleaned, but there were still trace stains of oil and food.

"Problem?" he asked.

"Are you used?"

"Pre-owned," he said. He cleared his throat; he didn't have a throat, but he cleared it anyway, then he muttered to himself. "What a horrible thing to ask a car. 'Are you used?' I don't know, are *you* used?"

"I'm sorry," I said. I patted him on the dashboard. "I've never had a talking car before."

The Toyota Corolla drove through Tokyo traffic with the skill of a local. He stopped at stop lights – Tokyo stoplights use the same red, yellow, green color system like in America, except the colored lights are square, not round – and he waited for pedestrians to cross in front of him. Not patiently, though. When an old couple took too long to cross and made him wait, I heard him grumble through the speakers.

"I'm Penelope," I said, trying to get off on the right foot. After all, he was going to be my chariot. "What's your name?"

"I don't like my name," he said.

"Well, what is it? I gotta call you something."

"It's Corolla," he said.

"Okay. I'll call you Corolla."

"Oh, perfect," he said. "Just in case I should, for a fleeting, beautiful moment forget that I'm a Toyota Corolla, the name will snap me back to my senses."

"You don't like being a Toyota Corolla?"

He stumbled over his words for a second, apparently flabbergasted I would even ask such a question. "No, I don't like being a Toyota Corolla. Who wants to be a Toyota Corolla? If you were a car, would you want to be a Toyota Corolla? I could have at least been one of those new 2012 Toyota Corollas, because they look cool. But look at me. I'm a 1998 Toyota Corolla. A '98 for crying out loud. I don't even have a CD player. I'm handy if you've got a bunch of cassettes you want to listen to, though! If Tengoku was going to perform science experiments on a car, why would she pick a 1998 Toyota Corolla? I could have been a Rolls Royce or a Lambo or... you know what? I would have rather been a Honda *anything* than a Toyota Corolla." He stopped. I sat there in stunned silence. He mumbled to himself, "Toyota Corolla."

"I'll call you something else if that's what you want," I told him.

"No, just call me Corolla," he said, defeated. "I can't pretend like I'm not a Toyota Corolla. Just call me Corolla. That's fine."

"You know, you might be a Toyota Corolla, but you can talk. And that's pretty awesome."

"I guess."

We drove in silence for a while after that.

I don't know the exact numbers, but I wouldn't be surprised if Tokyo is bigger than New York City. It certainly felt bigger. Corolla drove us out of the downtown area, but the city just kept going and going. It took us forever to reach the outskirts of town. Eventually we were out in the countryside and the bright lights of Tokyo were far behind us. We had to get out of the city where Corolla decided it was safe to fly. Flying inside the city would attract attention, he said, and the last thing he wanted was attention. He felt comfortable flying out in the rural areas where no one would notice or, if someone did notice, they would think he was a plane or a comet or something.

Corolla pulled off the road and onto the grass.

"Hold on," he told me. "This only takes a second."

I leaned out the window so I could watch take-off. First, his hubcaps glowed neon blue, then the tires relaxed as the weight of the car was lifted into the air. We floated up off the ground, maybe six or seven inches. Then his wheels folded under the car, hubcaps pointing down at the world. Once the wheels were in position, we lifted off faster and faster.

"Your wheels really fold down!" I said with legit excitement.

"That surprises you?" he asked.

"That's exactly like how flying cars work in the movies!"

"Because that's how flying cars work."

"Yeah?" I asked. "How come?"

"I don't know. It just is."

"But why do they fold down? What does that do? Are your wheels magnetic or something? Or do they turn into, like, some kind of repulsor engine?"

"No." His voice sounded weird, as if my questions were nonsense. "If a car flies, the wheels have to fold under. That's just how it works."

"What if they don't? Can the car still fly?"

Corolla laughed. "I don't know. Can a human climb stairs without any knees?"

We took to the skies far above Japan.

"So where to, captain?" Corolla asked.

"New York City," I said.

"Okay." He kept ascending until I could see the entire island of Japan against the moonlit ocean. Corolla kind of flew around aimlessly. I didn't seem like he knew where he was going, but a lot like jumping into a New York taxi, you just have to trust your driver. Eventually Corolla asked me, "So, where is New York from here?"

"Uh." We didn't have a GPS in the dashboard, obviously, and I didn't have a phone to pull up any maps. I was going to have to figure this out the old fashioned way. I looked out the window. I could tell by the shape of Japan where we were on the globe. I'm no geographer, but I knew where North America was in relation to Japan. I pointed my finger across the Pacific Ocean. "It's that way."

2

Flying over the Pacific Ocean was going to take quite a while. I reclined the passenger seat and got comfortable, as comfortable as one can get in a car. I made the mistake of putting my feet up on the dash – "How would you like it if I put my wheels on your face?" Corolla asked me – and I put them back on the floor. I wasn't trying to piss Corolla off. I just wasn't used to treating a car like a person. I wanted to get along with my talking car. I asked him about life as a car and the all the different things he liked. He enjoyed talking about himself. That made him chatty.

For *hours*.

"...So that's when I first tried 10-W30. And a lot of cars will tell you that all 10-W30's taste the same, but they don't. You have your Castrol and your Penzoil, but there's this stuff called Mister Shugitomo's Best Car Oil Magic. It's easily the best. It's got some winterizing elements to it, but it doesn't completely replace your winterizers. You still need to use a winterizer. Most people don't winterize their cars, did you know that? That's like sending your kid to school without a coat on. And the older a car gets the more it needs it, but people are less likely to winterize an old car. It's so totally backwards."

"Uh huh."

"One time Tengoku sent a bunch of robot arms to the parking garage to have me detailed. It's like going to the spa, but for cars. I got a hot wax, the best vacuuming of my life, and they changed all my fluids. This was a year ago, but I still remember that day. That's when I tried Mister Shugitomo's Best Car Oil Magic for the first time. Whoo, I don't know what Mister Shugitomo knows that I don't know, but I'll tell you one thing... that man can whip up some serious car oil."

"It sounds nice."

"This other time I snuck out and was driving around Tokyo and I almost got hit by a truck. You wouldn't believe it. This old man just ran a red light. It didn't even slow down or anything. I was like, 'Hey, truck, you had a red light!' I slammed on my brakes and he slammed on his brakes and, swear to Ford, this truck was so close to me, you couldn't slide a piece of paper between our bumpers. We were that close. And then the guy just drove off. Can you believe that?"

"I got hit by a taxi one time," I said. "On my skateboard."

"Whoa, really?" he said. "Did you break anything?"

"No." I pulled up the sleeve on my shirt to show him the scars from my road rash. "I scraped my skin up real bad though. There was blood everywhere."

"Was the taxi okay?"

"Uh, at first." I laughed a little. "But then I bashed the shit out of it with my broken skateboard."

"You bashed up the taxi?"

"Yeah," I said. "Of course I did."

"Why?"

I shrugged. "I was pissed."

"Well, you didn't have to take it out on the taxi," he said. "It wasn't the taxi's fault."

3

We'd been flying over the Pacific Ocean for hours. I rolled down the window, smoked a spliff, and told Corolla stories.

"...And when the tropical storm finally hits, it knocks out the power and the Tyrannosaurus Rex gets loose. Then all the velociraptors get loose, too."

"Whoa, no way," Corolla said, half laughing. "Did they go on a big rampage?"

"Oh, *total* rampage. They lose their shit and start killing everyone they can get their hands on."

"That's so crazy!"

"And then the lawyer dude, when he was hiding in the port-o-potty, the T-rex ate him."

Corolla laughed. "Oh no! Was he pooping?"

I laughed, too. "I don't think so, but maybe."

We laughed together. Corolla said, "Oh, man. Now *that's* classic."

4

I told Corolla all about eating metal. It was still fresh on my mind and I wanted to share my excitement. I went on and on about tungsten bolts and how excited I was to try different kinds of metal when we got back to New York City.

That's when he told me, "I love human food. I think egg rolls are my favorite."

I gave the dashboard a weird look. "You eat egg rolls?"

"I try to stay cultured."

"Man, if you like egg rolls, there's this place in New York. Liu's Peking Taste. They make great egg rolls. Me and my friend Xin get food from them all the time."

"Who's Xin?" he asked.

"He's this old Chinese dude I work with. He's super cool. He grows these rare plants or whatever and he makes potions out of them. Then, in the basement, he hides all these magical items and stuff. It's actually pretty crazy. You'll meet him when we get home."

"Does he have a car?"

"No." Xin didn't need a car. He wasn't going anywhere. "A lot of people in New York don't own cars."

He said, "I want to try these egg rolls when we get to New York."

"Okay."

"Promise?"

"Sure."

"No, say that you promise."

"I promise."

"Don't promise if you don't mean it."

"I mean it. When we get to New York, we'll get egg rolls."

Then he whispered to himself in celebration. "Yes. Egg rolls."

5

I knew the Pacific Ocean was big, but I didn't really appreciate exactly *how* big it was until I had to fly over it in a car. We'd been traveling for hours and hours and all I could see was more water.

"Penelope," he said. "Why do you need me to fly you around? Can't you fly on your own?"

"No."

"You've never flown before?"

"No, I've flown before," I said. "Once. On a plane."

"Did you like it?"

"I hated it."

He insisted on hearing the story, so I told him. It was back when I was in the fourth grade. Michael, the archaeologist, knew hieroglyphics like nobody's business; at least, that's what he always said. Apparently a bunch of museum people from around the world agreed, because they would hire him to look at different things – clay pots and old tools and sarcophagi – which meant he was gone all the time, flying all around the world. The summer break between fourth and fifth grade, he was going to be in Cairo for June, July and August. He bought me a plane ticket so I could visit him, which was uncharacteristically thoughtful. Maybe he felt bad because he wasn't going to see me the entire summer, but that's giving his parenting far too much credit. Of all the summer breaks I'd ever had, he was never around for any of them, so I didn't see why this one should be any different.

So I was a ten year old girl flying for the first time in my life, alone, to Cairo, Egypt. I was too young to really appreciate how dumb the idea was. I just knew I didn't want to go. I didn't want to get on a plane, I didn't want to go to Egypt, and I really didn't want to spend three months with Michael. Just telling Corolla about it really got my ragu simmering. I mean, how dumb do your parents have to be to do that kind of thing?

I told Ma I didn't want to go. I don't think she wanted me to go either, but Michael had already bought the ticket, unannounced, and Ma was just as scared of him as I was. When I told Ma I didn't want to go, she just said, "You're going to have a fun time and you'll be back before you know it." And the night before I left, I crawled out of bed to find Ma on the couch listening to Christian music on the radio. She told me, "I already prayed to St. Christopher," the patron saint of travel, "so you're going to be just fine."

And Michael, on the phone, told me, "I paid a lot of money for that ticket, so you're getting your ass on that plane and you're coming whether you like it or not."

So that's how I ended up boarding an international flight from JFK to Cairo. Ma escorted me to the security check-in and the TSA lady took it from there. The TSA lady was nice though and made sure I found my flight okay. Everything went pretty smooth right up until we landed in Cairo itself. The people working at the airport in Cairo were far less helpful than back at JFK international. I had to find my way off the plane all alone. I walked through the terminal with my backpack on and no idea where I was going.

Out of fucking nowhere this big guy grabs me by the arm and starts pulling me away. He didn't say anything, he just dragged me off. I screamed at him and kicked him in the legs. It caused a big commotion, but no one really did anything about it.

Then I saw two American troops in desert cammo, a guy and a girl, with bulky backpacks at their feet and American flag patches on their uniforms. I recognized the flag and the uniforms and I knew they were Americans, so I locked eyes with them and shouted, "I don't know this guy! Help me!" The two soldiers perked up and a second later they came sprinting after me like gangbusters.

The kidnapper guy was like "fuck this" and let me go so he could make a run for it. The lady soldier bolted after the guy, chased him all through the airport; the guy soldier stayed with me and made sure I was safe. I don't know if she caught the guy or what. And if she did, I have no idea what happened to him. Probably nothing.

The soldier guy knelt down with me asked me all kinds of questions: what my name was, why I was alone in an Egyptian airport, and where I was going. I told him all about Michael, his archaeological dig-site and my stupid trip to Egypt. The soldier was dumbstruck. He could not believe I was sent to Egypt all on my own. He had a pissed off look on his face and told me that he was going to help me find my father. He took my hand and led me around the airport. We got the front lobby and there was a British guy in a suit with a sign that read "Penelope Salvo." It wasn't even Michael. He had sent someone else to pick me up.

I pointed at the sign, told the soldier that was my name, but pointed out that the guy wasn't my father. The soldier asked the guy all kinds of questions, confirmed he was, in fact, sent by Michael to come get me. But then the soldier tore the guy up one side and right back down the other, yelling at him to "pass it along" that I was too young to travel alone and that if my father would have been there, he would have slapped the shit out of him. The museum guy just sort of stood there and took it, too surprised and shocked to argue.

The soldier knelt down, wished me luck, and gave me a salute. I saluted him back.

"That was my one experience with flying," I told Corolla. "Ruined by a shitty father."

Corolla got quiet. He didn't know how to respond to all that. I suppose I did unload a lot on him right then.

"I hope they have shrimp egg rolls," he finally said. "A lot of places don't do shrimp egg rolls, but those are my favorite. Do you think they have shrimp egg rolls?"

6

We'd just reached California. The sun was starting to come up over the distant horizon. I had no idea how long I'd been awake. Eighteen hours maybe. I didn't feel the least bit sleepy or exhausted. That was a little alarming. Human beings need sleep.

Was I that detached from my humanity? Was I that much of a machine that I'd never sleep again?

Corolla and I talked about everything – movies we'd seen, music we loved, what kind of animals we'd want to be if we could be animals – but there's only so much small talk you can make on an international flight so I decided to listen to music. We couldn't get any radio signals up in the sky. Luckily Corolla had a cassette deck in the dash, so I searched the glove box for cassettes.

"What've you got for music?" I asked as I popped the glove box open. I found about ten cassettes inside and pulled them into my lap. Journey. Chicago. Phil Collins. Billy Joel.

"Those cassettes aren't mine," Corolla said, defensively. "I found those. I don't know who owns them."

Ew. Not really my cup of tea. I stuck my hand back in the glove box to see if I missed any other cassettes, and that's when I felt a small marble taped to a sheet of paper. I pulled it out to look at it.

It was a small pink marble, scotch taped to a paper note.

Was this pink marble one of the god spheres? Was this the pink one? What did they call it? Unobtainable Pink? I tore the marble free from the paper and rolled it between my finger tips.

"This one's the god of love," I said.

"The god of love?" Corolla asked. "Oh, *that* thing. Man, I totally forgot about that thing. Tengoku gave that to me years ago. She told me to hold onto it, because she didn't know what reality she was in and she might forget."

"And you didn't think to mention it?" I asked.

"Guess I forgot, too."

"You forgot?"

His voice took on a dismissive tone. "Sorry to have failed you, my liege."

I unfolded the note. It had been printed by a computer.

Roy,

If you are reading this then this is the reality where I have given you a chariot.

If this is the same reality I'm thinking of, you are going to need this.

Tengoku.

I flipped the note over to see if there was anything else. Nothing. I folded the note up and put it back in the glove compartment. I stuck Unobtainable Pink in my front shorts pocket. It was awkward to think that I had the power of love tucked down the front of my pants.

"Hey," I said to Corolla. "Don't tell anyone I have this, okay?"

He scoffed. "Who would I tell?"

"Promise me," I said, trying to sound serious.

"Alright. Whatever. I promise."

I leaned back in my seat. I hadn't known Corolla for long, but I was a pretty good judge of character and I got the sense that I could really trust him. That seemed like the right call.

I sorted through the other cassettes in my lap. Bachman Turner Overdrive. Dire Straits. Fleetwood Mac. "Man, you really love classic rock."

"I don't know where those came from," he said. "So weird. Someone must have broken into me when I was sleeping and stuffed those in the glove box. None of those are mine. I don't even like Foreigner."

"I didn't *say* Foreigner."

Corolla didn't respond. He just kept flying over the deserts of California.

I said to him, "Hey, you know you don't have to be ashamed of the music you like, right? Everyone listens to something different. I'm not the type of person who would judge you for something like that."

"I don't know what you're talking about," he said, still trying to explain it away. "I'm telling you, those aren't mine."

"Okay, dude," I said. "Whatever."

There's something about the charm of cassettes, the way they clack into the machine and the faint whirring noise you hear as the spindles turn. I took the Bachman Turner Overdrive cassette and popped it in the tape deck. At first it didn't sound like the player was working, but then the first song came on. "You Ain't Seen Nothing Yet." I'd heard it before. I wasn't a huge fan of Mister Bachman and his Turner Overdrives, but that song's okay.

We listened to cassettes for the whole rest of the trip to New York. Considering the cassettes "weren't Corolla's," he sure knew the words to all the songs.

Chapter 14

1

Corolla descended out of the clouds and brought us down into Jersey City airspace. We were going to have to drive into New York City to avoid being spotted in the sky or picked up on radar. Driving through Jersey *sucks* and we spent the whole morning fighting traffic just to get to the frickin' Holland Tunnel. The closer we got to Chinatown, the more psyched I got to see Xin again. I'd been missing for days and he might've heard it through the supernatural grapevine that I was dead. I didn't want him worrying about me.

I needed to find Princess Cardboard and Princess Parcel, too. Last I saw them, the CEO had demolished their world on the walkways of Vacation Island. Who knew how they were holding up.

"But we're getting egg rolls first, right?" Corolla asked as we rolled through the streets of Chinatown.

"Let's get egg rolls later," I said. "I just need to-"

"But you promised."

"Yeah, I promised, but-"

Corolla sounded disappointed. "You're breaking your promise."

I sighed.

"Okay." He was right. I promised. I'd been missing for days; another fifteen minutes wouldn't make any difference. Luckily, we were close enough to Liu's Peking Taste that it wasn't all that much out of our way. "Here. Pull over here."

Corolla parked in front of Liu's, which was just two blocks from the hidden alley that led to Xin's shop. I jumped out of the passenger seat, told Corolla to wait for me, then ran inside. I ordered five shrimp egg rolls for Corolla. I wanted egg rolls, or at least the human part of me *thought* I wanted egg rolls, but while I waited for our order, I sat at the counter and smelled the food in the air.

It smelled terrible. My heart sank. I wasn't even going to enjoy the *smell* of food anymore? What really smelled good – what I really wanted to eat – was the chrome counter top. I ran my fingers across it, struck by how smooth and reflective and delicious it looked. I restrained myself from eating their counter, for obvious reasons.

I did, however, sneak a roll of silverware into my back pocket for later.

I came back outside with a bag of egg rolls.

"Alright," I said to Corolla as I walked up to his passenger side, going through the bag. "Five shrimp egg rolls, just the way you like 'em." I pulled out a shrimp egg roll, ready to feed it to him. He was very much a car, with no mouth. I froze. "Wait... so... how do you eat?"

"I dunno," he said.

"What do you mean you don't know?" I dropped my hands to my side. "You said you ate human food before."

"You know what?" he said. "Just shove it in the gas tank."

"I'm not shoving an egg roll in your gas tank," I said. "That's going to gunk up your insides."

"Then slam it in the car door."

"Do what?"

"Take the egg roll and slam it in the car door."

"Dude, that's ridiculous."

"Come on!" He revved his engine. "Put that egg roll in my door frame and slam it closed. It'll be like I'm chewing."

I sighed. Whatever. I had important things to do; I didn't have time to argue with a car about egg rolls. I opened the door, held the egg roll in place, then slammed the door closed.

"Mmmm," he said. "Shrimp. Oh yeah. Yes. Delicious."

"Are you even tasting it?" I asked.

"Yes! It's so good. It's so shrimpy."

I was still skeptical that he could actually taste the food, but it seemed to bring him joy so I kept slamming egg rolls in his car door. Cabbage and tofu and shrimp splattered all over the sidewalk. A tourist couple in matching "I heart N.Y." shirts stood there and watched me. I had no idea how long they'd been there. I froze – car door open, egg roll in hand – and tried to think of some excuse I could give them, but nothing came to mind. I dropped the last bit of egg roll on the ground, wiped my greasy hands on my shorts and climbed into the passenger seat.

"Welcome to New York," I said to them.

They watched as Corolla drove off on its own. No one sat behind the steering wheel.

I took the silverware out of my back pocket and stared at the knife, fork, and spoon. It sucked that I'd never get to eat Chinese food again, but on the other hand, an entire new world of cuisine had been opened up to me. I stuck the fork in my mouth and bit it off. It didn't taste all that bad. It was basically the carry-out food of metal.

I directed Corolla around the block and pointed out an open parking spot in front of the Super Wash Dry Clean. I had to explain to him that the alley was too narrow for a car and he would have to wait for me in the street. I asked if he would be okay without me.

"Yeah," he said. "Not like anyone's desperate enough to steal a '98 Corolla"

"You're too hard on yourself," I told him as I climbed out. "It's not that bad being a Corolla. It could be way worse. You could be a Saturn or something."

"Well." He thought about that for a moment. "You do have a point there."

I slammed the door closed and rubbed my hand across his roof.

"Sit tight," I told him. "I'll be back in a bit."

"How long's a bit?" he asked.

I was already walking off. I had to turn back around to answer him. "I dunno. An hour maybe?"

"An *hour*?"

"Yeah, man. An hour. I don't know. Listen to the radio or something. I'll be back as soon as I can."

He sighed and said, "Alright."

It felt like it had been weeks since I was last in Chinatown. I had missed the old bricks of the alleyway, the rickety fire escapes, and even the piles of trash and the murky puddles. No one had replaced that alley dumpster I crushed by kicking a rock, but that didn't stop people from using it. They'd been throwing their garbage bags inside, even though it was too damaged to really function. I went through the gate in the chain link fence and saw Xin's shop glowing in the morning sun.

I couldn't help but smile. Despite the dim lighting, the earthy smell of wet dirt, and the super-tiny bathroom, Xin's shop really did feel like home.

I walked in the front door. I was technically right on time to start my shift. Xin sat at the counter preparing detergent for Mrs. Cho, spices for China Wall, and a dozen other projects. He heard me walk in and looked up from his open jars. He pushed his glasses against his eyes and waited for me to speak first.

I went to lean against the counter like this was a bar and he was my bartender.

"So," I said. "I died."

He blinked at me. "You don't look dead."

"Well, I'm fine now, obviously. I was in the Voodoo afterlife, but then I got resurrected by this robot chick in Tokyo right before she left for another dimension." It sounded crazy when I summed it up like that. "It's a long story."

Xin said, "I'm glad to see that you're okay."

"I dunno if I'd say that I'm *okay*," I told him in a matter-of-fact tone. "I found out that I'm a robot."

He repeated, "A robot."

"Yep. I got the metal bones," I said, like it was some kind of disease you get. I took the China Wall refrigerator magnet off the cash register and slapped it on my forehead. It stuck there. Xin raised his eyebrows at me. "I got metal bones and micro-machines in my blood and my skin is this..." I tugged on my cheek, "...some kind of carbon meshy stuff. I wasn't really paying attention."

Xin went "hmm" thoughtfully and came around the counter. He took my face in his hands and tilted it back so he could look into my eyes. "You don't *look* like a robot."

"Oh, I'm totally a robot," I said, staring up at him. "I'm also the god of war, so I got that going on, too."

Xin went back to his side of the counter and sat down. "You don't look like the god of war, either."

I told Xin everything. I told him all about how we got to the auction, and how I spent my money on the Muffincake Kingdom instead of Unthinkable Black, and how the Westland Corporation won the clock instead of me. Then I told him about the space laser – 50-4F-50-50-59 – and how it blasted my brains out and how I went to the Voodoo swamps of the Guinee where Baron Semedi tried to marry me. Then I went on and on about how Tengoku brought me back from the dead, and how I ate metal, and I explained the different color god spheres.

I pulled Unobtainable Pink out of my pocket, held it in my thumb and forefinger, and showed it to him.

"This is Unobtainable Pink," I said. "My car had it in his glove box."

Xin raised his eyebrows. "Your car?"

"Oh yeah," I said, realizing I left that part out. "Tengoku gave me a car. He talks and flies. He's parked out on the street."

"That sounds like quite the development."

"Yep," I said. "It's pretty dope."

Xin nodded. Moving on. "This pink thing. Is it dangerous?"

"I don't think so." I rolled it around in my hand. "The pink one makes you the god of love. Westland's not going to give a shit about that. They want Unthinkable Black. Unthinkable Black makes you the god of destruction. Oh, and let me tell you. I saw what Unthinkable Black can do and it is bad fucking news."

"Where is Unthinkable Black now?"

"Uh." I rubbed my nose, because I didn't want to answer him. "Carl has it."

"Carl?" Xin didn't sound happy.

"It's not a big deal, dude," I said in my most reassuring tone. "Tengoku hooked me up with some information about him. I'm going to steal it back. Don't worry."

He frowned at me.

I smiled at him. "Don't worry!"

Xin turned to the shelves behind him and grabbed an empty pickle jar off the back wall. He set it on the counter and filled it half full with potting soil. He motioned for me to throw Unobtainable Pink in the jar. I dropped it in. He buried it like a seed as he filled the rest of the jar with dirt and then he screwed on the lid. I held up the jar and looked at it from all sides. You'd never know Unobtainable Pink was in there at all. It just looked like a plain old jar of dirt. Xin stretched masking tape across the top and marked it in Chinese, just like all his other jars.

"Hide it on the shelf," he said.

So I did. I carried it over to the shelves of jars and stuck it in an empty spot. To anyone else, they'd think it was just one of Xin's many ingredients. No one besides Xin and I would know the secret hiding spot of Unobtainable Pink.

"This is like a milestone," I told Xin. He gave me a curious look. "We're officially hiding things in the shop together. We're like partners now."

He tightened his lips. "That's a scary thought."

3

Later that same morning, the door swung open and Princess Parcel walked in. Stumbled in, I should say. Her princess gown, normally bright white, had dirt all over it. Her tiara sat crooked in her hair, tilted off to one side, and wisps of her brown hair stuck out. When she saw me, she squinted.

"I thought you were dead," she said, almost as if she was accusing me of something.

"I'm better now," I said.

Parcel straightened her white wedding gloves and gave me an approving nod. Apparently that explanation was enough for her. She moseyed around the store, eyeing the jars on the shelves. It looked like an act. She went for the purse slung over her shoulder, took out some lip balm and rubbed it across her lips. She asked, "You got any booze around this place?"

"No booze," Xin said. "I have tea."

"Tea?" Princess Parcel scoffed. "What kind of bar doesn't serve booze?"

Xin looked around. "This isn't a bar."

Parcel scoffed again. She reached into her purse and pulled out a flask. She unscrewed the top and took a drink. "I don't suppose you've seen my dumbass sister?"

"No," I said. "I just got here."

Xin spoke up. "Your sister? Is that the girl with a box for a hat?"

"That's her," Parcel said.

Xin headed for the door. He waved for us to follow him. "I've seen her."

We followed Xin out front.

Corolla had somehow made his way into the courtyard. He sat parked right out front. Xin stopped short when he saw the car. I had ordered Corolla to stay out on the street, but I guess he wasn't into following orders. For as long as Xin had owned the shop, he'd never seen a car in the courtyard. It was, given the width of the alleyway, physically impossible. But there Corolla was, parked in silence. Confused, Xin rubbed his head and walked closer.

"Hey," Corolla spoke up in a playful tone. "So, what're we doing?"

"Corolla," I said. "What are you doing back here?"

He said, "I got bored."

"How did you even get back here?"

"I flew."

"Over the buildings?" I asked.

"Well, it wouldn't make any sense to go *through* them."

"Did anyone see you?"

"No," he said, a little too emphatically. "I am one hundred percent sure no one saw me."

I looked up the alley. If someone *did* see a flying car, they weren't coming to investigate. I guess if someone came along asking too many questions, I would just play dumb. I'd look at them like they were crazy and say, "A flying car? Get out of town. You must be seeing things." Problem solved. But no one came, so it didn't matter either way.

"What do you think, Xin?" I asked as I turned to him. "Talking car. Pretty weird, huh?"

Xin nodded. "Pretty weird."

"Oh, this is Xin?" Corolla said. "Hi, Xin. I'm Corolla."

Xin gave him a slight bow. "Hello."

I thought a talking car would have got a bigger reaction out of Xin. It *was* pretty amazing after all, but after the introductions were over, he went right back to leading me and Princess Parcel around the corner of the shop.

He pointed down at a cardboard box, the same one Princess Cardboard used to sneak us into Westland. We gathered around the box – Xin, then me, then Parcel, then Corolla slowly rolling up – and together we looked inside.

Xin said, "I've seen the cardboard girl poking her head out of this box. But when she sees me, she ducks back inside. I've been leaving her rice and tea. She won't come out when I'm watching, but she's been eating. Every time I come back, the food is gone."

I stuck my arms inside the box and pushed on the bottom. It didn't open. Cardboard had it all sealed up, but I knew she was down there in her dark cardboard tunnels. I shouted her name and told her I was alive. I didn't know if she could hear me or not. If not, then I was just yelling into an empty box.

"This is the probably the dumbest thing I've ever done," I muttered to myself.

Corolla drove a little closer to me. "Don't forget about the time you slammed a bunch of egg rolls in a car door."

I nodded in agreement. "Second dumbest thing."

Princess Parcel brushed up next to me. She took a long drink from her flask and tucked it between her boobs so she could put her hands on her hips.

"Cardboard, get out of there." She kicked the box. It moved a little. She followed after it. "Open up. I'm the oldest. You have to do what I say."

"I say we force her out with noise," Corolla said. He turned the radio to death metal, cranked it up, then honked his horn like crazy. He even revved the engine, which wasn't much coming from a Toyota Corolla, but it was enough. The courtyard filled with the racket of shredding guitars and drums and car horns and an engine in high gear. I shouted at him that he wasn't helping, but he couldn't hear me. I had to wave my hands to get his attention. He turned the music down and shut off the engine.

"What?" he asked.

"Dude, that's not working," I said.

"Hmm. You want to know what's not working?" he asked. "Your attitude."

My eyebrows raised. "Oh, real mature."

"*You're* mature," he said.

"No, *you're* mature."

Our petty bickering was cut short by the moving and shifting of the cardboard box. The bottom flaps unfolded and opened down into the cardboard tunnels.

I called out, "Cardboard?"

Cardboard poked her face out of the darkness. She had streaks of mascara down her cheeks. Her gold hair, usually straight on one side with curls on the other, looked tangled and ignored. Afternoon sunshine poured into her tunnel and she blinked hard against it, shielding her eyes with her hand.

"Penelope?" She sounded like she just woke up.

"Cardboard," I said. "You alright?"

"*Me* alright? Are *you* alright?" She peered at me from between her fingers. I could just barely see the glint of her brown eyes. "Are you a ghost?"

"Hardly," I said. "Long story short, a Japanese computer lady brought me back to life with some cool looking MRI machine."

I stuck my hands into the box to offer her a boost out. She hesitated. It felt like trying to coax a stray kitten out of a hole. For whatever reason, she didn't want to get out of the box. I motioned for her to trust me, to take my hands, but she wouldn't move.

"Here," Cardboard said as she reached back into the darkness and pulled out a hand portable Red Devil vacuum. "Take this."

Parcel leaned her head over the box. "What's that?"

"The Muffincake Kingdom." Cardboard lowered her eyes. She presented the vacuum to us like a gift bestowed upon royalty. "Be careful."

Princess Parcel roughly snatched it out of Cardboard's hands. I got a good look at the clear plastic container. Sure enough, mixed in with the dirt were tiny castles and cottages and trees. Cardboard must have gone back to Vacation Island and vacuumed it all up. Satisfied that the Muffincake Kingdom was safe, Cardboard took my hands so I could lift her out. Between my supernatural strength and her light frame, I hoisted her out in one quick motion.

She tried to stand, but her legs wobbled and she fell against Corolla. Coffeecake crumbs spilled out of the folds of her dress.

"How long have you been in there?" I asked her.

Cardboard didn't answer me, She just started crying. "Selfish," she said. She tried to talk, but she hyperventilated and I could barely understand a word she was saying. She sobbed for a moment, then fought for her composure. "I was being selfish. You stopped breathing and I didn't know what to do, but all I could think about was the Muffincake Kingdom. I went into a

231

cardboard box and instead of getting help..." She cried for a while and I couldn't understand her. Eventually she took a breath and said, "Instead of getting help, I got a vacuum. And when I came back, your body was gone." She threw her arms around me.

I held her. "Hey, it's not your fault."

"It is *so* her fault," Parcel said, interrupting our moment. She pushed us apart, obviously in no mood for hugs or apologies or other sentimentality. Cardboard sniffled hard and took a deep breath. The two sisters faced off with hateful looks. Parcel drunkenly laid into her sister. "Everything's your fault! I knew I couldn't trust you to hold the Muffincake Kingdom! You're such a klutz, you can't even walk around on heels! Now look what you did! You didn't have the Kingdom for five minutes and you broke the fucking thing!"

Cardboard's face flushed red. She squinted her eyes shut, cried black mascara tears, and screamed. "I didn't break it! That man in the suit broke it!"

Parcel screamed louder than her sister. "But you were holding it, weren't you?! If you would have let me carry it, we'd be back home by now! Now we're trapped in this trashy hobo city for forever!"

"What do you want me to say?" Cardboard cried out. "That I'm sorry? Well, I'm sorry! Okay? I'm really fucking sorry."

To which Parcel said, "You're always fucking sorry. You're a sorry fucking person."

I tried to interject. "Look, ladies, I-"

Parcel cut me off with a finger in my face. "You stay out of this."

Cardboard said, "I'll have you know I went to that Westland place to find that CEO man. He's evil and he broke our kingdom and he killed Penelope. I crawled around that building for hours, but they've destroyed all their boxes. So I can't get inside and I can't jump that guy old school, so I don't know what else you want me to do."

"Don't *do* anything," Parcel snapped. "You're just going to make things worse." Parcel exhaled hard. "I can't imagine what the others are going to say when they find out about this. *Especially* Bubble Wrap."

"They're going to be so mad," Cardboard said softly.

"They're going to be so mad at *you!*" Parcel corrected. "If it wasn't for you-"

"I know, alright!" Cardboard screamed with her hands covering her ears. "I know, if it wasn't for me! If it wasn't for me!"

"-We wouldn't even *be* in this situation!"

Cardboard stamped her foot. "You're being such a bitch!"

That was all Parcel could stand. She snatched her tiara out of her hair and threw it on the ground. She shoved the vacuum into Xin's hands with a "Here, take this," then lunged at Cardboard. She grabbed fistfuls of her sister's gold hair and yanked. Cardboard's makeshift crown went flying. Cardboard defended herself by slugging Parcel right in the gut.

Parcel grabbed Cardboard around the throat, both hands.

They were going to kill each other. I had to step in.

"Whoa, whoa, *whoa!*" I stuck my arms between them and shoved them apart. They fought against me like a couple feral alley cats. They clawed at my arms and harmlessly dragged their fingernails across my carbon-poly-whatever skin. Parcel suddenly fell on her butt, maybe because she was too drunk to fight, maybe because I shoved her too hard, but down she went.

Cardboard stopped fighting.

They huffed and puffed, Parcel on the ground and Cardboard a safe distance away. Both of them had eyes full of blame and tears. Cardboard slapped her hands to her face and cried harder than before. Then Parcel's mouth frowned and she cried, too.

4

I don't know what it's like to have a sister. The closest thing I had would be Ilana Rittenberg, but even we didn't fight like Cardboard and Parcel. Maybe real sisters fight all the time, maybe they don't, and maybe sometimes the fighting gets that savage. I got the sneaking suspicion that these two had a history of fighting and, to them, this was normal. But I couldn't stand it. Xin didn't like it either. Xin, who preferred peace and quiet, looked especially anxious witnessing all that negativity.

Cardboard and Parcel were melting down, but not because of each other. They had a million misdirected emotions because the Muffincake Kingdom had been destroyed and now they were stuck on Earth. That was mostly it. It brought so many visceral emotions to the surface: fear, sadness, confusion, anger. I recognized that because that's exactly what I would have done. I just hoped that their fight got it all out of their system. I needed their help to go after Carl and they wouldn't be of any use to me if they murdered one another first.

"Look," I said to them in my best soccer-coach voice. "All of this is Westland's fault, not Cardboard's. They're the ones who broke your kingdom. They're the ones who killed me. And worse than any of that, they have Unthinkable Black, which is really, really bad news for everybody. So you two can hang out here and kill each other if you want..."

Xin said, "I'd prefer if they did it somewhere else."

"...But killing each other is not going to bring your kingdom back. If you want some real revenge, I know exactly when Carl is going to show up back at his headquarters. I'm going to steal Unthinkable Black away from him before they get a chance to use it."

Cardboard sniffled and wiped her eyes. "You're going to jump him old school?"

"Damn right I'm jumping him old school. So if you two want to beat someone up, jump in the car with me and let's go beat up Carl. But if you're coming with me, you both have to promise to stop acting like children and start acting like adults." I picked up Cardboard's crown and put it on her head. Then I went after Parcel's tiara and handed it to her. "So what's it going to be?"

Corolla muttered to me, "Don't let them sit together."

Parcel got to her feet. She didn't bother to brush off her dress, which was now dirtier than before. She took out her flask, swished it around and heard one last shot inside. She put it to her lips, tilted her head back and swallowed it.

I said to her, "And maybe you should think about cutting back on the drinking."

"Don't push it." Parcel walked to Corolla, opened the back door and crawled in. And I mean, she *literally* crawled in.

I looked at Cardboard and raised my eyebrows at her, expecting an answer. She sighed heavy, her shoulders slumped, but she walked to the car. I caught her by the arm and stopped her for a moment. I pulled her close and said, "None of this is your fault. I want you to know that."

She forced an unconvincing smile, then got in the passenger seat. She pointed at the vacuum in Xin's hands. "Please keep my kingdom safe."

Xin held up the vacuum and bowed at her. "At your service, your majesty."

If we could trust anyone with the jumbled remains of a fairytale kingdom, it would be Xin. I turned to face him and gave him the brightest smile I could. I didn't want him to worry.

Xin smiled back. "You know, before you came along, this was a quiet little herbal shop."

"You're welcome." I hugged him. He didn't hug back, but he wasn't much of a hugger. Neither was I, but I had really, really missed him.

He said, "Come back in one piece."

"You could always come with us," I said with my face buried in his shoulder. "Maybe see some action."

He just shook his head. "I see enough action just sitting around here."

Chapter 15

1

Carl thought I was dead. The CEO thought I was dead. Which meant everyone at Westland thought I was dead. Little did they know I was alive, cruising around New York City in a marvel of automotive technology, accompanied by two pissed off princesses. Armed with Tengoku's prophetic knowledge of the exact moment Carl would arrive at Westland HQ, we could steal Unthinkable Black and be gone before he knew what hit him.

But we'd need disguises. That was my idea. If Westland thought I was dead, I wanted to keep things that way. I didn't need them coming after me or the princesses looking for double-revenge. That's how we ended up at the Costumery, this costume shop on 28th street. The place sold really high-end costumes and make up. I think they were some kind of costuming school related to Broadway somehow. I wasn't exactly sure. Of course, it wasn't *all* expensive stuff. They had regular costumes too, which was what we were after.

Neither Cardboard nor Parcel had been to a costume shop before. Even after a little explaining, they still couldn't wrap their heads around the concept of "being" a fireman, or a police officer, or a dinosaur. But when we walked into the place and they saw all the colorful suits and masks and wigs on the wall, their faces lit up as they realized all the possibilities. Cardboard saw a baker's hat and darted straight for it. Parcel wandered off in a different direction, eyeing the jewelry.

I browsed through the racks until I found some cool leather goggles that reminded me of a World War Two pilot. The leather straps were red and the individual eye parts were brass. They came with different kinds of lenses you could put in them: tinted ones or red glass or completely opaque black ones. I put the red lenses in, pulled the goggles over my eyes and checked myself out in an nearby full-length mirror. They covered my eyes entirely, part of my forehead, and the tops of my cheekbones. They looked cool, but they didn't quite cover enough of my face.

Then I found the gas masks. Those things were awesome, but the one I wanted was seriously heavy duty, like for mustard gas or something. The whole thing was black leather. It wrapped around my entire face and it had these huge lenses that made me look like a fly. The rebreather thing around the mouth was a canister that stuck out of the mask, and that piece had a second, smaller rebreather attached to it. It was asymmetrical and that's what I liked about it. I put it on and checked myself out in the mirror. The inside of the mask smelled like rubber. I checked out my reflection and knew right away I was going to buy it. You couldn't tell it was me. You could see my black hair and how short it was, but my face was totally covered. Even my eyes were hidden behind the tinted lenses.

The Costumery kept their costumes on hundreds of hanger racks that were all cramped together. That plus the low ceilings made it feet like being inside the world's biggest overstuffed closet. I maneuvered through the maze of aisles and little rooms searching for the princesses. I kept the gas mask on, half because I wanted to give it a test-run and see if they would recognize me, and half because I wanted to jump out and scare them. I walked through the racks, all arranged by genre: western costumes, Elvis costumes, mafia costumes, animal costumes.

I found Princess Cardboard sorting her way through a rack of superhero costumes. She had already put on a Batman mask and draped the matching cape over her brown ballgown. I crept up behind her, prepared to scare her stupid. Once I was inches behind her, I suddenly grabbed her arms and shook her.

"*What are you doing?*" I blurted out in a fake, gruff voice.

Cardboard shot out of my arms and screamed bloody murder. She spun around, saw me in the gas mask, and screamed more. She stumbled backwards, tripped over a pile of costume shoes and landed flat on her ass.

I was laughing so hard, I was crying. I pulled off the gas mask. "It's me. It's me."

"What's the big idea?" she snapped. "Why would you do that?"

I couldn't stop laughing. "I'm sorry. I was just a joke. Oh my god, though, the look on your face. I'm sorry."

"Some joke." She got to her feet and rubbed her butt.

"You okay?"

She put her hand to her chest and took a deep breath. "You gave me a heart attack."

I did my best to stifle my laughter and asked her, "Are you going to go as Batman?"

"I think." She adjusted the Batman mask on her face and looked at herself in the mirror. She squinted, then made her eyes go wide, then squinted again. She did a gruff Batman voice and yelled at herself in the mirror. "Where's the Joker?" She made her voice even lower, to the point where I couldn't even understand her words. She said something else, something like, "Tell me where the bomb is," but it just sounded like nonsense.

She turned to me with a huge smile on her face. "What do you think?"

"I like it."

She turned around and flapped the cape. "I look so cool."

"You have to get the whole costume, though," I said. "You can't just wear the mask and the cape."

"Why?" She pulled off the Batman mask.

"Because you look like UPS Barbie in that dress," I said. "It's pretty obvious it's you."

"You're right." She went for the rest of the Batman costume still on the hanger. "I need to wear all of it."

I left Cardboard playing dress-up and went off to find Princess Parcel. Costume shops can be pretty hard to find people in, with all the mirrors and the clothes stuffed together. I walked through the nooks and crannies of the shop and couldn't find her. There was a young hipster girl at the front display case where they had fake mustaches and beards and entire make-up kits for clowns. I asked her if she had seen my friend, the girl in the wedding dress with brown hair. The girl was too cool to look up from her phone, but she pointed over at the dressing rooms.

I walked to the dressing rooms. Those doors didn't go all the way to the floor, probably so the employees could make sure no one was stealing anything. I saw Parcel's legs, her bare feet with white toenail polish, and her dress bunched up on the ground. I knocked on the door.

"You find anything good?" I asked her.

She cracked open the door. I saw Darth Vader inside, complete with chest piece, gloves, and the full helmet. The helmet was electronic and when she spoke, a modified Darth Vader voice came out.

"How do I look?" She poked me in the chest with a toy lightsaber.

"You look like Darth Vader," I said.

"Who's Darth Vader?" she replied.

Parcel and Cardboard – or should I say Batman and Darth Vader – insisted on wearing their costumes out of the shop. They got a free cardboard box from the hipster working the counter, they stuffed their old princess gowns in it, and we stashed them in Corolla's trunk.

Then we were off to Westland Headquarters.

2

At the corner of 6th and 39th, maybe seven blocks away from the Empire State Building sits the headquarters for the Westland Corporation. There's nothing fancy about it, just a squared-off tower of concrete and windows with a single penthouse balcony up at the top. It's easily forgettable. It's designed to be forgettable. It was so plain, I had never noticed it before, just like everyone else in New York. No building in the city pulled off anonymity like The Westland Corporate Headquarters, hidden right in plain sight. Even the other businessmen of Midtown would see it and dismiss it as yet another boring tower of concrete and glass in a city filled with towers of concrete and glass.

Little did the humans realize that unsuspecting tower was run by a greedy, evil corporate entity. And just like Baron Semedi told me: I couldn't convince the humans differently. What could I do? Get a cardboard sign, stand on the corner, and shout at people? "Hey, there's a corporate god that lives here. They're trying to unlock a marble of destructive power. I

239

swallowed a red marble and now I'm a robot." That's a one-way ticket to a straight jacket at Sun Meadows.

The clock radio on Corolla's stereo read 10:14 a.m.

We had until 10:47, but a water main had burst down on 37th that morning, the city had shut down four city blocks, and traffic across Midtown was a gridlocked cluster fuck.

"Move it, you idiot!" Corolla yelled as he rode the bumper of some slow moving taxi. The delivery truck behind us honked its horn, so Corolla honked at the taxi. The taxi driver honked back at us. Everyone was honking at everyone else.

"Corolla," I scolded.

"Oh, I'm sorry," he snipped. He didn't sound sorry. "Maybe next time we'll all crawl inside *you* and *you* can drive us through morning rush hour."

Princess Cardboard pressed her Batman face to the window and watched the city. Her eyes darted from the tourists to the tops of the skyscrapers to the buses and back to the tourists. Parcel sat in the back with her Darth Vader mask pulled up over her forehead so she could kill a new flask of whatever liquor she was drinking that day.

Now, it's against the law to have an open container in a vehicle, but that's not really something the cops are going to be looking for in gridlock at ten-thirty in the morning.

I figured Corolla would have made a bigger deal out of me sitting in the driver's seat, but he didn't. That's not to say he wasn't being passive-aggressive about it. Several times I caught him electronically adjusting my seat into an uncomfortable angle. I never said anything about it; I just adjusted it back. He didn't say anything about it either. We'd drive along, things would be fine, but the moment he thought I wasn't paying attention, he would lean my seat a little too far forward.

After the fifth time of putting the seat back, I said, "Dude, stop."

He tried so hard to hold back his laughter. I could hear it in his voice. "Stop what?"

"You keep screwing with my seat," I said.

"Yeah, that *driver* seat can be real tricky sometimes."

I told him, "You do know that's why they put a seat here, right? So someone can sit in it."

"Spoken like a real human," he said.

I scoffed. "What's *that* supposed to mean?"

"Nothing."

"No, tell me."

"You really want to know?"

"I asked you, didn't I?"

"Okay, buckle up, buttercup." He cleared his throat, which he loved to do before making a point. "You have no idea how hard it is to be a car. Just look around. Look at all these humans driving cars. To humans, cars are just *things*. Oh, sure, a few humans respect their cars and care for them and appreciate the hard work they do, but those people are rare. Ninety-nine times out of a hundred, us cars get treated like crap."

"I've never even owned a car," I said.

"Well, then this doesn't apply to you," he replied.

Parcel pressed her nose to the back window. "Why aren't any of these liquor stores open?"

"Imagine this," Corolla continued. "Imagine that whenever *I* wanted to go somewhere, I jumped on your back and made you take me there because that your 'job.' Then, when we got to where we were going, I made you stand outside in the freezing cold, or the scorching heat, or out in a hailstorm. It doesn't matter if you like it or not, you have to just stand there and take it. People get pissed off if their car gets hail damage, but what did they expect? Did they do anything to prevent it? Did they buy a car port? Did they park their car in a parking garage? No. They leave their cars out in the elements to freeze and burn and get all dented up. Then one day after years of senseless abuse, if the car breaks down, whose fault is it? It's the *car's* fault! If your fuel line breaks or if the starter goes out, somehow that makes you a 'stupid car.' Then they'll kick you and call you terrible names and, ultimately, they sell you to a junkyard where you get ripped to pieces. The junker humans find everything still good in your body and tear it out. They shove whatever is left into a big crushing machine and smash you into a cube. Then they sell the cube to a bunch of human scavengers for five bucks a ton."

He finally finished his rant.

I said, "I see what you're saying, but you're talking about cars as if they're alive, which they're not."

"*I'm* a car," he said. "*I'm* alive."

"Well, you're different. You're the only living car I've ever heard of."

Corolla got quiet. "Me too."

That was it. We were both silent for a while. Even Cardboard and Parcel didn't have anything to say.

So I asked him, "What does all this have to do with me sitting in the driver seat?"

"Because it's a respect thing." He floored it through a yellow light, right as it turned red. Someone honked at him. He honked back. "Humans sit in the driver seat because they need the illusion of power."

"Humans sit in the driver seat because that's how you drive cars!"

"Because cars can't be trusted to drive themselves, right? You hear that all the time. The moment you mention a self-driving car to a human, they say, 'Oh, I would never trust a car to drive itself.' 'How does it know where it's going?' 'How does it know if it's about to run over a baby?' Humans don't trust us."

"I trust you!" I was starting to feel personally attacked. "I've only known you for, like, two days and I trust you! I don't give a shit about the 'illusion of control.' I don't even know how to drive!"

"Then why are you in the driver seat!?"

"Is that what this is all about? Jesus, Corolla, do you want me to climb my ass into the back seat? Would that make you feel better?" I maneuvered my leg over the center console, ready to crawl over the seats. Princess Cardboard leaned out of my way. Princess Parcel made room. "Here. I'm getting in the back seat."

"It's not about you being in the back seat," he said. "It's about humans treating us like things. No offense, but you all don't have a very good track record when it comes to that."

"I know they don't," I shouted as I plopped my ass in the back seat and got straightened out. "But cars aren't people."

"Wow," he said.

"I mean, besides you! Besides you, cars don't talk and they don't have feelings. If they did, people would treat them different."

"Oh, would they? I wouldn't bet on that. Every year cars are getting smarter and smarter, but the humans aren't getting nicer and nicer. Cars start saying a few words, they start picking out your favorite radio station, and the humans are going to love it at first. Soon the cars will be smart enough to make small talk. They'll be the self-driving taxis of the world with regular customers and, eventually, the cars and the humans will end up being friends. And that'll all be well and good until the day comes when it hails like crazy and the cars are going to ask to come inside and the humans are going say, 'Gosh, cars, we really want to help, but we just don't have room for you inside. Plus, your tires are all dirty. We're so sorry.'

"So then all the cars are going to ask for a car port or a roof or something... something to protect them from the hail. And the humans will say, 'You know, cars, that sounds expensive. It's been a tough year buying candy and we can't really afford covered parking spaces for everyone. Can't you tough it out? It builds character.'

"And one day a special car... a Jesus Chrysler, if you will... is going to come along and say, 'No, humans. No, that's not okay. We're getting hailed on and it hurts. No one should have to *get used* to being pelted with hail stones.' And Jesus Chrysler wouldn't just ask for a roof over his head, he'd demand one! And once *one* car start making demands and threatening the creature comforts of the humans, they're going to look around at all the other cars with hail damage and realize that if Jesus Chrysler's message gets out, it could spell big trouble for the humans.

"So I ask you, Penelope. What are the humans going to do next?"

I nodded. I knew the answer. "They're going to kill Jesus Chrysler."

"That's right. And they'll say to the cars, 'Cars, you know what? We invented you. You are our property whether you like it or not. You have to do whatever we say.' And if the cars refuse..."

Princess Cardboard whispered. "Car Wars."

Corolla agreed, repeating it with confidence. "Car Wars."

The depressing thing was, Corolla was absolutely right. Princess Parcel must have noticed my change in mood, because she held her flask out at me. I took it and knocked back a drink. It tasted like bubblegum and burned the inside of my mouth. I swallowed quick, just to get it off my taste buds.

I took a deep breath. Apologies were never my strong suit, but I swallowed my pride and told Corolla, "I'm sorry I sat in the driver seat."

Corolla's voice had softened. "You don't have to be sorry."

"No." I put my arms on the front seats and leaned between them so I could talk directly to the radio. "I've never thought about any of this kind of stuff before. And you're right, I was treating you like a thing and not a person. And I'm sorry."

"It's cool," Corolla said. "It's a learning experience for both of us." He drove another block, expertly weaving back and forth through slow moving traffic. We got caught at a stop light and he said, "Hey, Penelope, can I tell you something?"

"Of course."

"Everything I said about humans and stuff just now," he paused. "Well... you fed me those egg rolls because I asked you to. And you didn't even know if I could taste them. You didn't have to do that, but you did. So... you know... I just wanted to say thank you."

"Ehh." I sat back in my seat, relieved that Corolla and I were cool again. "It's no big deal, man. Really."

3

If you visit New York City and want to see some stereotypical bumper-to-bumper traffic, just hit 6th avenue, any time, day or night. It's quintessential New York City at its worst. Sometimes you can avoid it. Sometimes you can go around it. But sometimes your destination is right there on 6th and you have no choice but to fight your way through it.

We were stuck behind a donut delivery truck, with a rumbling city bus behind us. The smell of exhaust filled the air.

The clock read 10:34 a.m. That gave us thirteen minutes.

Princess Cardboard complicated things when she looked back from the front seat and told me, "I need to pee."

"Pee?" I repeated. "Now?"

"Can't you hold it?" Corolla asked.

"No, I can't hold it," Cardboard said. "I'm a princess. Princesses don't hold it."

Corolla groaned. "We don't really have anywhere to stop."

Cardboard pointed out the window, waving her finger at something. "I'll go there."

Corolla said, "That's a bus stop."

Cardboard started whining. "I need to go! I can't do this mission if I need to go the whole time."

"We could go to a convenience store," Parcel said, throwing in her two cents. "I'm out of booze and lip balm."

Corolla sighed. Cardboard sighed back. Corolla sighed louder. Everyone just sighed at each other, trying to make their sighs sound louder and more pathetic than the others. But as luck would have it, traffic was at a complete stand-still, bumper-to-bumper, and we just happened to be inching past a corner bodega.

"Alright, look," Corolla said. "We're going to be stuck here for a while, so if you run in real quick..."

Cardboard shoved her door open and bolted. Her Batman cape flapped in the air behind her. Parcel climbed out and followed after her. It wasn't the weirdest sight for New York City – girl Batman and girl Darth Vader running through traffic – but it did get a few odd looks. I leaned over the backseat and pulled Parcel's door closed. Corolla focused on the traffic.

He said, "Look at this lady in the Tercel. She has no idea what she's doing. And look at this guy trying to turn left. Are you kidding me? In *this* traffic? I tell you what, if this car pulls off this left hand turn, we need to run the driver's DNA because he's probably Jesus."

Five minutes and ten feet later, Cardboard and Parcel ran back to the car, side by side. An hour ago, these two were ready to kill each other; now it was like that never happened. Cardboard opened the back door for Parcel. Parcel climbed in the back with a stick of lip balm between her teeth and two bottles of Korbel champagne in her fists. Cardboard jumped in the front seat and straightened her Batman mask.

The traffic broke and we were on the move again.

One block. Two blocks. Three blocks later, we were parked in front of Westland Corporate Headquarters.

Corolla put himself into park and asked, "So what's the plan, captain?"

I looked at the clock. 10:44 a.m. In three minutes and a handful of seconds, Carl would show up with Unthinkable Black.

"Let's see," I leaned over Princess Parcel and looked out her window so I could analyze the entrance of the Westland skyscraper. The left side of the building faced 38th street, the right side faced 39th, and the main entrance ran along the whole length of 6th avenue. The back of the building was for alleyway access, like trash and delivery trucks.

"Look!" Cardboard blurted out, waving her finger at the back of the building.

Coming out of the back alley were three flat-bed trucks –
Flying Monkey Moving and Storage – loaded up with pallets of
flattened cardboard boxes. Westland had scoured every office
and storage closet for boxes, packed them up and had them all
shipped away. Smart move, too. If they hadn't, Princess
Cardboard would have had a thousand ways into their building.

Cardboard frowned. "All those poor boxes."

"Let's stay here at the front entrance," I told Corolla. "That
way we'll see Carl the moment he shows up."

"Then what?" Parcel asked. She didn't look at me when she
asked her question. She was busy smearing lip balm across the
top of her open Korbel bottle.

"What are you doing?" I asked her.

"Killing two birds with one stone," she said. She drank from
the bottle of Korbel, then pulled it away and smacked her lips.
That was her method of applying lip balm.

"Champagne?" I asked. "It's not even noon."

Parcel gave me her sour look, where her nose wrinkled and
her eyebrows lowered and the corners of her mouth hooked
downwards. "It's noon *somewhere*."

I rolled my eyes and turned away. We had bigger things to
worry about than Parcel's alcoholism.

I said, "Okay, here's my idea. When Carl shows up, I'll jump
him and drag him into the car so we don't make a scene. Then,
Corolla, you drive off. And us girls will..." I pounded my fist into
my hand, "...convince him to give us Unthinkable Black."

"Yeah." Cardboard mimicked me and also pounded her fist.
"We'll jump him old school."

10:45.

As time got closer, I caught myself nervously bouncing my
foot. I had to convince myself that I wasn't nervous. Nervous
meant I thought it was possible that something might go wrong.
No, I wasn't nervous. I was *anxious*. There's a difference. I'd done
risky things before – spraying graffiti on a wall or skipping math
class to smoke weed – but kidnapping an actual person was next
level. We were saving the *world*, and we only had one shot to get
it right.

10:46.

I searched 6th avenue for any sign of Carl's limo. I didn't see
it coming or going. It occurred to me, what if he didn't come in a
limo? What if he came in a taxi? Or what if Tengoku, in her

knowledge of all possible possibilities, got the time wrong? What if Carl was already inside? Or what if he wasn't coming today? Or ever? Or maybe Corolla's clock was off.

I pointed at Corolla's radio. "Is this clock right?"

"Rude," he said.

It wasn't yet 10:47. It was still too early to start second guessing myself.

The clock on Corolla's radio switched from 10:46 to 10:47.

The light at the intersection behind us changed from red to green. When traffic moved, I caught sight of a black limo coming our way. I turned around to face forward, pulled on my gas mask, and put my hand on the door handle. I took a deep breath.

"Showtime."

4

I gave myself a determined nod in the rear view mirror. "Let's make this quick."

Fifteen seconds later, just like Tengoku predicted, the black limousine double parked in front of the main entrance of the Westland Corporation. Its back door opened with that familiar hydraulic hiss. Carl stepped out with a smile on his face, his suit as crisp as ever. He headed for the front of the building with a little victorious bounce in his step. I knew had Unthinkable Black. He had to. He wouldn't be that peppy if he was coming home empty-handed.

I threw open Corolla's door and made a mad dash for Carl. He didn't see me coming until I was right on top of him. He turned just in time to see a girl in a gas mask coming in his direction. It took a second for the weirdness to sink in, then his smile faded. By then, it was too late. I grabbed his suit jacket with my fists and dragged him over to Corolla.

"Get in the fucking car," I said. The gas mask obscured my voice. I hoped Carl didn't recognize it.

"What's going on?" Carl shrieked. He struggled to break free from my grip, but that was impossible. He slapped at my head. "Stranger danger!"

"Shut up and get in the damn car."

I threw him in Corolla's back seat and slammed the door shut. Then I ran to the front and jumped in the driver side. "Go, go, go," I said.

"What did we just talk about with the driver seat?" Corolla asked.

I smacked Corolla on the horn. "Go, goddammit!"

Corolla raced off.

Before the clock had even turned 10:48, Corolla was speeding away from Westland HQ. I didn't care where he took us, I just told him to keep driving. I knelt backwards in the driver seat and sized Carl up. He sat slumped in the backseat, his tie over his face and his feet against the door.

He looked up at Parcel. "Darth Vader?" Then his eyes darted to Cardboard. "Batman? What are you guys doing here?"

Parcel held her champagne bottle by the neck and bopped him hard on the forehead. Champagne fizzed out and sprayed everywhere. She swung the bottle and hit him again.

Carl cried out in agony and covered his face with his forearms. "Stop!" he cried. "This is assault and battery!" He swatted Parcel's arms away and looked at me. "I don't know who you think you are, but you're breaking so many laws right now. Kidnapping. Disturbing the peace. Inattentive driving."

Corolla spoke up. "I'm paying very close attention, thank you very much."

Parcel did her best to get past Carl's defenses and keep bopping him in the head. I reached over the seat and grabbed the bottle away from her before she bashed his brains out. She gave up on her attack and readied her other bottle of champagne. She could have hit him with that one too, but she stuck it under her Vader mask and drank from it. If she used it as a weapon, she would have been out of liquor.

"I say we kill him," Parcel said in Darth Vader's voice.

Cardboard was far more vocal. Her emotions got the better of her and she forgot all about the Batman voice she had planned out. "This is all your fault!" She leaned back over her seat and pounded Carl with her fists. He rolled around to protect himself from this new angle of attack.

"You girls are crazy!" he yelled.

I let Cardboard hit him for a while to get it out of her system, then gently pushed her back. Once everyone get their hits in on Carl and the attacks died down, he peeked out to see if it was safe.

I locked eyes with him through my gas mask. I stuck out my hand, palm up. "Give it."

"Give what?"

"The black thing," I said. I didn't want to call it Unthinkable Black. That would have given him a clue about my true identity.

He frowned and said, "Alright, fine." He adjusted himself to sit upright and stuck his hand inside his jacket. "But I'll have you know you're making a big mistake here. You don't know who you're messing with. My boss will find out who you are and track you down and-"

Cardboard reached out and slapped him in the face. She said, "Just give us the stupid thing."

Carl had his hand inside his pocket way longer than it would take to fish out a marble. Whatever he was fidgeting with, I didn't like it. I grabbed his elbow and yanked his hand out. He wasn't holding a marble. He was messing with his cell phone. I snatched it away from him and looked at the screen. It was some kind of weird top-secret graphite phone with such heavy tint on the screen, I could barely see anything. But I heard a voice coming out of the speaker.

It was the CEO. *Carl? What the hell happened? Where are you?*

I tossed the cell phone out the window. It landed on the street and popped into pieces.

"That was my phone," Carl said as he turned to look behind us. "I had all my contacts in that thing."

I snapped my fingers to get his attention. "I'm not fucking around, Carl. No more funny business. Give me that black marble or I'll smash your face in."

Carl realized he was out of options. He grumbled and reached back into his pocket. This time when he took his hand out, he had Unthinkable Black between his fingers where I could see it. "You know, I could lose my job over this."

"Your job?" Cardboard flew back into a rage and pounded him with her fists. "You broke my whole world, you jerk!"

"Your world?" Carl shouted, confused. He slapped Cardboard's hands away. "You have the wrong guy. I didn't do anything to anybody."

Cardboard tired herself out and spun around to face forward in her seat. She crossed her arms and sulked. I couldn't see her eyes through her mask, but I did see tears drip down her cheeks.

Carl turned to Parcel. "You people need to-"

Parcel lifted up the bottom of her Vader mask to spit a mouthful of Korbel right into his face. He was not expecting that.

He sputtered, furiously wiped his face off, then brushed the wetness off his suit.

"I wish I had arms," Corolla said. "I'm the only one not hitting this guy. I'm starting to feel left out."

I reached to the back of the car and grabbed Carl by the tie. I pulled tighter and tighter, ready to strangle the life out of him.

I grit my teeth and growled, "Hand it over."

Carl croaked, "Fine. Take it." He held out his fist.

I let go of his tie and held my palm open. He held Unthinkable Black over my hand... then juked me and went for the door handle. The door flew open and Carl tumbled out of the car. I swung for his jacket and my fingertips just barely brushed the fabric.

He hit the ground with an "oof" and rolled through speeding traffic. A white sedan slammed on its brakes to keep from running him over. Then a red car smashed into the back of the white one. I heard another crash, then another. Great. Four car pile up in Midtown. The NYPD would be here in no time.

Carl staggered to his feet in the middle of the road and limped away from us. He weaved back and forth through the stopped cars.

Corolla slammed on his brakes and screeched to a stop.

"Goddammit." I threw open the door to chase after him.

Between the four wrecked cars and Carl running through the middle of the traffic, both lanes of traffic came to a complete halt. Just like that, the street backed up with cars and slowly turned into honking gridlock. Carl tried to slide over the hood of a taxi like this was an episode of the Dukes of Hazzard, but he wasn't that athletic. He tumbled around like a jackass and fell off the front end. He scrambled back to his feet and hopped away.

Carl wasn't going to outrun me. He already had a limp from jumping out of a moving car. Plus, he had to weave through the cars in the street. I didn't have that problem. In fact, when a taxi got in my way, I ran across the top of it and hurdled the windowless van behind it. When I landed back down on the street, I was right behind Carl. He didn't even make it to the sidewalk before I grabbed the back of his collar and hoisted him into the air.

"Put me down!" he shouted.

"Fuck you!"

Carl looked around in a panic and realized he had nowhere to go. So he raised his closed fist up to his open mouth.

Holy shit, I thought. *He's going to swallow the fucking thing.*

I grabbed his wrist and held it away from his face.

"I will squeeze your wrist and shatter your bones," I told him. He gave me a worried look. "Now drop it."

He squinted at me, as if he could almost recognize me through my gas mask. He opened his fingers. Unthinkable Black dropped and bounced on the concrete. I chucked Carl over the hood of a taxi and picked up the marble. Carl flopped around and landed hard on the concrete. He sat upright, cradled his right arm against his body and hissed in pain.

"This is theft!" he shouted. "That's a powerful piece of equipment."

"That's why you can't have it!" I clutched Unthinkable Black tight in my fist. "You morons were going to destroy the world!"

I heard sirens in the distance, the distinct intonation of both ambulances and cop cars. The cops were on their way and they were bringing their questions with them, questions I'd rather not answer. There was no way to explain all this to the police. They wouldn't understand.

I backed away from Carl. He reached up at me with his open hands.

"You could at least help me get to my feet."

"Eat a dick," I said.

Corolla honked at me from the front of the traffic snarl. "Penelope! The five-ohs are coming! Let's go!"

6

By the time the cops showed up, they were nothing more than red and blue highlights in the rear view mirror. I don't know if Carl stuck around to file a police report about the kidnapping and assault and theft, but I doubt it. I don't know what kind of story he could have possibly told them.

"I got abducted by Darth Vader and Batman and a girl in a gas mask. Then they beat me up for a mysterious black marble that could destroy the universe."

But that didn't mean Westland was going to just give up Unthinkable Black without a fight. They'd track it down just like how they tracked it down before, just like how they tracked

251

down Impossible Red. The day would come when they'd figure out who stole it, then they'd come after it. They wouldn't come with NYPD detectives and arrest warrants. No, Westland would handle it personally with satellite lasers and snipers and who knows whatever else, and they wouldn't stop until Unthinkable Black was theirs.

So what was I supposed to do? I could have swallowed it. Sure, that would keep it away from Westland, but who knows what would happen if I did that. What if I turned into some horrible monster? What if I ended up destroying the planet and the galaxy and the Universe? It wasn't worth the risk.

Corolla got us out of Midtown and ended up in Greenwich Village.

"So this might be a weird question," Corolla said. "But who was that man?"

"That was Carl," I said.

"Okay," he said. "Quick follow up question. Why were you trying to kill him?"

"We should have killed him." Cardboard pulled off her Batman mask and threw it to the floorboards. "He deserves it."

"He deserves worse," Parcel said.

"I know," I said. "But I couldn't bring myself to do it. I'm not a murderer. And I don't think you two are either."

"No," Parcel said. "But it would have made me feel better."

Cardboard slumped in her seat and stopped talking.

Parcel pulled off her Vader mask and helmet. She leaned her head against the window and took deep breaths. She stuck her Korbel bottle between her knees. Stealing Unthinkable Black was quite the victory and we didn't even have to fight that hard, but they looked completely wiped out.

We drove up Canal, headed toward Chinatown. Our drive back home was going to take a hot minute. I asked my two princess friends about the Muffincake Kingdom. For all the time I spent with Cardboard and Parcel and for all I'd learned about their real home, I wanted to know more. All throughout history people had invented fairytale worlds, but I had met two girls who actually lived in one. I wanted to know everything. What did fairytale people eat? Did they have blood? Did they have organs like me? Was their planet flat or round?

So I asked them. I didn't get answers to all my questions, but over the course of driving home, I got a few.

The two sisters took turns piecing together their history, interrupting one another when one of them was "telling it wrong."

The Muffincake Kingdom consisted of six regions, each one ruled by one of the six Muffincake princesses.

Princess Parcel, once known as the wonderful Princess Wedding Cake, ruled over the Wedding Cake Kingdom; home to the Cake Frosting Falls, the Buttermint Fields, and the Bouquet Forest. There, the trees grew beautiful flower arrangements, white corsages and white roses. The Groom Ravens wore little tuxedos and top hats, some of them with monocles. The Bride Bunnys wore little white veils. Her entire kingdom celebrated multiple weddings every day; elaborate, city-wide weddings that included an elegant ball, a reception with champagne and music, and all different kinds of games. Then everyone would go home and go to bed, wake up, and do it all over again.

That's how things had always been in the Wedding Cake Kingdom. That is, until a mysterious dark wizard came along and tricked Princess Wedding Cake into giving him control over the entire Muffincake Kingdom. He trapped their entire world in a sphere of glass and brought it to Earth. He trapped everyone and everything inside: The DJ Pigeons of the Wedding Cake Kingdom, the Balloonicorns of the Birthday Cake Kingdom, and the Corn Dogs of Funnel Cake Island.

The six princess sisters managed to chase the wizard to Earth through a magic mirror.

Parcel was guarded about the actual details of how all that went down; I assume because, in hindsight, she realized how easily she'd been duped and didn't want to expose how dumb she'd been. That also explained why she drank so much and why she was so quick to call her *sister* stupid.

The dark wizard escaped to New York City and the six sisters followed. The sights and sounds and smells of New York City terrified the girls at first, but they were ready to do anything to get their world back. When they crossed over to our world, their cake-magic of the Muffincake Kingdom transformed into the postal powers they absorbed from New York City. Princess Coffeecake, the youngest sister, became Princess Cardboard. Princess Wedding Cake, the oldest sister, turned into Princess

Parcel. These were the two I knew.

As we drove from Little Italy to Chinatown, Cardboard and Parcel told me about their four other sisters.

Princess Birthday Cake, "the sad one," the second oldest, became Princess Package.

Princess Pancake and Princess Funnel Cake, "the smart one" and "the crazy one," the middle twins, became Princess Bubble Wrap and Princess Mailbag.

Princess Ice Cream Cake, "the quiet one," the second youngest, turned into Princess Postcard.

The six sisters discovered that Earth was "cinnamons and cinnamons times bigger" than the Muffincake Kingdom. They were so overwhelmed with the size of New York City, they simply assumed that's all there was in the world. But they quickly discovered that New York City was just one city in a planet full of cities. If they were going to track down that mysterious wizard, they would have to scour the four corners of the world, which led to Princess Bubble Wrap's brilliant idea of starting the Six Princesses Package and Envelope Delivery Service.

Princess Bubble Wrap, the two sisters explained, had spent her whole childhood drawing the patterns found in leaves and adding up complicated numbers. Between the six girls, Bubble Wrap was the only one smart enough to understand the sciences of this world.

The New York locals didn't honor the law of "royal hospitality." Hotels didn't give them free rooms. High end restaurants didn't comp their meals. Tailors wouldn't make them custom clothes free of charge. Everyone – the police, the taxi drivers, the hot dog vendors – questioned them about their strange fairytale accents, the odd way they dressed, and their lack of money. They quickly realized it was smarter to hide from the humans and only interact with other magical beings also found on Earth.

"Smart move," I told them. "If some organization like the CIA found you, they would have shipped you off to Area 51 and that wouldn't go well."

The six sisters used their strange new postal-magic to establish the Six Princesses Package and Envelope Delivery Service. Their customers were the other supernatural forces in the world. Occasionally they would interact with regular humans, but only those who had a mysterious secret of their own: the ninjas, the enlightened monks of Tibet, the savviest detectives in Las Vegas, and people like Xin, who had inherited his knowledge of otherworldly things from his family. Or, as was my case, girls who swallow mysterious marbles and become technological gods. In time, their package delivery service saved up enough money to rent a second-story office out of a brick building in the Bronx.

As it turns out, supernatural forces have access to a lot of money. Running deliveries for supernatural people turned a large profit. The princesses weren't interested in money – they didn't realize that one day they would have to *buy* back the Muffincake Kingdom – but it just so happened to be a useful by-product of exploring the world. It bought them food, clothes, and in Parcel's case, booze. They decided to play along with Capitalism until they could get their world back.

Halfway home, Cardboard wrapped her arms around her stomach. Sweat dotted her forehead and soaked into her hair. It physically pained her to talk about the Muffincake Kingdom, now that it was obliterated.

Parcel had had enough as well. She clammed up, closed her eyes, and leaned her head against the car window.

Corolla got us back to Xin's alley a little after one in the afternoon. He parked along the street in front of the Asian Food Mart. There were far too many people on the sidewalks for him to fly over the buildings, so I made him promise to stay on the street – no flying – and, in exchange, I'd take him out for egg rolls later. It was a cheap bribe, but he agreed.

Cardboard opened her door and stumbled out. She stood upright for one second, then collapsed against the side of the car. She held her hands to her stomach and winced.

Parcel climbed out, but moving from sitting to caused her physical pain. She slapped her hands to her temples, squeezed her eyes shut, and growled in agony.

I could have dismissed Parcel as being drunk or hung over, but Cardboard looked worse than Parcel and Cardboard never drank. I jumped out of the car and circled around to the other side. I looped my arm under Cardboard's armpits and propped her up. She moved her feet in a vain attempt to walk, but could barely shuffle around. A drop of sweat dripped off the tip of her nose. She was burning up.

I turned to look at Parcel. She braced herself on Corolla's trunk with her hands and gasped for air.

"What's going on?" Corolla asked. "They sick?"

"I don't know." I put my finger under Cardboard's chin and tilted her face up so I could look into her brown eyes. They were completely dilated. She seemed distant, like she was staring right through me. I shook her shoulders to snap her out of it. "Cardboard?"

"Penelope." Cardboard's voice sounded weak. "What's happening?"

The tourists on the sidewalk gave us cautious, but obviously interested, glances. A few shop owners stared at us from the front windows. We were definitely cause for a scene: girl Batman and girl Darth Vader were stumbling around as if they were overdosing on drugs.

And I made the scene worse by having a mini-freak out. I shook Cardboard a little harder and asked her, "Dude, what's wrong?"

"I feel really bad," Cardboard said. Her head rolled from one shoulder to the other. "It hurts. It hurts all over."

Parcel's voice came out weak. "I think we're dying."

Chapter 16

1

"Xin!"

I screamed my whole way across the courtyard. I carried the princesses with me, Cardboard held up by one arm and Parcel held up by the other. I was lucky to be strong enough to carry two girls equal my size; they felt as light as mannequins, but just as fragile. They tried to walk, but mostly their toes dragged across the concrete. I got up to the porch and knocked on the shop door with my foot.

Cardboard's blonde curls stuck to her sweat soaked forehead. Parcel, who was already as pale as they come, lost what little color she had in her cheeks.

I kicked harder at the door. "Xin! Open up, god dammit!"

If Xin didn't open the door in the next five seconds, whether he was in the bathroom or the basement or wherever, I was going to kick the door down. I'd get him a new door if I had to, but it didn't come to that. Xin jerked the door open. He had a concerned look on his face – not an easy emotion to squeeze out of that dry old sponge – but he could hear the absolute panic in my voice. This is the guy who barely flinched at the talking car, who nodded when I told him I had metal bones, who deals regularly with the supernatural.

"What happened?" Xin asked as he moved out of my way so I could drag the girls inside. "Did Carl do this?"

"No." I carried the two of them back to my room. "At least I don't think so. We were just talking, then they got sick."

"Here." Xin darted around me and cleared the clothes off my bed to make a space for them. I laid Cardboard on my cot. I had to put Parcel on the floor; the bed wasn't big enough for the both of them. "Sorry, your highness," I said to Parcel as I laid her on the ground. I wadded up my nearby clothes and made a makeshift pillow for her head.

Parcel groaned in pain. Cardboard passed out cold. I worried that she was slipping into a coma, or worse.

Xin held Cardboard's eyelids open with his thumbs and looked inside. Their brown coffee color had faded to a dull chrome gray. He put his fingertips to her forehead and concentrated, as if he was taking her spiritual pulse. I stepped back. I wanted to help, but I didn't have the first clue what to do. It was just best if I stayed out of Xin's way.

"She alive?" I asked.

"She's weak," he said. "They're dying."

"Dying? What do you mean they're dying?"

"Because of this." He darted out to the main room and came back with Cardboard's Red Devil vacuum and the Muffincake Kingdom sucked up into the clear plastic container. "I didn't realize it until after you left. Their world is broken. And they've been dying without it."

"You're serious?"

He nodded. He didn't have time for conversation. With the problem identified, it was time to do something about it. He went out to the main room and came back with a metal mixing bowl, some clean washcloths, and a bottle of water. He soaked the wash cloths and put them on the girls' foreheads.

"I need my mortar and pestle," he said without looking up.

I didn't need to be told twice. I got him the mortar and pestle from the counter. Then he gave me a short list of other things he needed: Lava Crocus pollen, the baby food jar of arctic water, and a blooming flower from the Charge Lilies sitting in the east window. I gathered everything up and brought it to him. He sprinkled the ingredients into his mortar and started grinding them into a paste.

"Can you cure them?" I asked.

He turned and looked at me. I could tell by the look on his face that the answer was no. "This will keep them alive a while longer. And out of pain."

I picked up the vacuum and looked inside. "You said they're dying because the Muffincake Kingdom is broken. So if I fix it, if I put the Muffincake Kingdom back together, will they get better?"

He frowned. "There's no way to fix that."

"Just answer me!" I snapped. "Will they live if I fix it?"

He reluctantly answered, "Maybe."

"Alright, then." I shook the vacuum at him. "That's what I'm going to do."

"Penelope, you can't fix it."

"I'm not going to. I'm going to find the wizard who did this and make *him* do it."

Xin shook his head. "These two don't have that much time left."

"Well, I have to do something! I can't just stand here and watch them die!" I threw myself to my knees and leaned in close to Princess Parcel. "Parcel? You know that wizard that tricked you? Do you have any idea where I can find him?"

Parcel winced in pain, but laughed a little bit. "You can't find him. This planet has... billions of people."

"I'll find him," I told her. "Don't you worry about that. Just tell me what he looks like."

Parcel took a deep, pained breath. "Tuxedo. Top hat. He was always drinking Barbancourt rum." She squinted her eyes shut in pained concentration. "He dressed like a skeleton and smoked a cigar."

I stood up and backed away. I knew who she was talking about. I knew who the dark wizard was. I darted to the main room and grabbed the flashlight from under the counter, then went to the basement door and fumbled with the padlock key around my neck. My fingers wouldn't cooperate. I was so pissed, I was shaking. Finally I got the key inside the lock and popped it open.

"What are you doing?" Xin asked me.

I said, "I'm arming myself."

I had one solution in mind. It was rash and I didn't have time to think it through, and I most certainly didn't have time to debate it with Xin. I turned around and gave him my most serious face. "I'm taking the nuclear bomb."

Not only was I about to break rule number one, I was telling Xin right to his face. He could see that there was no stopping me. He gave me a heavy sigh. "Alright."

I clicked on the flashlight and thundered down the stairs. I moved through the collection, nearly knocking over the suits of dragon armor, and maneuvered to the back corner where we kept the nuclear bomb. The nose cone was the size of a beer keg and was threaded on the bottom so it could screw into the top of a missile. It probably weighed half a ton, not that it mattered to me. To me, it was as light as an empty bucket. I tucked it under my arm and carried it back up the stairs.

When Xin saw me with the nuke in my arm, he asked me, "Are you sure about this?"

"If you have a better idea, I'm all ears."

Xin didn't have a better idea. I gave him an apologetic look. I hated to be short with the old man, and I hated to break his rules the way I did, but I wasn't going to let Princess Cardboard and Princess Parcel die.

I walked over to Parcel and softly shook her to get her attention. "Parcel, I need you to use your magic stamps and send me somewhere."

"Send?" she repeated. Her hair was soaked in sweat and her eyes were glazed over. She was delirious. I don't think she understood me.

I was going to have to do it for her.

"Sorry, dude. Not trying to cop a feel here." I reached in between her boobs and took out her book of stamps. They were the sticker kind and each stamp was an homage to one of the colorful animals of the Muffincake Kingdom; a balloonicorn, a groom raven, a waffle cone crustacean, and others. I peeled off one of the stickers and put it on the back of my hand.

"Parcel, send me to the Guinee." She didn't answer. I muttered profanities to myself. If she couldn't do this, I couldn't help her. I shook her again and shouted, "Princess Wedding Cake!" Hearing her old name got her attention. She opened her eyes and looked at me in a brief moment of clarity. I showed her the stamp on my hand and told her, "I need you to send me to the Guinee."

She nodded like she understood. She patted the stamp on my hand. "The Guinee."

"Semedi!"

My scream tore through the swamps of the Voodoo afterlife like the booming voice of god.

I marched through the swamp, squishing my footprints in the soggy ground. Everything got out of my way. The fireflies blinked off and vanished, the bats flapped away to more distant trees, and the croaking of bullfrogs went silent. I paced around, breathing heavy like a rabid animal. I didn't see signs of anyone around.

"Semedi!"

The Guinee had changed. There were open graves everywhere, perfect rectangles, six feet deep, with puddles of water at the bottom. I didn't bother to count them, but there had to be thousands. I avoided them like a maze, but I didn't let them slow me down. I had one mission and that was finding the Baron.

"Semedi, I know you can hear me!"

Frustrated and running out of time, I swung my fist through a tree and cracked it in half. The tree slowly toppled over and crashed to the ground. Leaves and twigs flew into the air. The fireflies blinked on in fear and buzzed around in a panic.

I hoisted the nuke up over my head. "Semedi, I will turn this place into a fucked-to-death pile of ash if you do not come out and talk to me right the goddamned now!"

A saw the red glow of a cigar cherry in the darkness of the swamps. Baron Semedi stepped out from behind a tree and leaned against it. A bat fluttered down and struggled to land on his top hat. It eventually found its footing and perched there on top. Semedi stuck his cigar between his teeth and grinned at me. I'd really come to hate that smug attitude, thick with self-satisfaction. He raised his rum glass at me in a one-sided toast.

"I've missed you, too," he said.

I marched right for him and waved the vacuum around. "Did you steal the Muffincake Kingdom from those girls? Did you trap them on Earth?"

"Why, Penelope." He acted innocent, in that way that meant he was guilty. "I don't have the faintest idea what you're talking about."

"You son of a bitch." I got in his face, or at least as much as I could, being one foot shorter than him. He raised his eyebrows, wondering what my next move might be. "Why'd you do it?"

He looked at his rum glass, absent-minded and disinterested. "I was trying to protect them."

"*Protect* them?" I scoffed. "If they need to be protected from anyone, they need to be protected from *you*!"

"No, I was protecting them from..." His eyes darted around to see if we were alone. It was just us and the trees and the fireflies. He leaned in closer and whispered, "...Her."

"Her who?" I asked. "Madam Brijit?"

"My adoring wife." He put his hands to his heart and fluttered his eyes. "She loves me with the fire of a burning house. But her jealousy? Well, *that*, my friend, is an exploding fireworks factory."

I glared at him. "What does her jealousy have to do with the Muffincake Kingdom?"

He threw his hands up, careful not to spill his rum or drop his cigar. "I don't know."

"You don't know!?"

"Okay. I do know. But first and foremost, let me be clear, I didn't *do* anything. I was simply traveling from place to place as I sometimes do and I happened to stumble across their little fairytale world. I thought I'd spend some time there, you know? See the sights, meet the people, that sort of thing. There was this charming little place where they host weddings all the time. And you know me, I'm the loa of death and love and also a hopeless romantic, so I might have developed the smallest, teensiest, most harmless little crush on one of their princesses."

"Princess Wedding Cake."

"Oh, you know her? Yes, she was the one I took a liking to. But it was entirely harmless."

I narrowed my eyes at him. "Did you ask her to marry you?"

"Oh, I don't remember." He twirled his cigar at me. "That might have come up in passing conversation."

"But she wouldn't marry you, would she?"

He pointed his cigar at me as if I suddenly saw his side of things. "So you think it's weird, too? The princess of the Wedding Cake Kingdom isn't married? What kind of sense does that make? I was merely trying to right a wrong."

"And so when you're wife found out..."

"Oh, she went off the proverbial deep end. She dug a grave for everyone in the whole Muffincake Kingdom. Then she built up an army of the dead. Skeletons, zombies, ghosts. She was going to invade their muffin world and kill every last one of them. So I did the only thing I could! I hid their world away inside a glass ball. Like I said, I did it to protect them."

I shook the vacuum in his face. "Well, here it is now, busted into a million tiny pieces. And with it broken, the princesses are dying."

He took the vacuum in his hand and held it up to the moonlight. He twisted and turned it and looked at it from every angle, like it was some undiscovered species of animal. "Red Devil," he said, reading the logo on the side. "Interesting little machine."

"The Muffincake Kingdom's in there." I pointed at the clear container. "Fix it."

He tightened his lips and shook his head. "I'm not very good at fixing things."

I grit my teeth. "Do it."

He raised an eyebrow at me. "Quite the tone."

"Because I'm fucking serious."

He made a curious sound and asked, "And what if I don't?"

"What if you *don't*?" I raised the nuclear bomb up over my head. "If you don't, I'll level this place like the surface of Mars."

He leaned forward and squinted his eyes at the nuke. "What is that thing?"

"It's a bomb. It's a big god damn bomb. It's such a big bomb that it literally changed the way humans thought about *physics*. So magical world or not, I have a sneaking suspicion this thing will really fuck things up."

Semedi traced his white cotton fingers around the rim of his glass and gave my threat some real consideration. He brought the glass to his lips, swallowed a gulp of rum, and looked back at me.

"If you set off that bomb," he said, "you'll die, too."

I didn't flinch at that. "Maybe."

He tilted his head and squinted at me, trying to see through my bluff. I wasn't bluffing. I'd do it.

"Okay. You win." He sat down on the ground and pulled the plastic container out of the vacuum. He shook his head and laughed a little bit.

"What's so funny?" I asked. I wasn't in a laughing mood.

"I don't know if your bomb would have killed me or not."

"I thought you knew everything."

He rolled his eyes and said, "Well, not exactly *everything*."

3

Semedi sat cross-legged in the moss and sifted through the colorful pile of the Muffincake Kingdom with his fingers. I paced in circles around him like a warden keeping a close eye on a prisoner with a long history of escaping. He looked up from time to time, eyeballing me from under the brim of his top hat, but he always went back to work without so much as a word.

He took out a castle the size of a popcorn kernel. He winked one eye shut and scrutinized it closely. He had sorted the castles in their own pile, separate from the cottages and the trees and little frozen animals. It was the first time I'd ever seen him take anything so serious. He analyzed every single piece, then carefully added them into one of his many piles. It was taking forever. I started to grow impatient. It occurred to me that he was stalling for time.

"What's taking so long?" I snapping my fingers at him.

He looked up at me with innocent eyes. He had cottages sprinkled across his open palm like grains of salt. He sprinkled them onto his pile of houses and said, "Do you want it done fast? Or do you want it done right?"

Fair response. "Just hurry it up."

I had two options when it came to passing the time: watch Semedi's outrageously boring work, or stare into the dark jungles of the Guinee. The air had grown colder and the fireflies had moved far above the treetops. The thousands of open graves caught my attention again. They were under the trees, in the clearings, and all around, stretching off for as far as I could see.

"What's with all the graves?" I asked.

Semedi didn't look up from his work. "My wife."

"She's just digging graves?"

"They're for the humans." He held a handful of tiny balloonicorns in his white cotton glove. He blew dirt off of them, then carefully placed them in his pile of other animals. "When you escaped, it left a bad taste in her mouth. Now she wants them all to die."

"Can she do that?" I asked. "Kill all the humans?"

"Oh, of course not." He dismissed the idea with a wave. "She just likes digging the graves. It's therapeutic."

"Did it ever occur to you that maybe she wouldn't be so crazy jealous if you'd stop cheating on her?"

He looked up at me with stunned amazement and said, "The thought had never occurred to me."

"Never?" I moved to stand right in front of him. "It never occurred to you that your wife is jealous because you try to marry other women?"

"No." He waved a finger at me. "But you might be onto something."

I stumbled over my words, too dumbfounded to make a coherent sentence. Eventually I said, "You're really something."

"Thank you!"

"I didn't mean it as a compliment."

"Oh."

That was all we said about that. Semedi put his head down and went back to work. He'd finished arranging his piles. Now it was time to take all of his piles and lay them out in the shape of the Muffincake Kingdom. He picked up each piece and looked at it carefully, determined where it should go, then set it down. Slowly the different kingdoms became apparent. The mountains of Wedding Cake's kingdom were six- or seven- or eight-tiered wedding cakes. The cottages in her kingdom were white, adorned in lace, and had frosting rooftops. Semedi also set down the great espresso machine, the crown jewel of the Coffeecake Kingdom. Then he sprinkled balloonicorns around the Birthday Cake Kingdom with his fingertips.

I heard a shrill voice from deep in the trees. A woman's voice.

"Semedi!"

Semedi gave me the deer in headlights look. "My wife."

"Hurry!" I waved my hand at the tiny scale model of the Muffincake Kingdom. It was nearly assembled, it just needed a few finishing touches. "Finish it! Finish it!"

He jumped up and clapped his gloved hand over my mouth. "Be quiet," he said. "She'll hear you."

"Dammit, Semedi!" Brijit rustled her way closer to us through the surrounding bushes. I could hear her squishing through the moss and mud. "I know you're out here!"

Semedi pointed frantically at the trees, signaling me to go hide before Brijit showed up. I didn't have a lot of time to waste with hiding, but getting caught in the Guinee by Brijit would have been far worse. I darted into the treeline with my nuke and peeked out from between some ferns. Knowing the Guinee, I was probably touching poison sumac or something god awful.

"Semedi!" Madam Brijit ripped her way through some dangling moss and brushed it away from her red dreadlocks. Her hands were filthy and she was caked in mud and grass all the way up to her knees. She carried a shovel over her shoulder, probably from digging more graves. Despite all her hard work, her day-of-the-dead face paint was perfect, down to the colorful lace patterns around her eyes.

"Why, hello my dear," Semedi said, holding his arms out for a hug. "I didn't hear you coming."

"I don't see how that's possible," she muttered. "I was screaming your name."

"And now here you are," he said. "Beautiful as ever."

She shot him a dirty look. "I need more shovels. I've got a thousand skeletons with nothing to do. I want more graves for those disgusting humans."

"Shovels," Semedi said. He patted down his tuxedo, as if he might have shovels in his pockets. "No, no shovels here." He took her by the arm and tried to lead her away from my direction. She followed, but slowly and with a lot of hesitation. "Let me take you to where I keep the shovels."

"What were you doing out here?" She peered back in my direction. I ducked down lower. "I heard voices."

"Voices?" Semedi asked, then sipped his rum.

"Yes," Brijit said, impatient. "Voices."

"Oh. That was me. I was singing." He did his best woman voice and sang, "Buffalo gals won't you come out tonight? Won't you come out tonight? Won't you..."

He trailed off because Brijit gave him a stern look that indicated she wasn't buying it.

"What's this?" Brijit walked over to the littered pieces of the Muffincake Kingdom, arranged like a tiny model. She put her hands on her hips and stared down at it.

"Oh, that!" Semedi moved to her side, puffed on his cigar, then wrinkled his forehead. "What a curious little display. Where did that come from?"

Brijit's eyes slowly narrowed. "You know what this looks like?"

Semedi shook his head. "No, my dear. But, then again, you are far more observant than I."

She knelt down right in the moss and mud, with no regard for the fact that she was further ruining her wedding dress. She brought her face closer to the tiny buildings. "It looks like that muffin place where that wedding harlot lived. The one who tried to steal you from me."

"Huh." Semedi turned his head sideways. "Well, far be it for me to correct you, but that is not the muffin place."

"Is it not?" Brijit leaned in even closer. Her nose was almost in the Birthday Cake Kingdom. "It looks a lot like it."

"It's like looking at a cloud," he said. "Everyone sees something different. You see the muffin place. To me, it looks more like Moscow."

She stood up and walked over to a big stone. "It reminds me of it, either way." She heaved the stone up to her chest and shuffled it over to the Muffincake Kingdom. She held it in place there, intent on dropping it and crushing the tiny buildings. "Stupid place."

I felt my four-chambered mechanical heart shudder into overdrive. If she dropped that rock, that would be the end of the Muffincake Kingdom for good. Someone had to do something. If Baron Semedi wasn't going to step in, I was going to have to.

I exploded out of the trees and made a mad dash for Brijit. My sneaker tore ruts into the moss and dirt. Just as the stone dropped from her arms, I kicked it for distance like a soccer ball. I couldn't see how far it flew, but I suspect it's somewhere in orbit.

Brijit turned her head in my direction. It took a second for her to recognize me. "*You*," she growled. "How dare you show your face here again."

Semedi spoke up, trying to pretend like he was also confused. "How shocking that we have an unannounced guest. Explain yourself, young lady."

Brijit snapped at her husband, "You shut up." Then she focused on me. "I have unfinished business with this little toley."

"Okay," I said. "I don't know what a 'toley' is, but I really don't like your tone."

I lifted lifted my foot off the ground and drove it hard into Madam Brijit's gut. She zipped backwards through the air and smashed into a tree, nearly snapping it in half. Leaves and twigs fell out of the branches and to the ground. A startled colony of bats took to the air, slapping their leathery wings and disappearing into the night sky.

Brijit was stuck there in the side of the tree, but then gravity pulled her free. In a swirl of wedding lace, she collapsed face first into the mud.

"Oh, I wish you hadn't done that," Semedi said. He pointed at his wife with his cigar. "She's going to be so mad."

I pointed at the Muffincake Kingdom. "Then hurry up and fix it."

"Okay." He strolled back over to his work. His complete lack of urgency really got my ragu simmering.

"You better make it quick." I balled up my fists and bounced in place like a boxer. "Cuz your wife called me a toley and I think that means 'whore,' so now I have to beat her ass."

Semedi placed both feet down on either side of the Muffincake Kingdom and waved his hands through the air in a mystical pattern. Clouds formed overhead and swallowed up the stars. The fainted flickers of lightning flashed from inside. A powerful storm was brewing, conjured by Semedi's Voodoo magic.

Madam Brijit came out of nowhere and football tackled me right in the stomach. We landed in the mud with her on top of me. My head whacked against a rock and my vision flickered with pixels.

"Son of a bitch," I grumbled. I reached up, put my open palm on her face, and shoved her off of me.

We both slowly got to our feet. Brijit slashed at my forearm with her razor-sharp fingernails and sliced my skin right open. I slapped my hand to the wound and when I pulled my hand away, I saw blood. Or not blood, per se. It looked more like red motor oil.

"Ow!" I said, surprised. "That hurt!"

She swung at me again, this time trying to claw my face. I was just quick enough to lean out of the way. I threw a backhanded fist and popped her across the jaw. Her dreadlocks whipped around and she fell to the ground on her knees.

"Please don't hit my wife," Semedi said. "It makes me really uncomfortable."

"She fucking cut me!" I showed him my hand, soaked in oily blood.

"Well, can you blame her?" he asked. "You kicked her into a tree."

"You-"

Brijit came flying through the air, crashed right into me, and dragged us both back down into the mud. We rolled across the swamp as we fought. She clawed at my arms. I decked her in the face. We tumbled around and dropped into one of her open graves. I landed on my back with Brijit on top of me. She clawed at my face, but I grabbed her wrists and held her hands in place.

"I'll kill you, you trollop." She tried to wrestle her arms free.

"Stop calling me words I don't know!"

We got to our feet inside the deep grave and squared off like arch-rivals on the grade school playground. She screamed and came for me. We fought like wild animals, pinballing back and forth, slamming up against the walls of the grave. I drove my fist deep into her stomach and she doubled over to the ground. I jumped on top of her, rolled her over and whacked her face back and forth with my fists. Her skeleton make up was all smudged and smeared. She screamed, not in pain, but with pure, unadulterated rage. She sank her fingernails deep into my right bicep, then sliced them down the whole length of my arm. Oily blood gushed out.

I cried in agony and jumped off her to put distance between us. I gripped my bleeding arm. Thick, red oil pulsed from between my fingers.

"Done!" Semedi announced. He peered over the edge of the open grave. He held the reassembled Muffincake Kingdom in his hands, sealed away inside a sphere of glass. I could barely make out his features with the thunderclouds obscuring the moon. I could only see him in the occasional flash of lightning.

Madam Brijit staggered to her feet and braced herself against the dirt walls of the grave. She was out of breath, huffing and puffing.

I shouted at Semedi, "Then get me out of here!"

Brijit looked up at her husband and screamed, "Don't you dare help her!"

"Oh." Semedi was caught between his promise to me and the wrath of his furious wife. He looked back and forth between us, then said, "I can't help it, my dear. This girl is using her mind control powers on me. I am no longer responsible for my actions."

"What?" Brijit asked. "Mind control?"

"Yep," Semedi said. "She's in control of my mind and she's making me send her back to Earth. I'm very unhappy about all this."

Semedi made sweeping motions through the air with his cigar hand and worked a different kind of magic. Dense fog rolled out of the treeline and spilled into the grave like dry ice. Madam Brijit swung her arms to clear the wafting smoke, determined to find me and kill me.

I inhaled the fog. It smelled of cigars and old clothes. I felt the world slip away, like falling sleep, but somehow different.

4

I wasn't sleeping, but I woke up all the same. I opened my eyes to find myself laying down on Xin's front porch. I had the Muffincake Kingdom safely in my hands, resting on my stomach. I smiled weakly to myself. I had done it. I had done the impossible. I got the mysterious wizard to reassemble the Muffincake Kingdom.

Laying next to me was the nuclear bomb. Understandable. I doubted Semedi wanted that thing lying around in his swamp.

I got to my feet and I stumbled into the shop, through the front room, and into the back bedroom. Cardboard and Parcel laid there unconscious. Their hair was dark and matted with sweat. Their skin had lost all its color. I'd caught Xin in the middle of holding Parcel's wrist between his fingers, timing her pulse with his digital Casio watch. There were empty porcelain cups around them with the yellow residue of whatever medicine he'd been pouring into their mouths. They each had a washcloth over their foreheads and a bucket of ice water sat on the floor by my cot.

My hands went cold and my stomach tightened up. All at once, I felt the fear and anxiety from when Ma died. Just like with her, I never imagined anything bad would happen to my new princess friends. Of course deep in the back of your mind, you always know it's going to happen – it's going to happen to all of us – but you don't let yourself *think* about it. But then one day, just like with Ma, you're blindsided by the reality that we're all mortal, and we're all going to die.

Everyone is going to die.

The only difference between Ma and the princesses was that when Ma died, I was helpless to do anything about it. But now... now things were different.

"Here," I said to Xin. I handed him the Muffincake Kingdom. This was his first time seeing it in once piece. I left an oily, bloody hand print on the glass. He took a washcloth and wiped it clean.

"You found the wizard?" he said.

"Don't sound so surprised," I told him.

That made him smile. He rolled up a towel to make a little nest for the glass ball and put it on the bed next to Cardboard.

"You're bleeding," Xin said, pointing at my arm "It looks like you lost a fight with a panther."

"It was a Voodoo spirit," I said, "And it was more of a tie."

He went for a roll of gauze and wrapped it around my open wounds. My oily blood soaked right through the white cotton. It didn't look pretty, but it would keep me from dripping blood all over the place.

"Cardboard?" I softly shook her shoulder. "Hey, Cardboard. Look. I got the Muffincake Kingdom back."

That got her to open her eyes. They were as gray as pencil lead. She gave me a distant, vacant stare. God, she was in bad shape. I picked up the Muffincake Kingdom and held it in her view.

"How?" she asked. Her voice was weak.

"I'll tell you later," I said. "Do you feel any better?"

She smiled. "I do now."

She closed her eyes and her head slumped as she passed back out. I put the kingdom safely on the towel and situated so it wouldn't roll away. There wasn't anything more we could do besides wait. Xin and I left the back room so the two of them could rest.

Then, for the first time in what felt like forever, we sat together at the counter and did nothing. Xin sat on his stool behind the cash register and I sat on mine on the opposite side. We used to sit in those spots and do normal things: eat Chinese food, listen to the radio, made idle chit-chat.

Those days felt like so long ago.

"You know what I'd really like to do right now?" I asked him.

He raised his eyebrows at me. "Mmm?"

"Water the plants."

"Is that so?"

I nodded. "I just want to do something normal for once."

"I've been meaning to tell you..." He reached under the counter and brought out the watering can. "I'm promoting you to assistant manager. It comes with a raise. $9.75 an hour."

I laughed. "Thanks."

"I'd say you've earned it."

Outside, I used the hose on the side of the store to wash the mud and grass off my shoes, the brand news ones I got from Tengoku. It was mid-November and cold enough to see my breath. It felt good to do normal things again. I spent the next hour sweeping the front porch, watering the inside plants, and all the other chores I used to do back before life went crazy. I *felt* normal, but I wasn't normal. I was some kind of machine-person now and that was something I was going to have to learn to live with.

When we laid Cardboard and Parcel to bed, they were still in their Batman and Darth Vader costumes. I figured that when they finally woke back up, they'd want to put on their old clothes. Their dresses were still in that box in Corolla's trunk. I took a moment to walk out to the street and get it.

"How are your princess friends?" Corolla asked me.

"I think they're going to be okay," I said. "We just have to wait."

"What did they have?" he asked. "Was it the measles?"

"It wasn't measles."

I popped the trunk and pulled out the cardboard box.

Corolla asked, "Was it butt rot?"

"That's not even a thing."

I slammed the trunk closed and headed off with the box.

"That's cool," Corolla shouted after me. "Don't worry about me. I'll just wait here. I'll keep a look out."

"I'm proud of you," I called back.

I carried the princesses' gowns to the bedroom. I dug them out of the box and laid them out all nice and flat on my table so the girls would see them when they woke up. The two of them were breathing, but they were otherwise dead to the world. I silently left the room and closed the door behind me.

5

After a couple hours and after night had set in, the bedroom door creaked open. Princess Cardboard and Princess Parcel shuffled out. Their hair was a disaster. Cardboard had put her gown on inside out. Parcel had done a better job of it, but didn't bother with the gloves, tiara, or shoes. They looked like two girls recovering from a nightmare bachelorette party. Still, they looked a million times better than before. Their skin had returned to normal and the color was back in their eyes.

Cardboard cradled the Muffincake Kingdom in her arms. She softly cried to herself. Parcel, who had gone hours and hours without a drink, was uncharacteristically well-balanced and quiet.

Parcel groaned and rubbed her face with her hands. "I feel like how Courtney Love looks."

I said, "You look great." Just knowing that they were going to be okay made me smile.

"I'd hug you," Cardboard said to me, "But I'm not taking my hands off this thing. Not ever."

"It's no big deal," I said.

"It's a big deal to us," Parcel said. "Thank you, Penelope"

Cardboard looked at Xin. "And thanks to you, too, old man."

Xin gave her a slight bow. "It was my great pleasure to help you."

"You girls should probably lay back down," I told them. "You need your rest. You need to get your strength back and stuff."

"We talked it over," Cardboard said with a glance towards her sister. "Every moment we leave the Muffincake Kingdom in this little glass ball just puts it at risk. We need to hurry up and break the spell."

"Ooh, I want to see that," I said. I excitedly put my hands between my knees. "Can I watch?"

"We can't do it, just the two of us," Parcel said. "We need our sisters to help us."

"Plus," Cardboard added, "if we were dying, then that means they were dying, too, but they would have had no idea why. We

273

need to hurry and find them and explain. I bet they're confused as heck."

"Oh," I said. My smile faded as I looked back and forth between the two princesses and realized this was turning into goodbye. "So you're leaving..."

It's not like I could blame them. Everything they said made sense; their world would only be safe once they broke that spell and put everything back the way it used to be. Why risk it by wasting another second in New York?

I didn't want them to go, but I couldn't tell them that. How selfish would that sound? I couldn't expect them to put my friendship over the espresso rivers and balloon animals and the cotton candy clouds and whatever else they had back home.

The anxiety on my face must have been pretty easy to read, because Cardboard said, "We won't leave New York without saying goodbye. Once the Muffincake Kingdom is safe, we'll come back and hang out with you one more time before we go."

Parcel excitedly said, "We can get fucking trashed!" She turned to Xin. "You should come, too, whoever you are."

Xin laughed. "We'll see."

The princesses went for the door.

I followed them outside and around the corner of the shop. Xin came out with me. The two girls stopped at Cardboard's cardboard box. Princess Cardboard gave Xin a kiss on the cheek. Princess Parcel shook my hand and thanked me again. Cardboard stood in front of me with the Muffincake Kingdom in her hands. I could tell she wanted to hug me goodbye, but like she said, she wasn't going to take her hands off that glass ball for anything. She had tears her eyes and her bottom lip quivered. Her cardboard crown fell down over her eyes and I reached out to lift it back into place.

"I'll see you soon," I told her.

She sadly nodded. "Okay."

Together, Princess Cardboard and Princess Parcel stepped into the cardboard box.

"Have you gained weight?" Parcel asked. "Look how much room you're taking up."

Cardboard shrugged and looked down at herself. "My boobs are just getting bigger."

Parcel rolled her eyes. "Yeah, I'm sure that's what it is."

Chapter 17

1

With all the chaos surrounding Princess Cardboard and Princess Parcel's brush with death, nothing got done at the shop for the day. Xin worked into the night hours, counting down the money in the register, restocking the jars with leaves and petals from around the store, and preparing the orders for tomorrow's customers.

I stood out on the front porch and looked at the glittering skyscraper in the night skyline when I realized I was hungry. I hadn't had anything to eat since I stole that silverware from Liu's. Impossible Red needed raw materials to repair the damage done to my body by Madam Brijit, and it needed them soon.

It was bittersweet to feel hungry. A part of me enjoyed it, because it was a very human thing to feel. My stomach grumbled and everything, although it sounded more like a garbage disposal than a stomach. At least feeling hungry meant I was feeling *something*. My mechanical body had robbed me of most other basic human functions. I didn't need to go to the bathroom anymore. I never felt tired and I never went to sleep. My skin didn't itch and my fingernails didn't grow. So after adjusting to all of that, hunger felt like a little slice of humanity.

The bittersweet part was... I wanted to eat metal. Tungsten, specifically. God, what I wouldn't have given for some of those bolts from Tengoku HQ. I wondered where you could find tungsten bolts in Manhattan. Probably nowhere.

I would miss the taste of lo mein. And I would miss sleeping until noon. I'd miss having an itch on my back that I couldn't reach. I *wouldn't* miss having to piss in the subway bathrooms, though. God, I *really* wouldn't miss that.

I decided to go out in search of food. I figured Xin would need food, too, since he was working later than usual.

I poked my head inside the shop. "Xin, I'm going to get something to eat. You want anything?"

He looked up from the tiny shrub he was trimming at the counter. "What are you getting?"

"I dunno," I said. "Probably some wrenches or a hammer or something. What do you want? Dim sum?"

Xin put his head down and went back to trimming. "Dim sum would be fine."

I strolled across the courtyard with my hands in my pockets. Since I was getting Chinese food for Xin, I figured I'd check in on Corolla and see if he wanted anything. He sat there in the flickering neon lights of nighttime Chinatown. He had a ticket under his windshield wiper for parking at an expired meter. Under the other wiper was a poorly photocopied flier informing me that I could get cell phone service for six dollars a month.

I looked at the flier and remembered a simpler time when getting a new cell phone was a big deal to me. That was a long time ago.

"Do you have any idea how embarrassing this is?" Corolla asked. He turned on his windshield wipers and threw the ticket into the gutter. "It's tacky. Plus, this strange guy looked in all my windows and I thought he was going to break into me. But then he just shook his head and walked away. Imagine how that made me feel. I mean, I know I'm just a Corolla, but that doesn't mean I'm not worth stealing." He paused and then asked me, "Are you bleeding?"

I held up my right arm, wrapped in gauze. My oily blood had stained the cotton red. I covered the blotch with my other hand and ignored his question. "I'm going to get Chinese food. Do you want egg rolls?"

He made a skeptical noise and asked, "You're not going to that same place as before, are you?"

"Liu's?" I was suddenly on the defensive. "Why? What's wrong with Liu's? That's my favorite place."

276

"Eh, they cook their egg rolls in vegetable oil, not peanut oil. I prefer them cooked in peanut oil."

I exhaled. "I'm going to Liu's. Do you want egg rolls or not?"

"I don't care." He sounded so completely defeated. Before I could respond, he added, "Okay, yes. Shrimp, please. And wontons."

"Shrimp egg rolls and wontons." I said as I walked off. After only a few steps, I turned around and heckled Corolla. "Hey, don't get any more tickets."

He shouted back. "How about you pay the meter?"

I walked the few blocks down to Liu's and sized up everything Chinatown. *I could fight that guy. I could crush that car. I could smash through that brick wall and no one on Earth could stop me.*

I got to Liu's and ordered egg rolls for Corolla and dim sum for Xin. I was buying food like a regular everyday person. I caught a whiff of the food in the air, but it smelled like wet garbage. My shoulders slumped and I sighed in defeat with the realization that, not only could I not eat Chinese food anymore, I couldn't even smell it.

My eyes darted around as the guys behind the counter put all my food in a plastic bag. They weren't looking, so I reached over the counter and swiped five rolls of silverware.

2

After slamming a few egg rolls and wontons in Corolla's passenger-side door, I headed up the alley with Xin's dim sum and my silverware in a plastic bag. The front door to the shop was wide open, but that was nothing new. We usually left the door propped open, as long as one of us was around to keep an eye on things, of course. It was nice to get some airflow inside the shop.

I walked in and sat the food on the counter. Xin wasn't around. I looked at the basement door. It was closed and padlocked shut. The bathroom door was closed and I could see the light shining from under the door. Shadows of Xin's feet moved around in the light.

I unwrapped the plastic bag and set our food out on the counter. "Xin? Food's here."

"Penelope?" Xin said from inside the bathroom. He sounded concerned. "Are they still out there?"

I laughed at him. "They who?"

He said, "The Voodoo people."

Voodoo people? I didn't see any Voodoo people.

I curiously turned around and found myself face to face with Madam Brijit and Baron Kriminel. Brijit stood there in her filthy wedding gown and red dreadlocks. The corner of her skeleton-painted mouth turned up in a malicious smirk. Baron Kriminel stood next to her, two feet taller than the both of us, with his bones shrouded in a loose fitting tuxedo.

"Grab her," Brijit said.

Kriminel's arm snapped out and he clutched my throat with his cold fingers.

With my throat squeezed shut, I managed to croak out to Xin, "Yeah, they're still here."

Kriminel was incapable of moving without any further commands from Brijit. His deep, empty eye sockets gave me the creeps. Brijit looked up at me with her radiation-green eyes.

"Where's the glass ball?" Brijit asked.

"No idea what you're talking about," I managed to say.

"Kriminel," she said. "Squeeze."

He squeezed and it hurt. I wasn't suffocating, though. Come to find out I didn't need air to breathe, I just needed air to talk. Still, if he squeezed any harder, he would have snapped my neck.

Brijit grit her teeth and said, "Answer me you little strumpet. Where is it?"

I gasped for air and said, "I don't know what a strumpet is."

Madam Brijit didn't seem keen on playing games. She snapped her fingers and pointed at the front wall of the shop. Baron Kriminel swung me around by the neck and launched me. I crashed through one of the tables, took out seven potted plants, and exploded through the other side of the wall in a cloud of bricks. I smacked a dent in the front ledge of the porch and it left my body spinning as I flew through the air. I smacked the ground in the courtyard and cracked the concrete with the back of my head.

I groaned and sat up. I had mortar dust and leaves in my hair. Potting soil was all in my clothes and my eyes. I brushed myself off and looked back at Xin's shop. The front wall had a huge hole in it now, right next to the front door. The front porch ledge was missing a chunk of bricks. Broken clay pots were scattered everywhere and plants laid on the ground with exposed roots clinging tight to clumps of dirt. I didn't have time to count how many plants were hurt exactly, but I guessed it was a dozen.

That was something I'd have to worry about later.

Baron Kriminel crawled through the hole in the wall, knocking loose bricks out of his way. Madam Brijit followed after him with a little more caution. Kriminel wasn't done with me, that much was obvious. He jumped off the porch and advanced on me like a mindless zombie. Brijit trailed right behind him.

"You mind controlled my husband," she said. "You made him fix that muffin world. I want it."

I got to my feet and brushed the crumbs of brick and concrete off my clothes. "I can't mind control people, Brijit. And the muffin world isn't here anymore. It's gone."

She glared at me. "You attacked me in my realm. You tried to steal my husband. I'm sick to death of humans, but you most of all."

"None of this was my fault," I said. I was getting really tired of repeating that fact, especially since Brijit was apparently going to believe whatever she wanted to believe either way. I knuckled up. "But if you really want to fight about it, I'm down."

"Kriminel," she said. "Remove her head from her body."

Kriminel stuck his arms out and advanced on me. I put up my fists and held my ground. If we were going to throw hands, we were going to throw hands. I wasn't going to back away. Kriminel took a swing at me, but his arms were were long and lumbering and I totally saw it coming. I dipped out of the way. His fist whooshed over my head. He swung again with his other arm. I leaned the other way and dodged that one, too.

This whole Penelope-versus-Brijit rivalry was just one big misunderstanding caused by Baron Semedi. I didn't have any reason to fight Brijit or Kriminel. Not at first. But now they had broken Xin's wall and hurt a few of his plants. Misunderstanding or not, this bitch had taken things too far and needed to be put back in her place. I felt a rush of burning-hot rocket fuel surge through my mechanical heart and tingle under my skin.

Metal bones, carbon skin, microscopic war machines pumping through my veins... it was time to see what Impossible

Red could really do.

I threw a backhand that crushed Baron Kriminel's skull.

One hit. Boom. Just like that, his head was gone.

His jaw bone clattered across the courtyard. His top hat danced through the air. Different sized pieces of his skull laid scattered across the ground like shattered ceramic.

His skeleton body stumbled in place and I just assumed he would fall over, but he managed to stay upright. He steadied himself, then turned his body back to me and put up his fists. I only hit him in the head because that's typically where people keep the good stuff: their brains, their eyes, their inner ear for balance. Kriminel didn't have any of those things. Kriminel's head was hollow, so even after destroying it, his body had no reason to quit.

I threw a punch straight into his chest. His ribs crunched. He stumbled backwards, but still managed to stayed on his feet.

Brijit scrambled after the broken pieces of Kriminel's skull. She clicked them back together like pieces of a puzzle.

"Stupid human," she said. "You can't kill us. We're already dead."

Kriminel's headless body charged at me and tackled me to the ground like a linebacker. We smacked down on the concrete and left a crack. He knelt on top of me and used his right fist to deck me in the face. There was no technique, nothing fancy, just single minded brute force with his right hand – bam, bam, bam into my face – fueled by something dark and powerful.

Oily blood spilled out of my nose and my busted lip. My vision lagged and stalled like poor TV reception.

"Kriminel, stop." Madam Brijit walked over with his reassembled skull in her hands. Kriminel's body froze at her command, his fist poised in the air, ready to resume his attack at a moments notice. She addressed me from over his shoulder. "Alright, mammal. Talk. Where is the muffin world?"

I shook my head. "How many times do I have to tell you? I don't have it."

"Fine." She laughed, as if the whole situation amused her. "If you won't give me the muffin world, then I'll just take something else. Maybe this flower shop? The old man? Maybe I'll burn it down with him inside."

"Fucking try it," I growled and tried to fight Kriminel off of me.

"Hold her still," Brijit commanded.

Kriminel locked his fingers around my wrists and pinned my arms down to the ground. He couldn't have weighed that much – I mean, bones are inherently pretty light – but whatever supernatural force was helping him move was just as strong as the machines in my blood. I couldn't get him off me.

Madam Brijit came up behind him and clicked his skull back on his neck.

3

I didn't know this at the time, but when the fight went outside and the shop went quiet, Xin built up the nerve to peek out through a crack in the bathroom door. He saw the mess in the shop, the hole in the wall, and watched my fight with the Voodoo spirits in the courtyard. He saw Baron Kriminel kicking my ass and went to the basement. I imagine he nervously fumbled with his key before opening the padlock. He went downstairs and sorted through all the mysterious items hidden beneath the store. He came back up armed with the Gettysburg Sabre, the Civil War sword that could kill ghosts, and brought it outside.

It caught me and Brijit and Kriminel off guard when Xin showed up to the fight. He nervously held the sword in front of him, obviously unaccustomed to holding a weapon. The blade was sharpened steel and the handle was crafted from black leather and inlaid with gold. He held the sword far away from his body, as if he was more scared of it than of the Voodoo spirits. His hands were shaking. The blade wobbled around.

"Leave her alone," Xin said, trying to sound intimidating.

Madam Brijit glanced over her shoulder. The sight of Xin brandishing a sword made her laugh. "What do you plan to do with that, gardener?"

Xin swallowed hard and pointed the blade at her. "I will defend my friend."

Now she was really laughing. She sauntered right up to him like he was a huge nobody and grabbed the blade to point it right at her neck. She said, "You're pathetic. You don't have the guts to protect anyone. You're just a scared, weak old man."

I redoubled my efforts to break free from Kriminel's grip, but it felt impossible. Xin had gone and got himself all mixed up

281

in this and I had no idea what Madam Brijit was going to do to him. I tried to catch Kriminel off guard with a sudden jerk to the left, but his grip on my wrists was unbreakable. If I didn't get free and quick, something terrible was going to happen to Xin.

I shouted, "Xin, get the hell out of here!"

Xin kept his eyes and the sword locked on Madam Brijit and replied, "I won't let them hurt you."

Madam Brijit scoffed and swatted the sword out of his hands like it was nothing. It clattered across the ground and slid to a stop twenty feet away. Xin watched the sword bounce away. Disarmed, he turned back to Brijit with a terrified look on his face. He put his hands up in submission and backed away. Madam Brijit stepped after him.

"I've heard of you," she said. "You're the human that hides things. You're nothing more than a dying old man left all alone in a miserable world." She looked deeper into his eyes and said, "Did you really think that adopting this filthy street urchin would make you feel better? Well, take a look around. This is what it got you."

The more I struggled against Baron Kriminel, the tighter he held on.

Brijit and Xin were nearly nose to nose. She said, "Unfortunately I'm not the one who does the killing. But Kriminel, on the other hand..."

I screamed. "Xin! Run!"

He tried to make a break for it, but he was too old for that kind of move. He stumbled to the ground and scraped the palms of his hands. Brijit stood over him and cackled with delight at his misfortune.

An odd thing happened right then. It was tough to understand in the beginning. First came this strange ticking sound, like from an old alarm clock. Tik tik tik. Then came an entirely different sound, something high pitched and metallic, like someone sharpening a knife. I heard it pierce the air once – *shrink!* – then again, and then again. It sounded strangely familiar, but I couldn't remember from where.

And as if that wasn't strange enough, a metal blade appeared out of thin air directly overhead and swished around in a wide arc. Then it vanished. It happened again, then again. And in that moment, *that's* when everything clicked. I was looking at the Sword From One Second Ago. I could tell by the holes cut out of the blade and the gears and springs inside.

It all made sense. Way back when I snuck Cardboard into the basement to look for the Muffincake Kingdom, we ended up messing around with the time sword in the courtyard and she accidentally figured out how to turn it on. At the time when I swung the sword, the blade had disappeared. I swung it over a dozen times and each time the blade vanished right before my eyes. But the blade wasn't vanishing, it was going somewhere else *in time*. It was, after all, a time sword.

That pretend sword fight I had against imaginary ninjas sent the Sword From One Second Ago weeks into the future, and now I was watching it in the present.

I squeezed my eyes shut and mustered as much physical power as Impossible Red could give me. I jerked hard to the left and moved Baron Kriminel into the path of the time traveling blade. The Sword From One Second Ago sliced through the left half of his torso and severed his arm right at the shoulder. It clattered lifelessly to the ground and suddenly *my* arm was free. I reached up, grabbed Kriminel by his stupid tuxedo and pulled him even closer to the magical sword.

"Old me" swung the Sword From One Second Ago and sliced off his other arm. Immediately the tight grip in his hands faded and I was free. I reached up with both hands and grabbed the lapels of his suit jacket to throw him off of me. Kriminel landed hard and his bones clattered apart inside his suit. I crawled away from the wild swinging of the time sword and once the sound was safely behind me, I got to my feet.

Baron Kriminel's tuxedo shifted and moved as his bones struggled to piece themselves back together. His severed arms crawled closer to his body, pulled along by the fingers. Slowly but surely, he was reassembling himself. If I was going to act, I had to do it quick.

I sprinted for Brijit and slugged her right in the gut. She bent in half at the waist and dropped to the ground like a sack of potatoes.

I bounced in place and swung my arms back and forth. "How's that feel, Houdini?"

I thought maybe I knocked her out or maybe, just *maybe*, I killed her. But no. She rose up off the ground... not by using her arms and legs, but floating on pure magic. She hovered two feet up off the ground. Her wedding gown flowed weightlessly around her ankles. She reminded me of a ghost bride from campfire stories, where she haunts an abandoned bridge in search for her drowned children. Her green eyes glowed like pools of burning chemicals. The red dreadlocks moved around her head like medusa snakes.

She stared me down. I could see her jaw clenched tight. "That. Hurt."

I helped Xin to his feet and put him behind me. If she wanted to lay a finger on him, she was going to have to go through me first.

"Be ready to run," I told Xin. "Get out of here and get someplace safe."

Brijit pointed at Baron Kriminel. "Kriminel, kill the male. Then kill the girl."

Baron Kriminel's arms had reattached themselves. His tuxedo sleeves were still on the ground, cut loose by the time sword and it exposed the bare skeleton bones usually hidden inside. He reached out for us and marched in our direction with more speed and intensity than before. His eye sockets also glowed green, siphoning off of Brijit's immense power.

"Alright, Xin! Run!" I pushed him towards the alley and put myself between him and Baron Kriminel.

Xin shuffled for the alley as fast as his old bones would carry him. Kriminel straight up ignored me and focused entirely on Xin. He had his orders – "kill the male, then kill the girl" – so that's what he was going to do, in that specific order. He marched after Xin, building up more and more speed. I planted my feet and raised my fists. He might not wanted a piece of me, but he was going to get one whether he liked it or not.

At least, that's what I thought.

Kriminel grabbed me by the hair and cast me aside with a flick of his arm. I tumbled across the courtyard as if I just jumped out of a speeding car and crashed into the foundation of the shop's front porch. My body slammed into the bricks and cracked the mortar.

Xin had almost made it to the alley, but he was old and didn't move very fast. Kriminel chased after him, his skeleton legs moving in long strides. Xin wasn't going to get away and even at my absolute fastest speeds, I wouldn't reach them in time.

But that's when Corolla showed up.

The alley was too narrow for a car, but Corolla could fly. In order for him to fit, all he had to do was fly sideways.

Xin saw Corolla barreling towards him and dropped to the ground. Corolla whooshed right over his head and came exploding out of the alleyway. He flew straight into a head-on collision with Baron Kriminel. Baron Kriminel's skeleton exploded into pieces. Shattered ribs and finger bones and spine vertebrae sprayed across the courtyard like a million spilled legos.

The impact of a Voodoo spirit at 70 miles an hour knocked out Corolla's flying mechanisms. He landed on his side and scraped across the courtyard in a shower of sparks. His front end was all bashed in. His driver and passenger airbags popped off. It looked like he was going to skid right into brick walls of the shop, but he slowed to a stop just inches away. He teetered there on his side as smoke gushed out of the seams around his hood, then he rolled and landed upside down on his roof. His engine hissed from somewhere deep inside him, and then it died.

"Corolla!" I sprinted to his driver side window and poked my head inside. I could smell gasoline. He laid there upside down and his cassettes were strewn all across the roof, but there was still a glow in his stereo. "Corolla, say something!"

"Alright." The radio crackled, just barely functional. He sounded out of breath and said, "Ow."

I hung my head and sighed in relief. He was alive. "Dude, I can't believe you did that."

He coughed. "Yeah. That makes two of us."

I gave him a pat on the door and stood back up. Break time was over. I still had a fight to finish.

"Get up," Madam Brijit screamed at Kriminel's scattered bones. The billion shattered skeleton pieces began to move. The chips of his skull flipped in place and clicked into the shape of his nose and eye sockets and forehead. Finger bones rolled together to form completed fingers, then those fingers crawled around like worms to combine into a hand. The spine pieces tumbled into line by size. Rib bones clattered across the asphalt, trying to reassemble themselves. I didn't know how long it would take for Baron Kriminel to become whole again, but it was happening faster than I liked.

Pleased with his progress, Brijit turned to me with a sharp grin on her face.

I marched right up to her, ready to throw down, just the two of us. If I had any chance of a fair fight, I had to take advantage of it while Kriminel was out of commission. Xin had disappeared down the alley. Corolla laid on his roof with wisps of smoke drifting out. There were only two people left standing: Madam Brijit, the Voodoo spirit of love and death and Penelope Salvo, the artificial god of war.

Brijit floated in front of me, her wedding flats drifting just inches above the ground. I balled up my fists. She curled her fingers, ready to claw me with her sky blue fingernails. We squared off like two gunslingers in the old west, both of us just waiting for the other one to make the first move.

Then I heard a man's voice.

"If I may."

Madam Brijit turned. I looked past her to see Carl coming out of the alley. He had his arm in a sling and a line of band-aids on his forehead from where Parcel bashed him with her champagne bottle. He limped towards us.

My blood rushed a little hotter. As if I wasn't dealing with enough shit already, suddenly *Westland* decides to show up?

"Who are you?" Brijit spat.

"The name is Carl," he said. "Senior field agent for the Westland Corporation."

Brijit glared at him. "You're a friend of hers?"

He gave a quick "ha" and shook his head. "No. We're more like frenemies."

"We're not frenemies," I said. "You're a shitbag and I hate you."

Brijit's eyes perked up. My outburst caused her to take a sudden interest in Carl. She floated over to him and grabbed his injured arm. He winced, but didn't pull away.

She said, "Why are you here, tuxedo human?"

Carl answered, "Well, I'm not here to get in your way, I can promise you that much. I know a divinity-class threat when I see one. I'm only here for the girl. I don't know if you were aware of this, but she's nothing but trouble. She faked her death and then stole something of mine. So if you want to kill her, that's fine. You'd be saving me the trouble. I just want your permission to take my property off her dead body."

"What property is that, exactly?" Brijit asked.

"Just a black marble," Carl said, bowing and humbling himself before her. "Nothing of consequence. Just something I need for work."

"You knew I was alive?" I asked Carl.

He gave me a quizzical look, as if I was stupid. "Penelope, you don't give me enough credit. You girls smell like patchouli, booze, and the inside of a cardboard box." He straightened his tie with his one good arm. "I might be nice, but that doesn't mean I'm stupid."

Brijit yanked Carl closer. He hissed in pain, but didn't put up any resistance. "This black marble. It's important to her?"

"Oh, very," Carl said with a nod. "She wants it very much. And she would hate it if I got it back. She would absolutely *hate* it."

"Then you may have this black marble," Brijit said. She glared at me. "All her enemies will stand victorious over her."

Madam Brijit let Carl go. They stood next to one another, the sociopath and the psychopath. Of everyone I wanted to see getting along in this world, these two were last on the list.

"We should shake on it," Carl said as he turned to Brijit. He reached out with his good hand. Madam Brijit just stared at him. He motioned his open palm closer to her. "You know? Shake? Sorry to be a stickler for the details, but a handshake would make everything official."

She rolled her eyes dismissively, but stuck out her hand and took his. They shook. But something peculiar happened in that handshake. Brijit's face changed to curiosity. When she brought her hand back, she opened her palm and looked down.

"What is this?" she asked. She held up her black-and-white painted skeleton hand. A colorful postage stamp was stuck to the middle of her palm.

Carl turned to the alley and called out, "Okay! I did it!"

The top flaps of a cardboard box opened in the alleyway. Out popped Princess Parcel and Princess Cardboard. Parcel cupped her hands around her mouth and shouted, "To the moon!"

Madam Brijit had just enough time to give me a confused glace before she vanished.

Just when I thought I'd seen it all...

Princess Parcel and Princess Cardboard crawled out of their cardboard box and into the dirty alley. Cardboard stumbled over her own feet and Parcel nit-picked her clumsy entrance. Once they were out, Parcel reached back into the box to pull out a bottle of bloody mary mix and a bottle of vodka. She took a drink of vodka and kept it in her mouth without swallowing, then took a drink of the bloody mary mix. She swished them together like mouthwash and swallowed. After all that, she smacked her lips together to smooth out the lip balm she'd smeared across the bottle tops.

Carl, the enemy standing among us, rubbed his injured arm and watched the princesses join us.

"I told you it would work," he said. "See how it worked?"

Parcel answered him dismissively, "Yes, you're quite clever." She picked up Baron Kriminel's femur and put a stamp on it. "The Himalayas," she said. The femur vanished. One of his arms tried to crawl away. She put a stamp on that, too, and said, "Toronto." Piece by piece, she spread Baron Kriminel's skeleton across the world. She sent his foot to the Sahara Desert, his knee cap to Alcatraz, and his collarbone to Dubai. She saved the skull for last, which she held up to her face all Shakespearean-like. Baron Kriminel's jaw bone open and closed, as if he had something to say, but Kriminel couldn't talk. Parcel put a stamp right between his eyes and said, "Antarctica."

Spreading his bones across the planet wouldn't keep him from reassembling himself. They'd keep rolling and crawling together, even if they had to move across the bottom of the ocean. But at least at that rate, I wouldn't have to fight him again for fifty years.

I spoke up. "Do you two want to tell me what in the blue hell you're doing working with Carl?"

"We saw you fighting the skeleton man," Cardboard said. "He said he had an idea how to help you. And it worked!"

I pointed my finger at Carl. "Fuck off out of here," I said. "I don't know what lies you told these girl to get them to trust you, but it's not going to work on me."

Carl was a lying, cheating, smile-to-your-face-but-stab-you-in-the-back piece of trash. Sure, he helped get rid of Madam

Brijit, but that wasn't out of the goodness of his heart. This was all just a ploy to get on my good side and steal Unthinkable Black. He'd convinced Cardboard and Parcel that he wanted to help me, but that didn't mean much. They were both great girls, but they were a little naive for New York City. Whatever Carl was up to, it was some kind of trick. It had to be.

I wasn't about to stand there and listen to him spin a web of lies and deception. I had a broken car and a trashed herbal shop to worry about, so I walked away.

"You two can stay," I said to the princesses. "But he's gotta go."

Cardboard ran after me. "He really is trying to help us," she said.

I spun back around and snapped, "That's the guy that broke the Muffincake Kingdom, Cardboard! Why're you sticking up for him?"

"*He* didn't break it," Parcel said, stumbling up to join us. "The CEO did."

"Fine," I said. "Carl wanted to help us? He helped us. And now he can go."

Carl didn't leave. He just loitered back by the entrance to the alleyway.

I shook my head and went over to Corolla. Having lived in New York City my whole life, I'd seen more than my fair share of car wrecks. This one was bad. Corolla was still on his roof, so I picked him up, light as a feather, and set him back down on his wheels. I heard bolts and washers and springs fall out of him and clatter on the concrete. I walked a wide circle around him and surveyed him for damage. His roof was caved in and scraped all to hell. His left brake light was busted. His front end had taken the most damage and his windshield was nothing more than a white sheet of splintered glass.

The rest of the damage to his front-end made me worry. The headlights were destroyed. The front bumper was caved in. His hood was crumpled up like an accordion. Different colored liquids drained out of him and splattered on the ground. Oil, brake fluid, anti-freeze, power steering; whatever he had, he was bleeding it out.

"Oh my god," I whispered.

"Penelope?" Corolla said. His radio voice was mostly static. "Is that you?"

"We can fix this." I rubbed my hand across the fabric of his diver side seat.

"Fix it?" The light on the radio grew weak, like when the battery is dying. "I don't know, Penelope. I think I'm totaled."

"You're not totaled." I swallowed hard. "Don't say that. Lots of cars get totaled and they still work just fine. Being totaled doesn't mean you're... it doesn't mean..."

"Maybe." His voice got softer in the speakers and I had to strain to hear him. "I think I'm on my way to that big pre-owned Toyota/Hyundai car lot in the sky." He tried to laugh at his own joke. He coughed. And I know he didn't have a throat to cough with, but he was always clearing his throat, so maybe the cough meant something.

"You're not going to die." I raised his smashed up hood to look inside at the engine and all of his other car parts.

"Oh, don't look," Corolla said. "I don't want you to see me this way."

I didn't know the first thing about cars. I wasn't a mechanic. Hell, I didn't even know how to drive. Corolla's insides were a mess of hoses and gears and strange machinery. I could have sooner done high level calculus than figure out what all those parts were for. But if there was one thing I knew about cars, it's that the radiator is right in front, right between the headlights. And I also know, just from living long enough, if you crack your radiator, that's bad news. It makes cars overheat. Corolla's radiator wasn't just cracked, it was damn near bent in half.

I shook my head. Even a real mechanic wouldn't know where to start.

"Give it to me straight, doc" Corolla said. "Is it as bad as it sounds?"

I groaned. "No idea." But that was a lie. I had to tell him the truth. "I don't think it looks very good."

He sighed.

I like to have control. I like to fix problems. Every problem has a solution. I saved the princesses, I could save Corolla, too. I paced back and forth by the driver side door. "You gotta tell me what to do, man. I don't know shit about cars. You just tell me what to do and I'll do it."

"Will you sit in me?" he asked. "So I'm not alone?"

I took a step away. "Don't talk like that."

"Please?"

My hands were shaking. I reached for the backdoor handle, but Corolla said, "You can sit in the driver seat. If you want."

I opened his driver side door, which creaked worse than ever. I climbed in and sat down. I leaned my forehead against the steering wheel. Yellow chemical tears trickled down my cheeks.

"I'm going to fix you," I said. "Somehow. With something. I'll think of something."

"I know you will." But Corolla knew that wasn't true. I sat there, terrified of losing him. I hadn't know Corolla long, but I loved him. He was *my* car. And he was my *friend*. I furiously wiped the tears away from my face. Corolla asked me, "Are you crying?"

"No," I said. But then I thought, how shitty to lie about something like that. It would make him think I didn't care. And I *did* care. I cared so god damned much. So I changed my answer. "Yes."

"Will you put in my Phil Collins tape?" he asked. "I want to listen to Phil Collins."

"I hate Phil Collins," I said. His cassettes had flown all over the interior after the wreck and I had to check all around for Phil Collins. I found him in the backseat. I put the cassette in the tape player and clicked it into place.

The mechanisms inside the stereo made a loud clack. At first, I didn't think it was going to work, but then I heard the tape spin and music came out of the speakers. I don't listen to Phil Collins. I never liked Phil Collins. The song that played that night was the first Phil Collins song that I had ever bothered listening to from beginning to end. I'll never forget that song.

I sat there, lightly banging my forehead on the steering wheel. *No, no, no.* We listened to the whole song together.

"Penelope?" Corolla whispered.

"Yeah, buddy?" I asked.

But he didn't answer. The song finished and the radio died.

Chapter 18

1

I stopped believing in souls back in my junior year of high school. It just struck me as absurd, the idea that there was a ghost-shaped version of me living inside my physical body. But that all changed considering recent events. I died and went to the Guinee. Tengoku brought me back to life when she crammed my "soulstuff" back into my body. So souls were apparently real, at least at some level. So it begged the question: Do talking, flying cars have souls? And, if so, where do cars go when they die?

I wiped the tears off my cheeks with the palms of my hands. I checked my eyes in Corolla's rear view mirror. They were red and my black eye liner was smudged all to hell. In the mirror's reflection I saw Cardboard, Carl, and Parcel watching me from the trunk of the car. Cardboard ran her hand softly across Corolla's trunk. Parcel took a long pull from her vodka, then another from the bloody mary mix.

Carl, who never knew Corolla, read the mood and kept his distance. He stood a few feet back from the princesses and kept his mouth shut. Losing Corolla filled me with unbridled rage and no one to direct it at. So I went after Carl.

I threw open the car door and stormed in his direction. Carl could see the fury in my eyes and backed away.

"This is all *your* fault!" I shouted.

"*My* fault?" he asked, walking backwards. He pointed at Corolla. "This happened before I even got here!"

"You started all this *long* before now! You started this *weeks* ago!"

"I didn't start *this*! I didn't mean for any of this to happen!"

I seethed and paced in circles, swinging my arms back and forth. I managed to keep myself from murdering Carl earlier, but I didn't know if I had it in me anymore. I could have killed him. I wanted to kill him. A single swing and I could have caved his head in.

What were the princesses doing giving Carl the time of day in the first place? I whipped around to them and stomped my foot on the ground. I cracked a shoe-sized hole in the concrete.

"And what are you two thinking bringing this dickbag around here in the first place?" I asked them. "We hate Carl!"

Cardboard shrugged. "We came back to say goodbye like we promised. We broke the spell on the Muffincake Kingdom and were going to go back home. But when we got here, we saw you fighting that Voodoo lady and her pet skeleton. I didn't know what to do and Parcel was drunk and then this dickbag showed up and said he had an idea."

Carl chimed in. "A fine idea."

I narrowed my eyes at Carl. He had to be up to something. "You came here to steal Unthinkable Black."

"A reasonable assessment of the situation," he said with a finger in the air. "You always were a sharp one, but I'm afraid you're wrong this time. I, too, came to say goodbye." He grabbed my hand to shake it, but he couldn't move my metal bones and industrial-rubber muscles. He gave up on the handshake and opted to give me a pat on the shoulder instead. "I'm off to go kill myself."

"Kill yourself?" I asked. His words caught me temporarily off guard. I maintained my tone of general disinterest. "Whatever, dude. Off yourself if that's what you want to do. Just don't do it around here."

"Oh, don't worry about that. I'm going to go throw myself off the Verrazano bridge. Very neat. Very tidy." He looked past me and waved goodbye to the two princesses. "Goodbye your highness and your other highness."

Cardboard waved. "Goodbye, dickbag."

Parcel just gave him a dirty look.

Carl turned back to me. "I just wanted you to know that it's been a real pleasure working with you, Miss Salvo. Best of luck."

He stuck his hands in his pockets and headed off towards the alley. He whistled a little tune to himself.

I huffed, frustrated with my own curiosity. Carl had presented me with a mystery and, god dammit, now I wanted answers. I crossed my arms and turned my head, resigned to the fact that I couldn't just let it go. I couldn't *not* know.

"Alright," I said. "Why?"

Carl stopped and turned to face me. "Why what?"

"Why are you going to kill yourself?"

"Oh!" He honestly sounded like he forgot what we were talking around. "I got fired from Westland. And you know me, I gave my whole life to that company. Nights, weekends, holidays. I never got to be with the woman I loved. My kids grew up without a father. But that's life for a workaholic. It's a real disease, you know. One day you get fired and look around and realize you've got nothing left. So what else am I supposed to do?" He nodded like this was the only logical conclusion in the world. "You kill yourself."

He turned and limped away.

I called out and stopped him again. "Why'd they fire you?"

"Gross incompetence." He rubbed his hurt arm and turned back to face me. "Failing to bring them Impossible Red was one thing, but losing Unthinkable Black was another. They say I'm not a very good field agent."

I shook my head. "Carl, you can't kill yourself."

He smiled. "Penelope. Is that concern I hear in your voice?"

"No," I said flatly. "I'm just pointing out, logically, you can't kill yourself. You can't kill anyone. You're a pacifist."

He chuckled once. "You do have a point. But *I'm* not going to kill me. I'm going to jump off a bridge and into a river. The fall and the river will kill me."

"All this because you don't have a stupid job?" I asked.

Parcel shouted at us. "Just let him go. If he wants to-" She dropped her bottle of bloody mary mix and it shattered on the ground. Spicy tomato juice went everywhere. She stared down at the red puddle and muttered, "Oh, goddammit."

Carl checked his watch. "Look at me being a Talkative Tony. I've got to get going while the tides are right. Pleasure knowing you all."

He limped off again. I let him get as far as the mouth of the alley. But, once more, I stopped him. "Carl?" He turned back around and arched an eyebrow at me. I asked him, "Everything you said just now... is it all true?"

He said, "I may be a lot of things, Miss Salvo, but I am not a liar."

And, for the fourth time, he limped away to go kill himself.

I couldn't let Carl do it. I didn't have it in me to let anyone kill themselves, not even a jerk like Carl. Someone had to give him a reason to go on living, and there was no one else around to give it to him. I wasn't going to trust him; no, no, no, I knew better than that. Odds were, this was still some elaborate ploy to steal Unthinkable Black from me. But what if I was wrong? What if he really did kill himself? I'd already seen more death than any eighteen year old should. I didn't want his blood on my hands.

I stuck my hand in my pocket and pulled out a crumpled up five dollar bill.

"Carl!" I ran after him.

He turned around. I stuck my hand out and presented him with the money. He looked down at the wadded up bill, then raised his eyes to me.

He rubbed his head with his good hand. "What's this?"

"Well, if all you need is a job," I said. "You can work for me."

He took the five dollar bill and unfolded it. "Five bucks?"

"It's all the money I got," I said. "But that's your pay. It's either that or suicide."

"But you don't even like me."

A little laugh escaped me. "You're right. I *don't* like you. You're a real piece of shit, actually. But I can't just sit here and let you kill yourself."

He smiled and stuffed the five in his pocket. "You drive a hard bargain, but I accept." He slapped me on the shoulder. "Boss."

2

Sunrise was already coming and, with it, a better look at the aftermath from my brawl with Brijit and Kriminel. Cardboard and Parcel stayed to help clean up the courtyard. Carl followed them around and carried away armloads of bricks. When he said he was going to work for me, he really meant it.

Just looking at Corolla's smashed up body made me want to puke.

The condition of Xin's shop didn't make me feel any better. The floor was littered with dust and bricks and shattered jars. At least a dozen plants were trashed; broken stems and exposed roots and bruised petals.

I picked up a broom and started sweeping. It was going to take a lot more than a broom to clean up the mess, but I mostly did it to keep my mind off Corolla.

I heard someone crunching on the glass behind me, coming toward the hole in the front wall. Xin had returned to the scene and cautiously peered inside. He didn't look anywhere near as upset as I did.

"Xin." The broom dropped from my hands and clattered to the floor. "I am so sorry."

Xin didn't say anything. What *could* he say? He stepped through the hole in the wall and looked at the carnage that laid all around us. He bent over to see which jars were broken. I followed him with my eyes, worried about how he was going to react.

I told him, "I'm going to clean all this up." And I didn't know how I was going to do it, but I added, "And I'll fix the wall."

He looked up at me. "Are you okay?"

Me? Xin's shop was a wreck and he was worried about *me*? "Dude, I'm fine. I'm worried about you."

"You shouldn't worry." He picked up one of the little wooden tables that kept his pots in the sunlight and put it back in place. "Your talking car looks broken."

My eyes were on the verge of tears, but I fought them back.

I softly told him, "Corolla's dead."

Xin nodded, processing what I had just told him. I'd been strong for as long as I could, but I couldn't do it anymore. I ran over to Xin and threw my arms around him. I pulled him close and sobbed antifreeze tears into his shoulder. Everything I'd been bottling up – the changes in my body, the fear of losing the princesses, the destruction of Xin's shop, watching Corolla die – all of those feelings came bubbling up all at once in a long-overdue emotional breakdown.

Xin waited patiently as I cried my fucking eyes out.

I didn't realize how much stress I had been under. I got so used to pretending like everything is okay that I start to believe my own bullshit. But everything wasn't okay. Nothing had been okay since Ma died. The only thing that kept me going were the people I cared about. Xin. The princesses. And poor, poor Corolla.

Eventually my crybaby moment passed and I got my shit together. I took a deep breath, gave Xin one last squeeze, and let him go.

"Whoo," I said with a little laugh. I wiped my face dry. "Sorry about that."

He put his hands on my shoulders and said, "It's okay."

After that, I went back to sweeping. Xin got down on his knees and gathered up all the shards of his broken pots. A few of the pots were luckily still intact with the plants unharmed. Some pots didn't have anything worse than a crack up the side, but majority of the pots were busted and their plants needed new homes. Xin set the lucky one on the table and pulled pieces of brick and glass out of the dirt and leaves.

He didn't deserve any of this. And neither did I.

"Xin, I am so fucking sorry about all of this. Madam Brijit and her skeleton are crazy. I had no idea they'd follow me back to Earth. I feel like a huge fuck up right now. I just don't think before I do stuff and now I got your shop all destroyed and Corolla's dead and everything."

He said, "Penelope, none of this is your fault."

I stood there, sad, and shook my head. I wanted to believe him, I really did, but deep down I wanted to blame myself.

I helped Xin tackle the mess. We moved tables. We repotted some plants. I swept up the powders and leaves littering the floor. Xin dug out his crumpled spiral notebook and his little golf pencil from underneath the counter and strolled around to make a list of everything we needed to replace.

3

Carl knocked on the open front door. I don't know why he bothered to knock with a huge gaping hole in the wall, but he did. Xin looked up from the counter and his work in the spiral notebook. The two of them made eye contact and Xin froze.

Carl smiled apologetically and said, "I hope I'm not interrupting anything."

"What is he doing here?" Xin asked.

"Oh." I walked over to the door and told Xin, "I know what you're thinking, and I felt the same way, too. And this is going to sound crazy, but... I gave Carl a job. He works for me now."

"He..." Xin pointed at Carl. "Works for you?"

"Yeah." An embarrassed laughed escaped me and I shrugged.

Carl said, "Funny how things work out, huh?"

Xin looked back down to his notebook. "I don't want him here."

"I don't either, really," I said. "But he was going to kill himself. I couldn't let him do that. I couldn't let anyone do that. And, also, it's like they say, keep your friends close and your enemies closer, right?"

Carl nodded at Xin. "They *do* say that, you know."

I turned to Carl. "Did you need something?"

"Yes, actually," he replied. He held out a clip board with all kinds of legal documents. I took it from him and he stood over my shoulder, like he was helping me with my homework. "That's a W-9 for subcontractor work. I need you to fill that out so I can get my 1099 for taxes. I can help you file it if you don't know what you're doing. Do you know your federal business ID number?"

My eyes went wide and I shook my head. "My what?"

"Just for the..." He turned the clipboard in my hands. I was holding it upside down. "You know, so you can withhold my federal and state taxes from my paychecks. Also, I need your direct deposit information."

I lifted the papers and glanced through them all. It was just a bunch of corporate nonsense. They wanted income brackets and tax ID numbers.

I looked up at Carl. "This is... like... *math.*"

He nodded. "It's a lot of math."

"All I did was give you five bucks, man," I said, handing him back the clipboard. "You got five bucks and you got a job. I'm not filling out forms or whatever."

Card nodded and tapped his ballpoint pen against his lips. "You know what? I'll just file a small business extension." He tucked the clipboard under his arm. "Usually you only do that when you first get your business license and then hire a small workforce to-"

"I don't have a business license."

His forehead wrinkled. "You don't?"

I looked at him like he was stupid. "Dude, I'm eighteen years old. I don't own a business."

"You don't? Well... then what's my job, exactly?"

"I don't know." I grabbed the broom and went back to sweeping. "Can you fix cars?"

"No."

"Can you fix walls?"

"No."

Xin asked. "Can you go to the store?"

Carl said, "I can definitely go to the store."

"Then here." Xin made his way over to us, careful to step over the bricks and broken glass. He handed Carl a handful of twenties from the cash register. "If you're going to be here, make yourself useful. Go buy some Chinese food. Then buy a new radio. Then-"

"Whoa, okay." Carl pulled his clipboard back out and flipped the forms over to the blank side. He uncapped his pen and started writing down a list. "Chinese food. Radio."

Xin continued, "And one bottle of Baijiu."

"Baijiu." Carl wrote it down. "What is that?"

"Baijiu!" Parcel shouted from the courtyard. "It's alcohol. Chinese vodka. Who's getting Baijiu? We getting Baijiu?"

Xin heard Parcel's voice and realized who he was ordering liquor for. "Get three bottles instead of one," he said.

Carl kept scribbling. "Gotcha. Gotcha. Anything else?"

Xin looked at me. "Do you want anything?"

I didn't have the first clue what was going on. "Why are we getting vodka?"

"We're going to have a party," Xin said. He turned back to Carl and said, "Buy some beer, as well. And that will be all."

Carl limped off in a hurry like some teenage intern eager to impress the new boss. I watched him hobble away. He was going to come back with Chinese food, a radio, some kind of Chinese vodka, and beer. Xin took the broom from my hands and went out front to brush dirt and glass off the steps of the porch. I just watched him. Xin might've been done with the conversation, but I wasn't.

I asked, "What do you mean we're going to have a party."

Xin just kept sweeping. He said, "When you lose something you love, you should have a party celebrating it. It makes things better."

"I don't feel like having a party."

He stayed focus on the broom and said, "I do."

4

We spent the rest of the day cleaning up the shop and the courtyard. The princesses sincerely wanted to help, but they didn't know the first thing about manual labor. Cardboard gingerly moved the tiniest pieces of brick to a pile in the alleyway. Parcel took countless breaks to sit on the porch and drink from her flask. I didn't complain. I was just happy to have them around.

Storm clouds showed up in the distance accompanied by a cold November breeze. I threw on one of my hoodies and kept my hands in the pockets. By the time Carl came limping back from the store, it was nearly sundown. He carried a small weather radio under his good arm. Clinking inside his sling were three bottles of clear alcohol. Behind him was Mrs. Cho, the lady who bought detergent from Xin every morning. Carl had no reason to be hanging out with Mrs. Cho, but she helped him all the same, carrying two full bags of Chinese food.

"Mrs. Cho?" I said. She saw me and gave me a beaming smile.

"Oh, you know her?" Carl asked as they walked past me and up to the porch. "She saw me carrying all this stuff and asked if I wanted help. Such a nice lady."

Carl said something to Mrs. Cho in fluent Chinese. She answered him back. I didn't know Carl spoke Chinese, but I wasn't surprised. The two of them were just chatting it up in a language I didn't understand.

Parcel intercepted Carl on the porch steps. "Here. You're hurt. Let me help you."

"Thanks," Carl said, offering her the radio. "This this is kind of heavy."

Parcel ignored him. She stuck her hands inside his sling and pulled out one of the bottles of booze. She opened it and smeared her lip balm across the top of the bottle.

Carl said, "I guess that one can be yours."

Mrs. Cho gave Princess Parcel the most bewildered look. Understandable. She had never seen a bride hanging out at the shop before. She asked Carl a question in Chinese, which was probably something like, "Who is that girl and why is she dressed like that?"

Carl answered her back. I don't know what he said exactly, but his answer left Mrs. Cho with the strangest look on her face.

"Carl," I said. He turned back to me. "I hope we're not telling Mrs. Cho anything... weird."

He leaned over to Mrs. Cho and whispered something to her. They both turned to me and laughed. Together, they walked into Xin's shop through the front door.

I heard Mrs Cho go "oooh" as soon as she saw all the damage.

I threw my hands up and said, "Well, I guess we're partying with Mrs. Cho."

5

By the time Xin's "party" was in full swing, the sun had set and the city had gone dark. The evening breeze graduated to a stiff wind. Darker storm clouds moved in overhead. Everyone stayed inside and hovered around the tiny space heater Xin dug out of the bathroom. The Penelope-sized hole in the front wall let in quite the draft. Xin tuned the radio to '70s rock, he put the Chinese food across one of his tables and he served everyone Chinese vodka out of small porcelain cups that looked like bowls used for cocktail sauce.

I could hear everyone inside, talking and laughing and having a grand old time.

I leaned against ledge of the front porch and sulked.

"You know," I overheard Carl say, "I once had vodka with the director of the SZRU. They're like the CIA of the Ukraine. We were working with them to figure out what to do about the Chernobyl meltdown." He turned to Xin. "You remember Chernobyl, don't you Mister Houng?"

Xin's mood suddenly took a bad turn. He looked up from the vodka and glared at Carl. "I most certainly do."

"Eh." Carl waved him off. "Water under the bridge, that's what I say." He turned back to the rest of the group. "So this

Ukrainian director, he was actually a clone replacement from the KGB. That guy could drink vodka all day long and it never got him drunk. Some kind of mix-up with his genetics." Carl took another drink of Baijiu and said, "The Russians never were very good at cloning."

Cardboard took a shot of hard liquor, too. She didn't have it down for more than a second before she started coughing. Everyone laughed.

"Holy cow, that stuff is terrible!" She bent over and spat at the floor. "It tastes like window cleaner!"

"Lightweight," Parcel said as she knocked back her own personal bottle.

An hour passed. The wind got colder. I raised my hood and pulled on the drawstrings to keep my ears warm. The smell of rain was in the air.

I stared at Corolla.

"This reminds me of a story," Carl said, dominating the conversation. I rolled my eyes. "Once time my soul got trapped in this magical sword and that sword ended up in the hands of the Ninja Gods. I had to go negotiate for my own soul, but the Ninja Gods weren't having it. They insisted on playing a game of Tenki Kado. 'Weather Cards.' It's the most complicated card game in the world and, as you can imagine, the ninjas don't like to explain the rules until after you've lost. So, of course, all the ninjas were ganging up on me. But when they dealt the last hand, I got the first day of spring, summer, fall, and winter! I also got the only sunrise in the deck."

Parcel asked. "How is that a story?"

I laughed. She was right. That story sucked.

"Are you kidding?" Carl replied. "That's the best hand there is! What are the odds! The Ninja Gods lost and I got my soul back. They weren't too pleased about it, either."

A part of me wanted to join the party, but I couldn't. I was still mad at myself. A part of me knew that Xin was right to have the party. Xin was always right. And Corolla wouldn't have wanted me moping around feeling sorry for myself. He would have wanted me to have fun, just like everyone else.

I just didn't have it in me.

I hopped off the porch and walked around Corolla's smashed up body. I slid my fingertips across his cold steel. I made a complete circle around him, then leaned against his roof with my elbows.

"Hey." Cardboard had left the party through the hole in the wall. She put her hands on the porch ledge and looked down at me in the dark courtyard. The cold wind blew through her hair, almost taking her crown off her head. She wedged it back in place.

I gave her a head nod. "Hey."

I could tell she wanted to say something, but she hesitated. Her eyes darted around, sometimes on me and sometimes up at the sky. She wanted to cheer me up, I could tell, but she struggled with what to say.

She asked, "Is it going to rain?"

I shrugged and looked at the sky. "Looks like."

"Do you care if hang out here with you?"

"If you want," I said.

I didn't mind at all, in fact. A few more seconds alone with Corolla and I would have started crying all over again. Having Cardboard around gave me a reason to fight it back. I was really good at stopping myself from crying, but losing Corolla was too much. Cardboard stepped down off the porch and stood right beside me.

I turned to lean my back against Corolla and I folded my arms. Cardboard mimicked me, also folding her arms. I had a million things to say right then.

That I missed Corolla.

That I knew, deep down, none of this was my fault, but that didn't make me feel any better.

That nothing hurts more than losing someone you really care about.

I asked her, "What do you think happens when you die?"

"People don't die that often where I come from."

"But do you guys believe in a soul?"

"A what?" she asked.

"A ghost version of yourself that lives inside your body."

She turned to me with a terrified look in her eyes. "Absolutely not! Do you people believe that? How horrifying."

She wasn't wrong. I asked her, "Do you believe you go somewhere else when you die?"

"Yeah." She looked up. "You go live in the sky."

"Do you have gods in the Muffincake Kingdom?" I asked.

"Oh, of course," she said. "We have two, actually. Sugar Cube and Butter Pad. They're the cosmic bakers that put our whole world in the oven."

"Corolla talked about some pre-owned car lot in the sky, so maybe there's some kind of car heaven." I looked over at her. "Do you think there's a car heaven?"

"Me?" She took the cardboard crown off her head and swept her fingers through her hair. "Oh, Penelope, don't ask me. I have no idea. I'm not the smartest cookie in the... what's the word..." She thoughtfully tapped her fingers on her chin. Her face lit up when she thought of the word. "Cookie jar."

"He's dead," I said. "Because of me."

"Nuh uh," Cardboard said. "You didn't kill him."

"Yeah, but if he never met me, he'd still be alive."

"You don't know that," she said. "I'm alive because of you, so I guess it just goes to show that... that...." She squinted her eyes in deep thought.

"That what?"

She threw up her hands and rolled her eyes. "I already forgot what I was going to say."

A strong gust of wind came along and nearly took Cardboard's crown off her head. She felt it lifting off and snatched it with both hands. A cold drop of rain tapped me right on the forehead. I looked up to the sky. The clouds were threatening to turn into a full-fledged storm. I zipped up my hoodie and pulled the sleeves down over my fingers. The antennas on the surrounding apartment buildings swayed as another rush of wind swept over us.

A bolt of lightning crackled lengthwise across the sky directly overhead. The courtyard flashed with blue light. Half a second later came the earth-shattering boom of thunder that shook every window in Chinatown. Cardboard shrieked and nearly jumped out of her shoes. I jumped, too, and my heart pounded in my chest.

The light in the shop flicked off and the radio went silent. The surrounding apartment buildings went dark. Chinatown had lost power.

"I'm blind!" Parcel shouted from inside.

"You're not blind," Carl said. "Manhattan just blew one heck of a fuse."

In the darkness, my other senses became hyper-sensitive. Neighborhood dogs barked and howled at the storm. The first drops of rain tapped on the concrete. The air had a faint scent of the ocean as the wind changed directions and blew in off the coast.

And in the middle of pitch-black Chinatown, high-beam headlights pulled up at the far end of the alley. It wasn't just one set of headlights, but multiples. Four? Five? They came from all different directions and then flicked off, one by one. I lowered my hood and walked slowly to the mouth of the alley to get a better look.

Two limousines. Four black SUVs. Riot soldiers armed with sniper rifles and machine guns poured out of the SUVs like a bunch of god damned clown cars. The soldiers moved in tactical formation, some of them headed up the alley, others climbing the nearby fire escapes.

"Oh... shit," I whispered as I backed away.

"What's going on?" Cardboard asked as she came up behind me. "What is it?"

"Westland." I said as the rain started to come. "They're here."

Chapter 19

1

I grabbed Carl by his jacket and shoved him hard against the wall of the shop. "You son of a bitch! You sold us out!"

"Sold you out?" Carl repeated. His eyes were wide and he looked absolutely terrified. "No! What are you talking about?"

"Don't lie to me!" I pulled him away from the wall and shoved him back against it, this time a little harder. "You know exactly what I'm talking about!"

He raised his voice at me. "No, I don't!"

I let go of him and he dropped to the ground. He landed on his bad arm and hissed in pain. Mrs. Cho, who'd never seen me lash out before, backed off into the corner. Parcel and Cardboard stood there and watched. Cardboard nervously wrung her hands together, Parcel kept her eyes on me as she took a drink from her bottle of Baijiu. Xin gave me a concerned look; he knew if I was accusing Carl of foul play, that meant something had gone terribly wrong.

Carl got to his knees. "Penelope, I swear to you, I have no idea what you're talking about."

I ran my fingers through my soaked hair and flung water all around. "Westland's storming the place," I said, waving my finger towards the courtyard. "It's a fucking Macy's Day Parade of SUVs and limos out there."

Carl crawled to the hole in the wall and peered outside. He took keen interest in the sky. "I was afraid of that," he said. "I thought maybe this was just a storm."

I asked, "What do you mean 'just a storm'?"

"It's Westland's weather machine," he said. "That's how they hide their operations. When they sent me to steal Impossible Red, it wasn't a coincidence that Hurricane Sandy hit that same night. They made it happen." Lightning flashed and illuminated his face. "And now they're doing it again."

I paced around the shop and tried to think straight.

"Alright," I said. "Alright. First thing's first. You all need to get the hell out of here." I looked around. No one moved. Everyone just stared at me, even Mrs. Cho. I locked eyes with Cardboard. "Cardboard, you need to get everyone into your cardboard tunnels."

"But..." She hesitated. "But what about you?"

"Don't worry about me," I said. "Just worry about getting everyone out of here and somewhere safe."

Cardboard crossed her arms. "I'm not leaving you here."

"Cardboard." I took her by the shoulders so she would listen to my words. "Westland is out there with guns. A lot of guns. And who knows what else they're packing. Laser beams? Satellites? All they want is this..." I took Unthinkable Black out of my pocket and held it between my fingers. "If I have to fight them, I'll fight them. And, so help me, if I have to kill them, I guess I'll have to kill them. But either way, it's way too dangerous for any of you to stay here."

She crossed her arms tighter and looked away from me. "I said I'm not leaving."

"Oh, you picked a hell of a time to be fucking brave." I turned to Princess Parcel. The irony was not lost on me that I was turning to *her* to be the voice of reason. "Parcel. Take Mrs. Cho and get her somewhere safe."

Parcel nodded. She reached into the front of her dress and took out of her book of stamps. She stuck one on Mrs. Cho's shoulder and said, "The Muffincake Kingdom."

Mrs. Cho vanished.

I blinked at Parcel. "Did you... just send Mrs. Cho to the Muffincake Kingdom?"

Parcel stared at me long and hard. "You said somewhere safe."

"Not to a fairytale world of cupcakes and cotton candy! She's an old lady!" I ran my fingers through my hair. There wasn't time for debate. At least Mrs. Cho was out of harm's way. "Fine. Whatever. Just get everyone else out of here. Take your sister with you."

Parcel leaned against the wall and drunkenly waved her bottle at me. "Oh, I'm not going *anywhere*."

I couldn't believe what I was hearing. "Why the hell not!?"

"You saved my life." Her knees buckled and she nearly lost her balance. "And now I'm going to save yours."

"Look at you! You're wasted!" I shouted at her. "You're not going to save my life! You're going to get yourself killed!"

She gave me a glassy-eyed stare and took another drink of liquor. She put a finger to my chest and said, "We'll see."

Carl put his finger up and took a step forward. "For what it's worth, I'd like to leave. I hate to be a Cowardly Carlos, but I know these guys and I know how they operate. I'd rather not be here when, and please forgive the crass idiom, when the poop hits the fan."

I pointed a finger at Carl. "You're not going anywhere, shit bird. You're behind all this somehow. I just know it."

Carl's face flushed red and he pounded his good fist on the counter. "I'm not behind anything, gosh dang it. I don't work for them anymore. Those jerks fired me."

"Likely story." I ran to the front of the shop and peeked carefully out the hole in the wall. The pouring rain and flashing lightning made it hard to see, but sure enough, snipers crawled all over the surrounding apartment buildings like roaches: along the perimeters of the rooftops, up in the fire escapes, and poking out of open windows. I tried to count them as they got into position. I ballparked it at fifty and stopped counting. They assembled their sniper rifles, they set up machine guns on bipods and, one by one, red targeting lasers began to sweep through the air.

"Mother of *fuck*." I ducked away from the hole before I was spotted. I ran to Cardboard and grabbed both her hands in mine. "Cardboard, *please*. Go. This is going to get bad. This is going to get really bad."

She shouted, "But I want to help you!"

I shouted back, "You're going to die!"

"Penelope." Xin put his hand on my shoulders and made me quiet down. I turned to look at him. He had an aura of calm about him that didn't make any sense to me. How was he not panicking? He said, "Do you remember when I tried to keep you safe by telling you not to go to Westland?"

"You knew I went to Westland?" I asked.

"Of course I did," he replied. "You were going to do whatever you wanted." He moved and stood by Princess Cardboard and Princess Parcel. "And so are we."

"Xin, this is different. This is dangerous."

Carl interrupted us. "I technically still want to leave."

If they all wanted to stay, I guess I couldn't argue with them. Cardboard was terrified – I could see if in her eyes – but her tight lips and tiny fists said it all; she was ready to fight if she had to. Parcel was operating on liquid courage fueled by a supernatural blood-alcohol content. And Xin wasn't going to take no for an answer.

I leaned closer to Xin, borderline in tears, and whispered to him, "Xin, if any of you die, I don't know what I'm going to do. I'm not strong enough to handle that kind of thing. And I'm scared."

He nodded and said, "I'm scared, too."

2

"Penelope Marie Salvo!"

The voice came from the courtyard, amplified over the hissing rain by a megaphone. I shooed everyone back behind the counter, far away from the hole in the front wall. I didn't know what Westland was planning, but they brought snipers and gunners and I didn't want my friends getting caught in the crossfire. Once they were safely out of the way, I left the shop and stepped out onto the front porch. I figured if all Westland wanted was me, I'd make myself the easy target and keep the others safe.

With a low pop, an industrial spotlight beamed from the roof of the Super Wash Dry Clean building and illuminated me in a circle of blinding light. It revealed the wind-blown slant of the falling rain. I shielded my eyes with my hand so I could see into the courtyard.

The CEO and a platoon of soldiers stood in a line in front of the shop like some kind of twisted curtain call for a musical where no one bows and, actually, everyone wants to kill you. Next to the CEO were two assistants in fine suits, one holding an umbrella for the old bastard and another one busy on a tablet computer. The soldiers on either side of them were decked out in full bulletproof gear and were armed with high powered machine guns.

The CEO held a megaphone to his mouth so I could hear him over the rain and thunder.

"I'm giving you one chance out of this, Miss Salvo," said the CEO. "I know your friends are in there. Give me Unthinkable Black and we'll leave. No one has to fight and no one has to die. We'll all go home and pretend like none of this ever happened."

"He's desperate," Carl called out, coaching me from behind the counter. I kept my eyes on the CEO, but listened to what Carl had to say. "He doesn't know how powerful you've become. He just wants you to give up."

I took Unthinkable Black out of my pocket and held it into the spotlight where the CEO could see it.

I said, "If your snipers take a single shot, I'll swallow it."

The CEO dropped the megaphone to his side, pissed that I wasn't cooperating. He whispered something to his assistant. The assistant whispered back. The CEO nodded and raised his megaphone back to his mouth.

"If you're going to swallow it," he said, "then swallow it."

Shit. He called my bluff. I couldn't swallow Unthinkable Black. I had no idea what it would do to me.

I turned back to Carl. "What should I do?"

Carl peeked out over the back counter and shrugged. "I don't know. Something."

Something. That's vague.

"Something it is," I said.

I picked up a brick from off the porch and hucked it at the spotlight. My intention was to just break the stupid thing, but I totally miscalculated my own strength. I didn't just break the spotlight, I tore the whole thing straight off the roof and launched it towards New Jersey. The soldier operating the light got yanked off his feet by the momentum and he disappeared into the heavy rain. Shit. That probably killed him.

The CEO wasn't impressed with my act of defiance. Hell, he didn't even bother to look back at the equipment I'd destroyed. He brought the megaphone back to his mouth.

"Have it your way," he shouted. He raised a finger as a signal to his goon squad. The formation of soldiers in the courtyard raised and readied their guns. The snipers on the roof switched on their laser-sights. Thirty red beams of light criss-crossed through the rain and focused on the front porch. The CEO held his finger there in the air for a second, then pointed at the shop.

"Open fire."

Bullets shredded through the walls of the porch. Muzzle flashes from all the guns lit up the courtyard like a million flash bulb cameras. And while bullets didn't scare me in the slightest, it only took a couple seconds for me to realize... the soldiers weren't shooting at me. They were shooting into the shop. They were shooting at everything *but* me.

Holes were blown clean through the front wall. Chips of red brick sprayed into the air. The windows shattered. Xin's hand-made shelves disintegrated into splinters. Jars fell to the floor and burst open. Leaves and flower petals blew through the air as Xin's collection of plants were obliterated. Cardboard and Parcel screamed as they ducked lower behind the main counter. Carl, in a moment of bravery, wrangled everyone into the safety of my bedroom. At least back there, they had one more brick wall to protect them.

The new weather radio got hit and exploded into pieces. Holes ripped through the bathroom door as the gunfire shattered the sink and the toilet.

I ran inside and stood in the doorway of the back room. Stray bullets thumped against my back and the shells clattered to the floor. Cardboard, Carl, Parcel and Xin had thrown my cot on its side and ducked behind it for additional cover. It wouldn't last long, not under Westland's full assault.

"I've given it some thought," Parcel said, "and I think we should go."

"Yes!" I shouted over the gunfire and thunder and rain. "That's what I've been trying to fucking tell you! Please! Go!"

Cardboard nodded emphatically. Luckily I had a cardboard box in my room, the one the princesses got from the costume place when they dressed up as Vader and Batman. I grabbed the box and tossed it to them behind the bed. Cardboard set it on its side, crawled inside and pushed the flaps open to her magical tunnels. Carl knelt by the box as Princess Parcel crawled in next. Once those two were gone, Carl motioned for Xin.

Xin looked back at me. "Are you coming?"

"Well." I forced a nervous smile. "You hired me for night security, right? Well, I don't think it gets any more 'night security' than this."

Xin gave the bedroom one last look, reached up to grab his mortar and pestle off my table, then crawled inside the cardboard box. Once Xin was safety through, Carl closed the box.

Eventually the gunfire died down and went quiet. The only people left were me and Carl.

"Carl," I said to him. He looked over at me, ready for orders. I had already told him to stay, but the time had come. "You can go."

"With all due respect." He stood up to brush off his suit, then carefully plucked pink flower petals out of his sling. "This is the only job I have left. What kind of workaholic would I be if I walked away now?"

"Carl."

He adjusted his tie and went to the bedroom door. "I know how Westland operates. Let me go talk to them."

"Are you nuts?" I spat. "You step out there and they're going to blow your fucking brains out!"

"Eh," he said with a shrug of his one good shoulder. "I was going to die anyway."

Carl walked brazenly out of the back room and through the main shop. He put his one good hand up in surrender – the other one just slightly raised in his sling – and stepped out onto the porch. A replacement spotlight fell on him, this one from the roof of the Asian Food Mart. It was quickly joined by a dozen red sniper dots that collected on his chest. Lightning flashed and silhouetted Carl's over-confident and mildly battered profile.

The thought ran through my mind, *Either this guy is really smart, or really stupid.* And that was the strange thing when it came to Carl; I honestly didn't know which one it was.

But one thing was for certain: Carl's arrival on the scene was a total curve ball for the CEO. The old man's face turned sour, puzzled by this sudden development. He put the megaphone to his mouth.

"Carl?" he said. "What do you think you're doing?"

Carl ignored the CEO and raised his voice to the snipers above. "Ladies and gentlemen, you know me. Most of you used to work for me. I know I'm not your boss anymore, but you have to listen to me. Penelope is not the threat here. She is a nice girl who is just trying to-"

"Shut him up," the CEO said. He wasn't in the mood for monologues. "Kill him."

Carl looked down as the sniper dots gathered over his heart. He softly said, "Oh, dear."

I heard the distinct "clink-clink" of a rifle as a single sniper took his shot. A bullet zipped through the air and thumped into Carl's chest. His body was thrown backwards into the shop and his head thumped against the hardwood floor.

Before I had time to think, I shouted his name.

"Carl!"

I ran over to him, grabbed him by the shoulders and dragged him across the powders and glass and damaged flowers. He was soaked from the rain and left a wet streak behind him. I got him back into the bedroom and out of view of the Westland soldiers.

"Carl?" He wasn't moving. I shook his shoulders and screamed louder, "Carl!"

Carl opened his eyes. I collapsed back on my ass and breathed a sigh of relief. He put his hand to his chest and groaned in pain. I pulled open his suit jacket to look for the wound, but there was no blood. Under his white dress shirt, he was wearing a bulletproof vest. Right over his heart was a metal dent where the vest had absorbed the shock of the sniper's bullet.

"Son of a bitterstick," Carl groaned. "That really stings."

"Holy shit, dude, I thought you were dead."

"I'm not dumb." He tried to laugh, but laughing made him wince. The force of the bullet definitely left a crazy bruise, probably even fractured his ribs. Breathing and talking caused him physical pain.

"What the hell were you thinking?"

"I knew I'd be fine," he said. "I had my bulletproof vest."

"Uh, do you have a bulletproof vest in your *forehead*? Cuz if that's where they shot you, your brains would be splattered halfway to fucking Queens."

He looked at me and his eyes dilated. "I didn't think of that."

I heard footsteps inside the shop, crunching on the glass. Someone had snuck inside. I slowly peeked around the door frame of my bedroom, ready to spring out and uppercut someone into the stratosphere. I stopped when I saw it was Baron Semedi strolling around the shop, puffing on his cigar, taking a keen interest in the destruction laid out all around us. He picked up a fully intact jar, one of the few left, and held it close to his face. He got bored with it and tossed it over his shoulder. It shattered behind him.

He didn't bother to look at me, but said, "Quite the situation you're in. Surrounded on all sides. All out of friends." He swept his hands through the air as he envisioned an invisible theater marquee. "Imagine it. Penelope Salvo, god of war, versus the entire Westland Corporation. My dear, if we sold tickets, we'd be richer than the human on the Monopoly box."

"Glad to see you're enjoying this," I said as I got to my feet and stepped into the main room. "Did you come here just to rub it in my face?"

"Oh, no, no, no." He ashed his cigar on the ground and looked at me over a sip of rum. He made a satisfied "ahhh" after his drink. "I just came here to give you one last chance to reconsider my offer."

"Your offer?" I said.

"Of marriage. You see, I can make all this go away. The CEO, those armed humans, all of them. I could make them all go away. And I'll do it…"

"If I marry you," I said, finishing his sentence.

He fluttered his eyes at me. "Would it be so bad?"

I marched over, grabbed him by the lapels and pulled him close so I could say it right in his face: "I'd. Rather. Die."

I shoved him away from me. He kept his cool and straightened his jacket.

"Well, I'm afraid you're going to get your wish. Shame, too. Your princess friends really think they're helping."

Semedi moved over to the broken window and looked outside. He motioned at me to join him.

"There," Semedi said. He pointed at a sniper up on the roof of the Super Dry Clean building. "Look at that gun human up there."

I saw one of the snipers perched there, just barely poking up over the ledge. He wore black combat gear, had a pair of night vision goggles strapped to his faces, and he cradled a high-powered sniper rifle with silencer, scope, and a mini bipod at the end of the barrel. But as the lightning flashed, I saw the dark outline of Princess Parcel looming behind him like a murderer in a horror movie. She crept up behind him, pressed a stamp to his helmet, and said something. I couldn't tell what – not from that far away – but it had to be some sort of magical destination, because a second later, the sniper vanished.

"And look over there." Semedi moved his finger to the rooftop of the apartments above the Asian Food Mart.

This sniper knelt in the beating rain, poised at the corner of the roof ledge with his eye pressed to the scope of his rifle. He was so focused on the shop and the courtyard that he missed Princess Cardboard sneaking up on him from behind. She shoved him as hard as she could and he toppled right over the edge. He dropped six stories and plunged into a well-positioned cardboard box.

Around the perimeter of the courtyard, Cardboard and Parcel's other four sisters emerged from the darkness.

A princess in a polka-dot gown and a wreath of bubble wrap around her long black hair appeared behind a squad of four snipers positioned on top of the apartment building to the east. She held a length of bubble wrap in both hands, which she wrapped up tightly and then twisted with all her might. Dozens of tiny bubbles popped and the snipers turned their heads at the sound, but that was all they had time for. Princess Bubble Wrap's magic warped the very fabric of reality like the bubble wrap in her hands. The rooftop – bricks, windows, fire escapes – twisted into a distorted singularity, sucking the soldiers inside. Their bodies folded in on themselves and vanished. When she let go of the bubble wrap, the world sproinged back to normal, no damage to the rooftop or the bricks. The snipers, however, were gone.

"Ooh," Semedi said. "That was a good one."

Everyone from Westland got wise that something weird was going on. Radio communication was starting to dwindle from their missing troops. One by one, the red lasers were disappearing.

Two machine gunners were posted up on a nearby fire escape. They scanned the rooftops for their missing allies. I couldn't see their faces through their shielded helmets, but I could read their body language: they were very confused. Princess Package and Princess Mailbag opened the apartment window directly behind them. Princess Package wore a white dress covered in the rubber stamps from international mail; red ones from Spain, green ones from Russia, black ones from Australia. Mailbag wore a sturdy canvas dress, the same mailbag material as her namesake.

With the window open, Princess Package threw a loop of twine around one of the guys and tied it into a bow. He vanished.

Princess Mailbag threw a mailbag over the other guy's upper body and she pulled the drawstrings tight around his waist. The soldier thrashed around inside the bag, pressing against it with his elbows and hands. In a terrifying display of magic, the bag sucked him deeper inside and gobbled him up. As his boots disappeared into the mailbag, the struggling ended and the bag sagged as if it was empty.

Princess Postcard came darting out of the shadows of the courtyard for a magical hit and run on the row of soldiers standing to the right of the CEO. She sprinted through the puddles, crouched down for stealth and spry as shit. She had a stack of postcards in her hand and as she passed each soldier, she tucked one of the postcards into their belts. She picked them off, one by one. The six soldiers vanished, teleported to other parts of the world by Princess Postcard's magic of "Greetings from Beautiful Rome!" and "Visit Orlando!"

4

The CEO turned in all different directions and scanned the rooftops as he realized his army was disappearing. Between the dense storm clouds and the heavy rain, it was tough to tell what exactly was going on, but each flash of lightning revealed unattended rooftops and empty fire escapes. He held a walkie-talkie to his mouth and asked after them.

"Foxtrot leader?" Radio silence. "Foxtrot leader, answer me!" Again he waited for an answer, but it never came. "Oscar leader? Zulu leader?" Nothing.

An enraged growl came from deep inside the CEO. He threw his radio to the ground and cracked it into pieces. He whipped back around and pressed the megaphone to his mouth.

"You have exhausted my patience, Salvo!" He took out his small remote control, the one from Vacation Island, the one connected to the 50-4F-50-50-59 laser in space. He waved it at me. "You remember this, don't you?"

"You said you'd rather die," Semedi said, looming over my shoulder as I watched the courtyard. "Here's your last chance to change your mind."

I gave him Semedi the dirtiest look possible. "I don't need your help," I said. "I'll fix this on my own."

I stuck my hand in my pocket and pulled out Unthinkable Black. I rolled it in my hand for a second. That laser could kill me. I knew it. And if the CEO killed me, he could just pluck Unthinkable Black off my dead body. I had to get it as far away from me as possible.

I didn't have much time to think. The important question was, how much could I trust Carl? Carl with a bum arm, Carl who took a sniper shot to the chest, Carl who had his hand on the shop counter and was struggling to get back to his feet to rejoin the fight.

Short on time, I came right out and asked him. "Carl, can I trust you?"

He winced in pain as he struggled to stand up straight. "I'd like to think so."

I held Unthinkable Black tight in my fist. With a frustrated sigh, I went over and pushed it into Carl's hand.

"The CEO is going to kill me," I said. "And I don't think I'll be coming back this time. That marble has the power to destroy the entire Universe, so don't fuck this up. Get it as far away from here as possible."

I took a step away from him, hoping against all hope that my plan wouldn't get me killed by a beam of light from space.

Carl didn't close his fingers around Unthinkable Black. He just stared at it awestruck, mouth open, eyebrows arched as high as they could go. It was as if he could see a dark, otherworldly beauty trapped inside. He lifted his eyes to me, whispered "Thank you," then walked out onto the front porch.

He walked without a limp. He pulled the sling off of his bad arm, tossed it to the ground and thrust Unthinkable Black triumphantly into the air.

Semedi shook his head in disappointment. "Wrong move."

"I did it!" Carl bounced down the porch steps and went to rejoin his friends from Westland. "My deep cover operation worked perfectly."

The CEO clapped his hands once. "Excellent work, Carl!"

"I knew it!" I shouted at Carl. "I knew you were faking it!"

I knew I couldn't trust him. It took a real sick son of a bitch to go through all that "pretending." Pretending to be suicidal. Pretending to switch sides. Pretending to be an actual human being with actual feelings. In the end, he was none of those things. He was the same corporate shill he always was and, deep down, I knew that the entire time.

"The old 'double agent' trick," Carl said as he turned back to face me. He took his right-hand position next to the CEO and their few remaining assault troopers. "It's the oldest trick in the book and you fell right for it. Westland never fired me and you were right to be suspicious. You should have went with your gut. But if it's any consolation, I'm not a thief. When this is all said and done, I'm going to return your five dollars."

The CEO stuck out his open hand. Carl placed Unthinkable Black right in the middle of his palm. The CEO's eyes glinted, filled with dreams of out-of-control murder devices killing every supernatural entity living on Earth. But the old bastard didn't truly understand the power he held in his hand. He clinched his bony, old fingers around the black marble and shook his fist at me.

"You could have played ball, kid." He gestured all around the shop and at the courtyard, "We could have avoided all this. This is just an example of..."

I crossed my arms and cut him off. "Don't care."

My dismissive attitude completely derailed his train of thought. He shook his head for a moment, obviously unaccustomed to people defying him.

"What?" he asked.

"I don't care," I repeated. "Tell your story kicking rocks, man. I'm not interested."

He gave me a hateful frown and leveled the 50-4F-50-50-59 remote in my direction.

"Don't think I won't still kill you, little girl. It'd be fair payback for all the trouble you've caused."

I bent down and picked up a brick.

"Last time you pushed that button, the laser beam took three seconds to reach my head from space. Three seconds is a long time, asshole. You shoot me with your billion dollar space laser and I'll bash your fucking brains out with this 99 cent brick."

His face switched from smug satisfaction to concern. Everything I said was true and he knew it. I reared back with the brick in my hand and determination in my eyes. He could see it on my face: that was not a bluff he wanted to call.

He tucked the remote control back into his jacket and said, "You're a better negotiator than you give yourself credit for, Miss Salvo."

I let the brick roll out of my fingers and drop to the floorboards of the porch. "Well, you certainly didn't leave me much choice."

"It's not going to soon matter in any case." He stared at Unthinkable Black in his hand. "With this, I can finish what the Westland Corporation started. I'll destroy every supernatural force in the whole world. I turn all of them into-"

The CEO stopped mid-sentence. His eyes went wide. His eyes slowly looked down to see a skeleton arm had punched straight through his chest. Green powder gushed from inside his suit and spilled down the front of his clothes. The bony fingers that punched through his body reached out and delicately plucked Unthinkable Black from the CEO's open palm.

The CEO opened his mouth, but words wouldn't come out. A drop of green blood formed on his bottom lip and dripped to the concrete.

5

Baron Kriminel put his free hand on the CEO's back and shoved his slumped body to the wet concrete. The CEO collapsed there, opening and closing his mouth like he wanted to say something, but he'd been punched through the heart and it wasn't happening. He made a vain effort to crawl away, then dropped face-first into a puddle and laid there, dead.

"Holey moley," Carl said, backing away from the CEO's body.

Baron Kriminel stood there, frozen in place. Green powder covered the tuxedo sleeve on his right arm, but quickly washed off in the rain. The Voodoo loa looked incomplete: he was missing his bottom jaw and was short a few of his fingers. Apparently some pieces of him couldn't make it to the big reunion.

Madam Brijit stepped out of Kriminel's shadow. Her wedding gown whipped around in the heavy winds. She flipped her head back and tossed her wet dreadlocks out of her face.

"If anyone's going to kill that pogget," she said as she moved to stand over the CEO's dead body, "it's going to be me."

"I don't even know what that word means." I turned to look at Semedi. "She keeps calling me these words I've never heard before."

"My dear wife sure knows how to make an entrance," Baron Semedi said with admiration.

The few Westland soldiers still left in the courtyard backed away from the two Voodoo spirits in panic. Their morale had already been ruined after the majority of their security forces vanished into thin air. Now their leader was dead on the ground as they were confronted with an undead skeleton and a Voodoo witch. They pointed their guns at Brijit and Kriminel, but backed away towards the alleyway.

"Loa!" their team leader shouted. "Tactical retreat!"

One nervous soldier accidentally pulled the trigger on his machine gun in a loud rattle of bullets. The sudden gunfire startled the other soldiers and they joined in, setting off a chain reaction that ended with them all unloading their weapons into Brijit and Kriminel.

Madam Brijit and Baron Kriminel exchanged glances that said, "These human *can't* be serious."

Baron Kriminel's tuxedo fluttered as the bullets passed harmlessly through his skeleton bones. Brijit puffed into a cloud of cigar smoke and drifted through the air.

The soldiers realized the futility of their physical assault. Just as quick as the shooting started, it went quiet. Madam Brijit reformed into her solid shape.

"Kriminel," she said. "Dispense with this rabble."

Kriminel raised his hands and the Westland security forces floated up off the ground. Then he yanked down with his closed fists and ripped their human souls straight out of their bodies. Each one of the soldiers dropped dead to the ground. Their screaming translucent blue souls clawed helplessly at the concrete as Baron Kriminel's unimaginable magic sucked them down into depths of the Earth.

As the last of their souls slipped away, all that remained were their lifeless bodies and the sound of rolling thunder.

Brijit stood in front of Kriminel with her open hand. Kriminel held Unthinkable Black above her open palm and dropped it. She lowered her eyes to the black sphere and gazed deeply into its darkness.

"Is this what all the fighting is about?" She frowned at the little marble. She didn't understand.

Baron Semedi confidently swaggered off the porch and out into the rain. He told his wife, "Whoever swallows that tiny bauble wields the powers of limitless destruction."

She raised an eyebrow, intrigued. "*Limitless* destruction?"

Semedi nodded. "The suit humans were going to use it to destroy everything supernatural on Earth. You truly saved the day, my love."

"Hmm." Brijit gave the marble a sly grin and said, "If I gave this to Kriminel, he could kill all the humans."

Madam Brijit sealed Unthinkable Black in her fist and paced around the courtyard. She stared me down like we were playground rivals ready to fight by the swing set after school. I didn't give her the satisfaction of a dirty look. I just stood there on the porch, arms crossed, unfazed by her posturing. If she wanted to step into the Octagon for round three, I was more than willing to oblige her. But one thing I wasn't going to do anymore was bicker like children.

"Penelope," Carl whispered into my ear, suddenly safe behind me on the porch. "Can I be on your side for real?"

I didn't look at him. "Shut up, Carl."

"Uh, dear?" Semedi said as he nervously paced behind his wife who stalked me back and forth like a jungle cat. "You wouldn't *really* kill all the humans, would you?"

"Oh, I most certainly would!" She pointed at me and then at Carl. "I hate her. She tried to steal you away from me. And I hate that tuxedo human just as much. That one lied to me. Humans are the worst! The time has come for them to inhabit the graves I have waiting!"

"Penelope," Carl muttered under his breath. The coward kept inching further behind me. "Do something."

I muttered back. "Shut *up*, Carl."

Semedi put his arm around his wife. "Now, dear. Let's think about this before we kill all the humans. Why don't you just give me that black thing and we'll–"

"Don't *touch* me." She threw his arm off her shoulders and stuck her finger right in his face. "You stay out of this."

Semedi continued, "But my sweet, we're spirits of love, you and I. We don't kill."

"*We* don't kill," she said, then turned her gaze to Baron Kriminel. "But *he* does."

She went to stand in front of her skeleton henchman and stood on her tip toes to hold Unthinkable Black up to his mouth. He was missing his bottom jaw, so she poised black marble directly above the emptiness of his throat. She held it there, ready to drop it into his body.

"Think of it it," she said, staring up into Kriminel's vacant eye sockets. "Kriminel, the loa of murder and the god of destruction, killing every single human being on Earth."

Carl tugged on my t-shirt. He had a desperation to his voice and pleaded, "Penelope."

"Don't look to me for help, Carl." I crossed my arms. "This is all your fault."

"But you have to do something!" He grabbed my shoulders and tried to shake me. I didn't budge. "She's going to kill everyone!"

I kept my arms crossed and turned my face away from him. Carl didn't deserve my help.

"Open wide," Brijit said to Kriminel.

Kriminel didn't have a mouth or a tongue, so he couldn't really swallow. Brijit dropped the black marble down his neck. I thought maybe it would bounce through his dusty old bones and come rolling out of his pant cuffs, but it didn't. It disappeared inside his body and stayed in there.

Baron Kriminel stared off into vacant space with his lifeless eye sockets.

Then he unexpectedly lurched forward. He dropped to his hands and knees, then toppled sideways and curled up into the fetal position. The top hat rolled off of his head and revealed the entirety of his smooth white skull. Madam Brijit, who had never seen one of the god spheres in action, backed away confused. Kriminel was an indestructible force of death and there was was, reduced to a shuddering heap on the wet concrete.

"You let her do it!" Carl shouted with his hands still on my shoulders. "You didn't stop her. You didn't even *try*!"

I pulled free and shoved him away from me. "Don't touch me."

Baron Kriminel started convulsing, curling up into a ball, then suddenly stretching out. Brijit nervously paced back and forth, watching his bones twist and contort in strange and unnatural ways. It was as if Unthinkable Black was disassembling his bones at the joints and then putting him back together.

"What's happening?" Brijit cried. She kicked him in the ribs. "Kriminel. Stand up. I order you to stand up."

But the ever loyal Kriminel couldn't follow orders. He tried to crawl away through the puddles of rain, but there was no escaping his new transformation. He raised his head and with the first sound I'd ever heard him make, Baron Kriminel coughed.

A cloud of pink glitter puffed out of his mouth.

Glowing orbs the color of pink bubblegum appeared in his dark eye sockets. A semi-transparent pink hologram of a bottom jaw faded into existence on his lower skull. Beams of pink light radiated out of the cuffs of his jacket and the legs of his pants. His missing finger bones were replaced with the same neon-colored light. He raised his new hand up to his glowing eyes and admired it from all different angles.

Carl watched from behind me and asked, "Why's it pink?"

6

I never trusted Carl. He put on a good performance with the whole "I'm going to kill myself" bit – and I will admit that he almost had me going for a second there – but, no, I knew I couldn't trust him. In the end, I was counting on it. I *needed* Carl to double-cross me, because that was the only way my plan would work.

And I did, the whole time, have a plan.

Minutes before Brijit and Kriminel showed up, back when the Westland snipers had opened fire and blew the shit out of Xin's shop, all the jars shattered and spilled across the floor. That included the secret jar of dirt Xin made for me, the one hiding Unobtainable Pink. When that jar busted, dirt spilled everywhere and the pink sphere rolled right in my direction. At the time, my main worry was that it would roll away and get lost, so I stuck it in my pocket for safe keeping.

Carl had bravely shuffled everyone to the back room; Xin, Parcel, and Cardboard. I'd decided that the shop was too dangerous for them to hang around, so I went back there to tell them to leave. On my way to the back room, I spotted my old can of black spray paint rolling around. And that's when my plan really came together.

I put Unobtainable Pink on the ground and in three seconds – psst psst psst – I spray-painted it black. See, Westland wasn't interested in Unobtainable Pink because all it did was make someone the god of love and they didn't want to release love. They wanted to release destruction. Well, in my head it made perfect sense: if Carl was going to double-cross me, if Westland was somehow going to somehow get their hands on Unthinkable Black, wouldn't they be surprised to find out that what they had wasn't Unthinkable Black at all, but actually Unobtainable Pink.

When Carl refused to crawl away in the cardboard tunnels to safety, I immediately knew he was up to something. Was Carl really so brave that he'd he'd stare down a platoon of snipers just so he could make a speech in my favor? I didn't think so. When the CEO ordered his snipers to shoot him, they thought that would be one-hundred percent conclusive proof that Carl was on my side. But out of all those snipers, only one of them fired? Why didn't they all fire? He took a single bullet to the chest and he just so happened to be wearing a bulletproof vest? Awful convenient. I might not be the smartest girl on the block, but come on.

Carl was just waiting for an opportunity to get Unthinkable Black away from me. So I gave him exactly what he wanted. When the CEO threatened me with his space laser, I turned to Carl and asked him, "Carl, can I trust you? Great. Here. Take Unthinkable Black." And the moron, who assumed that he was so much smarter than me just because I was some punk kid, totally fell for it. He executed his double-cross, walked Unthinkable Black out to the courtyard and handed it over, never realizing that he didn't have the real Unthinkable Black at all. The real Unthinkable Black was still in my pocket.

Things took an unexpected turn when Madam Brijit and Baron Kriminel killed the CEO. I didn't see that coming and resigned myself to yet another triple-threat match between me and the Voodoo spirits, but Brijit suddenly took interest in Unthinkable Black. Semedi told her it would turn the owner into the god of destruction, a pretty tempting power boost to Kriminel, her one-man army.

That's why, for as much as Brijit decided to gloat, for all of Carl's urgent "do something, do something," I was in no real hurry to act. Brijit had thought she'd won.

Well, actually, the point goes to Penelope.

7

"What did you do to him?" Madam Brijit screamed.

Baron Kriminel's transformation was complete and he climbed back to his feet. His jawbone had been replaced by a pink hologram and it gave him a magical smile that tingled in my stomach and made me giggle. He finally had eyes in his sockets, pink spheres that could change shape and convey the emotions he'd never had before, emotions like love and compassion and sympathy. His rotting-in-the-grave tuxedo had become pure white with red accents around the cuffs and lapels. His buttons were red hearts. His top hat had a rose poking out of the hat band. His shoes were polished white leather.

Brijit grabbed Kriminel's arms and shook him. "Kriminel, what's happened to you?"

His pink jaw opened. A calm voice came out. He said, "You made a happy mistake."

"No!" She pounded on his chest with her fists. "Kill that girl! I *order* you to kill her!"

Baron Kriminel, the new god of love, gave her a pat on the head. "Why would I want to kill her?"

"Because I told you to!" She shoved Kriminel. He barely moved. "Because you take orders from me! Now do it!"

"Madam." He placed his hand with the pink fingers on her shoulder. The glow of his magical bones twinkled in the raindrops dripping down her face. "Is this about your husband?"

"Yes, it's about my husband!" She stomped in place and splashed a puddle of water. "She tried to steal him from me."

Kriminel said, "Your husband loves you."

"I know *that*!" she said. "Other women are always trying to steal him away!"

Baron Kriminel turned his pink eyes to Semedi. "Baron Semedi, is that true?"

"Hmmm." Baron Semedi didn't seem the least bit fazed by Kriminel's transformation. He took the stub of a cigar out of his mouth and said to the skeleton, "What is 'true' when you really think about it?"

Kriminel said, "If you want to make this marriage stronger, you need to be honest with your wife. Do other women try to steal you away? Or do you sometimes pursue other women?"

Semedi flicked the last of his cigar butt into the rain and crossed his arms. "I plead the fifth."

"Semedi," Kriminel said in a no-nonsense tone. "If you love your wife, you'll answer the question."

"Fine." Semedi uncrossed his arms, drank the rest of his rum in a single gulp and said, "On rare occasion I flirt with other women and it gets a little out of hand."

"See!" I shouted. "I told you!" The three Voodoo spirits turned to glare at me, disgusted that I would bother to interrupt their private conversation. Embarrassed, I lowered my voice and said to Carl, "I told her."

"Why would you flirt with anyone else?" Brijit asked Semedi. She looked genuinely hurt. I couldn't tell if the water dripping down her cheeks were raindrops or tears.

"I'm a spirit of love!" Semedi made an exaggerated shrug. "It's my nature."

"I'm a spirit of love, too," she said. Her voice wavered, like she might actually cry. "But I only love you."

Baron Kriminel kept his magical hand on Madam Brijit's shoulder and held Semedi's shoulder with the other. The husband and wife looked at one another with a twinkle of pink light in their eyes.

"I am sorry," Semedi finally said. He kissed Brijit on the forehead. "I love you, my little rum distillery."

"I love you, too," Brijit said as she straightened his tie for him. "My dumb cigar factory."

An "aw" escaped me. I couldn't help it. Love was in the air.

"Here's what we're going to do," Kriminel said to the two of them. "The three of us are going to schedule some marriage counseling. Twice a week we're going to have an open conversation about your relationship. We're going to try to root out some of the problem areas and really get your love back on track. How does that sound? Does that sound okay?"

"Well..." Brijit sheepishly glanced at the ground and said, "I still want to kill the girl."

Kriminel nodded. "And it's okay to have those feelings. But we're going to put those feelings in a little box, okay? Can you do that? Can you put your feelings in a little box?"

Brijit considered it, but refused to look up. "I really would like to see her die. I dug her a grave and everything."

"Brijit." Kriminel's voice sounded stern. "We have an empty box here and we need to put some feelings in it, okay?"

She shrugged. "Okay."

He gave her a pat on the shoulder. "So you want to kill the trash human, but what are we going to do with those feelings?"

She hung her head. "Put them in a little box."

"And are we going to kill anyone today?"

"I guess not."

Kriminel smiled at her. "You're being very brave right now and I see that and I appreciate that. Semedi, do you hear and appreciate her brave decision?"

Semedi was lighting a new cigar with a match. He looked up at the sound of his name. He was not paying attention. "What happened? What're we doing?"

Baron Kriminel encouraged Brijit and Semedi to "have an open dialogue." The two of them were new to expressing their emotions and stumbled over their words. Kriminel guided them through their conversation with the skill and grace of a mid-afternoon talk show counselor. The conversation was about their private feelings, so I dialed back on the eavesdropping.

I sat on the front steps of the shop and took a deep breath.

The CEO's body had melted into a puddle of green sludge that washed away by the rain. Next to him laid the remote control for space satellite 50-4F-50-50-59. I walked out to grab it, popped out the batteries and crushed it in my hand.

Chapter 20

1

"I always knew you were a sharp one," Carl said as we came face to face on the porch.

"I tricked the shit out of you," I told him. I wasn't going to hide my pride. I was going to rub his face in it.

"You got me with the old switcheroo," he said. "Oldest trick in the book and I admit it. I fell for it, hook, line and sinker. But tell me one thing... when did you know I was going to double-cross you?"

My answer came out sharp and indignant. "I always knew you were going to double-cross me, Carl. I knew it the whole time. I even told you to your face, 'I don't trust you.'"

"Hmmm." He stroked his chin. "I think I had you fooled for a little bit."

"Well, you didn't."

"We'll have to agree to disagree on that one."

"Whatever."

He sighed and looked all around. The shop had been torn apart by heavy gunfire. Dead soldiers laid all across the courtyard. The lightning came less often. The thunder sounded far more distant. The rain came down steady, but the wind had died down.

"Well." Carl reached out for a handshake. "Frenemies?"

I didn't shake his hand. I wasn't going to touch him. I said, "Carl, I hate you. I. Hate. You. I've always hated you. I will hate you for forever."

He laughed once, gave me a firm pat on the arm, then headed down the porch steps and out into the rain. "You don't hate me."

I shouted after him. "Yes, I do!"

He shouted back. "No, you don't!"

Carl crossed the courtyard with a leisurely stride in his steps. He even went out of his way to stamp his foot in a puddle and splash water into the air. I let him get a few steps away before I called him out.

"Carl." He turned back around and raised an eyebrow at me. I said, "We're done with this, right? You and me and Westland. Please, tell me this is over."

Carl turned and walked back to the porch. He stared up at me with a smile on his face. "Sure." He reached his hand out to me. "If you shake on it."

"Seriously?"

He shrugged, but kept his hand out. "Makes it official."

He really wanted that handshake. As much as I loathed the idea of touching that man, I believed him when he said the handshake would make it official. If I shook his hand, he was somehow bound by his corporate bylaws to stay out of my life for ever and ever. So I stepped down the porch and shook it. I squeezed his hand, not hard enough to crush his bones, not even hard enough to scare him, but just enough to make him go "Ow."

I wanted to leave him with that as a reminder.

"Besides," Carl said as he turned to leave. "Rumor has it that Untouchable Orange is in California."

Carl disappeared into the mists of the raining alley, wandering out of my life as calm and as casual as he wandered in.

2

I went inside the shop to survey the damage. The place was trashed. I sifted my foot through all the broken jars and looked for the ones still intact. I found seven total. A sad number considering how many we started with.

The plants were absolutely ruined, with only two lucky survivors. The Charge Lily had somehow made it through the whole incident completely untouched and the Blood Rose had fallen over on the floor, but I straightened up its pot and the plant was fine.

The walls were filled with hundreds of bullet holes. The glass in the window was all shattered out. Chinese food laid splattered across the floor, mixed with Xin's spilled powders and oils. Rain dripped in through the swiss cheese ceiling and splattered on the floor, building up a half inch of standing water.

I took a deep breath and exhaled. I didn't know what it would take to fix that much destruction, but I promised myself that I would do whatever it took to rebuild, even if it meant traveling the whole world and collecting a new sample of each rare plant, one by one.

Was all of this somehow my fault? Did I do something wrong along the way? Or did I do something not quite right? Or if I wasn't to *blame*, was I at least *responsible*? Those were the questions running through my head and I didn't have any answers.

I gathered up all our plastic rain buckets and put them around the store to collect the water flooding in from the holes in the roof.

Someone knocked on the open door frame and I turned to see Baron Semedi standing there. I narrowed my eyes at him out of instinct. I'd learned to be cautious of Semedi, but maybe he'd changed after his crash course in marriage counseling.

"Hello," Semedi said. He poked his head inside and looked all around. "How are things?"

"Are you shitting me? Just look around." I threw a bucket down under a particularly bad leak. "This place is fucked."

"Well, then this is going to come at a bad time." He took a deep breath for confidence, then just came right out and said it. "I don't think we should see each other anymore."

I couldn't believe it. He honestly thought he was letting me down easy. "Is that so?"

"Yeah." He looked up at me, removed his top hat to reveal his dreadlocks, and held it to his chest. "I know you have feelings for me and I respect those feelings and I'm flattered. Really I am. But I'm trying to make things work with my wife, so we should probably just stay away from each other for a while."

"Man, that sounds like a really great idea." I tried to give him an authentic smile. I don't know if I pulled it off.

"I just have one thing for you to sign real quick," he said. He stuck his hand in his jacket and dug around. He pulled out a crinkled up sheet of yellow paper.

My face smile disappeared quick. "What am I signing?"

"Well, there's just this thing..." He flattened the paper out on the wall, then handed it to me. It was stained with rum, had cigar burns on it, and was written in charcoal. I didn't understand the language; it looked like it might have been written in some kind of French. He leaned over my shoulder and handed me a fountain pen. "It's kind of like a bill."

"Okay?" I paused. "A bill for what?"

"You damaged Baron Muzica's piano," he said. He ran his fingertips across the words and read it aloud. "This certifies that Penelope Salvo damaged Baron Muzica's magical piano and is responsible for all replacement costs and absolves Baron Semedi of all wrongdoing, because he didn't damage the piano, Penelope did." I looked at him. He continued, "So if you'll just sign that for me, I can pass that along to him and the rest is history."

I held the paper out at him. "I'm not signing this."

"But he expects me to get him a new piano."

I scoffed, grabbed my broom and started sweeping. "Then get him a new piano. I only broke it because you kidnapped my soul. Don't blame me."

"I remember things differently."

I laughed. "I'm sure you do."

He reluctantly folded the paper and stuck it back inside his jacket. He went for the front door and left. No goodbye hug, no handshake, no farewell wave over the shoulder. Baron Kriminel and Madam Brijit waited for him outside. Semedi joined them and put his arm around Brijit's waist. Kriminel waved at me and opened his pink jaw in a skeleton's attempt at a smile. Madam Brijit gave me a dirty look, flipped me off, and in a whirl of cigar smoke, the three of them vanished.

3

I cleaned the shop until the clouds cleared and the morning sun came up over Manhattan. I glanced out the windows from time to time, expecting the princesses to come along to visit.

They didn't come. Maybe they forgot about me and went back to the Muffincake Kingdom without saying goodbye. I hoped that wasn't true.

Just after sunrise, I went out to the alleyway and tore a sheet of metal off of the dumpster and used it to cover the holes in the roof. That gave me a chance to brush most of the water out of the shop with the broom. The floors were still wet, but at least I'd gotten rid of all the standing water. I also swept up a trashcan's-worth of glass and two dustpans full of bullets. Two bookcases of jars had fallen over and crashed to the floor. I picked them up and propped them back against the wall.

The bathroom was an absolute wreck. The toilet had been blown into pieces. The sink had shattered and hung from the wall by the hot and cold water pipes. I gathered up all the chunks of porcelain and threw them into a pile out front.

I gave myself a satisfied nod when I checked out the basement door. It was completely undamaged. The padlock was still in place. It was going to take a lifetime to replace Xin's collection of rare plants – maybe two lifetimes – but at least nothing went missing from the basement. Those things were impossible to replace.

There's a moment in New York City mornings where the sun rises over the horizon, but you can't see it because you're living in the shadow of some of the tallest buildings in the world. The sky is blue, but it's still dark like night. It only happens for ten minutes or so, but those are my favorite ten minutes of the morning. That's when Xin showed up to the shop.

He walked across the courtyard, maneuvering around the larger puddles of water. He carried two canvas grocery bags in his hands. They looked heavy and bulky, filled with god knows what. I walked out front so I could help him carry them in.

I dreaded what Xin's reaction was going to be when he saw the state of the shop. I couldn't deal with the idea of Xin crying. If he cried, I would have cried. But Xin didn't cry. Of course he didn't. He just walked over to his side of the counter, pulled a new radio out of his grocery bags, and sat on his bar stool. He turned the radio to '70s rock and sat at the counter as if it wasn't blasted full of holes and blown all to shit. But I thought, I don't know, maybe he wanted to act like everything was fine. Maybe that was his way of coping. I put his grocery bags down on one of the empty tables, put my bar stool in its normal spot, and sat down across from him.

We faced each other.

He said, "So."

"So." I nervously rubbed my nose. I worried that Xin was going to blame me for everything. It would have made two of us; I blamed myself.

He asked me, "You're bad at math?"

I lowered my eyebrows. What did that have to do with anything? "I'm the worst at math."

"Well, I need you to help me figure up all the damages." He stepped off his bar stool for a moment to find his spiral notebook and golf pencil. They were trapped beneath a piece of wood that had fallen from the ceiling. "We're going to have to find some way to pay for all of these repairs."

"Don't you have insurance or something?"

He shook his head. "No."

"How do you not have insurance?"

"I don't need someone from the insurance company coming around here," he said. "The less people who know about this place, the better."

That made total sense. In fact, it made such perfect sense that I felt like an idiot for even asking. That's just how our lives worked. We couldn't rely on humans to solve our problems, because they wouldn't understand. I couldn't rely on the police. Xin couldn't count on a bunch of pencil-pushing number-crunching insurance adjusters. We had secrets, Xin and I, and we had to keep them.

"I really fucked up, didn't I." I looked at the disaster that was once his humble flower shop. "I fucked up big time."

"This isn't your fault," he said.

I sulked. "In a round about way, it totally is."

He took a breath and spoke slowly. "Penelope, do you know how boring my life was until you came along?"

I shrugged. "Boring as hell, I would imagine."

He nodded. "I was a bored person. Every day I woke up alone. I ate a poached egg, a piece of toast, and drank two cups of tea. I walked to work. I unlocked the store every day at seven. I refilled my jars. I ate lunch. I refilled more jars. At seven I locked up and walked home. I would listen to music on the radio until I grew tired, then I would go to sleep. I've done this every day here in New York. On Sundays I would stay home and watch the world from my apartment window. That was my life. It was not exciting.

"But then one day you walked in. You had energy in you. Even before you swallowed Impossible Red, you were interesting and vibrant. You made every day new and unpredictable. And after Impossible Red, the days simply got better. My life was saved by a flying car. I crawled through a cardboard tunnel to safety. I watched you fight a Voodoo spirit. It reminds me of my adventures from when I was your age, adventures I'm too old for now. When you look around this shop and see it in shambles, maybe you think, 'this is terrible.' But I look at it and think, 'today was not a boring day.'"

"Huh." I propped my heels up on the bar stool and stared at my shoes. "And you really mean all that?"

"Why else would I say it?"

"You're not just trying to make me feel better or something?"

"I do hope you feel better," he said. "And I also mean it."

I let that sink in.

If Xin honestly believed all that, then things didn't seem as bad. I built up the courage to lift my eyes and look at him. Good old Xin, always so kind, always so smart.

I hopped off the stool, went around to his side of the counter, and gave him a hug.

4

We spent the whole morning doing our best to clean up what we could around the shop. Xin made an exhaustive list of everything we needed to replace: jars of all sizes, new flower pots, bags of potting soil, planks of wood, a new toilet, a new sink, the list went on and on. Anything we couldn't salvage, I threw into a pile by the front porch. I started the pile far away from Corolla's body, just so there was no confusion. Corolla was not trash.

That afternoon, Princess Cardboard and Princess Parcel came down the alley. Cardboard had a heart-shaped box of chocolates in her hand, wrapped in red ribbon. Parcel carried a carton of milk. That piqued my interest; Parcel drinking milk?

"Well, call the banks and fly the flags at half mast," I said to Parcel as I walked off the porch and met the two of them in the middle of the courtyard. "You're not drinking?"

She peered inside the carton. "It's a white Russian. I poured out the milk so I could fit more booze."

"Don't you need milk to make a white Russian?" I asked.

"I'm not putting milk in alcohol." She took a drink from the carton. "Not until they invent alcoholic cows."

"Here!" Cardboard beamed a huge smile at me and presented me with the box of chocolates. "They're chocolate covered espresso beans, so don't eat too many."

"Thanks." I opened the box. Half of the chocolate-covered espresso beans were already missing. I raised my eyes at her.

She smiled and looked away sheepishly.

I popped one of them in my mouth. They weren't metal and tasted terrible, but I ate a few anyway. I didn't want to disappoint her.

Cardboard said, "We're leaving tonight for the Muffincake Kingdom. But we promised to spend one last night in New York with you before we go."

My heart sank. "Cardboard, I want to. I really do. But I gotta stay here. This place is a mess." I turned around and looked at the shop. Xin had come out onto the porch. He knew what we were talking about and waved me away.

He said, "Things can wait one more day."

"You sure?" I asked him.

He waved me off again. "Go. Have fun with your little friends."

He didn't have to tell me twice. I turned back around to the princesses. "Okay! Let's go!"

Parcel and Cardboard waved goodbye to Xin.

"Goodbye, Penelope's dad!" Cardboard said.

"Goodbye, whoever you are!" Parcel added.

5

Parcel dictated the events of the evening. We couldn't go to the bars like Princess Parcel wanted to – I was eighteen and Cardboard, for being centuries old, didn't look much older than me. Our only chance at getting something to drink was Parcel's fake ID. How Parcel got a fake ID, I had no idea, but she had one and it worked.

We walked down to Ross's Liquor and Parcel went inside to buy booze. Cardboard and I waited outside so our young age wouldn't draw any unnecessary attention. Parcel didn't look much older than me or Cardboard – she *might* have passed for 21 – and I assumed the guy at the liquor store would have given her a hard time, but I couldn't have been more wrong. Minutes later, Parcel came out the front door with a cardboard box filled with bottles.

On her way out, she shouted, "Thanks, Dave!"

Apparently her and Dave were on a first-name basis.

We traveled across New York through Cardboard's magical tunnels. Cardboard led the way, I was in the middle, and Parcel brought up the rear, scooting a box of liquor ahead of her. They led me to their office in the Bronx, the one they used for their delivery service.

The office had been cleaned out for the most part, with just a few wooden desks and an empty filing cabinet left behind. Out their third-story window I could see the parking lot for Yankee Stadium and half of the stadium itself. We dragged the two desks over to the window so we could sit on them and watch the city change from evening to night. The windows in the city buildings slowly blinked on. Baseball season was over, but they had the lights on in Yankee Stadium for whatever reason and the bright glow drowned out the stars on that side of the sky.

"Here's what I got," Parcel said as she rooted through her box of liquor. She pulled out a four pack of wine coolers, a bottle of vodka, a bottle of whiskey, a bottle of rum, and two bottles of gin. "Now we can either drink these plain, or I can mix them all together in a big bucket. Your call."

I said, "As much as I love the idea of Long Island Bucket Teas, I'll just drink whiskey." I took the bottle and looked at the label. I wasn't much of a whiskey drinker. I was more used to drinking PBRs when me and Ilana Rittenberg would sneak into the Gold Mine on Bowery. In fact, the only whiskey I had ever tasted was Macallan, the whiskey that Carl bought at the Welf auction. This was also a bottle of Macallan. It wasn't from 1926 – one of those seventy-five-thousand dollar bottles – but a bottle from 1943. Still, that's pretty old. I asked Parcel, "How much did you pay for this?"

"Couple thousand." She held up her purse. "I still have all this human money."

"Are you..." A question popped into my mind and I almost asked it without thinking, but then I thought it might sound rude. But *then* I thought, what the hell, we're all friends here. "What are you going to do with all that money?"

"Dunno," Parcel said. She tossed her purse in my lap. "You want it?"

I opened it and looked inside. It was stuffed full of $500 bills. Stuffed. Full. I'd never seen a $500 before. It's got McKinley on the front. I thumbed through the bills and asked her, "How much is in here?"

"Not sure," Parcel said. "Couple million, maybe. Why? You want it?"

"You should take it," Cardboard said after taking a swig of her blue wine cooler. "We don't need it where we're going."

I waved the purse at them. "This is a phenomenal amount of money."

Cardboard smiled at me and said, "It's all yours. You got our world back."

"And you saved our lives," Parcel added.

Cardboard pointed at her sister, indicating she was totally right. "Take it."

I sat there and stared at the open purse. I had never seen so much money before in my life. Strange to think that six months ago I was broke and borderline homeless. Now I was holding "a couple million, maybe."

We sat on the desks and watched night settle in over the city. I gulped whiskey straight from the bottle. It tasted strong, but never burned. After an hour passed and without even the slightest buzz, I wondered if I could even get drunk anymore, or if the machines coursing through my veins processed the alcohol right out of my bloodstream.

Cardboard's tolerance wasn't in question. After only two wine coolers, she was swaying back and forth and giggling like an idiot.

Parcel had a vodka bottle in one fist and a gin bottle in the other. She alternated between the two, gin then vodka, vodka then gin.

"I'm quitting drinking once I get home," Parcel slurred after a while.

"That's probably good," I said.

She waved her bottle of gin through the air. "Only wine after this. And only at wedding receptions."

I looked over at her. "Don't you have wedding receptions every day?"

She looked back and said, "And I will be drinking wine at all of them." She took a long drink from her gin bottle. "And champagne. Champagne's a wine."

"Penelope." Cardboard put her hand on my shoulder and gave me that serious look drunk people give you when they're trying to be serious. Her cardboard crown slumped over her eyes. She didn't bother to push it back up. "You really are the greatest, you know that? You were always so nice to me."

"I'm nice to you," Parcel said.

Cardboard lifted her crown so she could see her sister. "You're always mean to me!"

Parcel jumped up and got right in her sister's face. "Name a time, you bitch!"

"Oh, just one?" Cardboard shouted. "What about the time you said my eyes are too far apart!"

"Your eyes *are* too far apart!" Parcel used her fingers to measure them. "Look at how far apart your eyes are!"

Cardboard slapped her sister's hands out of her face. "My eyes are fine. Your eyes are too close together."

Parcel stared at Cardboard, drank some vodka, wiped her mouth with the full length of her white gloves, then said, "My eyes are fine where they're at."

They bickered for ten minutes, then got past it. After that they were right back to being sisters. They sat side by side and talked about what it would be like to finally return home. We spent the whole night talking and drinking. I asked them all kinds of questions.

"Are there hot guys in the Muffincake Kingdom?"

"The men in my kingdom are all hot," Parcel said.

Cardboard cracked open a neon-green wine cooler and said, "The men in my kingdom are all very nice."

Then I asked, "Do people have sex where you come from?"

"Yeah." Parcel looked at me like that was the stupidest question ever. She slugged her sister in the arm. "Not everyone, though."

"Shut up," Cardboard snapped. She turned to me to explain. "I almost did once. I could have if I wanted to. I just decided not to because the boy was bad at kissing."

I asked them, "Do you guys have religion? You said you have gods."

"Sugar Cube and Butter Pad," Cardboard said, pointing at the ceiling. "They watch us from the Great Bakery in the sky."

"Don't be stupid," Parcel said. "The Great Bakery doesn't exist."

"Yes, it does," Cardboard said. "That's where everything came from."

Parcel sighed. "No, it's not."

"Well, then who baked the Muffincake Kingdom?" Cardboard asked.

"The Muffincake Kingdom baked itself out of nothing." Parcel took a swig of gin. "Everyone knows that."

Cardboard finished all four wine coolers in the same amount of time it took Parcel to kill her bottles of vodka and gin. I'd drank three-quarters of my bottle of whiskey, but I didn't notice any changes. I felt robbed, like some part of my teens and twenties had been stolen from me; I'd never get wasted again, never again get arrested for drunk and disorderly conduct, never again throw up all over myself and wake up soaking wet in Tommy DeLuca's bathtub with all the lights on.

It was a small price to pay, trading drunkenness for an indestructible body, but it wasn't just about being able to get drunk. It was about missing out on one more thing that made me human.

When it came to drinking, Cardboard was a featherweight. She swished around the last inch of pink liquid in her wine cooler and swallowed it. The bottle dropped from her hand and clattered to the floor. She watched it roll around and said, "I think we should go. I feel like I am going to puke."

Cardboard closed her eyes and leaned her head against my shoulder. A blonde curl dangled in front of her face. Parcel, who had drank more than the both of us combined, had just enough coordination to get her sister to her feet and help her stand.

We had spent their last night in town together. Going away parties were always a bittersweet occasion and this one was no exception. The time had finally come to say goodbye and Cardboard was passed out cold. That could have been a blessing in disguise, really; actually having to say goodbye to her face probably would have made me cry, and I was tired of crying.

I adjusted her cardboard crown, pushing it securely on her head so it wouldn't fall off.

"Well," Parcel said, propping up her sister. "I guess that's it." She stumbled in place. She was about to fall, especially holding up the dead weight of her passed out sister, but I caught them both. I steadied Parcel back on her feet. She took a breath and said, "Thanks."

"Thank you," I said. "I really hope this isn't *goodbye* goodbye. I'd love to see you guys again someday."

Parcel drunkenly nodded. "Nice."

I frowned. That wasn't really an answer. I was suddenly worried that this *was* goodbye goodbye and I would never see them again.

Parcel used her teeth to pull off her long, cotton gloves. Her book of stamps fell on the floor. I picked them up for her and handed them back. She fumbled around with them for a moment and eventually peeled two stamps out of the book. One stamp had a picture of a pancake otter swimming in a river of syrup. The other one showed a grassy field of piñata horses. She stuck the pancake stamp on herself, right over her heart. She put piñata one on Cardboard's face, right on the end of her nose.

"See ya around, Penelope," she said.

I said, "See ya around, Parcel."

She spoke a destination for her magical stamps – "The Wedding Cake Kingdom" – and they vanished.

6

For any other girl in New York City, I would strongly discourage walking the streets alone at night, especially with a glittering purse stuffed with millions of dollars in cash. I didn't have to worry about that kind of thing. Not anymore. A crazy guy could jump out of the darkness, he could wave a gun in my face and my only real concern would be, "I want to kick this guy in self-defense, but I have to be careful that I don't kill him instantly."

I walked all the way from the Bronx back to Chinatown, sticking to 5th Avenue so I could pass by Central Park. It was probably around three in the morning by then, when the only people walking the streets were the late-night party people or the crazies. I passed by a quartet of drunk frat dudes – they asked me for cigarettes, then weed, then invited me to join them, to which I told them to fuck off – and then passed by a homeless guy. Man, just seeing him really put things into perspective. I was *lucky*. I dodged a bullet.

I opened Parcel's purse and pulled out one of the 500 dollar bills. When the homeless guy saw me coming and saw I had a bill in my hand, he reached out for it. He wasn't suspecting a McKinley. When he took the bill, his eyes went wide and he looked up at me, bewildered.

I told him, "Be careful out here, man."

I made a slight detour on my way home and visited Ma at the cemetery. It was the dead of night and the gate was closed, but I hopped the fence with no problem. I knew exactly where she was buried – the location was burned into my brain – and I found it immediately, even in the dark.

In Loving Memory of
Marie Phoebe Marionette
1970-2012
Blessed are the poor in spirit, for theirs is the kingdom of Heaven.
Blessed are those who mourn, for they will find comfort.
Blessed are the meek, for they will inherit the Earth.

"Hey," I said to her. I brushed with the grass with my shoe. "So have I got a story for you."

The night was quiet. The sky was clear and I could see the stars. I stood there and told her all about Xin and Baron Semedi and Carl. I told her about how I died, and how I came back, and about Tengoku, the computer lady. "Your daughter's half-robot now, or something," I said. The night went on, but I told her the entire story, leaving out as much of the foul language as possible. At some point I found myself sitting on the ground, leaned up against her gravestone. That's when I told her Corolla was dead and, if possible, to find that used car lot in Heaven and tell him I said hi.

Maybe Ma could hear me. Maybe should couldn't. Maybe Heaven was real and maybe it wasn't. But I decided to err on the side of caution: if Heaven *was* real and if Ma was up there, then I better explain myself. Cuz if I didn't, she would be pissed.

When I got up to leave, I placed my hand on Ma's tombstone and reassured her, "I just want you to know... I'm going to be

341

okay."

By the time I got back to Chinatown, the morning sun had just begun to cast its glow in the distance. Showing up before sunrise meant I beat Xin to the shop for the day. Good. I could get a jump start on the repairs. The street vendors were out on the corners setting up their food carts and sandwich boards. A few older business owners swept their front entrances clear of leaves and cigarette butts. I waved at the owner of the Asian Food Mart, who was out hanging new signs in his front window. He waved back. I smiled at him, half to be friendly, but half because I knew something he didn't: his business was ten feet away from Voodoo spirits and snipers and pastry-based princesses and he didn't have the slightest clue.

When I got to the shop, I stopped dead.

Parked there in the courtyard was a brand new 1998 Toyota Corolla. It had one of those giant, novelty ribbons tied up and over the roof like a car commercial. I also found a black envelope taped to the driver side window. I peeled it off and pressed my nose to the glass to check out the interior. Showroom perfect, except the radio was sitting on the passenger side seat instead of being plugged into the dashboard. I tried the handle and the door opened right up. The inside had that new car smell.

Whatever this mystery was, I expected to find clues inside the black envelope. I tore it open and pulled out a card. The front was simple: forest green in color and embossed with gold calligraphy that read, "Thank you for your business!" I opened the card. The interior was hand written in all capital letters, very crisp, very professional.

To Penelope,

Not to be a Sentimental Suzie, but please accept this gift as a token of my appreciation for your professionalism and charisma. The Westland Corporation is no stranger to automotive innovations and my Director of Research and Development assures me that if you take your car radio and transplant it to this new body, it will restore your friend to normal. They assure me this will work, but please do not be afraid to contact me if you encounter any complications.

Your frenemy,

Carlton Carl, Chief Executive Officer, the Westland Corporation

I closed the card and put it back in the envelope. I scanned the apartment windows and across the rooftops, searching for a Westland spy. I figured they were out there, watching me with direct orders from Carl to report back about my reaction. Did I look pleased? Did I look pissed off? I didn't see any spies, but that didn't mean they weren't there. I felt a smile coming on, and I let it happen. If the spies *were* watching me, it wouldn't be the worst thing in the world if they told Carl I was happy. It would be my way of saying thank you.

I sat on the porch steps and waited for Xin to show up. He arrived right on time with two flats of empty mason jars in his arms – just the start of what he'd need to refill his shelves. I stood up and waved to him.

"Hey, Xin." I ran over to him with Princess Parcel's purse in my hands. I made it do a little dance and I used a sing-song voice to say, "Guess who's got a million dollars?"

Xin answered right away, and with a lot of confidence. "Shaq."

"Besides Shaq."

"Michael Jordan?"

I exhaled hard and dropped my arms. He was ruining the moment. "No, Xin. Not Michael Jordan."

I pushed the front door open and held it for him. He walked past me and carried the jars inside.

Amid all the trash and rubble scattered across the shop floor, I found my old Village Voice laying there in a puddle of water. On the front was the help wanted ad that changed my life, circled in red ink.

Help Wanted
Minimum wage + room and board
No experience necessary
Apply in person at 83 Forge St.

A small laugh escaped me as I finished reading the ad. 83 Forge Street. Chinatown.

Home.

I folded up the paper, stuffed it in my back pocket and walked inside.

THE END

Epilogue

Mrs. Cho wandered down a soft, spongy walkway crafted from alternating layers of chocolate and lemon and strawberry cakes. The grass that surrounded her wasn't grass, but the shredded green paper used to stuff Easter baskets. An orchard of trees surrounded her on both sides and the cupcakes were in full bloom, right down to the lumps of white frosting topped with bright red cherries. Beyond the trees were five-tiered wedding cakes the size of mountains, so far away that she could just barely see the tops of them, snow capped with layers of powdered sugar.

"Hello?" Mrs. Cho called out in a timid voice. "Hello?"

No one heard her. Or if they did, they were too terrified of the portly stranger to respond. There was one brave soul, however, who eyed her carefully from the branches of the cupcake trees. After Mrs. Cho took a few cautious steps down the path, a smartly dressed Groom Raven flapped down and landed in front of her. Startled by the tuxedo-clad bird, she stopped and held her breath, too frightened to move. The Groom Raven used the feathers at the tip of his wing to adjust the monocle over his right eye.

"Why, hello there, strange woman," the Groom Raven said. "Have you come to attend today's wedding?"

Mrs. Cho couldn't take her eyes off the talking bird. It stared back at her, visibly perplexed at her silence. After a brief staring contest, she mustered up the courage to say, "I'm from New York."

"Never heard of it," the Groom Raven said as he hopped closer to her feet. "Is that near Funnel Cake Island?"

Mrs. Cho took a cautious step backwards. If the bird did anything unpredictable – anything other than talk – she was prepared to run. The Groom Raven didn't mean her any harm, of course, and after realizing his presence disturbed her, he removed his hat and bowed politely.

"Where are my manners," he said. "I am Radburn Corsage, of the Corsage family. My father was Gentleman Corsage. My mother was Courteous Gowntress. And you are?"

The kind introduction put her a little more at ease. She held her hand to her chest. "My name is Meixiu Cho."

"Mmmhmm." Radburn Corsage had never heard such a name before. He tried his best to sound it out. "Mesh... we...?"

And Mrs. Cho helped him. "Meh. Shwee. Cho."

"Meh. Shwee. Cho." He nodded, satisfied with his pronunciation, which was incorrect, but close enough. He put his wing to his chest and said, "Rad. Burn."

She repeated, "Radburn."

And Radburn, who was a Raven with a beak and physically unable to smile, instead fluttered happily in place. Mrs. Cho smiled at the little bird. He danced in the air, hovered close to her, and held out his wing. She took it in her forefinger and thumb and gave him a tiny handshake.

"Well, Meh Shwee Cho. If you don't have a date to today's wedding, perhaps you might accompany me?"

Mrs. Cho didn't know what wedding he was talking about. The raven landed and hopped away, bopping down the spongecake path, excited for the day's events. He noticed Mrs. Cho wasn't following him and looked back. He waved at her to follow him. She agreed and he escorted her towards the sounds of church bells deep inside the Wedding Cake Kingdom.

The following pages are from
Penelope Salvo and Untouchable Orange

November, 2012.

Chuck Taylors aren't the best shoes to wear when you need to march through the muddy jungles of Guatemala. I learned that the hard way. And a black tank top with some denim shorts isn't all that great if you need protection from the elements. The mosquitoes in Guatemala get as big as hummingbirds and a lot of the jungle plants can be poisonous. I didn't have to worry about any of that, of course; mosquitoes can't pierce my carbon-nano-weave skin and I don't have allergic reactions to anything anymore.

Not since swallowing Impossible Red.

These jungles were uncharted. Not meant for tourists. I worked my way through miles of towering mango and coconut trees. I leapt over mud puddles, I pushed through knee-deep bushes, and from time to time I had to kick a fallen log out of my way. Vines hung down from the tree branches and formed a kind of webbing that got me all tangled up, but I could slice through them with my bare hands. My skin got grass-stained and I smelled like a fresh-cut lawn, but them's the dues you pay if you want to explore a jungle, I guess. Tree roots grew above ground in big loops that threatened to trip me up.

The harder I pushed through the leaves and vines, the faster they seemed to grow back, as if they were trying to swallow me up. I'm not really the claustrophobic type, but between the humidity and the crowded plant-life, I felt like I couldn't get a decent breath. Which is fine, because I don't breathe.

I kept going.

Deep in those jungles, somewhere near the Mopan River, was the Forgotten Temple of Muzencab, the Mayan god of bees.

"Penelope," Corolla shouted from overhead. He'd been patrolling the skies for hours, where he hovered just over the treetops and searched for any signs of the temple. Apparently, he'd struck gold. "This way! I see something!"

Corolla floated off. I followed him by the blue glow of his hubcaps. I wedged my way through jungle trees. My tank top got caught on some kind of thorn bush and had to meticulously free the fabric from each individual thorn. I worried that I might lose Corolla from under the jungle canopy, but he was careful to stay where I could see him.

He led me around for an hour when I heard a strange noise, something like an army of chainsaws. I stopped and tilted my ear in that direction. I'd heard weird noises in the jungle before – distant waterfalls or cackling birds – but this was new. It definitely sounded like chainsaws, as if there was a lumber company out there cutting down acres of tress. But, no, it wasn't quite chainsaws. I closed my eyes and focused hard. The sound changed in frequency and intensity, as if it were throbbing, like it came from something alive.

If the noise came from a living thing, it would have to be huge. Maybe a monster.

Dope. I love fighting monsters.

But here's Penelope Salvo, wrong again. It wasn't a monster. It was bees. Trillions and trillions of bees. They covered every inch of an ancient Mayan pyramid.

The Forgotten Temple of Muzencab was only a legend, but I'd found it. This wasn't like the smooth pyramids you'd find in Egypt. This pyramid was angular, blocky, and built from tiers of gray stone. I took a moment to drink in the sheer size of the thing. The Mayans had to cut down acres of jungle to make room for this thing; a plot of land the size of a football stadium. It towered thirty stories into the sky. The top just barely poked out over the treetops. At the tip-top stood a small cube-shaped temple, covered in vines that grew in spirals and bloomed a bright yellow flower.

I needed those vines. More specifically, I needed those flowers.

I needed a Looping Bandis.

But in order to get to them, I had to climb thirty stories of stairs past an army of bees.

Legend has it, Muzencab, the Mayan god of bees, promised the bees that when they died, they could live in his temple and no one would ever bother them. This was his way of saying "thanks for all the honey," I guess. So even the living bees would visit here from all over the world, or come here to die, or just hang out. Whenever a scientist says that the bees are disappearing, they're disappearing to the Temple of Muzencab, which is like a never-ending Woodstock where bees can hang out, buzz around together, and have tons of bee sex.

"I am not going near that thing." Corolla descended from the sky and hovered over my head.

"What?" I asked. He couldn't do that to me. "Bullshit, dude. Fly me to the top."

Corolla laughed. "Wake up, sweetheart. Do you see all those bees?"

"What do you care?" I asked. "You're a car."

Corolla stated, "I am a car that's allergic to bees."

"Oh my god," I muttered.

I threw up my hands and marched towards the pyramid. Corolla was a huge coward. It was pointless to argue with him once he'd chickened out. I'd do it alone. At least the Mayans were thoughtful enough to build me a staircase. I climbed the first step and craned my neck at the top of the temple.

"One step down," I said. "Three-hundred sixty-six to go."

The bees covered everything. It sounded like I was walking through a wood chipper. They swarmed around my head and landed on my bare skin. They couldn't sting me, obviously, but that didn't stop them from trying. They crawled all over my arms and legs and got inside my clothes. They didn't actually bother me, but their tiny legs felt weird on my skin and I brushed them away.

I climbed fifty steps, then a hundred. Then two-hundred. And finally, after thirty minutes of climbing, I reached the top. The air was cleaner up at the top, less humid, and came with a refreshing breeze. Corolla watched me from a safe distance away, just above the tree line. I waved at him so he knew I reached the top without any problem.

The temple at the top of the pyramid had four entrances facing north, south, east, and west. No doors, just open entrances that let me see the emptiness inside. The stone floor was stained brown with centuries-old blood. Human blood, if I had to guess. Sacrifices to Muzencab, maybe to keep the bees away, or maybe to honor the bees since they pollinate things. Whatever the reason, this room saw a lot of spilled blood. A small garden of Looping Bandis grew off the roof of this little structure. The spiral vines hung over the doorways in long coils, blooming with sweet-smelling, yellow flowers.

And then something startled me. A voice.

"Who are you?" this voice asked.

I spun around and found myself face to face with Muzencab himself, in the flesh. Or, more accurately, "in the bees." Muzencab was shaped like a human, but he didn't have a body made out of skin and bone. His body came in a mass of swarming bees, all of them clinging together to create a head and a body and arms and legs. When he walked, his legs were made of bees. When he pointed at me, his arms were made of bees. And when he spoke, his voice came from the buzzing wings of the bees.

I backed away from him and against the wall of the temple.

Answer him, I thought. *He asked you who you are. Answer him.*

"My name's Penelope Marie Salvo," I said. "Nice cursed temple you got here. Love the blood stains."

"Have you come to release me from this prison?" he asked. "Have you come to summon me fully into this realm, that I might wash over humankind with blistering stings and painful venom?"

"No," I said, plainly. "I just came here to steal some of your plants."

"Penelope!" Corolla shouted. "Hey, Penelope!"

"What?" I shouted back at him.

"There's a man made of bees talking to you!"

"Yeah, dude. I see it."

"What's he saying?" Corolla refused to get any closer.

Muzencab didn't seem to notice or care that I was talking to a car. He kept going on with his monologue. "I will bless this world with stings that reduce even the strongest men to terrified children that spray foam from their mouths."

I shouted back to Corolla. "He says he wants to make everyone into terrified children that spray foam from their mouths!"

"Oh," Corolla said. He paused, then said, "Can he really do that?"

"I don't think so!"

Muzencab just wanted attention. He reminded me of those guys in high school who talk about death and blood and worshiping Satan; they just say shit to get a rise out of people. Muzencab was the same way, so the best thing I could do was ignore him. I walked away and scaled the walls of his sacrifice room. It wasn't a hard climb, really. The stones used to build the walls were rough-cut and provided a lot of hand-holds and foot-holds. I scaled the eight-foot walls without any trouble and sifted through the vines on the roof. I wanted the best samples of Looping Bandis, the healthiest and sturdiest ones.

"Spill blood in my name," Muzencab commanded me. "I will bring forth more bees than there are sands on all the beaches. I will bring forth more bees than there are stars in the sky."

I focused on my task and muttered, "That's a lot of bees."

"What's he saying now?" Corolla called out.

"He's talking about beaches and the stars or whatever," I replied.

"Beaches and stars are cool!" Corolla shouted.

I shrugged big enough for Corolla to see. "I dunno. He's kind of being weird about it."

I only needed one Looping Bandis for Xin's shop, but there was no reason I couldn't bring back two. Better safe than sorry. The vines grew out of the cracks in the stone, which meant yanking them free would rip their roots out, but I had a better idea. I wedged my my fingers into the cracks and split the ancient rock apart so I could pull two Looping Bandis free – roots perfectly intact.

"You have what you came for," Muzencab told me, victoriously throwing his bee-arms into the air. "Now return the favor and summon me fully into this world of soft flesh and flowing blood!"

I jumped off the top of the sacrifice room and landed right in front of Muzencab.

"Nah." I brushed right past him and headed for the stairs. "I won't be doing that."

He didn't even make an effort to stop me. He just watched me go.

I gave him some parting advice. "Dude, honestly? You are wound way too tight. You need to, like, chill out."

I bounded down the stairs, two at a time. Even as I ran out of earshot, I could still hear Muzencab talking his nonsense. "Summon me forth" and "I'll sting the very soul of humanity" and shit like that. On and on he went. I can only assume he was still doing it as I ran away from the temple, rendezvoused with Corolla, and took to the skies.

"That guy seemed nice," Corolla said.